Made in United States
Troutdale, OR
10/01/2024

23265824R00137

PATHS

THE KILLERS SERIES, BOOK 2

BRYNNE ASHER

PATHS

A Killers Novel, Book 2
Brynne Asher

Published by Brynne Asher
BrynneAsherBooks@gmail.com

Keep up with me on Facebook for news and upcoming books
https://www.facebook.com/BrynneAsherAuthor

Join my Facebook reader group to keep up with my latest news Brynne Asher's Beauties

Keep up with all Brynne Asher books and news. Sign up for my newsletter http://eepurl.com/gFVMUP

Edited by Hadley Finn
Cover by Haya in Designs

ALSO BY BRYNNE ASHER

Killers Series

Vines – A Killers Novel, Book 1

Paths – A Killers Novel, Book 2

Gifts – A Killers Novel, Book 3

Veils – A Killers Novel, Book 4

Scars – A Killers Novel, Book 5

Souls – A Killers Novel, Book 6

The Tequila – A Killers Novella

The Killers, The Next Generation

Levi, Asa's son

The Agents

Possession

Tapped

Exposed

Illicit

The Carpino Series

Overflow – The Carpino Series, Book 1

Beautiful Life – The Carpino Series, Book 2

Athica Lane – The Carpino Series, Book 3

Until Avery – A Carpino Series Crossover Novella

Force of Nature - A Carpino Christmas Novel

The Dillon Sisters

Deathly by Brynne Asher

Damaged by Layla Frost

The Montgomery Series

Bad Situation – The Montgomery Series, Book 1

Broken Halo – The Montgomery Series, Book 2

Betrayed Love - The Montgomery Series, Book 3

Standalones

Blackburn

CONTENTS

DEDICATIONS

To Elle –
Once upon a time two women lived across the street from one another and became sisters in spirit.
On a beautiful fall day, one called the other and said, "It'll suck, but I think I want to try and write something."
Like the best friend ever, she replied, "I promise to tell you if it sucks."
After reading the first chapter, the one walked across the street and stood in the other's kitchen looking relieved. "I'm *so* glad I don't have to tell you it sucks."
And so it began.
I love you.

To Layla Frost and Sarah Curtis –
What would I do without you two? Thank you for your daily friendship, our Saturday night raves, and for helping me become a better author.
And thank you for your continued patience when I send you millions of pictures of my dog, doing nothing

exceptional, and ecstatically agreeing that she's super cute.

To Rae Larand, Ivy, Laurie, Gi, Gillian, and Kristan –
Thank you for helping me make my book what it is. You all are the earrings and perfectly applied mascara to my final product.

And finally, to all my readers and bloggers –
Thank you for taking a chance on my books. Without you, I couldn't do this.

A NOTE FROM THE AUTHOR

I'm continually humbled that anyone wants to read my words. Not only do I dread doing it, but I suck at marketing my books, which makes me all the more grateful for YOU—my readers. So, I'm not going to drag it out. You're awesome and I love you. I hope you enjoy Grady and Maya's story as much I loved writing it.

PROLOGUE
I FUCKED UP

IT’S FUCKING HOT. The stench in this room is getting worse by the hour. It’s all I can do to focus on breathing.

In.

Out.

In.

Out.

I never knew breathing could be a distraction, but it’s the only thing to focus on since it’s echoing in my ears from this damn thing tied over my head. The monotony of my breathing—keeping it steady, listening to myself exhale—almost makes me forget about the pain.

Almost, but not quite.

And as bad as the pain is, what’s worse is I don’t know where Crew is. They could have him—we’d just separated when they got me. I’ve never fucking hated myself more than right now, knowing he’s here because of me.

The door slams. They’re back with more yelling—

again demanding to know who I am, who sent me, and how I found them. I get another warning, and just like all the other times, I've learned to brace because I know something's gonna follow.

Fuck.

I bite back my groan, trying not to make a sound, but that felt like a pipe. Hanging from one arm, those hits fucking hurt. I'm pretty sure they cracked some ribs. Little do they know, I was taught how to take a beating —but a pipe? That's new, even for me.

I go back to focusing on my breathing because there's nothing more for me to do. I never realized how fucking big and heavy I was until all my weight is hanging by a thread—that thread being a rope, tearing through my skin.

More threats, demands, warnings. It's all been bad—worse than I ever imagined—but listening to them speak in their language, this shit's about to get even worse.

It doesn't matter how much I try, I can't control my heartbeat. My breaths, which have been echoing in my head for what's got to be almost twenty-four hours now, get louder and faster.

Focus, Grady. Focus on something.

Nothing. I can't find one fucking thing to think about besides my good hand being tied to something hard. For the first time since they got me, I struggle. Thrashing and twisting makes the pain worse, but fuck me, I think I'm about to lose my hand, or at least my fingers one by one.

I'm not sure which would be worse.

Yeah, I fucked up.

My chest heaves, my lungs not able to keep up. It

doesn't matter how long this sack has been tied over my head, I suddenly feel smothered.

Then my body jerks, and not from another strike, hit, or thrash. I force myself to concentrate, making sure I still have all my extremities. It's a noise. I've used them enough, I know instantly what it is.

A flashbang.

A lot of fucking gunfire mixed with screaming voices follow, all in their language. The commotion around me is too much. I tense and I feel the pain in my shoulder more than anything I've felt so far.

I hear bodies slam into others and two more gunshots ring out. That's it.

Silence.

"Grady? You with me?"

Crew.

They didn't get him.

Even with the pain, I exhale in relief. But I still can't utter a word.

My good arm is untied and before I know it the weight of my body is lifted. That weight was so fucking heavy. Never felt anything like it, not even when I was seventeen. That weight would've been too much for most people at that age. Not me—not even then. That was when I created a new path for me and my family. Since then, I've felt free. Never a heavy day since.

Until now, when I fucked up and almost got Crew killed along with me. I almost got the one person I care about outside of my family killed and right when he found something to live for. That path led me here, hanging by a thread—beaten, bloodied, and almost dead.

He must've cut the rope. I groan in pain as the blood

starts to flow, even as my arm falls limp to my side. When my ass hits the ground, Crew rips the stench-soaked cloth off my head. I have to squint from seeing light for the first time in almost twenty-four hours. My friend is bleeding from the mouth and a bruise is already forming on the side of his face.

He's serious, all business, when he demands, "I'm gonna pop your shoulder back in. It can't wait, then we've gotta get out of here."

I wince and barely nod.

"Brace, I'll go on three," he warns.

I swallow and nod. Then, I brace.

"One ... two ..."

I scream, allowing the first sound I've made since they got me. "Fuck! You said three."

Crew yanks me up by my good arm and I don't know if I feel pain or relief in my shoulder.

"Sorry, man. It would've been worse on three. Come on, we've gotta get the fuck outta here."

I shouldn't feel the weight. No matter the condition of my body, all parts are still attached, and I'm alive. I should be light as a fucking feather.

As Crew drags me out of the broken-down makeshift warehouse—littered with bloody, dead bodies—I've never felt heavier.

1

THE MIDDLE-OF-NOWHERE VIRGINIA

Maya

"You sure you've never waited tables before?"

I look up at Maggie as I balance a plate on my forearm, another in the same hand, and pick up a third in the other. How do I answer without sounding like an entitled bitch?

"No. Just eaten out a lot I guess."

Maybe that will appease her. It's not a total lie. I have eaten out a lot, but it was either at my parents' Country Club or five-star restaurants. And never would I tell the full truth, that I've been served my entire life at the house I grew up in.

"Well, you're a natural. I didn't know what to think when Addy gave you a job with no interview and not knowin' your skills. That's *so* Addy. To be honest, I was plain pickin' mad I didn't have a say in who was gonna help in my kitchen. You're lucky you're a natural. I know it's hard to see, but I'm not usually so good-natured about things."

I try not to let my eyes widen in surprise, disbelief or, when you get right down to it, fear. From the moment I met Maggie, I've done my best to please her. It's a good thing I paid attention to how I was served all those years and enjoyed working in the kitchen with our cook. Maggie's downright scary. I accidentally spilled a bowl of soup last week and I thought she was going to come undone. She didn't care one bit that I burned my hand or offered to clean it up immediately.

I do my thing, get in and out of her kitchen as fast as I can, and smile every chance I get in hopes she doesn't snap at me.

"Everyone's been great to work with," I tell her the truth, or mostly the truth. I've been here a while now, and I've learned how to best work with Maggie—that being to always agree with her, stay out of her way, and for the love of all things holy, don't spill a drop of anything on her floor. The soup and I learned that the hard way.

With that, I swiftly exit her kitchen for the tasting room. It's best to leave Maggie to her work, not chat too much, and never spill.

"Your meals," I announce as I approach each guest from their left. This is a lesson learned as well—my mother would have a fit if we were served from the right. I guess one learns a lot about waiting tables when their help has been chastised in front of them their entire lives.

I've never thought about waiting tables, but I do enjoy it. Other than the rare difficult customer, everyone is pretty laid back. I realized this after a few weeks of work. Customers come for the environment and wine, wanting a chance to take a break from their hectic lives.

This is something I'm not accustomed to, but during my short time here, I've mastered the art of appreciating it. Relaxing long enough to sit and enjoy life isn't something I've ever been allowed to do. But if there was ever an environment to encourage it, it's here.

The middle-of-nowhere Virginia where no one knows me has proven to be the perfect place to be. There are no preconceived notions that I'm an entitled bitch. Here, I get to be me, and after all this time juggling work between Whitetail and Rolling Hills Ranch, I've stayed tucked deep in the woods in my bungalow, as Addy calls it, and I've almost stopped looking over my shoulder. Almost.

There are days I find myself going hours without scanning my surroundings for anyone familiar, their people, or especially *him*. I never worry about my mom, though. She'd never bother herself with looking for me. She'd say she's too busy with her philanthropies—pretending to solve the world's issues.

But I think I'm good. I've found a little slice of heaven an hour outside of the Capitol. After driving far enough south, I found a part-time opening at an assisted living center. Even though I'm a physical therapist who graduated at the top of her class, I took a job as a part-time activities director.

It's been an experience, to say the least. I can't practice physical therapy in Virginia since I'm not licensed here yet and I hesitate starting that process. I'm worried I can be tracked somehow. I'm sure that's the first thing they'll be looking for since it was my only source of income. I spoke to the director about a possible position in the future, as the therapist on staff is slated to leave early next year, but I'm still apprehensive. I've done everything I can do to avoid a paper trail. The position hasn't been promised to me, but they said they'd see how I interact with clients since they tend to be persnickety. The pay sucks, but for now I'm content with working hard to make their elderly clients like me.

When I left, I had no idea how to create a new identity—who does? It's risky enough being lawfully employed, but it was a risk I had to take. I needed a job, but applying for my PT license in a new state would be pushing it.

My experience with seniors was nil, zippo, zilch. Both sets of my grandparents are snooty. They never baked cookies with us, took us to the zoo, or even had us for sleepovers. Nope, they were more of the *children should be seen and not heard* mentality. But I've bullshitted my way at the Ranch, just like I have here at Whitetail.

I had to do my research on activities for seniors. I'm actually surprised I even got the job, but I think I sealed the deal when I BS'd my way through the questions about activity and exercise during the interview. Health is what I know, so I went with it. I got the position on the spot.

Landing this job at Whitetail was a different story. When I met with Addy to rent her bungalow, I thought she handed me a job out of sheer pity. That was not a fun day for me. Pity is something I've been taught to loathe. One can pity others all the livelong day, but to be pitied is a sign of weakness.

When Addy offered me a job, she had no idea how badly I needed out of my hellhole of a sleazy motel room. Not only was it the dirtiest place I'd ever experienced, but it was seriously scary and completely unsafe.

I slid the dresser in front of the door every night, just in case. But what I've learned over the last month and a half is Addy didn't pity me that day, she offered me pure kindness.

Kindness isn't something I'm accustomed to.

I smile at the guests as they seem happy with their food and quickly go to clear two tables who have finished eating. Another lesson learned from my mother—no one wants to look at a dirty dish at their place setting.

After dropping them in the kitchen, I go to the bar to wash glasses and find Evan doing inventory.

"Maya, Maya, Maya. When are you going to come to poker night? You're starting to give us a complex, you know." When I look up, Evan is leaning back against the bar with his arms crossed and has a smirk on his face.

Evan towers over me, but he's young. At twenty-four, he's four years younger than me. He's smart, self-assured, and good at his job as the tasting room manager. He's my boss. I'd never say this to his face because I know guys hate it, but he's nothing but pure cute. He oozes cuteness. He's like my little brother who I hug just to annoy him, because I can't help it. When Evan smiles, he's off the scales adorable, and I want to ruffle his messy hair.

I shake my head and look back to my task, holding a glass up to the light to make sure there aren't any water spots. "I told you, I don't know how to play poker. I'd just slow the game down, and everyone would be frustrated but wouldn't say anything because they're too nice. I'd be a bother and I hate being a bother."

"Mary didn't know how to play and we taught her. Not knowing how to play isn't an excuse. Maggie has an excuse, she..." He pauses and tips his head with a grimace. "Well, she's Maggie. Claire would have to bring her kids, they'd tear down the Ordinary for sure. You have no excuse. It's on a Monday, so you're not working here, and you're not leading Bingo because all the old codgers are asleep by the time we start. You're coming next week."

"We'll see." I smile as I lie. Everyone here is so nice, but I need to keep a healthy distance. Friends tend to want to know things about you. I need to be friendly, but I do not need friends. So far, I've managed to toe this line carefully, although the longer I work at both the Ranch and here, it's proving difficult.

Damn, people are nice out here in the middle of nowhere. Who knew?

"I'm not taking no for an answer again. After Mary cut your hair, she all but gave me the girlfriend warning that if I didn't get you to poker, I'd pay the price. If for no other reason, you need to do me this favor so I can score points with my new girlfriend."

After going months without a trim, I mentioned in passing to Addy that I needed a haircut. She made me an appointment with her girl, Mary. Little did I know they were best friends or that Mary and Evan just started dating. I swear, this group is woven so tight, I've never seen anything like it. Bev is so sweet it actually hurts to turn her down when she invites me to dinner, poker, or for a glass of wine at sunset when she knows I'm getting off work.

But no, I need distance. I need it like my life depends on it, because it does. It's already hard enough to keep my story straight. Even Addy, who in the beginning gave me my space, has started working her way into my heart by talking about how she lost her mom to cancer, how she came to live here in the middle of nowhere, and how her employees became her new family. There are days where I just can't take it, not because she's trying to find things out about me, but because I'm jealous. Inside, I'm green with envy because I've never had what she has, even though I lived under my parents' roof until the day I left.

These people even rallied around Addy like a family should after some man from her father's past came after her, holding her at gunpoint in her own vineyard. She's been through so much. I can't say I've ever had that kind of support.

Evan shoots me his boyish grin that I'm sure won Mary over in a heartbeat. "You're not going to disappoint my new girlfriend, are you? I mean, you wouldn't let me down like that, right?"

"I don't know—" I start, hoping to put him off yet again, wondering how creative I'll have to get, when my attention is drawn to the door. My breath catches.

It's him.

He's been coming in every day for a while now. When the lunch hour hits or when we're near on closing at six, he gets a sandwich, soup, or sometimes both. And he always orders more than one dessert—usually two or three, which I find strange. But I take his order—one that never includes a single fruit or vegetable—and submit it to Maggie. I make every excuse I can think of to clean up the storage room or kitchen so I don't have to deliver his to-go order.

This is because he's probably the most beautiful man I've ever seen.

Rich, dark-brown hair with hints of deep gold, it

looks as if he spends his days lounging on the beach, even though I doubt this is true. He doesn't look like the lounging kind of guy. He's big, really big, and his presence commands attention, even though I can tell he wants none of it. Every time I've seen him enter the tasting room, his eyes never wander and he never smiles, trying not to draw attention to himself, even though his efforts are a lost cause.

His expression always remains stoic and apathetic, but underneath his features are strong, rigid, and masculine. His medium complexion is in stark contrast to his eyes—so bright blue, the first time I looked into them, they were blinding.

Blinding, but also wounded.

I don't question the fact there's pain hidden there, because I recognize it. I've seen it in the mirror for a while. Only recently have I noticed it fading in my own eyes—but still, it's there.

Even if I didn't notice his inner pain, it's plain to see he's been wounded physically. As big as he is, he moves gingerly, as his arm is casted and in a sling that's wrapped tight to his body with a wedge under his arm. His face looks better, but the first time I saw him, he was bruised and battered in a way that matched his eyes.

All of this, his beauty mixed with his injuries, only fuels my fascination.

There's obviously something wrong with me.

Whenever he comes in, he strides straight to the bar, never makes small talk or asks for the daily specials. He orders and waits, then he pays and leaves. If I'm here long enough, I see it happen twice a day.

Right after I take his order, I resume spying on him

from the backroom. And I've spied enough that, even to myself, I'm reaching creeper status.

Ugh. Creepers are weird and I'm becoming one.

Since he's already made it halfway across the tasting room, I do what I've done for weeks, and prepare to spy on him.

Before I can hide, Evan's phone rings. He looks at the screen and beats me to the punch, leaving for the back room as he mutters, "It's Mary. Do me a favor and hold down the fort."

Shit. I've never been alone with him.

When I turn around, there he is, looking at me with his perfectly-beautiful, anguished blue eyes.

I swallow and do the one thing my mother instilled in me more than anything else—be composed. I take a breath and go to him, the bar being the only thing separating me from the target of my inner creeper. "May I help you?"

His brows pull together and my eyes go directly to the scar on his temple. Red, angry, and still inflamed, it's clear to see he's recently had stitches. This, too, fascinates me.

His voice comes at me strong and deep, even if a bit harshly. "The Monte Cristo with chips, potato soup, and whatever desserts she has, one of each."

The Monte Cristo and potato soup? Never mind the dessert order, there's so much there that bothers me. I've spied on him ordering almost every day I've worked for the past few weeks, and in his condition, his body needs healthier foods to heal.

For the first time ever, I muster up the courage to do more than simply take his order. "Would you like to hear today's specials?"

His answer comes quick and clear. "No."

Doing everything I can to collect my courage, I push, "Are you sure? Maggie's worked really hard on them. Her new sandwich is great."

He couldn't be any clearer when he answers firmly, "I'm sure."

What the hell. I'm on a roll, so I keep on as if he invited me to. "It's a Mediterranean wrap. Lean cut turkey, stacked with romaine, English cucumbers, heirloom tomatoes, red onion, and for a bit of salt, Kalamata olives. She even added a spread of roasted red pepper hummus. It's delicious. I had it yesterday."

This time he tips his head and frowns in a way I know he finds me ludicrous. "No. I want the Monte Cristo."

Well then.

I put another smile on my face and try again to add some color to his diet and continue with the specials. "Our soup of the day is colorful minestrone."

"Pay attention." His face hardens, and if he didn't sound serious before, he sure does now. "The Monte Cristo. The colorless potato soup, and it better be a bowl, not a cup. Desserts, one of everything she's got. That's it."

Only because it's my job, I feel safe in offering, "Would you like a side salad with that?"

He loses his frown when his brows fly up, his beautiful blue eyes going big. "Are you kidding?"

He's close to losing his patience, but I know for a fact his body will heal faster if it has the proper vitamins and nutrients. "The organic seasonal fruit medley?"

And if he didn't mean it before, there's no question now when he growls at me, "No!"

Even though I'm disappointed *and* a bit freaked at his rumbling voice, I can't deny, having a conversation with him has been exciting. I scribble down his order and give myself one more opportunity to appreciate his now-frustrated blue eyes. That's when I ask, even though I know, but I really like to hear him say it, "A name for the order?"

"Grady."

I love his name. Grady is casual, comfortable, and friendly, even though its owner is anything but. Still, I love it because every name in my family is snooty, stick-up-the-ass formal, just like my family, so very unlike the mysterious-but-wounded, blue-eyed Grady.

"I'll give this to Maggie. You can have a seat while you wait."

He lets out a sigh and shakes his head before turning. I'm not quite sure, but I think he lets out a string of curse words as he moves gingerly to the tables. Like every day, this makes me wonder what type of accident he was in and what his physician has him doing for rehabilitation.

I go to the kitchen and hand Maggie his order. As usual, she quizzes me, making sure I got the order right. "A Monte with chips, bowl of potato, and one of every dessert. That right?"

I sigh, wishing I could've talked him into some vegetables that offer anti-inflammatory benefits to help with his injuries, and reply, "Yep. That's it."

I decide to revert back to my creeper status, pronto, and let someone else deliver his order. As exciting as it was talking to Grady, I don't want to push it.

Ugh. Just when I thought it couldn't get any worse, I'm not just a creeper, but a scaredy-cat creeper.

2

ONE STEP AT A TIME

Maya

"BINGO!"

"You could not have gotten Bingo already, Erma. She's barely called any numbers."

"I did so, Betty. She'll check the numbers, just you wait. The Bingo gods love me 'cause I'm not a crabby old hag like you."

"I might be crabby, but I'm not a cheater."

"How can you cheat at Bingo? Maya checks. If you can cheat at Bingo, lemme know how, 'cause I'm all for cheatin'."

"No one's cheating." I sigh. Sometimes I wonder if I work with the elderly or preschoolers. "Tell me your numbers, Erma."

Erma calls out her numbers and she was right, the Bingo gods definitely love her. She wins a lot.

"Bingo," I confirm. I reach for the old boom box we use and cue up the song on the CD. "We all know what that means. Everybody up. It's good for your circulation. Let's hokey pokey."

"I hate 'The Hokey Pokey'," Betty complains. Betty always complains about something. "Can we do the 'The Twist'?"

"We'll twist next Bingo," I offer.

"I want to do that *slide* dance," Foxy yells from the back. Foxy is spry and surprisingly limber for his age. When I first started working here, I asked how he got the name Foxy and he said he didn't know. He's been called Foxy his whole life and, since his given name is Cornelius, he was good with Foxy. Who could blame him? I'd be good with Foxy, too.

"Most of us can't hop, Foxy!" Emma Lou shouts even though she's sitting right next to him. She must not be wearing her hearing aid. She's right, though. Foxy is the only one who can hop. He's also the only man who plays Bingo and I'm pretty sure he does it only for the dances. We do a little dance every time someone gets a Bingo. It's a good way to get them up and moving.

I push play on the CD player and yell over the music so they can all hear me, "Two more Bingos, it's almost lunchtime. We'll twist and cha-cha next. Come on, sing with me!"

I lead them in "The Hokey Pokey." My group of about fifteen seniors sing and dance, some having fun, others only pokey grudgingly. I do my best to dance around the room to get them in the mood—I'm over feeling like a fool when doing things like this. It's my job to keep them excited, and really, I think they like me for it.

We put our arms in and out, our legs in and out, and we turned ourselves around. By the time we're done, they're breathing hard and I can tell they've had enough. We play two more rounds of Bingo, with breaks for "The Twist" and finally the "Cha Cha," which makes Foxy a very happy man.

There aren't many men here at Rolling Hills Ranch. I'd say the ratio is hardly five to one. It's also hard to get them involved in games like this—Foxy is one of the only joiners. I do my best to coax them out of their rooms.

They do like to be outside, though. This fall we played horseshoes. I had to fetch the horseshoes for them, but I did it because it made them happy. We even tried croquet, but they don't like to bend over, so that wasn't a good idea.

I quickly clean up the Bingo sheets and markers as the residents move to the cafeteria. I spot the sneaky seniors who I've secretly named the Clickety-Clique walk by. "Miss Lillian Rose, you better not sneak a regular plate again. You're BP was up—you need to stick with the low-sodium meal." Lillian Rose is from the deep south in Alabama, and her family moved her here so she could be closer to them. She loves her southern food, but her blood pressure does not. She's thicker than thieves with some of these women and they've started smuggling her food on the side. "Yeah, I'm looking at you, Dot. You're not doing her any favors by pilfering food that's not good for her."

Just to show me they don't give a damn, the entire group rolls their eyes.

"That's what my medication's for," Miss Lillian Rose says as she struts out of the commons to the cafeteria.

Sighing, I gather my things to return to the storeroom. I've been here since seven this morning to plan and get ready for the day. We usually start after breakfast around nine. So far today, we've gone for a morning walk, sung karaoke, played trivia, and just now, Bingo Dance Party. Not everyone does everything—that would be too much for anyone in this group. I try to vary the activities so there's something for everyone. The Ranch isn't the poshest assisted living facility on the planet, but it isn't a dump, either. Their monthly payment includes activities to entertain and keep them healthy, both physically and mentally. They have other activities here in the afternoons, but they're group-led, or volunteers come in to organize a book club or a Bible study. The residents are most energetic in the mornings, so that's when I'm scheduled, which works well with the winery. I usually stick around through their early lunch, then by noon I'm back at Whitetail, where I work the regular lunch hour through closing in the tasting room.

As I put everything away so I can work on my schedule for next week, the director stops me in the hall. "Hey, have you started the process to get licensed in Virginia? Cheryl gave me her notice yesterday. She'll be gone at the end of February. Everyone really loves you, and as much as I'll hate losing you in activities, I need a good PT on staff."

I bite my lip because I'm going to have to talk my way through this, and I'm so tired of bullshitting those around me. What I hate even more is I'm becoming really good at it, and coming from a long line of really good bullshitters, it's not a family trait I was hoping to inherit.

I'm a bullshitter *and* a creeper. I'm beginning to hate the new me.

"I've gathered the paperwork and have started

digging through it. Virginia is a bit different than New York. I think I have to take some additional classes, they won't allow me to test out. I'm working on it," I lie. Lying sucks and it seems the longer I'm here, the more I'm lying. Maybe it's time to sever my ties and move on. I'm not quite sure what the normal protocol is for staying in the same place when you're hiding from your ex and his family.

"Perfect. How long do you think it will take?" he asks.

It shouldn't even take a month. I've looked into it and, other than some paperwork, it's only a few exams which shouldn't be hard. Besides getting all my New York credentials transferred, it should be a simple process. What's not easy is doing all this while hoping it won't create a paper trail. I'm almost positive as soon as I start, someone's pockets will be lined green, and I'll be found instantly. "I'm not sure—it's a lot of red tape."

"Be sure and get it done. I really want to slide you into that position. It took me forever to find Cheryl, I went through three therapists before I found someone who wasn't scared off by the sweet dispositions of our clientele." His eyes widen with sarcasm.

"I'm on it." I smile and try to appease him with another lie. Even though the paperwork is all sitting back at my bungalow, finished and ready to file, I'm totally *not* on it. I'm so scared, I'm not even close to being on it.

Later, on my way out, I hear my name called as I walk past the cafeteria. "Maya."

Stephanie, the office manager, is waving to me from down the hall, so I stop and turn back. She's standing with a younger man, and when I say younger, I mean probably in his mid-forties. Not a potential resident, that's for sure.

"Mr. Acogi, this is our activities director, Maya Augustine." Stephanie turns to me and continues. "Jeff Acogi is touring our facility for his uncle who lives in the area."

I offer my hand. "Nice to meet you, Mr. Acogi. I haven't been here long, but all the residents really seem to enjoy it."

"Miss Augustine." He takes my hand and tips his head. "It's a pleasure. I like what I see so far."

Stephanie turns back to him. "Maya is the best activities director we've had in a long while. Our residents really take to her, she works hard to get everyone involved. You can know that if you choose Rolling Hills Ranch for your uncle, there will be plenty of events to engage and keep him moving."

Finally releasing my hand, Mr. Acogi says, "You must be very dedicated. It sounds like everyone enjoys having you here."

I say nothing about hoping to someday be brave enough to get my Virginia PT license so I can work here in another capacity, and simply say while shrugging, "I like it here, too. The feeling is mutual."

Stephanie smiles at me. "Thanks for stopping to say hi, Maya."

"Of course." I turn back to Mr. Acogi one more time. "Enjoy your tour."

He smiles. "I already have."

Ron MacLachlan

Upstate New York

"Boss, you got a call."

"I told you I didn't want to be bothered," I yell without looking back.

Fucking recruits. We had a break from the cold and all I asked for was a couple hours to sit and fish. Can they not handle any-fucking-thing? I hardly get to the lake house anymore as it is.

"Sorry, boss. It's Jeff. I told him you ordered no interruptions, but he wouldn't have it. Said I'd be in a fuck-load of trouble if I didn't get you right away. I like to walk straight and don't want a hole in my foot."

When I look over, our newest and most motivated recruit in a long time, Trevor, is holding a cell out for me.

I fucking hate cell phones, too. We never had trouble doing business back in the day when we couldn't be reached at a moment's notice. If anything, it was easier back then.

If one of my lieutenants insists, I know it's a big deal, so I shift my reel to one hand and take the fucking cell. Jeff went south to visit family, which really makes me wonder what this shit is about.

"What?" I clip.

"The kid said you're at the lake fishing. Sorry to interrupt."

"Glad you're sorry, but you're still interrupting. What do you want?" Not one nibble all day, and now that I have a fucking phone to my ear, my bobber dips.

"I'm in Virginia visiting my uncle."

Shifting the phone to my ear, I slowly reel in the slack on my line. "Did you forget my Nancy made him baked ziti with sweet sausage? Just got my first bite all day and you call to tell me something I fucking know?"

"We had it last night. He loved it. Send my gratitude to Nancy. That's not what I'm calling about."

My line pulls taut and I stand to give it a good yank to sink my hook. "I'm gonna throw this cell in the water if you don't tell me something I care about real fucking quick."

"Boss," he starts and his voice dips, finally getting to it. "I found something you've been looking for."

"It better be the holy grail, Jeff." I wind my reel slowly as my rod arches.

"Sorry, Ronny, no. But maybe the next best thing. I found Weston's woman."

I stop reeling and grab the cell with my hand. "What the fuck?"

"Yeah. I'd love to say it's because I tracked her down, but I didn't. We all know she left no trail. It was pure luck I found her. She works at a retirement facility I was touring for my uncle. I couldn't believe my eyes when I saw her. Thought it couldn't be, but they introduced her as Maya. Surprised she stuck with her real name. I have no doubt it's her. She doesn't know me—we don't need to worry about her getting spooked."

I thrust my rod at the recruit and turn, moving quickly from the dock. "I want all the details. Don't leave anything out. You sure she didn't recognize you?"

"I'm sure. I've only seen her from afar and in pictures since she vanished. Now she only knows me as someone's nephew. I don't think she'd have any reason to be suspicious."

"Stay," I order. "Watch her 'til I send Byron to you, then you can come home. Keep this quiet for now. Weston's gonna go crazy when he learns we found her. I need more information first. I'm not calling the Augustines, either. You handle Byron when he gets there. Make this your first priority, hear me?"

"Sure thing, boss."

Jeff goes into detail about where he found her, what she said, and everything he knows. It isn't fucking much, but it's enough. She's been gone for months. With what happened, I would've thought she'd gone farther. Maybe she went far enough. It's not like we found her by our own talents—she fell into our laps.

As much as I hate to admit it, sometimes a bit of luck is all that's needed. Or maybe it's the million candles Nancy has lit since she left. Whatever it is, I'll take it.

Weston will be another story.

My son—the longer she's been gone, the more agitated he's become. He knows he fucked up and caused this shit storm. But if Jeff's right and this is really her, we can bring her home.

I've just gotta figure out how without causing too much angst with the Augustines. Once she's back, we'll deal with her.

One step at a time.

3

CREAM PUFF

Grady

"You think yer tough, huh?" he slurs, his big body shifting to the side, catching his balance. I don't know exactly what he does to get like this, but I don't think it's just from drinking. This seems different.

Without taking my eyes off him, I say to Peyton, "Go find the girls. You know what to do."

"You little fucker." The man sways before looking over my head. "Don't you move, Peyton. You girls left a fuckin' mess. 'Spose to clean this shit up before I get home."

"Get home from where?" I ask, taking a step closer, trying to get his attention back to me.

"Grady," Peyton calls for me through her tears, not doing what I told her to. I feel her hand grab at my arm to keep me from moving closer to him, but I shrug her off.

"Go," I stress. She needs to hide now before I can't keep him from her. I've started to put on some weight, but he's still got at least sixty pounds and five inches on me. No way can I protect her once he gets started.

"Little fucker," he repeats, too few brain cells to come up with anything new. "Yer fuckin' thirteen. You think you can stop me from teachin' those girls not to make a mess in my house?"

I think I hear Peyton scurry off. I hope she does what I've told her to. If not, we're all in for it, not just me. "Fourteen. I had a birthday six months ago, but you wouldn't know. You've been drunk for years."

And he has. He was always a drinker but it's been worse since Mom's been gone.

His arm comes up, but I'm quicker. I've learned to be out of self-preservation, but football taught me to be even faster. Most guys my age go out for football for the love of the sport. I doubt many pray they make the team so they can bulk up and learn to dodge an uppercut to better survive at home. Or to have another excuse for the bruises. And I need every excuse I can get.

He fumbles then trips. "Damn you!"

My newfound agility pisses him off and he really comes for me. I try to dodge him again, but no matter how quick I am or how off he is from whatever he's high on, his sixty pounds and five extra inches win.

The next thing I know, I see stars...

I jerk awake, pain shooting through my shoulder from my body wracking. The remote goes flying, hitting the floor, and when I look up, game highlights are on the screen.

Fuck. The dreams won't stop.

I've never needed a lot of sleep to function, even to be on my game. But I can't say I've ever been afraid of sleep. Hell, I've never been afraid of anything.

I look at my phone and it's early. I must have drifted off after dinner. The days are so damn long sitting around here, but the nights are even longer. They last for-fucking-ever.

The cameras ding, telling me there's movement in the woods, and when I open the app, there are multiple alerts. It's probably what woke me, not that I mind. Ever since Crew and I got back to the States, my shithead father invades my dreams. Fifteen years later, from the grave, he's still fucking with me. After all this time, his tormenting doesn't stop.

Because of Crew's business and training the up-and-coming assassins, this property has got to be one of the most heavily secured pieces of land outside of the beltway. When Crew made Addy his, he extended that security to the vineyard, too. The alerts mean the cameras and sensors have picked up something in the woods, and like it does every time since I've returned from the assignment from hell, it makes my insides tighten.

When I click to the cameras, there she is—running.

Always running. I almost missed it.

I should turn off my phone and give her privacy. She has no idea every time she runs, I can't take my eyes off her.

Seeing her face as she moves quickly through the trails of the vineyard, she's focused and deep in thought, different than how she looks when she's working in the tasting room. There, she's antsy—even nervous.

Just like every time I watch her over the cameras—which is everyday—no matter if she's coming, going, running, or sitting on her porch, I know I shouldn't look, but I do.

I can't stop.

At first, I realized this made me a slimeball—watching a woman over cameras for pure escapism—

but I don't give a shit. If I wasn't worried about being a slimeball, I should be really fucking worried about my mental capacity that I'm watching her and don't care.

But I adjust the cameras and do what I do every day. I watch so I don't think about anything else.

Nothing but her.

Maya

"I JUST TALKED TO MORRIS. Next year I want to go bigger and better in the fall. The Thanksgiving tasting was such a hit—I want to start earlier in October. In the spring, we'll plant a pumpkin patch for kids and only request a donation to go to charity. Expanding the menu to include some kid-friendly meals or treats might be a good addition. Maybe it will give adults another reason to visit."

Addy is filling Evan and me in on her plans for next year. I worked hard to become a physical therapist and never planned to wait tables. It sort of makes me sad to think I might not be here next year to experience her bigger and better plans. I don't know what I expected when I left, but the longer I'm here, the easier it is to breathe, not to mention, I like it. I'm not sure I can make it a whole year without needing to move on. Deep down, I hope I get to stay.

It's Friday and the tasting room is becoming more crowded by the hour. Thanksgiving was just last week and Addy has the place decked for Christmas. There are trees everywhere and they're decorated solely with wine and deer-related ornaments that are all for sale. She even mixed in some cows.

I grew up in the suburbs and have never been around livestock before. Addy sure loves her cows. When she found out I'm a runner, Addy invited me to walk with her and the cows in the mornings, but I'm usually at the Ranch by that time. Plus, as cute as they are from far away, they smell exactly how one would expect a cow to smell—like a cow.

I've passed on walking with the cows and stuck to my late-evening runs. It's dark, and out here in the middle of nowhere with no city lights, it's *really* dark. I stay on Addy's property, but I can't say it doesn't freak me out to run in the dark by myself. I can't afford a treadmill, let alone have room for one in my bungalow.

"Maybe build some fire pits," Evan offers. "If it's cold, customers can still be outside and the kids can run around. You can offer s'mores on the menu."

"Ooh, that's good. I'll ask Morris how best to do that. Fire pits beyond the patio should be an easy addition. What do you think, Maya?" Addy asks.

She always catches me off guard when she does that. Asking my opinion—like it matters, since I only wait tables. It's even worse when she asks me something that would give away any personal details of my life.

I feel my eyes go big and shrug, trying to think of something to add. Pulling from my most recent experience at the Ranch, I offer the only thought that pops into my head. "Maybe some yard games? You know, for the kids and even adults, since you're trying to entertain them outside."

"Yeah, you need to up the entertainment," Evan agrees as he washes glasses and looks to me. "I keep telling her she needs to stay open late a couple nights a month and have live music. They'd come in droves for that."

Addy sighs. "I know they would, Evan, but I already work six days a week, plus all the events. Crew and I are trying to cut back our hours, not add to them."

Addy is dating a man named Crew, though I don't think dating is the right word. He lives with her even though he owns the property next door. I've seen him come in with Grady a few times for lunch or dinner, so I assume they know each other. I've done my best to stick with my *don't make any friends* plan, and I haven't asked, but I'm so curious it's becoming a thorn in my side.

Speaking of my thorn, I look to the front entrance when the big heavy door swings open. My creeper instincts must be honed to perfection, because there he is—Grady, bigger than life like always, with Crew behind him.

"Hey, you here for lunch?" Addy swiftly moves from behind the counter and greets her boyfriend—or whatever he is—with a kiss.

Crew doesn't let her go, keeping her tight to his side and looks down at her with full adoration. "Yeah. I decided to drag Grady out for a late lunch."

Grateful for the excuse to finally peek at him, I bite my lip and try to hide my frown when I find him staring at me. It's sort of a mix between a glare and a stare, but nonetheless, his beautiful, bright-blue eyes shine through his crinkled brow. I should greet them both, or do my job and offer to take their orders, but Grady frowning at me makes me hesitate. I have a feeling it's all about my pushing the specials on him.

Hmm.

That was a couple days ago, but apparently, I made an impression. I've resorted back to hiding for the last couple days and successfully avoided him every time he's come in.

"How are you feeling, Grady? You look like you're moving better," Addy asks.

Grady's eyes narrow on me before looking to Addy, muttering, "Better every day."

"What happened?" Oh, shit. I hate it when I speak before thinking. That popped out of my mouth before I could stop it, probably because I've wondered what happened to him since the first time I laid eyes on him. After moving here, I've controlled my curiosity about everything in an attempt to keep my distance, but it's plain to see Grady was in a serious accident. The health care professional in me—and more recently the creeper—has been gnawing at the bit to find out how he ended up broken, bruised, and scarred.

If I'm not mistaken, Addy and Crew tense a bit as all eyes move to Grady. He's staring at me again, those blue eyes a mix of annoyance and curiosity.

When he doesn't answer, my mouth starts to run, because the awkward silence is so uncomfortable, I can't handle it. "You were obviously in some sort of accident and broke your arm, but with your wedge, it's easy to see it's more than just your radius and ulna."

Grady says nothing, but shifts his weight as his frown deepens.

But I'm on a roll and can't help myself. "I've seen you this way for weeks now, broken forearms aren't slung that long anymore, let alone with a wedge. Did you do something to your shoulder?"

I must have annoyed him into speaking because he finally clips, "I'm fine."

"You need to go back to the doctor," Crew adds. "He told you to come back soon for a follow-up. You're gonna fuck up that shoulder if you wait much longer."

Grady's eyes shift to Crew, his blue eyes nothing but angry now. "I said, I'm fine."

The mention of his shoulder is too much—I slide right into healthcare mode. "What did you do to your shoulder?"

Grady looks back across the bar to me. "Nothing."

"He dislocated it," Crew answers for him.

"Are you fucking kidding me?" Grady growls at Crew.

And I thought he was grumpy before. All this back-and-forth has certainly pushed him over the top.

"How long ago?" I ask, now more concerned than ever. I've been stalking him for more than four weeks in this condition, if he hasn't been back to the doctor by now, that isn't good.

He's in full-on glare mode when he looks back at me and asks, "Who are you?"

Sweet Addy offers her first words in the conversation, trying to lighten the mood. "I'm sorry, Grady, have you not met Maya Augustine?"

Grady's eyes widen, and this time I know he's talking about me pushing the specials when he answers without looking away from me, "Oh, I've met her."

As if no one else has spoken, Crew keeps filling me in. "It's been five weeks."

Unbelievable. He dislocated his shoulder five weeks ago and hasn't been back to the doctor? Grady starts to direct his frown to Crew, but looks back to me instantly when I can't hold back any longer. My next words come from nothing but pure passion for a job I love, but also concern for my patients, even though he's definitely not my patient.

"It's been five weeks and you haven't been back to the doctor? You're going to lose motion if you don't do something right away. Even with the break, light therapy should have started a week after the injury. Those ligaments are going to tighten around the gleno-humeral joint between the humeral head and scapula, making it more painful later on, and that's if you don't permanently lose motion. The damage is already setting in, and if you don't get started right away, you'll never have full range without major reconstructive surgery."

When I finally end my unwanted assault of therapeutic knowledge, I find all three of them are standing on the other side of the bar staring at me. And I realize I've done it. I've totally screwed myself for the first time in months, giving hints as to who I am.

Damn, I've been so careful, too. If I'm honest with myself, I'm actually surprised I lasted this long. I'm not a good liar and never have been.

Addy is looking at me with wide eyes and a hint of a smile playing on her pretty face. Crew's head is tipped, but his facial features have barely changed even if his eyes do appear curious.

But Grady?

No, Grady is about to come out of his skin. If I thought he was irritated before, it's nothing compared to now.

"I mean..." I start to backtrack, spinning my wheels, trying to make my knowledge of the scalpula, humerus, and the glenoid cavity sound like I merely enjoy perusing WebMD for light reading. "It only makes sense, you know, that not moving it for so long would be bad, right? Like when you sit for too long and you're stiff when you get up. You clearly take care of yourself—it's plain to see simply by your pectorals, deltoids, and brachioradialis. You look like you lift and work out regularly."

Addy grins and Crew's dimple barely appears, but Grady's frown softens a bit when I realize I'm going on about Grady's body right in front of Grady. This would be bad anytime, but spewing about his beautifully-built body right in front of him is downright embarrassing.

"Not that I'm looking." I try and make it better, even though I doubt anything could improve the situation at this point, besides me disappearing and reappearing in a foreign land, never to see him again. Because right now, this is bad, bad, bad, and since disappearing isn't an earthly option, I need to make it better. "It's just, how can I not look? Wait, I don't mean *look*, I'm not *looking*. I mean it's easy to see. Although, I guess seeing is the same as looking. Maybe *notice* is a better word. I've noticed you take care of yourself and it would be ... well ... sad for you not to be able to do that anymore, so I assumed some type of therapy might help you with that. But, really, never mind." I take a big breath and decide to change the subject. I'm sure the smile I try for comes across painful, because it sure feels that way. "Would you like to hear the specials?"

Ignoring my little rant, Addy asserts, "You sound like you know what you're talking about."

It's clear what she means, but I fake it all the same. "Yes, I memorize the specials every day."

Crew is no-nonsense when he points out, "She means the medical stuff, Maya."

Now I'm sure my face is pained as I shake my head and shrug. Every time I open my mouth it gets worse, so I bite my lip.

"Are you a doctor?" Addy asks.

"Oh, no, no-no. I'm not a doctor," I say, happy for once, to tell the truth.

"A nurse?" Crew goes on.

I shake my head again, not liking their interrogation.

"You're something. Come on, Maya. It's apparent you know what you're talking about. There's no reason to be so tight-lipped, and I know you've never waited tables before you started working for me. What do you really do?" Addy pushes.

"You're a physical therapist," Crew states, as if he was at my graduation from PT school.

I open my mouth to refute him, but realize I've said too much—given away everything I meant to hold dear. As much as I didn't want them to know anything about me, I do wonder if it's better than admitting to being a creeper. Even if I have daydreamed of running my fingers over every honed muscle on his body as I reviewed my knowledge of the muscular system, I certainly don't need to let them in on my fascination of everything Grady.

"Maybe?" I sort of answer.

"You are?" Addy's shocked. "I thought you were an activities director."

"Oh, I'm that, too," I answer carefully. There's no need for them to know I'm new to the senior citizen circuit. "I'm sort of waiting for the PT position to open up at the Ranch. I like it there and it'll be full time."

I try and ignore Crew, who seems to be assessing me in a way I don't like. Grady opens his mouth to say something, but Addy interrupts him.

"This is perfect. You're a physical therapist and Grady doesn't want to go to the doctor."

Grady looks straight at Addy. "No."

"Yes," Addy insists. "You heard what she said. You're already behind and you don't want to lose motion. If you refuse to go to the doctor, you can at least work with Maya."

"I'm fine," Grady asserts.

I can't help but sarcastically raise my brows and roll my eyes, because I know for a fact he'll be anything but fine if he continues to do nothing.

Grady goes on to growl, "Crew, do something."

Crew looks to his friend and sighs. "If you want to work for me, you need to let her help you. Maya's right. You can't lose motion, and you know it."

Wait, Grady works for Crew? In my attempt to distance myself, I've never asked what Crew does, let alone Grady.

Crew looks to Addy and asks her instead of me about my schedule. "When is Maya off?"

"Six o'clock, then we have to clean up. It's getting busy, but she can leave right at closing and we can handle the prep for tomorrow. Will that work?" Addy asks him.

"Fine, I'll go to the doctor," Grady growls.

"Sorry, too late. Maya just confirmed what I've been trying to tell you for weeks. You still make that doctor appointment, but she's coming tonight to sort you out," Crew informs him before turning to me. "He'll be at the house on my property. You can't miss it, it's the next drive over and the lane takes you straight to the front door. Grady's my employee and I'm self-insured. Send me a bill for your hourly rate."

"Um..." I mumble, wondering what just happened, because Grady doesn't look like he wants my help.

"Perfect. It's all set." Addy smiles.

Grady shakes his head and turns to leave while protesting, "I'm not doing therapy and I'm going to town for lunch."

I watch Grady as he stalks out of the tasting room, a sight just as good leaving as it was entering.

"He's doing the therapy. Thanks, Maya," Crew repeats before giving Addy a squeeze. "I'm hungry."

"Me too." Addy leans into him before grabbing his hand, pulling him toward the kitchen. When she looks to me, my heart drops when she grins broadly. "Stay right there, Maya. When I get back, I want to know *everything* about you."

Oh, shit.

Grady

SOMEHOW, I KNEW she'd come. As much as I wanted her to ignore Crew and Addy, not to mention me, the past few days have shown me the woman is persistent. The last thing I want is attention or help.

It's one thing to watch her over the cameras, but ever since she was forced to wait on me and wouldn't stop talking, being around her is more than intriguing. Today was more incessant talking, and even though it pissed me off when Crew butted his way into things, she surprised me when she admitted to being a physical therapist along with a waitress.

I thought maybe she wouldn't show. She certainly didn't look like she wanted to, but as I watch her drive up Crew's lane in her small nondescript economy car with Pennsylvania plates, she surprised me again. I didn't plan on going back to Addy's to get dinner. I had no desire to be bombarded about my shoulder. But here she is, it's almost six-thirty, she didn't waste any time.

Instead of getting up, I watch her on the cameras as she pulls to the front. I finally moved into Crew's house a couple weeks ago, simply to get him off my ass about moving out of the barn. I know he's not coming back. He's in so deep with Addy, I've never seen anything like it. Then again, no one close to me has ever had a normal relationship, let alone an exceptional one—but for some reason I can tell Crew and Addy are different than anything I've witnessed before. Especially since the day her shit blew up at the vineyard. After everything Crew's done for me, I was happy to repay the debt. Putting a hole in that traitor's head was the least I could do.

Even though it's dark, it's easy to see her on the cameras as she gets out of her car, carrying a to-go sack from the tasting room along with a pile of papers. She's changed from the dress and boots she was wearing earlier into her workout gear. I've tried not to let her evening runs keep my attention, but I can't help that they do. She's definitely a trained runner, she keeps at it for over an hour most days, and not at a slow jog, either. Being a runner, I know one when I see one, she can definitely keep up a good clip.

All of these things shouldn't pique my interest, but they do. Watching Maya has been a much-needed distraction ever since Crew and I got back, and I've taken every opportunity to be distracted. I try not to think about how she's become an obsession.

I not only see her on the cameras but hear her knock. I do what I planned on doing, and don't answer. Instead, I stay put in my recliner watching her on the live feed.

Her long dark blond hair is pulled back and I've got a clear view of her. She's got to be five-eight, maybe five-nine. Since she's on the porch and the cameras are close, I see her light blue eyes before she looks down to check the time, probably wondering where I am. She shifts the things in her hands so she can knock again, before eventually peeking through the side window.

The woman is persistent, waiting longer than I expected. Finally, she sets the sack at the door and folds the stack of papers to slide them inside. I sigh, not knowing if I want to run to her or ignore her, when she gives up.

I switch cameras so I can make sure she leaves the property before I get up and open the front door. Grabbing the bag, I instantly recognize the smell. Going to the kitchen, I pull the papers out first. They're detailed pictures of stretches and exercises focusing on the shoulder. It looks fucking miserable, so I toss them to the side and reach in the bag, not surprised to find a large bowl of Maggie's potato soup. I know that smell, I've eaten it enough. Still, I stare at the bowl, feeling something foreign turn in my gut.

Tamping that back, I pull out the rest of the containers of food. Popping them open, all I do is shake my head at what I see. There's a sandwich that I have no fucking idea what it is, but when I peel back the top layer of thick wheat bread, all I see are green, red, and purple. Thank fuck there's some meat on the bottom, but I've never ordered anything that looks like this before. She also got me a side salad, and damn if there isn't fruit, too.

The last box is a small one, the smallest container I've ever seen come from Maggie's kitchen. In it is the puniest cream puff I've ever seen. One—singular. This wouldn't be a dessert for anyone, especially me, who can down multiple for breakfast, lunch, and dinner.

If the vegetables didn't do it, that one single cream puff pisses me off for some reason. It doesn't matter that she thought to bring me a meal when no one's gone out of their way to bring me food since I was little. Crew might've right after I fucked up and almost got us killed, but I was so deep in my head at the time, I barely remember. I've known Crew since the day we started our training together to become contract killers. We've had each other's back for ten years now. For someone else to do something for me is foreign.

I toss the cream puff in my mouth, savoring it since it's all I've got besides the packaged cookies and boxed cakes I bought when I went into town today. They're shit compared to the desserts Maggie brings in. That one cream puff was barely enough to chew, swallow, or taste. I proceed to toss the salad and fruit in the trash along with everything of color on the sandwich.

I glance at the papers Maya left for me, thinking maybe I'll look them over tomorrow. I take the remaining food to sit in front of the TV and flip on a game. I need to get back to my weights, running, and I really need to get back on the fucking mat where I can kick someone's ass. Maybe that'll help me sleep through the night. Because right now, I've never been more fucking miserable.

The days are long enough, but nights ... I fucking hate the nights. When I finally do fall asleep, I'm restless at best. My fucking dreams keep creeping into my head. They're different since I was captured, just as bad as before, but sometimes worse because they take me back further, to when he was alive.

Those are the fucking worst.

4

WE FOUND HER

Weston MacLachlan
Upstate New York

"YEAH?" I ANSWER a call as I pull onto my parents' property. I just wrapped my meeting with our main supplier's contact and need to fill in my dad and his lieutenants on my idea. It's fucking brilliant if I say so myself. It'll give us the ability to triple our shipments, maybe quadruple them, if we're lucky.

"You about here? Your dad wants to sit down, has something he needs to talk about," the recruit, Trevor, says.

"I'm pulling in now—I've got a meeting with him and Byron. I just got done with our contacts from the south."

"Byron's not here, but Jeff is. They're anxious to see you and said to be fast."

I don't get a chance to answer, Trevor disconnects before I can ask what in the hell's going on. Then again, he wouldn't know. I was right where he was two years ago. Even though I'm my father's son, he only cut me a few breaks. I had to earn my position the way everyone else has.

I have no idea why they're in a rush to talk, they knew I was on my way. Even though it's my dad and it shouldn't make me anxious, I wonder what the fucking hurry is.

I pull up the circle drive and park at the front door. Letting myself into my childhood home, I'm greeted by Jean, who's worked for my parents since before I was born.

"Mr. Weston, it's good to see you. Shall I tell your mother you're here? She's in the kitchen." Jean smiles as I lean in to kiss her cheek.

"I'll find her before I leave. I need to speak with my dad first."

"I'll let her know." She takes my jacket and heads for the closet as I go to my father's office near the front of the house.

He's sitting behind his desk and one of his lieutenants, Jeff, is standing beside him.

I give my father a curious look because I don't report to Jeff, and the air is tense. "Thought I had a meeting with you and Byron."

"Byron's on a job for me." My father looks up at Jeff and I swear there's a silent communication there I don't like. When he looks back to me, he continues carefully. "Tell us about your meeting first."

I try to relax and not worry about the unknown elephant in the room, but it's not easy. "I pitched my idea and they like it. John Deere tractors—antique ones. I've researched it, they're not too hard to find and we don't need them working. We look like we're refurbishing them, but gut them instead—the entire thing—leaving only a shell. Some are huge and when completely emptied, will leave massive amounts of real estate for storage."

My father tips his head, rubbing his jaw with his thumb. His brows draw together when he asks, "Transport?"

"We get a flatbed trailer with a cab, not old but not new, just nondescript. All with legit Midwest plates, no one'll be the wiser. We'll look like a farmer, a collector, a hobbyist, someone wanting to refurbish them. It's time to pull out of Miami. With the threat of terrorism, the shipping industry is tight. We need to utilize the border. Easier payoffs, more traffic on a daily basis, and with the tractors, we have a way to cross in plain sight. Importing bananas might've worked for the last decade, but our people were picked off twice in the past five months. Our luck's gonna run out soon, Dad. Someone's gonna give us up. We need a new way."

My father's jaw tenses. He's never liked change. "The bananas are legitimate income—we need that to funnel the rest of the money through. We can't give that up."

"I didn't say give it up," I answer. "I'm saying stop moving the heroin through the bananas for now. Find a different way to transport. If the border gets tight, we can move back, that system is set up and ready. We should at least try—mix it up. It's time to diversify the transportation. With the tractors coming across on trailer, we can deliver to different spots along the way. Who knows, maybe we can diversify later."

My father looks up at Jeff, who gives him a tip of his head. Even though I don't report to him, I know Jeff is progressive and open to change. Although it doesn't take much to be progressive in comparison to Ronald MacLachlan.

My dad nods slowly and finally concedes. "We'll start small and give it a try. You've got the go ahead for three tractors. Get them to the warehouse and make sure they're prepped and sealed so the dogs don't tip us off. I fucking hate drug dogs."

Breathing a sigh of relief, I nod, but don't get the chance to enjoy it for long when my dad keeps talking. He leans forward and Jeff turns to walk around the desk, coming close. Confused and not liking him standing over me, I rise defensively, looking back across the desk to my dad. "What the fuck?"

"Relax. We need to talk to you, but you need to keep your shit together." My dad lowers his voice in the way that commands attention. I've heard it my entire life, but it's different now that I've been brought into the fold.

I clench my jaw, trying to control myself.

Dad gives Jeff a meaningful stare and a nod of his head before looking back to me. "Son, we found her. She's okay."

I know instantly who *she* is, because it doesn't matter what I'm doing or who I'm with, she's in my every thought.

Maya.

They found her.

I exhale, feeling all the air leave my body as relief replaces it, flowing through me. They found her and she's safe—my Maya. No matter what happened, no matter if she insisted it was over between us, there was no way I was letting her go. I just need time to convince her of that, and I thought I had. I thought I was making headway with her, but then I realized she was faking it when she up and disappeared. No note, no clues, no trail, no communication with her family. Not even her brother.

All the years we spent together—until I got sloppy—were perfect. Twelve years is a long fucking time when I'm only thirty. From the moment I laid eyes on her when she was sixteen, I knew she was mine.

I suddenly feel whole, the limb that was severed from my body when she disappeared has been miraculously healed.

But only for an instant.

When I finally take a breath, the relief dissipates.

And anger takes its place.

They must see it, because my dad quickly stands, his chair rolling back, slamming into the wall. Sensing Jeff close to my side, I turn and with all my might, put my hands to his chest and push. "Where the fuck is she?"

Jeff stumbles back a couple steps before advancing on me. I push again when he tries to restrain me and he growls, "Enough, calm down."

"Don't fucking tell me to calm down! Is she here? Did you bring her here?"

"There's no way we're telling you where she is while you're acting like this. Get your shit together," Jeff commands, standing a good few feet from me, posed defensively. He's fifteen years my senior, I've got at least thirty pounds of muscle on him. He couldn't do shit to restrain me if he tried.

"Weston!" my dad shouts. "Enough—that's an order."

Breathing hard, I force myself to halt, and do my best to calm down. There's no fucking way they're gonna keep her from me. She's mine and always has been.

After allowing a few moments to go by, my chest is still heaving. "Tell me where she is."

My father narrows his eyes. "You prove to me you won't run out of here creating a shit-storm, I might tell you. But you've gotta prove to me you can handle her. I haven't told the Augustines yet—we need a plan that'll convince her to come back on her own. I think the best way to do that is to use Joseph. I still can't believe she left him as close as they are. For now, know she's safe and we've got eyes on her all the time. Byron's on it."

"You put Byron on her?" I yell. "Why the fuck would you do that? I don't want him anywhere near her."

"Settle down. He's been told to watch her, that's it."

Fuck. I'm surprised I can process any of this, all I can think about is getting her home. This time in *my* home —I'll insist on it. Living all these months not knowing where she is has been hell. I spent the first month looking for her—my dad and the others understanding what I needed to do. I knew I couldn't keep that up forever, not doing my fair share of earning and letting the others carry my responsibilities. Plus, I had to man up. I knew she left because of me.

"Tell me," I exhale, trying to hold onto my control as I stare at my dad, "where is she?"

My dad looks from me to Jeff, curtly nodding once.

"Virginia," I hear from my side and turn to Jeff. "She's outside of DC, but your dad and I have already talked, expecting you'd lose it. You show us you've got your shit together over the next couple days, we'll tell you where she is, but you can't fuck this up again. She knows too much and because of that, we want her home where we can keep an eye on her. We need her loyal to you like a woman should be—and to prove she's not a liability. If she is, we've all decided it doesn't matter what family she belongs to, we'll take care of her like we would any threat."

"No!" I yell.

"Look." Jeff puts out a hand to calm me, as if anything could calm me when they're talking about Maya being a liability. "First off, that piece of ass you keep on the side is gone—cut her out for good. Second, you propose to Maya as fast as you can and marry her soon after. If you want her, you tie her up tight, and that includes babies."

It's all I can do not to put my fist to his face, but I know better, and deep down, I know he's right.

My voice is tight and strained when I agree. "Done."

Jeff nods and takes a step back.

"Son, you've got twenty-four hours to get rid of that skank and make a plan. Don't disappoint me."

I want to scream at both of them to tell me where she is so I can go to her, convince her to come home, or if I need to, force her to. I need to prove to her I want her more than anything and things can be good again, like they were in college, and the couple years we had after. She wore my ring once—I'm determined she'll wear it again.

I say nothing and turn to leave. There's no way I can see my mother right now. She'll know there's something wrong, and I know there's no way my dad told her about Maya. She'd be on the phone with Vanessa Augustine faster than I could blink.

I go straight to my car. I need to figure out how to make this happen.

Grady

I YANK UP my sweatpants as best as I can with my bum shoulder and arm. It's not easy showering with one arm wrapped in plastic. After five weeks, my arm feels great —it's only my shoulder that still bothers me. I know I need to do something about it, but I hate going to the doctor. I'll have to make shit up on how it happened and I'm not excited to do that.

Before I get a chance to pull a shirt over my head, the doorbell rings. I didn't hear the alerts from the cameras since I was in the shower. Grabbing my phone, I switch to the front door view of the house.

She's back.

I ignore my sling and stare at the screen on my phone as she waits. I shouldn't answer, it's bad enough I can't look away from her on the cameras. Last night it took her five minutes to leave.

She knocks.

And rings the bell again.

Fuck me, more knocking.

Minutes upon minutes go by and she waits, knocks, and rings some more.

All the while, I stare at my phone as she chews on her lip, sighs, and even closes her eyes like she can't believe she's standing where she is. She looks miserable, and I can't say I don't know how she feels. Not going to her is fucking hard. But she doesn't stop, and I'm not sure why she doesn't give up and leave.

She keeps on so long, I can't make myself ignore her another second. Tossing my phone to the bed, I march down the stairs and go straight to the front door. When I swing it open, she's surprised, and drops her arm from her constant state of knocking.

"What?" I'm frustrated with myself for not being stronger and leaving her be.

"Um..." her voice trails off and her light blue eyes drop to my torso. I stand and wait for her to say something as her eyes drag over me, and she rolls her lips, swallowing hard.

"Maya?" I call for her and try not to let her gaze affect me, even though it does. After watching her for so long, being alone with her for the first time gives me an uneasy feeling I've never experienced.

Her eyes dart back to mine, and she looks like I've shaken her out of a daze. I like the way she sounds out of breath when she says, "You're not wearing your sling."

I tip my head to study her expression. "No. I don't wear it all the time anymore."

She shifts her weight, looking uncomfortable. "Did you get the papers I left with the food last night?"

Mention of the food makes me think of the one dessert she left me, and I feel myself relax. For the first time in so long I can't remember the last time it happened, my mouth scarcely tips on one side. "You mean the single, miniature cream puff that was barely a bite?"

Her brow immediately crinkles and she stands straighter. "It was more than a bite."

"No," I contest, but I like her response. "You packed me a quarter of a dessert. That's just not nice. It's like you're teasing me or something."

"But," she pauses and puts her hands to her hips, "I did bring you dessert. I can tell you like them."

I lean my good shoulder into the door jamb and let myself enjoy our back-and-forth. "You also brought me a lot of vegetables."

"And potato soup, which I know you like, right?"

When I look down at her, I realize this is the closest we've ever been. She's wearing jeans that fit her like a second skin, and I know this because I've watched her on the cameras in her skintight leggings. Her jeans are rolled at the ankle over a pair of short boots that boost her to at least five-ten. Topping it off, she's wearing a Henley made for chicks that's unbuttoned just enough, she's teasing me with the swell of her tits.

I like it all, but I'm tired of talking about food. "What do you want, Maya?"

A confused expression takes over her pretty face and she shakes her head, her long, dark blond hair swaying back and forth, making me wonder how soft it is. "You didn't answer last night. I told Addy and Crew I'd come work on your shoulder. I don't like not following through on my word, so I left my job at the Ranch early today to try again. Did you at least do the exercises outlined on the papers I left for you?"

"No."

"Grady," she breathes my name, frustrated. No matter how frustrated she is, hearing my name pass her lips stirs something in me. I wonder what my name would sound like if she was happy, tired, or fuck me, when I was making her come. She keeps on, pulling me out of my contemplation of her screaming my name while my mouth is between her legs. "You're going to get frozen shoulder. You cannot simply resume normal activities without working up to it, you'll risk doing major damage. You probably need another MRI to check on the condition of the joint, but at the very least, you need to start the stretches."

"You're here to do that?" I ask, all of a sudden anxious to start therapy.

She exhales harshly. "Yes, I am. As a favor to Addy."

I straighten and step back to make room for her. If therapy is my way to spend time with her, I'll take it. "Well, we wouldn't want to disappoint Addy. Come on in."

As if willing herself to take the first step, she finally walks in, her boots clomping on the old hardwoods. When I swing the door shut behind her, she turns and asks, "Where should we go?"

I shrug with my good shoulder. "You're the professional. You tell me."

She looks around and sighs, dropping her bag on the floor. "I guess here is fine. Really, I need to measure your range of motion, check for swelling, and muscle tightness. That'll give me an idea of where to start."

"Measure away."

She pulls her bottom lip between her teeth again and I find myself jealous, wanting to bite her lip, too. When she closes the distance between us and stands in front of my bum shoulder, she hesitates, taking another deep breath.

When she doesn't make a move to do anything, I break the silence. "You sure you're really a physical therapist? You're not here just to fuck with me since you don't approve of my sugar consumption?"

"What?" She looks insulted. "Of course I am. I mean,

yes, I'm really a physical therapist. This has nothing to do with your love for sugar."

"Are you here to offer me the specials or are we going to get to it?"

"No, sorry." She exhales harshly and raises her hands, flexing her fingers before touching me.

I tense, not knowing what to expect, but the instant she lays her small hands on my body, I have to force myself not to react.

Her touch is soft, warm, and fuck me, even soothing. She runs her hands lightly over my bare skin, and I'm grateful she moves behind me, because I have to close my eyes to overcome it. Now she's touching both my shoulders, nothing but symmetry in her movements, gently probing my muscles.

Hell if I don't feel her breath on the back of my neck when her soft voice comes at me. "Do you think all the swelling is gone? I don't see much, if any."

I try to even my voice when I answer, "Swelling's been gone for over a week."

"Good," I hear and feel her say.

She moves to my bad shoulder, and as if she's finally more comfortable touching me, her hand slowly moves down to my elbow, bending my forearm up. I open my eyes and study her face as she focuses on what she's doing.

Her blue eyes are intent and methodical as I'm forced to stand here, doing nothing while she has her hands on me. As much as I will it not to, my heart speeds. It's like nothing I've ever experienced.

Just when I didn't think I could handle anymore, she lightly brings her hands to my chest, running them over my pecs as she says, "It's not uncommon for pectorals to become tight from poor posture when recovering from shoulder trauma. You've been compensating for your injury for weeks. That's a long time. You could really benefit from electrical neuromuscular stimulation, but I don't have access to a machine. You should get into a clinic where they have everything you need. It can help loosen muscles to speed up recovery."

With her so close in front of me, I can't manage a word, so I nod, even though I'm still not going to a doctor. Now that Maya's touched me, I'm gonna want more, and it's gonna be all I can do to fight the urge to return her touch.

Moving back to my shoulder, she gently lifts my arm forward until I can feel the pain and tense. Stopping, she does this again to the side, and then to the back. Each time, sensing when it's too much and stops.

She continues to torture me, not only with her stretches, but her touch. All the while, I have to stand here and act like it doesn't affect me. She talks me through some exercises, doing multiple reps of each. Sometimes I answer her questions, sometimes all I can do is grunt, because as much as I love her touch, the stretches hurt like a bitch.

When she finally lays my arm at my side, she brings her hands back to my shoulder. She must be trying to slay me, because fuck me, she starts to press and rub my muscles, massaging the tension she just created. It might be releasing the tension in my shoulder, but it's creating all kinds of tension in my cock.

She's killing me.

"You'll want to ice this. You can alternate ice and heat, but be sure to keep up with the ice since we moved it quite a bit. Do you still have the directions I left last night?" She looks up questioningly, having no idea what she's stirred inside me.

"Yeah."

"Good. Repeat everything we just did tomorrow, and keep up with the ice. I'll come back the day after to check your range. You'll probably be ready for some new motions, I'll bring my rubber bands, you'll need to start small, but it's time to add some strengthening motions." With that, she drops her hands as she takes a step backwards, and on an exhale, asks, "Do you hate me?"

I feel myself slightly frown. "Why would I hate you, Maya?"

She gives her head a little shake and flips her hand out between us. "That couldn't have felt good. Physical therapists aren't normally popular with their patients."

I feel myself relax, but what I can't explain is her touch is one of the best things I've felt in my life. Since I can't tell her that, I offer, "If you bring dessert next time, there's no way I could hate you."

As if I've broken the ice, she finally relaxes and rolls her beautiful blue eyes. Shaking her head, she bends to pick up her bag, and turns to the door. "You eat enough dessert—I'll take my chances with you hating me."

"Your gamble," I call, checking her out from the back, now even sorrier I can't return her touch.

When she's standing in the open doorway, she swings her head around and gives me the first genuine smile I've ever gotten from her. "I'll see you around, Grady."

"Yeah." I couldn't agree more, sooner than later, in fact. "See you, Maya."

I watch as she leaves. I'm sure she has no idea what

just happened—the effect it had or what she stirred in me.

I should do what she said and ice my shoulder, because it's starting to fucking ache. But I don't. I quickly move up the stairs and finish getting dressed. When I get back downstairs, I head straight out the back door to Crew's barn to look for a saw. Because for the first time in weeks, I'm ready to move forward.

Who am I kidding?

It's the first time in fucking years.

After years of nothing but resentment and revenge streaming through me, it's time for something different. Who the hell knew it would all start with physical therapy?

5

THE TINGLE IS BACK

Grady

FINALLY. I'VE BEEN waiting and she's later than usual. I was beginning to wonder if her schedule had changed, but she's back, pulling up the drive of the vineyard. I slip my phone in my pocket and go to the window of the upstairs bedroom.

Crew's been cool with me laying low since we got back. I haven't worked with the men once, not even in the classroom. I've tried, but I can't wrap my mind around what happened. Deep down, I know I slipped, lost my edge, and got careless. Something triggered in me, and I can't shake it—I've tried. Doesn't matter how I spin it, it all comes back to my head fucking with me, and even I know when that happens, it's over.

At first, I ignored it. Later, I worked out harder than I ever have before, trying to face it head-on. It was all pointless.

It never would've bothered me had it not been for Gracie. I've never had one single regret about what I did all those years ago. I'd do it again—even enjoy it—if I had the opportunity.

But it started fucking with Gracie, and knowing I caused that, it messed with me, too. It fucked with my head and my sleep. If I sleep, I can't get rid of the dreams. If I fall into a deep enough sleep, there he is, fucking with me, or worse, the girls.

He's been gone fifteen years and still causing havoc. I hope he's rotting in the depths of hell—it's the only place he deserves to be.

Knowing I came close to getting Crew killed almost did me in again. He followed me to that hellhole to have my back, and because I'd lost my edge, he had to save my ass. It doesn't matter how many times he's told me we're good since it happened, or that he thinks I saved Addy, and probably him, that day in her vineyard. He's tried to convince me we're even.

Still, it's not a good feeling.

Finding focus after being beaten to a pulp and almost having my hand chopped off has been challenging. Retreating has been the easiest option.

Until yesterday.

There's no denying Maya's gorgeous—any warm-blooded man would agree. With nothing to do for weeks, I've become obsessed. At first I'd just watch her come and go, run, or, on the rare occasion when she wasn't working and the weather wasn't too cold, sit outside by herself as she stared off into the woods.

But when she laid her hands on my bare skin yesterday, something clicked. I found it—my focus that disappeared. Even though it's different and foreign, it's the only thing that's felt right in a long time. I'm not back to where I was—not even close. But the second I looked down into Maya's light blue eyes with her soft touch on my skin, I knew.

I look out the window to the little house on Addy's land as Maya gets out of her car to hurry inside. I can't remember a day when she hasn't been rushing around, coming and going, or working at the winery.

Why the hell does a physical therapist work two part-time jobs—one as a waitress and the other at an assisted living center? We're located near one of the biggest metropolitan areas in the country. She said she was waiting for a PT position to open up at the senior center, but it can't be hard to find work in her field until then. Hell, there're suburbs just fifteen minutes east of us.

It makes no sense, but it does make me curious.

I rub my forearm while flexing my fist, enjoying the feeling of not having that cast on for the first time in weeks. Sawing it off myself was an experience, and not as easy as cutting out my own stitches, but it's done. No stitches, no cast, and I've decided I'm done with the sling.

Maya doesn't make me wait long as I stand at the window. After locking her door from the outside, she jogs back to her car. Making a quick U-turn, she starts toward the tasting room instead of leaving the property.

I turn and grab my keys on the way out. I'm anxious but I don't give a shit. If being near Maya feeds my obsession, I'll take as much as I can get.

Maya

"SORRY AGAIN," I call to Evan as I hurry out of the back room where I store my purse.

"Quit apologizing. You called to let me know you'd be late and I told you we're slow today with no events. I plan on doing inventory in the cellar this afternoon unless things pick up. Are you good up here on your own?"

"I think so. I've practically memorized my cheat-sheet for tastings. I know how the wines are made and their pairings, but I'll never be as good as you." I grin at him, serious and teasing at the same time. How Evan knows as much as he does about wine at his young age baffles me. He told me he wants to become a certified Sommelier someday. Courses to do this are easily found in California, but not Virginia. He's been working closely with Van, Addy's winemaker, to learn his side of the business, explaining time and experience are key.

Since he's twenty-four, I'd say he's ahead of the game.

Evan grabs a file and his tablet. "Addy's in her office. Call me if you get busy."

I watch him disappear on his way to the cellar before going to the kitchen to check in with Maggie. I've decided it doesn't matter how long I work here, conversing with Maggie will never be effortless. Today is no different. I jot down the specials and listen to her explain her attempts at seasonal baking so Addy doesn't have to order fresh desserts from a local bakery. No one has come right out and said it, but from what I gather, baking isn't Maggie's strong suit.

I hightail it out of her kitchen, but hardly make it a step into the bar when I'm stopped in my tracks. I was barely away for a couple minutes, but in that short amount of time, he appeared out of nowhere. One second I think I'm by myself, prepared to enjoy a slow afternoon, and then, *poof*—he's here, studying the wine list.

Without moving a muscle, his bright blue eyes look up from the leather-bound menu. Those eyes drop from my face, slowly traveling down my body before making their way back up, and when they do, he does the same thing he did for the first time ever when I stood on his porch. His lips scarcely tip on one side, making me wonder what he's thinking.

I mean, I'm not stupid. I'm pretty sure I know what he's thinking, but I haven't had a man look at me like that in a really long time. No man had the opportunity, or if one did, he knew who I was, and knew better than to give me a second look. In fact, up until a year ago, I didn't realize just how dangerous it would be for another man to glance my way, but now I do. I get it, and it makes me angry all over again.

But having Grady's eyes on me is freeing. Not only are they eyes that I like and have lusted over for weeks, but after yesterday when I got to look into those eyes up-close, having them travel my body makes me tingle.

I can't even think about having my hands on his bare skin. Touching his warm body and firm muscles was too much. I barely kept it together, it was all I could do to keep my breathing even. My heart racing along with the damn tingle didn't help one bit.

I haven't tingled for a really long time. Hell, I haven't even wanted to tingle, and any self-induced tingling business never crossed my mind. I guess stress can do that—make one not care about the tingle anymore.

But Grady's eyes and his beautiful lips barely tipping make me think solely about the tingle.

Damn. Now my panties are wet.

Holy shit, that hasn't happened in ... I don't know ... almost forever. Well, it did happen last night when I was touching Grady's bare skin and rock-hard—even if a bit tight—muscles. But before then, it was absolutely almost forever.

"Maya," Grady greets me as he tosses the menu to the counter and leans back in his bar stool.

I immediately notice his bare arm for the first time, the cuffs of his sleeves rolled low with no cast, showing off his veined forearms. I do my best to ignore his veins and my voice is hopeful when I ask, "You went to the doctor?"

He shakes his head casually. "Nope."

"But..." I'm confused, at a loss for words, before stating the obvious. "Your cast is gone."

"Yep."

Without moving, I keep on. "If you didn't go to the doctor, how did you get it off?"

"I cut it off."

My eyes go big. "Why would you do that?"

He slowly moves his arm up, proving his shoulder is stiff, and turns his forearm a few times, twisting his wrist. "Because it's better. No reason to keep showering with a plastic bag on my arm. That was a pain in the ass."

The thought of Grady showering, plastic bag or not, does not help my case of the tingles, so I put that out of my mind and slowly move to where he sits at the bar. I go with the easiest subject that comes to mind. "You should still have it x-rayed to make sure it set properly."

"It set just fine."

"You can't know that for sure."

He leans forward with his good arm on the bar and softens his voice in a way I've never heard from him. "It's fine, Maya."

Because of his tone and the simple fact I'd look like a freak if I kept arguing, I stop and sigh, directing the conversation toward the only other thing we've ever talked about. "Do you want to hear the specials?"

The man sitting before me, who's only been broody at the least and irritable at the most, leans back in his stool and carefully crosses his arms across his wide chest. Before I know it, a grin spreads across his face. "Are you going to torture me if I say no?"

I pull my lip between my teeth to keep from smiling. The man's proclivity for food is relentless. "Maybe."

His grin fades into a smirk and he jerks his chin. "Hit me."

Without looking at my notepad, I say, "A kale, brussel sprout, and broccolini salad, with finely shredded carrots, red cabbage, minced red onion, dried cranberries with fresh parsley. It's dressed and massaged with freshly squeezed lemon, garlic, and olive oil." I watch his smirk disappear and he slowly starts to grimace, but I persevere. "Instead of a sandwich, Maggie's created a lovely grilled tofu lettuce wrap with an almond dipping sauce." His grimace turns to a scowl. "She's also made a cabbage roll soup. Would you like me to describe it?"

"No," he answers emphatically.

I smile. "Are you sure? The soup is packed with cabbage, offering all kinds of health benefits, from preventing colon cancer to healing ulcers to relieving muscle soreness. It would actually be really good for your shoulder."

He frowns, appearing deeply disturbed by the food I just described. "Are you serious?"

I smile bigger and roll my eyes. "No, but that was fun. You're really weird about food, you know."

I don't think he found any of that fun because he narrows his eyes on me, shaking his head.

"Although, the soup of the day really is cabbage roll, and cabbage is good for you. It even has meat—beef and pork. You should try it."

His smirk reappears. "Maya, you're a smartass."

"Maybe," I tip my head, "but you're like a five-year-old who refuses to eat his vegetables."

"I like what I like, but I promise you, I'm most definitely a man."

I shake my head and take a breath, needing to stick with the topic of food rather than Grady being a man. "What can I get you?"

He ignores me and asks, "Why are you working as a waitress when you're a physical therapist?"

Honestly, I'm really sick of lying. I'm relieved when I can mostly give him the truth. "I just moved here and don't have my Virginia license yet."

"Where did you move from?"

Trying to keep up with the conversation without pause and be as truthful as possible, I answer, "The northeast."

"Northeast?"

"Yeah. Can I get you something to drink?"

"Where in the northeast?"

Not liking his bombardment of questions, I decide a distraction would be best. I reach to my left for a clean wine glass and place it in front of him. Grabbing two bottles in each hand out of the refrigerator below the bar, I ask, "How about a tasting?" I don't wait for him to answer and pour a small amount of the Petit Manseng. "Addy grows these grapes here at Whitetail. Try it."

He works his jaw as if he's thinking before he picks up the glass and tosses back the contents. I was hopeful he'd give up, but he continues. "What brought you to Virginia?"

I quickly uncork the Viognier, giving him a healthy splash, and continue telling truths. "It can be cold in the northeast."

He picks up his glass, but before taking a sip—or a gulp—asks, "It's not cold here?"

"Fine. It's colder there. Now drink," I demand, ready with the next bottle. I'm glad Evan isn't here. This is like the speed-round of wine tasting. He wouldn't be happy seeing fine wine that should be savored being downed like cheap tequila.

Grady swallows it in one gulp. "True."

His glass barely hits the bar when I start pouring and giving him the super-duper abridged tasting edition. "Chardonnay. Popular, crisp acidity, good with fish or white meats."

He looks at me inquisitively when he keeps on. "Why haven't you gotten your Virginia license? Since you're working on my shoulder and all, I should probably make sure you're legit."

He picks up the Chardonnay and swallows, waiting on my answer. I continue to tell him the truth, even though the truth is getting fuzzier by the second. "I'm working on it."

He continues to taste the special blend named The

Delaney, a Riesling, and Cab, all the while he asks about my job at the Ranch, why I'm such a vegetable pusher, my favorite color, and what I like to eat on my pizza besides vegetables.

He tosses back the Merlot as I answer about the pizza. "Mushrooms."

He's had to have had at least three glasses of wine by now, I've had a pretty heavy hand as we've progressed. Not to mention, this is the fastest wine tasting I've ever done. I think I've only been semi-answering his questions for maybe five minutes.

He sets the glass down roughly. "A mushroom's a vegetable."

"No." I pick up the last bottle, a blend of reds. "It's not a plant, it's fungi. Some would even classify it as a meat since they have similar vitamins."

"Who would classify a mushroom as a meat?" he probes, picking up the red blend.

I shrug, watching him down the last tasting just as quickly as the previous eight. I've done this long enough to tell he didn't enjoy the wine at all, but did it solely to talk to me. "You're done. What do you think?"

He sits the glass down and leans into the bar. "I think you didn't tell me shit about yourself other than your favorite color is celery, which again, is a fucking vegetable."

"It's also a color," I refute.

"Maybe, but I hardly know anything about you, Maya."

I lean down, putting my elbows to the bar to get close to him. I'm almost as close as I was yesterday when I was working on his shoulder, but now I'm face-to-face. I get to take in all of his features. His dark brown hair with glints of gold peeking through here and there, a strong jaw below his perfect lips, and those long, dark lashes, so long they frame his piercing blue eyes, much bluer than mine.

After I've taken a moment to appreciate his features, I lower my voice to almost a whisper. "Then tell me, Grady, how did you break your arm, dislocate your shoulder, and get that fresh scar on the side of your head?"

He doesn't flinch or move a muscle, but those blue eyes flare just enough, I know he had to work for it.

It appears I'm not the only one holding truths close to the vest.

When he minutely gives his head two shakes, I lower my voice further and respond to his nonverbal answer. "Touché."

He narrows his eyes as I stand quickly and turn for the kitchen.

"Where are you going?" he calls for me.

I look over my shoulder as I push the kitchen door open. "I'm ordering your lunch."

"I didn't tell you what I wanted."

"Oh, I know what you want, Grady."

With that, I leave him sitting at the bar shaking his head. Just because he'll be getting cabbage roll soup, I'll order him two desserts. They are a little on the smallish side, after all.

6

HERE COME THE CONSEQUENCES

Grady

"DID YOU DO your exercises yesterday?"

"What's your favorite food from a box?"

She drops my arm from where she was doing something called a pendulum stretch, and I can't lie, her exercises don't feel good.

"I'm serious," she says.

She might say she's serious, but her face shows me she's a mix between pissed and suppressing a grin. There's something about that look—I can't get enough of it.

"I'm serious, too. There's gotta be something you eat that isn't organic or a fungus. In fact, I refuse to do any more of your torture-chamber demonic aerobics until you tell me."

She puts her hands on her hips. She's wearing a pair of tight black jeans with a shitload of rips up the front, and a pair of red Chucks. But unlike when I sat at the bar in the tasting room longer than necessary so I could ask her questions and watch her work, she's got on a girly hoodie, so I can't see the rest of her curves. But that's okay, her face is close and her hands are on me—something I've been waiting for since she said she was coming back to torture me some more.

She sighs and shakes her head. "You're the worst patient ever and I've had some doozies."

I take a step, closing the small distance she created when she dropped my arm. "You've got to like one processed food, Maya. No one is that hardcore. You might want to be the picture of health to the rest of the world, but you can tell me. I promise we'll get back to the torture, but throw me a bone—something."

Tipping her head, she mulls it over a second before she finally sighs and fesses up. "Fritos."

I don't know why I'm surprised, but after two days of harassing her about food, I didn't actually expect her to say anything. "Fritos?"

"Yes, but not the regular ones, the Flamin' Hot ones. Are you happy now? Can we finish?" she asks, frustrated.

I don't even try to keep from smirking when the words fly out of my mouth. "You like it hot."

As she shakes her head ignoring me, her hands return and I get her touch back. I thought about taking my shirt off before she got here so I could really enjoy it, but I didn't want to look like a freak. I know I'm definitely toeing that line by hanging around her at work for hours. She doesn't even know I've been stalking her on the surveillance system.

"Your range is improving already," she says, lifting

my arm with one hand while her other is warm on my side.

"Hot Tamales?" I keep on. Since I can't take my eyes off her face, I get to watch her immediately grin, her beautiful features more relaxed with me than they've ever been.

She keeps ignoring me and I lose her touch when she moves to her bag, pulling out an enormous rubber band. She ties one end to the knob of the closet door. "Come here."

She doesn't have to tell me twice. When I get to her, I let her position me because that means I get her hands back.

"Hold this," she instructs. "I want you to lift from the side, but when you lower your arm, do it slowly. Let those muscles constrict on the way down, too."

"Mexican food? Spicy Chinese?" I keep on as I lift my arm as high as I can, letting her direct me on how slow to release.

"You're relentless." She smiles without looking away from me. Stepping back, she keeps up her torture. "Do twenty of those."

"Twenty? You like it hot and painful. You're into some weird shit, Maya," I tease, hoping to get her to smile again.

I get my reward because she does, and it's beautiful. Her eyes flare as she does her best not to laugh when she asks, "What's your last name?"

"Cain, why?" I'm only a third of the way through her reps, and I can't lie, it's uncomfortable.

She crosses her arms, looking up at me, her smile genuine. "Grady Cain. I don't think I've ever met anyone like you."

I look down into her light blue eyes, and enjoy her sincere expression. "It's because you're into the pain. Stick with me, I'll show you how hot can feel good. But if you really need pain with your spice, I'll do my best."

I'm almost done with my reps, and as much as it's starting to burn, it doesn't keep me from enjoying the blush creeping up her face. Even with her blush, she doesn't sound embarrassed when she shifts her weight and counters, "I've definitely never met anyone like you."

I finish, letting out a breath of relief, but she doesn't let me enjoy it for long.

"Now, stand facing the door and do the same thing but pull backward. Then we'll do the opposite with your back to the door and you can pull forward."

I turn to face the door and mutter, "Maybe I got you all wrong. I think you're into inflicting pain on others. When do I get to feel good?"

"Trust me." She tips her head and crosses her arms, leaning her shoulder into the wall to sit back and watch. "It'll pay off in the end."

I look out of the corner of my eye, and don't lie when I say, "It better."

She laughs, and I can't disagree. So far with her, the pain has been worth it.

Maya

I JUST GOT BACK from a much-needed run.

After Grady's PT session, I can't remember the last time I've needed to run so badly. I've been running since middle school. Like everything I ever took an interest in, my mother didn't mess around.

When I chose to play the flute in the school band, normal school classes weren't good enough for me. My mother hired a flutist from the Buffalo Philharmonic Orchestra to give me private lessons twice a week, not to mention all the hours she forced me to practice. Attaining first chair and keeping it all four years at my private high school was no problem. She made sure I was the best. The scholarship offers were proof enough.

I was in the seventh grade when I received some lame award for writing the most creative story and she knew I was going to be the next Hemingway. Many, many hours of creative writing lessons later, I finally rebelled. That hokey award was just that, hokey, not to mention a fluke. I sucked at writing and refused to continue.

Before that it was piano, voice lessons, gymnastics, ballet, and Latin.

It was my gym teacher in the eighth grade who pulled me aside and asked if I had an interest in track and field. I'd never thought about it, but after he called the high school coach to check out my skills—it was on. It took one call to my parents from the coach, and quicker than I could pass a baton, I had a private trainer three days a week for the next five years.

It's amazing what money can buy you. As a freshman, I placed first in two events at the state tournament. I only got better from there and the scholarships came rolling in, not only for the flute, but also track and field. At the time, I thought I'd hit the jackpot. My mother finally pushed me into something I loved.

Being a runner has an addictive quality. If I go too

long without my feet hitting the ground, I don't feel right. Even after college, it was a great way to work out my frustrations, and there were many.

But tonight, my frustrations are of a different variety.

After Grady spoke to me in a way no one has before, I needed to run. I've never had the luxury of thinking about another man, not when the only one in my life oppressed me from the young age of sixteen. He might not have been outwardly oppressive and controlling until a few years ago, but when I look back on it, it was there. All the signs I didn't know to see because I was young and infatuated—I thought I was in love. It didn't help that our mothers basically set us up for a long, happy, privileged life. Hell, I'm sure they thought they'd have grandbabies by now.

Somehow, as the years passed, it didn't feel right. That's when things started to fall apart, because not only did I get pressure from him, but from his family and my mother, as well. I'd hit my breaking point. I was done. It was over, damn the consequences. And the consequences were as big as they could be.

Warm from my hot shower, I pull on a tank with my favorite lounge pants. I've got music going from the small TV Addy provided when I moved in.

I still can't believe my luck, happening upon Addy and Whitetail. I needed a place to settle and some income. I'd blown through all the cash I was able to withdraw before I left. No way have I chanced using a credit card. They'd find me in a flash.

The extra job and furnished place to live was like a miracle when I needed it most. It's private here and I finally feel somewhat safe. Not completely, but it's more than I've felt in a long time.

Right when I was about to make something to eat, there's a knock at my door. It's not late, but it's late for anyone who'd knock on my door here at Whitetail.

Morris comes by every once in a while to check on things at my bungalow. His wife, Bev, stops by a couple times a week if she's made too much for dinner, insisting it will go to waste. These plates of leftovers are always hot and right out of the oven. Deep down, I know these meals aren't extra food, but just her excuse for trying to take care of me, and that feels good.

All my lights are on—it's going to be hard to make an excuse not to answer with the TV going. I go to the window and lift a slat to peek through the wood blinds I keep closed tight all the time. I see a car I don't recognize—a midsize sedan—pulled up to the small porch, parked right next to mine.

Another knock, but this one's more insistent. Damn, I wish I had a peephole.

It's been months, I need to quit freaking out and making things out of nothing. In the beginning, I swear my mind played tricks on me everywhere I went.

More knocking.

Trying to talk myself into being rational instead of the hyper-paranoid freak I've turned into over the last few months, I go to my purse and grab my prepaid cell, just in case.

When I flip the deadbolt and turn the lock, the knocking immediately halts. I barely crack the door and look through, when my heart drops.

Fuck!

"Maya, wait."

But I don't wait. I use all my might to slam the door, but he's faster and stronger. He always was.

He catches the door and pushes.

"No!" I scream, but it doesn't matter. I'm in the middle-of-nowhere Virginia, no one will hear me.

"I need to talk to you," he hisses.

He wants to talk, my ass. It always starts with him talking.

I made it months without them finding me. Even though it seems like forever some days, there are others where it still feels like I only left yesterday. When I escaped, I had no idea what I was doing. I guess I should be happy it lasted this long, but there's no fucking way I'm going back, much less back to the way things were. Over my dead body—literally—will I return to that life. I'll shout it from the rooftops if I have to, and I'll enjoy every second of it, knowing it'll be my demise.

Now that he's here, knowing he'll never leave me be, I have no choice but to face him head-on. I open the door halfway, the cold air from the December night flooding through me in my minimal state of dress, but nothing chills me like seeing him again. Standing on the porch of my bungalow, he's a completely different person than he was the day I met him all those years ago.

Weston was eighteen, only two years older than me. It was at a political fundraiser my parents were hosting for a state senator, and he came with his family. Weston was young, handsome, charming, and sweet. Even though he was off to college the next month, it didn't matter—he ensnared me in his web. Being young and oh-so stupid, I never fought it. I did all I could to wrap myself up tight in him.

He's even taller now, and has always taken care of

himself. He's built, and would be incredibly handsome to any female. But not to me. Not any longer. Over the last couple years, his beauty has grown ugly. Standing before me, staring at me with his deep brown eyes, his perfect wavy black hair, with his perfect bone structure, and framed by his perfect mouth—he's never been uglier.

"I never want to talk to you again, Weston." I seethe, trying to calm my voice, yet still giving away the fact my heart is racing out of control.

He looks down at me while keeping his hand on the door to hold it open. "We have to talk. Everyone is worried about you."

"How did you find me?" I need to know where I went wrong.

"It doesn't matter." He softens his voice in a way I know is a crock of shit. "All that matters is we found you and you're okay. Your family misses you—I miss you, Maya. It's time to put this behind us and come home."

"I'm not going anywhere." I somehow find a way to strengthen my voice. Weston shifts closer, but I put my hand to his chest and push. "You're not coming in. You need to leave."

"Maya," his voice tightens. "We can work this out. I thought we were until you left. Let me make it right for us. I can do that if you give me the chance."

"Right. I'm not young, stupid, or naïve anymore."

He can't hide his frustration, he never could for long. Controlling his emotions isn't his strong suit, so when the next words pass his lips, they're harsh, abrasive, and curt, just like he's proven to be. "This shit is getting old. It's time to come home and get over your fit."

My fit?

Fuck him. How dare he describe my cutting things off from him, his family, and even mine for that matter, as a *fit*, after what happened. But just when I was about to lose it, I hear a familiar voice. "Maya?"

Weston jerks, surprised by the voice coming from out of nowhere. He turns, dropping his arm from my door, giving me a clear view of Grady standing close. In our heated conversation, we didn't even hear his approach. Between all the rock, gravel, and twigs lying about, it's usually impossible to make a move without causing a ruckus.

Grady glances Weston as if he's an animal at the zoo he's grown bored of looking at because he's seen him a million times. He doesn't appear surprised to see a man standing on my porch, nor does he feel the need to explain his presence, appearing out of nowhere, and at this moment of all times.

But I don't dwell on any of this. I've been found and I know what that means, it was clearly explained to me before I left. According to them, I have two choices. Conform and accept the truths that were hidden from me for years—or be considered a liability, that being worst of the consequences. But it doesn't matter—conforming and accepting will never be an option.

I decide to create a new option for myself, that being delay the inevitable.

Looking up into Grady's inquisitive blue eyes, I do the only thing I can think of at the moment, even though it's a risk. I reach out to grab Grady's hand on his good arm so as not to hurt his shoulder. The moment my skin touches his, he quickly wraps his hand around mine, and I don't have to work hard to pull him to me.

He comes willingly, but when I grasp his sweatshirt in my other fist, his eyes flare with surprise for only me to see. I don't get to contemplate them long because I surge up on my toes, pressing my body to his firm one, and put my lips on his.

I barely have a chance to put my plan into motion when I feel a big hand in my wet hair and his strong arm round my lower back. Where I only planned on giving him a quick peck to get Weston off my doorstep, Grady has turned my intended brush of the lips into a kiss for the ages.

My back arches. As his strong arm pulls me close, and grasping my wet hair, he tips my head. I immediately open my mouth for him and he answers, his tongue dipping inside as his lips move on mine.

My body, which has reacted to Grady in so many ways the last few days, does something it's never done. Since I've met this man, he's made me nervous, excited, frustrated, and even tingle. But right now, the impossible happens. While being kissed by only the second man in my life while the first one watches—I relax.

I simply melt.

"What the fuck?"

Even Weston's irate tone doesn't affect me.

Grady pulls back enough to look into my eyes with his intense ones. "You okay?"

I tell him the truth, plus some, hoping he gets the message because I need him to play along to buy some time. "I am now that you're home."

His face doesn't change, he gives nothing away, but I do get a squeeze before he murmurs, "Good."

"Who are you?" Weston demands.

I get another quick kiss from Grady before he turns,

but doesn't let me go. He pulls my front into his side and I'm tucked under his good shoulder. He holds me tight, and it not only feels good, but he's warm, and I just realized I'm freezing from standing here in the night air with hardly anything on.

Grady looks down at me and sounds bored when he tips his head toward Weston. "Who's this guy?"

"Weston MacLachlan. Remember, I told you about him?" My heart beats rapidly, hoping this goes well enough to get Weston off my porch so I can really figure out what to do next.

"Ah." Grady nods as if we've had many lengthy discussions about Weston. "You said he was a pain in the ass, now I see what you mean."

"Get your hands off my fiancée," Weston growls before looking at me. "Maya, what the fuck?"

My body tenses and I tell Weston what I tried to tell him for months. "I'm not your fiancée and haven't been for more than a year now."

"You are," Weston insists. "Whatever you think you're doing, it's a phase. You'll get over it when I get you home where you belong."

"You were being nice, baby." Surprised by his endearment, I look up, but Grady is staring at Weston. "He's a bigger pain in the ass than you let on."

I know Weston well, and he's getting close to losing it. That's never a fun experience. "I'm not going to tell you again, asshole. Get your hands off my fiancée."

"She said she's not yours," Grady counters.

"She is," Weston growls.

Grady, who's remained cool, calm, and collected, shrugs, as if he couldn't give a shit. "Well, that's gotta be weird for you then, seein' as I'm sleeping with your fiancée."

Oh, shit. That was not a part of my plan.

Weston's whole body goes rigid, and just when I think this could get really bad, another voice joins our fray. "Everything okay, Maya?"

I have to crane my neck to see him since Grady has me tucked tight to his side, but it's Crew. He might've been talking to me, but he's staring straight at Weston.

I open my mouth to speak, but Grady gives me a squeeze and answers, "We're good. Although, it's getting late and we'd like to get to bed, but this guy won't leave."

Crew stands with his arms loose at his sides, relaxed, yet weirdly focused. "Who's this?"

"Weston, the one Maya told us about."

"You've gotta be fucking kidding me?" Weston explodes. "You cannot be with this guy. You've been mine for twelve years. I'm warning you, Maya. Do not do this."

"Enough," Crew interjects. "She doesn't want you here, that means you're trespassing and since I'm with the woman who owns this land, that means you answer to me. If you don't leave on your own, I'll make you—and trust me, you do not want that to happen."

"Maya." I look to Weston and his anger has brimmed. Weston MacLachlan isn't used to taking orders, except maybe from his father. Even then, it's a crapshoot if he obeys. "I'll give you twenty-four hours to come to your senses. If you don't, you'll regret it." He starts for his car, but after taking a few steps, turns back to me in the darkness and looks straight into my eyes with his evil ones, proving he's the monster I remember. "Still can't believe you'd leave and not keep in contact with Joseph. I've heard he's home and not doing well. Maybe I'll check on him myself."

A panic I haven't experienced until now erupts inside me, my stomach dropping. I twist out of Grady's hold and hiss, "You wouldn't dare."

Weston cocks his head, his anger turning into something he loves—the upper hand. "Dare? I don't know about that—Joseph is practically family. Or he would've been, but you changed that." He looks to Grady then back to me, narrowing his eyes, his face hardening when he sneers, "You'd better get to *bed*, Maya."

My heart catches for me, but more so for Joseph, because I know what Weston's capable of. Watching him get in his car and drive off into the darkness, I realize my life just changed. The choice I made months ago, damning the consequences no matter what, just came to fruition.

Here come the consequences.

7

LETHAL RECIPE

Grady

I FOLLOW HER in and shut the door behind us. She doesn't say a word or look back at me, but this house is so small I can see from here that she goes to her closet. Pulling a sweater over her head, she settles on the edge of her bed and drops her face to her hands, appearing to try and get hold of herself.

I have no idea what just happened, but I do know it's opened a can of worms. I had a feeling she was holding shit back, but I had no idea it could result in what just went down. If anything, I have a million more questions about Maya Augustine than before, and they have nothing to do with food.

What I do know from having Maya in my arms and my mouth on hers, is I'll do everything I can to figure her shit out fast. Not only do I need to know everything about her now, but I want more of her, and soon. When I walked up and saw her barely dressed—visibly cold through her thin tank—I had no idea who that shithead was, but I had the burning desire to kick his ass off her doorstep to get him away from her.

Yeah, something might've clicked the first time she laid her hands on me, but tonight? Tonight, Maya Augustine ruined me.

I decide to give her a second and pull out my phone. No surprise—I already have a text from Crew.

Crew – He's gone, watched him leave on the cameras. What the fuck was that?

Me – I saw someone approach and could tell she was upset. I came right away. You ever pull her background?

Crew – No. Addison took her on right when you and I left. She seemed boring, no need.

Me – I want it by tomorrow along with that asshole's—Weston MacLach-something. I'm sure he'll be in her report. Get the name there.

Crew – Done. I'll get with Asa. He was still at the camp working and was waiting in the wings with the men in case we needed them. He heard it all and might already be on it.

I leave it at that, not in the mood to answer any questions about me being here with her. When I go to her bedroom door, she's still sitting there, looking shaken by what just happened.

"So," I begin, startling her in the process.

"Quit sneaking up on me." Her face is troubled, etched with anxiety.

"You knew I was here. I'm not sneaking up on you."

"Still." She sighs and rubs her face. "Stop it."

"Anyway," I keep on and move into the room to stand in front of her. "Never thought to ask if you were engaged. That would've been an interesting question."

She looks up quickly with big eyes, telling me she thinks I'm absurd. "I'm *not* engaged."

"Not everyone agrees with that."

She stands, coming almost toe-to-toe with me to defend herself. "We were on and off for almost three years. It was more off than on—for me at least—but I officially cut off the engagement a year ago. Something..." she swallows and tries to finish, "something happened and it was the last straw. I was done."

"Hey." I reach up and tuck her still damp hair behind her ear. Keeping my hand there, I lift her chin to look at me and lower my voice. "Relax. He's gone and won't be back."

She grabs my wrist firmly and it's easy to see the fear in her eyes. "He will. Now that he found me, he'll be back. He's relentless, he'll never leave me alone. It's why I left when I did."

I pull her close, liking the way she fits against me. Her body pressed up against mine was like nothing I have ever experienced and I have to fight from getting hard.

"Grady?" she calls, her voice muffled in my chest as she fists my sweatshirt in her hands.

I rub her back. "Hmm?"

"I'm sorry, I shouldn't have done that. Now he won't only be after me, but you, too. I have a feeling I just dragged you into my nightmare."

I close my eyes as I breathe in the fresh scent of her hair, burying my face there. She's tense, not like earlier when I had my mouth on hers, so I press my lips into the side of her head. "Don't worry, I can handle it. If he comes back, I'll know. I don't want you to worry, especially not right now."

"Why did you come, anyway?"

I sigh, thinking how best to answer. Now isn't the

time to tell her about the surveillance system, even though I'm not sure when would be a good time to tell a woman she's been under heavy security for months, not to mention that I've been watching her. "I was out for a walk to get some air. I heard your voice and knew something wasn't right. You need to relax and not think about it. Can I get you something?"

I feel her breath against my skin, her warmth spreading through me.

"Like what?" she mutters.

Keeping her where she is, I shrug. "I don't know. A carrot?"

A single laugh erupts, her body moving against mine. "A carrot?"

I grin into her hair. "Yeah, a carrot probably makes all freaks like you feel better, right? Maybe some fungi? Or, I could just get you a drink. Bourbon, coffee, tequila, gin? You probably have some juiced spinach sitting around here somewhere."

She tries to push away from me, but I only let her go enough where she can look up. Shaking her head, her face is still distressed. "You don't have to stay, I'll be fine. I've dealt with Weston for a long time, I'll figure something out."

"I'm not leaving after what just happened. Tell me what you want and I'll get it for you."

She grips my arms and bites her lip.

"Maya? Spinach or wine?"

"I have a bottle of wine in the fridge."

I tip my head and lift an eyebrow before turning to make the short trip to her kitchen, muttering, "I'm glad it's not juiced spinach."

I find a half-empty bottle of white wine sitting with

all kinds of food I'd never want in my refrigerator or purchase to begin with. After looking through three cabinets, I find a wine glass and fill it full. This place is so small, it wouldn't be hard to find anything in here.

When I turn back, I don't hand her the glass, but tag her hand to pull her the short distance to the small couch.

"What are you doing?" she asks, but I ignore her.

I sit first and pull her down next to me before handing over her drink. Her couch might as well be a two-seater, so it works out well for me to pull her tight to my side.

"There." I grab the remote before putting my good arm around her and scoot down in the cushions. When I start to flip through the channels, I sense how stiff she is next to me. "Drink up, Maya. You'll feel better."

When she doesn't say anything, I look over. Her face is makeup-free and her golden hair is starting to dry. I'm getting used to having her close and have no desire to give that up, but right now her beautiful face is confused as she clutches her wine in both hands.

"What?" I ask.

"I told you, you don't have to stay. I already feel bad you had to endure all that. I'll figure out what to do about Weston, you can go."

I narrow my eyes before looking back to the TV and continue flipping channels. I don't look at her when I ask, "Tell me how you're going to take care of that guy."

She tries to shift to get up, but I hold her tight. "I just need to think it over—"

"You can think it over tomorrow," I interrupt and pull her farther down into the couch with me. "What do you like to watch?"

"Grady—"

"Maya." I have to speak over her to get her attention, but she finally shuts her mouth when I turn her to me. I lower my voice and explain one more time. "Drink your wine. Relax. Don't think about that asshole, even though I'm sure that'll be hard to do. He thinks I'm here with you, so this is where I'm gonna be. Now, what do you like to watch?"

Maybe she finally understands I'm serious, because she sighs. "The Food Network."

I tip my head questioningly. "You like to cook?"

"Yes."

I turn back to the TV and pull up the guide to find her channel. When I feel her relax against my side, I mutter, "Now that I know you like to cook, I may never leave."

When I find her channel and we start watching some woman stir the contents of a huge pot, I hear her call for me. "Grady?"

"Yeah?" I kick up my feet and cross one ankle over the other on her old coffee table.

"You're being weird," she states before taking a sip of her wine.

"How's that?"

She tries to face me even though we're plastered side-to-side on her tiny sofa. "Ever since you started talking to me, you've either been frustrated with me or asking me a million questions. This mellow-nice-guy act is kind of freaking me out."

I smirk. "I guess we're even then, because since you started speaking to me, you've been nothing but flustered—at least when you're not pushing vegetables on me—or inflicting pain."

"You're not going to ask me anything about Weston? He's a jealous, territorial man. I practically threw you under the bus by kissing you and pretending you're something you're not."

I turn, looking straight into her light blue, worry-filled eyes, and whisper. "Are you engaged to that guy?"

Her answer comes quick and meaningful. "No."

I lean in as close as I can get and continue whispering, "Do you want to be?"

Her forehead creases and she gives her head a little shake. "I hate him."

I could tell that was the case, but even so, it feels good for her to show how much she means it. I didn't think she'd be a woman to yank my chain.

Since she's close and I want her skin on mine again, I lean in the rest of the way and put my lips to her forehead. "Then that's good enough for me. You're upset, I don't want to add to that. We'll talk about it tomorrow after you've slept."

"Really, you don't have to sta—"

"Drink your wine and watch TV," I insist, turning up the volume. "Do you like all the shows or are there healthy nutsos on here that are your favorites?"

She finally gives up—hopefully for good this time—and I put my arm around her. "I like them all."

As we settle in and watch some chick chop up something or other, she sips her wine and slowly sinks into my side. I bring my hand up to her hair and start to finger through it as I wonder about Maya. I wonder what went down tonight, her past, and why she's here.

When this show ends and the next one begins, her weight becomes heavy and her breathing evens. I shift as she turns, settling her into my chest.

Just when I thought having Maya's hands on my bare skin was everything, holding her as she sleeps just moved into first place. More of that focus I lost comes into view, but like before, it's different.

All of a sudden, I don't care about her background. I need to know it so I can get rid of that asshole giving her grief, but other than that, it doesn't matter what's in her past.

I'll handle whatever I need to and hopefully pave a path for what could be an us. What I do know is having that to focus on feels almost as good as her sleeping against my side.

Focus and Maya—a lethal recipe I never imagined would be what I'd need to get me back to me. But as it settles by the second, I know this is it.

Maya

I ROLL, BARELY opening my eyes. It's lighter than normal, making me shoot to a sitting position because it's always dark when my alarm goes off. My eyes shift to my small nightstand to check the time. I'm late—really late.

As I jump out of bed, still in my sweater and lounge pants, the last thing I remember is watching *Everyday Italian* with Grady. I was warm and comfortable. I remember trying to talk myself out of being freaked out about Weston finding me, which is as bad as it could get, while allowing myself the comfort of Grady. I certainly don't remember going to bed.

It takes ten minutes to get to work and I have to be there in fifteen. There's no time for a shower.

I push down my pants and grab a pair of jeans off the floor. When I turn around, I yelp as Grady makes the turn into my bedroom saying, "You're up."

He stops immediately and his eyes drop to my bare legs.

It's not like I'm indecent. I'm wearing panties and my sweater drops almost below them, but I still can't help holding my jeans in front of me.

"What are you doing here?" I half-yell in an accusatory voice.

His gaze slowly moves up to my face, not at all trying to hide the fact he's raking his eyes over me. When they finally reach mine, he shrugs, which I'm finding he does a lot. "Went home to shower and just got back."

"You slept here?" For some reason, my voice keeps getting higher, accusing him of something, when really, he's guilty of nothing besides sneaking up on me. *Again.*

"Sleep is a relative word with me. I dozed. You must make a habit of not being aware of your surroundings. You didn't notice when I carried you to bed last night, or when I left to shower, or when I came back this morning. You should really be more cognizant."

"I'm a heavy sleeper," I say, my tone still accusing him, like it's somehow his fault.

He tips his head and gives me a small smile. "Why are you talking to me like that?"

"Because you're here and I'm not wearing any pants!" If that wasn't the queen of accusations, I have no idea what would be.

He has the nerve to huff a single laugh and cross his arms, but he makes no move to leave my bedroom. "Then you should put your pants on."

"You need to leave. I need to get dressed—I'm late

and need to leave for the Ranch in less than five minutes."

He looks me up and down again before slowly shaking his head. He turns, but I can still hear him say, "Then you'd better hurry, we need to be on our way."

I was about to slam my bedroom door so I could dress in private, but I stop at his words. Instead I rush to the doorway and watch him dig through my refrigerator. "What do you mean *we*?"

Without taking his head out of my fridge, he answers, "Not letting you go to work alone while some asshole who thinks he's gonna marry you is roaming the countryside."

Still grasping my jeans, I declare, "You are not coming to work with me."

"I am," he answers into my fridge as he pulls out a container of left-over garlic mushroom quinoa. He opens it, sticks his nose in and grimaces before quickly covering it, returning it to the shelf. "Hurry up. Looks like we need to get breakfast on the way."

"I don't have time to make a stop. You can go on your own since you're leaving." I don't know what he thinks he's doing, but after last night, I don't need to add to my worries by dragging Grady into the mess that's my life.

He turns, looking back to me. "You're still not wearing pants, Maya."

"Holy shit," I exhale, giving up. I step back and slam the door. At least I can get dressed. If he wants to hang out here all day, so be it, but he's not coming to work with me.

I pull up my jeans as fast as I can and rip off my sweater and tank. Throwing on a bra and clean shirt as fast as I can, I brush my teeth, pull my hair back into a tie, and grab my mascara. I can at least swipe lip gloss on while at a stoplight. It'll have to be enough for today.

When I throw open the bedroom door, Grady is standing by the entrance of my bungalow looking intently at his phone. I ignore him as best I can and go to the fridge, grabbing a protein shake and an apple. This will have to do.

"See ya later." I try for casual as I breeze past him, grabbing my bag and open the front door.

"Moo."

"What the hell. These cows are everywhere," Grady mutters from behind me.

He's right. It's not unusual for one or more of Addy's cows to stray and show up on my doorstep.

"I think it's Harry," I say, looking at the huge beast standing between me and my car. The longer I'm here, the more I understand Addy's fascination with her farm pets. They're friendly and sweet, not nearly as intimidating as they were when I first moved here. They do, however, still smell like cows.

Grady ignores Harry and grabs the keys from my hand to lock my front door. Jogging down my steps he moves around Harry, who bellows another greeting. Since I can't escape without my keys, I'm forced to follow and move around our visitor.

"Hey, give those back," I complain when he pockets them and reaches for my hand.

Distracted by Harry, I didn't see the huge SUV parked right next to my little car. It's an Escalade—shiny black and chrome from top to bottom. The windows are tinted, the wheels are big and fancy, and for some reason all I can wonder is how he keeps it this clean out here on all these county roads. My tiny economy car, that I traded my practically new BMW for on my trip south, is always filthy.

Before I know it, he opens the passenger door and turns to me, expecting me to climb in.

I pull my hand out of his. "Give me my keys."

"Moo."

"Get in the truck," he returns.

All of a sudden, I have a big wet nose in my ear, making me yelp. When I look over, all I see is Harry's face. If I didn't know any better, I'd think she was snuggling up to me.

I step away, not wanting to smell like a cow for the rest of the day, and yank my purse strap up my arm. "I'm not getting in your truck. Look, I'm sorry I kissed you last night. I was trying to get rid of Weston, but now I realize all I did was drag you into my mess. And my mess isn't just with Weston. My mess is with him, his family, his work, and my mother. Trust me when I say, you do not want to be anywhere near my mess. Run, Grady. Run the other way, and fast. I've dealt with them for a long time—I'll figure it out on my own."

Grady says nothing for a moment before he takes a step, closing the distance between us. Reaching up, he tucks a stray section of hair behind my ear that escapes my pony tail on the best of days, let alone when I've thrown myself together haphazardly.

He lowers his voice as he cups my jaw with his hand. "You ready for me to ask you questions?"

I lift my hand to pull his away, but it doesn't work. "No."

"Why's that guy such an asshole?"

I bite my lip and say nothing. Even if I wanted to

answer, there are too many examples of Weston being an asshole for me to list. I wouldn't know where to start.

"Why are you hiding out in Virginia?"

I give my head a tiny shake. I'm not ready to answer that, either.

He narrows his eyes and his voice softens. "Who's Joseph?"

I bite my lip again to keep from showing any emotion, but I can't control my heart from racing. In the back of my mind, I'm more worried about Joseph than myself. Especially after Weston threatened him.

"Maya?" he calls for me again.

I don't know why I open my mouth now, after months of keeping everything locked tight. But I do, I open my mouth, giving away my only weakness, and whisper, "My brother."

He lifts his head once as his eyes roam my face. "You have reason to be worried about him?"

"I always worry about him, but yes. More so, now."

He nods. "Please, let me take you to work."

I realize I'm tired—exhausted really. I think I've been this way for months, ever since I left and have been looking over my shoulder, afraid of my shadow.

I drop my hand from his and close my eyes. "Fine."

He leans in and presses his lips to my forehead, just like he did last night. "Get in, I'll take you to work. But you'd better do it fast before the cow tries to climb in after us. I know for a fact she likes car rides."

I look over at Harry, wondering if he's serious.

"Moo."

I guess I shouldn't be surprised given the way Addy treats her cows, so I quickly climb up into his shiny Escalade. It's just as clean on the inside as the outside.

He slams the door, shutting me in, and I wonder what in the hell's going on with my life.

It's not even seven-thirty in the morning. Grady spent the night at my house, has seen me without pants, I've been snuggled by a cow, and now he's coming to work with me.

I have a feeling it's going to be a long day.

8

DONUTS AND DOMINOES

Maya

"THERE'S ONE MORE donut. Do you want it, Grady?" Betty asks giddily, as she slowly rises to get up from her chair.

"I'll get it for him," Erma insists, but she's even slower and Betty has a head start.

Miss Lillian Rose waves her hand toward the other two women as she leans in next to Grady. "They can go chase your donuts. I'll just sit here and talk to you."

Grady gives her a devilish grin with his bright blue eyes shining, and I swear, even after being widowed twice, Miss Lillian Rose blushes.

This has been going on all morning. Donuts and Dominoes is a popular activity and brings out the residents en masse. For one—donuts. They love their sweets. Even the sugar-free varieties we special order for the diabetics aren't too bad. And two—they get to sit. I haven't found a way to get them up and dancing in the middle of dominoes. Everyone's sitting at different tables and have their own games going on. Maybe we need an intermission. All I know is *Donuts*, *Dominoes*, and *Dancing* has such a catchy ring to it, I need to find a way to make it happen.

The instant the ladies caught sight of Grady Cain this morning, they all argued over who would get to play dominoes with him. Not only that, but I have no idea how many donuts Grady's eaten. I wouldn't be surprised if it's a baker's dozen.

Hoping Grady would simply drop me off at work this morning was too much to wish for. After the short drive to the Ranch, I tried one more time to talk him out of coming in. He was having none of it, and held my hand as we walked through the entrance. I had to wave off the big-eyed interest of Stephanie, the office manager and my boss, telling her Grady would leave eventually.

Grady, on the other hand, informed Stephanie he was here for the duration of my shift, and even asked what he could do to help. That's all it took. Faster than I could blink, he'd filled out the half-page pink form and was proudly wearing a badge with his name on it that Stephanie whipped up in no time flat, informing everyone he's an official volunteer.

Ugh.

Even though he's eaten a good portion of their beloved donuts, he's the most popular new toy that has hit the Ranch since I started working here.

Betty, Erma, and Miss Lillian Rose dug their claws in him first. There was an argument that sent Dot into a fuming tizzy since she didn't get to sit at Grady's table. She was so mad, she nabbed two donuts, and marched right back to her apartment, refusing to participate in dominoes, but informed me she *might* be back for book club after lunch.

There are five tables of dominoes going this morning. I'm playing with Foxy and Butch at a table next to Grady and his harem.

"So, tell me, Grady, what made you want to volunteer here at Rolling Hills Ranch?" Erma smiles sweetly.

Grady takes his turn, sliding a tile across the table placing it crossways since it's a double. Before picking up his umpteenth donut, he answers, "I'm here with Maya."

"You are?" Miss Lillian Rose looks surprised before turning toward my table and keeps on loudly. "Is this your beau, Maya? If so, you're one lucky belle. Where I'm from, we'd call him a *tall drink o' sweet tea*."

Not that I can argue that Grady's a tall drink of sweet tea, especially since I kissed him last night and know for a fact how he tastes, but I don't get the chance to refute the fact he's my beau when Foxy butts in. "I thought we were a thing. We do the dirty—bumpin' and grindin'—a few times a week during your dance parties, and now you bring another man here? I was about to make my move on you. I'm hurt, Maya."

I think my jaw hit the floor and look back at Foxy, who winks at me. He even raises his arms with his hands up, giving them a couple pumps toward the ceiling to raise the roof.

My eyes go big. "We do not bump and grind, Foxy."

He narrows his, I think trying to make them sultry or something, and does a little wiggle dance move in his chair. "We could—that was my next move. Just you and me, blue eyes. I was gonna break out the Marvin Gaye."

Butch laughs, but still has the decency to stick up for

me. "The only bumping and grinding you'll be doing is in your dreams. There aren't enough blue pills in the Commonwealth of Virginia to push you over the top."

Foxy finishes his dance and reaches for his cup of coffee. "My testosterone is strong, my friend. Sometimes I don't even need my little blue friend. I got it goin' on, as the youngins say."

"Here's your donut, sugarlump. It's the last one." Betty sets the small paper plate on top of the empty stack in front of Grady. He wastes no time picking it up and taking a huge bite.

"Grady is Maya's *boyfriend*," Erma informs Betty what she missed out on during her trip to the donut table. Erma turns to Grady. "How long have you been dating? Maya hasn't mentioned you."

Even though she didn't ask me, I insist, "We're not dating."

Grady washes down his donut with a big gulp of milk and tips his head, ignoring me. "Long enough, even though it feels like only yesterday when she threw herself at me for the first time."

I turn in my chair to fully face him. "I did not throw myself at you."

He settles his blue eyes on me and winks. "If that makes you feel better, baby."

Flabbergasted, I insist more emphatically, "I had a good reason!"

Grady turns back to his harem. "Does time really matter, anyway? Time is insignificant. Have we been together twelve years?" He looks back at me and my breath catches at his words. His expression and voice are meaningful when he speaks straight to me. "No, but even years mean nothing if they're bad. I think when you know, you know." He looks back to his adoring audience. "Maya will get that eventually."

"Trust me, when you get to our age, time is nothing if not significant," Betty confirms.

"I think you're lovely," Erma adds, as she looks admiringly up at Grady.

"He's a charmer *and* a looker," Miss Lillian Rose states before glaring at me. "What's wrong with you, Maya?"

That's it.

"Our time for dominoes is almost over," I announce and push my chair back to stand. "Finish up and put them away, but leave the boxes on the tables. I'll come back and collect them. You, Mr. Prince Charming," I point at Grady, "come with me."

Grady grins as Erma croons, "Ahh, she calls him Prince Charming."

I roll my eyes and turn to leave the commons area, assuming Grady will follow. I quickly march through the halls until I get to the clinic. The current physical therapist is off today, so there are no appointments or anyone about.

I get to the back room and open the last door. After Grady follows, I slam it, closing us in.

Grady looks around, probably wondering what we're doing, but I don't waste any time. I have Wii games on the schedule and need to get that going soon. Moving to the cart parked at the side of the room, I roll it to the vinyl-covered exam bed.

Between what happened last night with Weston, Grady being wonderful yet annoying by insisting we're something we're not, and finally, wondering what Weston's next move might be, my emotions are all over the place. I've officially lost my patience.

"Take your shirt off," I clip.

Grady half-grins, half-frowns and immediately starts to unbutton his shirt. "If you say so."

I do my best to be professional and not ogle Grady undressing, so I look away and snap the stickers onto the electrodes. When I turn back, he's standing bare from the waist up, his jeans are sort of loose and sitting low on his hips where I can see the band of his underwear peeking at me. I have to exhale quickly when I see his iliac furrow for the second time. It's so deeply defined, I could barely handle it during our first PT session, and now isn't any easier.

Looking up from the beautiful V below his abs, I chastise him for last night. "You shouldn't have carried me to bed. That wasn't a good idea, you really could've reinjured that joint."

He continues to grin. "I didn't think you'd sleep well with me on your miniature couch. Maybe next time we'll just start off in your bed."

I bite my lip, and regret bringing it up at all, so I change the subject.

"Sit," I demand. When he settles on the vinyl exam table, I take a step toward him and start peeling the stickers one by one. I adhere them to his muscles, framing his shoulder, and then have to bite the inside of my lip when I place three on each of his pectorals.

"Is this some sort of kinky sex game?" Grady looks up from what I'm doing and into my eyes. "Do I get to do you next?"

"Since you insisted on coming, we might as well get you on the electrical stimulator." I don't wait for him to say anything more and turn to the machine. It might not be nice of me, but I'm not in the mood so I don't ease him into it. I flip the dial all the way to the highest surge before turning it back down to a moderate level.

"Fuck, Maya," he exclaims, even though he hardly jerks from the initial shock of the strongest possible electrodes pulsing into his body.

"What?" I tip my head, copying what he's done to me regularly over the past few days, and grin. "You're a big, tough guy. I thought you could take it."

"I was just shitting you the other day, but now I do think you get off on inflicting pain."

"This will increase strength, and prevent disuse atrophy since you're behind on your PT. It'll even reduce the pain during therapy, if you can handle it." I step back and cross my arms, watching his muscles jump and twitch from the stimulation.

I can tell he's settling into it because he looks up from his bare chiseled chest and shakes his head at me. "You know this means I'm going to get even with you someday."

I give him a smirk and only tell a half-truth. "I'm only doing what's best for you, Grady. It's not like I'm getting some weird satisfaction out of this."

"Yeah, I bet." He looks around the room and when his eyes settle back on me, he states, "You're good at this."

"I haven't fixed you yet—you might want to wait on that assessment."

He shakes his head. "I don't mean the therapy stuff. As much as you've hurt me, I assume you're good at that. I meant working with the people here. They really like you."

I shake my head and shrug. "They're sweet, but really I just herd them around and try to keep them active. They're fun. I'll miss the activities with them every day if I get to work back here. That is, if I'm still working here."

He looks at me questioningly. "You goin' somewhere?"

I shake my head and sigh, not wanting to talk about this so I change the subject. "Why did you let them believe we're together?"

A smirk appears. "We felt together last night."

"I explained that."

Grady narrows his eyes and leans back on his good arm. "Why are you hiding?"

"I'm not hiding," I sort of lie. I've always thought of myself as running. As desperately as I needed to get away, the longer I'm gone, the guilt has become a heavy burden, harder and harder to bear. Weston showing up last night only made that worse.

"Maya," he starts and lowers his voice. "It's obvious you're hiding. You ran away from a man who insists you're his when you tell me you're not. You've got a brother you're worried about. From what I see, you know no one here other than the people you work with, and now you're talking about leaving. No one talks about leaving a place where they like to work and people they like to be around without a reason. What's going on?"

I swallow over the lump in my throat, because he's right about all that. But I'm not about to tell him anything, so my only choice is to go on the defense. It's worked before.

"If you tell me how you got hurt, I'll think about it."

This time he doesn't look defensive at all. He pulls in a big breath and softens his voice. "Come here."

My brow furrows. "Why?"

His hand comes up gesturing to his chest and he sounds a little frustrated when he continues. "Maya, you're basically electrocuting me. I'm stuck to this machine or I'd come to you. Would you please come here?"

I sigh because he's right and take the few steps separating us. When I get close, he reaches out and grabs my hand, pulling me the rest of the way. He then separates his legs and pulls me close. My hands come up to his chest because he's pressed my torso to his so we're face-to-face.

I know I should pull away, tell him to stop, to leave me alone because my life is nothing but a bad made-for-TV drama right now. If he's smart, he'll want no part of it. But ever since last night, his sweet touches and affectionate ways are too much. I haven't experienced anything like it in a long time. If I allowed myself to really think about it, I don't think I've ever experienced it.

One of his big boots wraps around the back of my leg as his arms come around me. Before I have the chance to complain, ask what he's doing, or even enjoy the feeling of being held tight to Grady Cain, he looks into my eyes and shocks me. "My work was dangerous. On my last job, I was captured."

My eyes go big and his arms constrict around me when my body tenses. I can't believe what he said, but I'm also surprised he called my bluff.

"What?" I whisper.

"You heard me. Not gonna lie, I was lucky to get out

alive. You wanted to know, so I told you, but I'd appreciate it if you wouldn't tell anyone else how I got hurt. It won't be the end of the world if you do, but I like to live lowkey. My life is no one's business but mine and who I choose to share it with."

I'm shocked at his words, by his confession, really. I thought he was probably in some sort of accident. "Why did you tell me?"

He shrugs. "I show you mine—you show me yours."

I ignore his tit-for-tat expectation, and ask, "What do you do for a living?"

He shakes his head. "I'm retired from that. I'm taking some time off for a while, but now I work for Crew—we specialize in intelligence. We train and contract with those we used to work with. I used to be a contractor, but I'm done working in the field."

"Like what? What kind of jobs did you contract for?" I ask, wondering what he possibly could have done that got him captured, beaten, and from the sounds of it, almost killed.

"Security. I told you what I could ... and I did it because I want you to trust me. I can't expect anything of you if I don't share first. Now, tell me why you're running."

My fingers flex on his skin, and in turn, his muscles contract, either from my touch or the electro therapy. Whichever it is, it feels good. But instead of telling him what he wants, I slide one hand off his chest and reach for the dial, turning off the machine.

Looking back to him, I say quietly, "You're done. It's time for Wii games."

"I promise I'll find out one way or another, but I'd rather hear it from you. You might as well tell me."

"You don't want to be bothered with my problems, trust me," I tell him the truth, trying to put him off.

"I'm feeling a little used, you know." A small smirk appears on his face and he lowers his voice and he pulls me in even tighter. "You throw yourself in my arms, kissing me for your own benefit? That stings, baby."

I know he's teasing but he's right, so I press against his chest to move away, but he wants none of it. His arms constrict, keeping me close.

"I apologized for that," I remind him.

One of his hands on my back moves up, and pulls my face into the side of his. His clean-shaven cheek brushes mine and I scarcely feel the tip of his nose run up the side of my ear, making me shiver. "You didn't feel sorry when I had you in my arms. In fact, you felt the very opposite of sorry." His tongue flicks my earlobe once. "It felt right—felt like you've been there forever."

"Grady," I whisper on an exhale. Damn if he isn't right again. I've never felt anything so good, so natural as being kissed by Grady. Even if he doesn't know he's only the second man ever to lay a hand on me. I never remember feeling this way with Weston, even in the beginning when I was caught in his snare and could pretend it was good.

When Grady's lips hit the sensitive skin below my ear, my breath catches, and I slide my hands up his thick, corded neck. I'm not sure if I'm trying to push him away, pull him to me, or simply hang on.

"I need to get back to the residents," I mutter as best I can, but his hand comes to my hair and he gently pulls my head back to gain access to my neck. I exhale and sound breathy as his tongue traces my collar bone. "I can't get off schedule or it breaks into their lunch. Wii games are important for their circulation."

His head comes up and he runs light kisses over my sensitive skin as he murmurs, "I've never played Wii before."

"It's fun," I breathe and swallow hard. "The ladies like bowling and Foxy likes to hula-hoop."

That's when I lose his lips. He pulls back just enough for me to tip my head and look into his eyes where I find him frowning. "You are not hula-hooping with Foxy."

His words, but even more his expression, are laced with a possessiveness that snap me out of my Grady-haze created by his lips on my body. I'm not sure if it's because his expression is created by jealousy over an elderly man, but I find it funny instead of irritating. What it isn't, is scary, like it became with Weston.

For some reason, I do something I've never done before, because I wouldn't dare try to egg on Weston. I'm not sure if it's my many months of new-found freedom or if it's just Grady, but I can't help but grin and taunt him. "I always hula-hoop with Foxy. It's our thing."

He narrows his eyes and his hands squeeze my waist. Even though my experience is limited to Weston, for some reason I knew it was safe and I was right, because I know he's not serious when he says, "If you're gonna fucking hula-hoop with anyone, it's gonna be me."

"I don't know." I let my eyes wander to his bare chest and let my hands run down his smooth skin, covered with a light smattering of hair. "You've clearly got it going on with the ladies, as Foxy would say. I'm not sure

I'll get a turn, they all seem to be vying for your attention."

"Foxy's a dirty old man," he states.

"Maybe." I look back to my hands as I keep speaking. "I guess we'll just have to see who gets to hula-hoop with whom."

With that, I grab an adhesive electrode in each hand, yanking hard and fast.

"Dammit," he jerks, letting go of my hips.

I take a step back, but reach for the rest of the stickers, ripping quickly, but he's expecting it this time. "I've got a date with Foxy, we need to get moving. Get dressed, Grady."

A sexy smile spreads across his face and his dark blue eyes heat. "Someday, Maya, I'm gonna get you back for all the pain. I'm looking forward to it."

For some reason, his threat doesn't scare me as I'm accustomed to, and I've been threatened many times.

I look at him over my shoulder and grin as I roll the cart back. "No pain-no gain, big guy."

Grady simply shakes his head, but with the smile on his face, I know for a fact there's no reason for me to worry. Grady might've been grumpy and a little brooding in the beginning, but he's turning out to be nothing but a big, fluffy, sweet marshmallow.

9

FIGURE YOUR SHIT OUT

Grady

We've bowled, white-water rafted, and downhill skied. I even played doubles in tennis with Erma and we kicked Miss Lillian Rose and Betty's asses. I thought I was gonna come out of my skin, because Maya wasn't shitting me when she said Foxy liked to hula-hoop. Since there was no actual hula-hoop, Foxy could get really close to her. I never thought I'd feel the need to beat an elderly man to a pulp, but that's how I felt today. He was going for the bump and grind with my new favorite physical therapist and it did not make me happy. All the while, Maya laughed and played along as I had to sit and watch her hips move in circles, side to side, and back and forth.

Who knew fake hula-hooping could be hot? I've never been so pissed and turned on at the same time.

I helped her clean up from Donuts and Dominoes and we got the video games put away in the TV room. I hugged and kissed every old lady on the cheek—I swear they were lining up for it. This morning has been interesting, that's for sure.

Maya is putting away the last of the controllers. The residents just left us to go to lunch. Tomorrow is Saturday and I just found out she doesn't work at the Ranch again until Monday, which is good. The winery is more secure. I got an email from Crew during downhill skiing with both Maya's and MacLachlan's backgrounds attached, with a message saying, "The woman sure isn't boring. You'll want to focus on his report. Don't take your eyes off her."

I haven't had time to read the report, what with all the reindeer games, but that made my blood boil, wondering what it could be. Now I'm glad I listened to my gut and came with her this morning. Besides the guy being an asshole, I'd rather Maya tell me why she's running than having to read it on her background. I know women. If she finds out later I knew more than she wanted me to, that's a sure-fire way to piss her off. I can't afford to do that yet.

I'm sure I'll piss her off eventually. I am me after all—it's inevitable. But this soon? No way.

"You sure are popular with the ladies." I look up and Maya is walking to me with her bag, grinning. "You had them lining up for a piece of you."

My mouth tips because really, all I want is Maya, but instead of saying that, I tell her the truth. "I'm good with women."

She stops in her tracks, only making it halfway across the room to me. She puts a hand to her hip and a frown mars her pretty face. "What do you mean you're *good with women*?"

"Settle down—don't throw a salad at me," I defend myself. "I meant I grew up surrounded by women. I've got four sisters. If a man doesn't learn how to survive swimming in a pool of estrogen in that environment, he'd drown."

"You have *four* sisters?" Her eyes get big.

"Yep."

"Wow," she shakes her head a bit. She moves again, passing me.

It takes two steps for me to catch up and tag her hand. She tries to pull away, but I hold tight.

"Grady, you need to stop this."

I ignore her and look over her head as we walk past the cafeteria. I see a large table of my new friends and wave. "See you ladies Monday."

A gaggle of goodbyes are squealed as we leave.

"You're not coming back Monday," Maya insists in a low voice, again trying to pull my hand from hers.

I don't have the chance to argue with her, because the moment I turn my head as we hit the electric sliding front doors, I'm stopped mid-step. I pull Maya close, and this time she doesn't fight it or pull away. She squeezes my hand as her free one comes up to my bicep to hold on. She nestles halfway in back of my arm, shielding herself from the men we practically walk into.

Today in the daylight, it's easier to see his frustrated rage. Unlike last night when I surprised him, today there's no surprise in his features. His glare, which was initially focused on Maya, moves slowly to me.

What a dumbass.

Unlike him, it's easy for me to rid my face of emotion when needed. I've spent too many years dealing with scum of the earth much more intimidating than he is.

"Wes," I greet him with a blank face, and almost want to laugh at the expression he makes, probably because I shortened his name. "I'm surprised you're still wandering the countryside. You visiting a resident here?"

Weston's jaw tenses and the older guy with him takes his side. He's got to be in his fifties and has a paunch hanging over his belt. He's not the threat he's presenting himself to be. I can see the piece he's got strapped under his jacket since he's overweight and his clothes don't fit.

I'd shake my head at him if I could. Carrying concealed isn't worth it if it isn't concealed. I should know. After what happened last night I'm carrying now, but unlike this jackwad, I'm actually concealed. Even with my bum shoulder, I could take them both down before he could reach for his weapon.

On the other hand, I can't tell where Weston's carrying. Still, I have no doubt I could have them face first on the floor within fifteen seconds.

Weston's eyes move to where Maya's clinging to my arm and he finally growls out an answer to my question.

"I've come to take Maya home."

Maya

OF COURSE, I should've expected this from him, but I've been so distracted by Grady, I haven't thought about the possibility of him showing up here.

So far this morning, if Grady wasn't being sweet or finding a way to touch me, he was charming the old ladies' club. He made them so happy, it was almost too much for me to watch. I haven't had very many genuine people in my life—my brother is pretty much it. Everyone else wanted to be my friend because of whose daughter I was. The worst was when people wanted absolutely nothing to do with me because of who I was. It sucked because no one wanted to invest in a true friendship, and honestly, most people were too careful with me to be genuine.

But I've come to love all the residents here, and I think I've done okay at winning them over. They don't have an ulterior motive to like or hate me—they're just happy I'm here to spend time with them and provide some fun in their lives.

Many of them don't have a lot of visitors, it doesn't take much to give their day a boost. It doesn't matter if Grady only brought them joy by some secondary means while he primarily wanted to follow me around all day. He brought a smile to the faces of many. It was hard for me to overlook that all morning as he flirted with his harem.

So almost walking into Weston after being distracted by the wonderfulness of Grady shouldn't surprise me, but nonetheless, it does. Weston was alone last night, but I shouldn't be surprised he has a lackey with him.

And of course, he brought Byron Murray, the man who made my options clear just before I decided I had to escape. He sure did his part threatening me before I left. Of course, it wasn't Weston or his dad who explained the ways of their world to me.

I couldn't help it, the second I saw Weston walk through the front door of my place of employment, I latched onto Grady before I realized what I was doing.

"I've come to take Maya home," Weston growls, staring straight at Grady.

I cringe, and if I could melt into Grady's side, I would.

"I think we went over this last night—but just to jog your memory—she's not going anywhere. She doesn't want you here. She told you as much last night, and after you left, she continued to express it to me the rest of the night in our bed."

I really need to have a talk with Grady about Weston. It's not a good idea to goad him, and at this point, that's exactly what Grady is doing by insinuating we're something we're not. Grady doesn't know the tiniest fraction of my background with Weston, but he needs to stop. He's only making things worse.

Weston looks back to me, anger radiating from every pore of his body. "Okay, I get it—you want to give me a taste of my own medicine with this guy?" He jerks his chin toward Grady. "Fine, it's done, but this shit is getting old, Maya. Whatever phase you're going through, get over it—I'm losing my patience. We're even. I told my father you'd be home. You know I won't disappoint him."

"Not sure who your father is," Grady answers before I can, "but Maya's not with me to get back at you. It's time you come to terms with your disappointment and realize she's not going anywhere." Grady then looks Byron up and down before adding, "I have no idea who you are, but she's *really* not going anywhere with you."

Weston looks to me and keeps talking. "I don't know

what you're doing, what you think you're going to accomplish here, but you know you'll end up back home eventually. Don't drag it out and make it harder than it needs to be. If you come now, we can easily explain things—to your family and mine. Everyone wants you home."

Saying my first words, I look at Byron when I respond, "Oh, I bet they do."

"Maya," Weston bites out my name to get my attention.

I might be grasping at Grady, but from somewhere deep inside, I find the will to strengthen my voice. "I'm not going anywhere with you ever again. You shit all over what was left of our relationship a year ago when I found you with *her*. Your perseverance did no good, and others telling me to look the other way was more than I could handle. But you know what pushed me over the edge." I look back to Byron and narrow my eyes. "The threats. I'm never coming back."

"You should call and talk to Joseph." Weston gets my attention, and my eyes shoot back to him. Grady squeezes my hand and pulls me in back of him a little more, keeping his protective stance in front of me. "He's home. He's having seizures again. But you wouldn't know that, would you?"

My heart catches and I can only imagine the expression on my face, because all of a sudden, Weston turns smug. He raises a brow and that evil smirk creeps across his face, one I'm more familiar with than anyone has the right to be. He knows he's one-upped me, even though I shouldn't trust a single word that passes his lips. It's a sure possibility what he says is true.

"You haven't called him in all this time? I've heard

he's more worried about you than anyone. Maybe it's the stress causing the flare-up."

Weston's been around Joseph long enough, he knows stress has nothing to do with it, he's just trying everything he can to get to me. Even though I know it's not true, guilt flows through me for not being there. I haven't contacted Joe since I left—I knew they'd expect me to do just that. It was all I could do to keep myself from reaching out to him. I miss him terribly. Now that they know where I am, it shouldn't matter.

Weston goes on. "He wants to see you, you should come with me now. I'll book you a flight home with us and take you right to him."

"Enough," Grady says, as if he's bored with the entire horse and pony show. "I've told Maya if she wants to see her brother, I'll take her. She'll talk to him this afternoon, if she wants to go, we'll go, but I'm not going to say this again—she's not going anywhere with you. Now get the hell out of our way before you create a scene."

I thought Grady was going to move to leave, but he doesn't. He's patient and stands stock-still, holding my hand tight. Byron finally slaps Weston on the back. "Come on, you know what your dad said." I don't like the eerie look on his face when he turns to me, but keeps speaking to Weston. "I'm sure she remembers her last conversation with me. She knows what'll happen if she doesn't come home. She'll come around eventually, I just hope it's soon enough."

They finally turn to leave, even though Weston seems reluctant. They walk to the same car that was parked outside my bungalow last night, and I finally exhale deeply for the first time since we practically walked into them.

I watch as they pull out of the parking lot of the Ranch until I feel Grady shift. When I look up, he's turned to me and I feel his hand in the back of my hair again. That's when he pulls me close, and before I know it, his lips land on mine. I may not have initiated it this time, but I sure don't pull away even though he surprised me.

Without saying a word, he lets me go and takes my hand. Leading me quickly to his Escalade while scanning our surroundings, he opens the passenger door and makes sure I'm in before slamming it with all his might.

When he gets in, I know I should explain, try and make another excuse for all the drama, or hell, even lie like I've been doing since I crossed into the Commonwealth of Virginia.

"Grady—" I start, but I have no time to say another word before he holds up an index finger, gesturing for me to wait and a phone starts ringing over the speakers of his ultra-clean SUV.

It barely rings twice before I hear Crew's voice. "Yeah?"

"Do me a favor and tell Addy that Maya won't be in for a while. Depending on how long this takes, she might not be in at all."

"Grady!" I yell and quickly refute his plans. "Don't do that, Crew. I'm coming into work."

Of course, Crew doesn't listen to me, but says to Grady, "Done. Everything okay?"

Grady quickly pulls out of the lot and turns onto the

two-lane road toward Whitetail, simply answering, “No,” before he hangs up.

I guess those two aren’t chatty phone talkers, because I didn’t have a chance to get in another word, so I turn to Grady. “You can’t do that, I need to go to work. I can’t afford to miss a day.”

Grady glances over at me before turning back to the road and states matter-of-factly, “Then talk fast, Maya. Until I figure out what’s going on with you, you’re not leaving my sight. You’ve got until we get back to Crew’s house to get your story straight, and it had better be the real one. It’s time we figure your shit out.”

Sighing, I slump back into my seat. As I watch the bare trees fly by, I wonder what I’m going to do. I think I’m out of options and have no idea how Weston found me, but he knows where I live and where I work. I’ve known him long enough to realize he’s at least been watching me, trying to leave now would be stupid. Closing my eyes, I lean my head back, and breathe. Telling Grady the truth at this point should be the least of my worries.

10

YOU'RE SWEET

Grady

I PULL UP to Crew's front door, not bothering to park in the barn. The drive home was silent and I wondered the entire way what I'd get from her. The truth might be too much to hope for at this point. It's clear she's hidden her life from everyone—if not outright lied about it. Maybe expecting the truth is too much.

All I have to do is read the report Crew sent me to know. Normally, I'd be all over that. But for some reason, as distraught as she's been since last night, I want to hear it from her first. I want her to trust me even though she has no reason to. I want her to open up, tell me why that fucker was in her life to begin with, especially for as long as he was. Fuck me. I've never felt this way before, but I want her to need me to make it right, and when that's done, I just want her to need me.

But if I can't get it out of her soon, I'll be forced to read the report. I need to know what I'm dealing with.

Because after watching her for weeks, and now spending time with her, holding her, having her touch me?

I need her. I just hope to fuck she needs me, too.

She gets out of the car at the same time I do, meeting me quickly at the front porch. "Grady, please, I need to go to work. I promise to tell you anything you want to know later, but I can't afford to miss a day. I have rent and bills to pay—I need the money."

I pause in the middle of unlocking the door and turn to her. Her beautiful face is tense and filled with worry, and I realize I never thought about that part of her. About her working two jobs, never having a full day off, and renting Addy's one-room house.

Money never crosses my mind. It's just there, sitting in the bank, waiting for me to spend it. All I did was deposit it for years, meet with my broker—who I do regular background checks on to make sure he stays on the up and up—and let it grow. I've put my sisters through school, and if I wanted something, I bought it.

Besides that, I never think about money.

I let my eyes roam her features, and as much as I want to tell her not to worry because I'll make sure she's covered, she doesn't need to know that right now.

"Doesn't Addy give you personal time? Sick, vacation?" I ask.

She shakes her head. "I'm hourly and part time. She said if I needed time off, we'd work it out."

I grab her hand as I open the door and pull her through, making a mental note to get with Addy and work something out for Maya's rent. "Then don't worry about it. Addy's a good woman, if she said she'd work it out, she will."

"I can't just not show up for work. It's busy on Fridays and—"

"Maya," I interrupt, pulling her all the way in and toss my keys on the table. "Crew will take care of it. I'm sure after last night, Addy already knows something's going on with you."

Maya sighs and drops her purse on the table next to my keys. I lead her into the only room with furniture, but stop because I realize there's nowhere for us to sit. Maybe I should've taken her back to her place. At least she has a small sofa, but I was worried she'd run off to work as soon as we got there.

With no other option, I cross the room to my only piece of furniture—the recliner I bought when I first moved here with Crew. After I sit, I pull her into my lap. "Now we can talk."

She's stiff and awkwardly tries to push away from me. "What are you doing?"

"This is the only place I have to sit besides folding chairs that are on their last leg. Or my bed." I give her a squeeze. "If you'd rather go upstairs and climb in bed with me, we can talk there."

"You're crazy, and now I have to worry about what Addy thinks of me." She sighs before putting her fingers to her forehead and temples, shaking her head. "Addy's been so good to me, I don't want her to think I'm a drama queen who can't show up for work."

"Don't worry about Addy." I try and make her feel better, and pull her hands away from her face. "Tell me about Weston."

She pulls her bottom lip between her teeth, and sighs before giving me a resigned look. "We were engaged for three years."

I feel my eyes go big. "That's a long engagement. What, could he not close the deal?"

She shakes her head, and I'm surprised I don't have to work harder to get her to talk. "He pressed a little bit, but it was me who wouldn't close the deal. I kept putting things off—wedding plans, coordinators," she rolls her eyes, emphasizing, "*my mother*. When the date started getting close, I'd push it out."

"Why?"

"I met Weston when I was sixteen and he was eighteen. He was my first ... everything."

I do my best not to respond to that, but it's hard. The thought of him being her anything pisses me off, let alone everything.

She keeps going. "It was young love on crack, and up until about four or five years ago, things were fine. That's when he started to change. As much as I tried to pull away, I always got pulled or pushed right back to him. Either by him or our families."

"Your family tried to force you on a man you didn't want?" That's jacked. I could barely stand to see my sister, Raine, get married, let alone think about forcing her into anything.

"It's complicated." She pulls in a big breath and looks away from me to her hands. "Our families are complicated."

That's interesting. "Okay, then what?"

She shrugs and looks up to me. "Like I said, things were fine until about four or five years ago. He slowly started to change. He became controlling—domineering. It started when I was in college, he didn't want me to go into physical therapy, he thought it was beneath me having to treat other people. After I graduated, he tried to keep me from working, saying I needed to focus on planning the wedding, move up the date, and once we were married, I wouldn't need to work anyway. But I kept putting off the date, even pushing it back three times, much to the dismay of him and everyone around us."

"What finally happened?"

"He'd get angry, but he always got over it pretty quickly and later on I found out why. Apparently, I wasn't enough. I mean, it wasn't like I made him wait for marriage, but still." She looks up at me, widens her eyes and shrugs.

I have a feeling I know what that means and something comes over me. Rage. I'm surprised I haven't burst out of my clothes like the Hulk. I'm overwhelmed by it, knowing what he probably did to her. I force myself to relax my expression and give her thigh a squeeze, hoping we can get past this shit fast.

Giving her head a little shake, she keeps going. "Anyway, I had to stop by his house one day and he was in the shower. There was a cell I didn't recognize sitting in the kitchen next to his. It went off three times in a row, so while I was waiting on him, I went over to look. The message on the screen said three new pictures were sent from the same person. I probably shouldn't have, but the phone wasn't locked, so I did. I opened the messages, and while standing right there in my fiancé's kitchen, my life came into focus. As I scrolled through, there were all kinds of pictures of a naked woman." She closes her eyes and shudders from the memory. "Then there were more sent back to her, and since I'd *been with him* since I was almost eighteen, I knew exactly who the dick pics were of."

My rage instantly turns into jealousy, and that's even harder to overcome.

I pull her closer, tucking her tight into my lap, and this time she doesn't push away, but she does bring her hands up to my chest. It's easy to see she still hurts so I lower my voice. "This is what he meant when he said you were getting back at him with me?"

She shakes her head quickly, but her words conflict with her actions. "Yes, but I'm not. I'd never do that, not that we've done anything, anyway. I still feel bad about last night, but when you showed up, I didn't know what else to do. I needed to get rid of him."

"I told you not to worry about it." I give her a small smile, wanting to make her feel better, but also tell her the truth. "Plus, it wasn't a hardship on my part. Not to mention, from now until forever, I get to tell the world you made the first move."

She shakes her head while trying to suppress a small smile.

"What?" I smirk back. "It's true and I'll shout it from the rooftops. Now, finish your story."

She sighs, but keeps going. "That all happened a while ago. The months following, he was intent on winning me back. He wouldn't take no for an answer, even though every time my answer was always no. My mom started to pressure me even when she knew what he did. I was messing up her big plans for the Augustines and MacLachlans to become one. She's best friends with Weston's mom. When his family started pressuring me—that's when it freaked me out, because their pressuring came in the form of threats. Even though it killed me to not have any contact with my brother since we're so close, things transpired and I couldn't take it. I left months ago, moved around for a while before I finally settled here."

"They threatened you?"

This time she doesn't say a thing, closing her eyes and giving her head two slow shakes, as if to try not to think about it.

"Maya," I call for her. She opens her eyes and I attempt to tell her some of the truth about what I do. "I told you Crew and I work in security, right?"

Her brow furrows in question.

"With that work comes a certain amount of access to information. When Crew left here last night, he knew things weren't on the up-and-up. I didn't know how forthcoming you'd be with me about what happened, so we pulled your background. Because of our work, we can put together a very comprehensive report on someone."

She instantly tenses in my arms before really trying to push away. I hold her tight and keep talking.

"Maya, let me explain. He ran your background, but I haven't read it yet. More importantly, he also ran Weston's. I haven't read it yet either, but I've been told his is the one I'll be more interested in."

"What do you do?" Her words come out fast.

I pause before explaining as best I can, even if it is brief. "I used to contract for the government—sometimes our allies. I told you I don't work in the field any longer, but because of Crew's company, we have clearance."

All of a sudden her face tightens and her hands drop from my chest. "If you had all this at your fingertips, why would you ask me to rehash all that? It wasn't fun living it the first time—I certainly don't like to talk about it."

I bring my hand up to her face and when I make contact, she jerks. I ignore that and pull her close, lowering my voice to a whisper. "I thought you'd be upset if I learned about your past without giving you the chance to tell me. I had a feeling it wasn't going to be good. Maya, we don't know each other well yet, but I'd never hurt you. I want you to trust me more than anything, so I gave you the chance to tell me first."

"So you weren't going to read that report?" she shoots back.

"Could you not have looked at your ex's cell phone?" I ask.

Her eyes narrow, but she says nothing.

"I let your story come from you and told you I have the report. Don't be pissed at me for something I didn't do, baby. If you give me long enough, I'm sure I'll do something to piss you off for real."

That worked. Since I've got her close, I get to enjoy the change of her expression go from pissed to amused. It's such a beautiful transformation, I look forward to the next time I get to make it happen.

Before I can think about how to do that, I get back to the matter at hand. "I'll still read the report, along with Weston's. But you trusted me with it first, and that's what I wanted."

Barely smirking, she shakes her head. "You're not what I thought you'd be."

"Yeah? What's that?" I slide my hand back down her back, over her hip, and when I reach the outside of her thigh, I yank her legs over the arm of the recliner, scooting her down in my lap farther.

Surprised, she grabs onto my neck. I lean over her and cup the back of her head where she's laying across my lap when she says, "You're sweet. When I'd watch you come into the tasting room and order food to-go, you looked anything but sweet."

Bringing my face to hers, I run my nose up the side of hers and whisper, "That's because I didn't have your magic, yet torturous, touch to make me better. I'm not usually known for being sweet. If I'm sweet, it's because you made me that way."

"What are you known for?" she whispers back.

I shake my head and say right before my lips touch hers, "I'm not sure anymore. Lately, I'm not sure I even know myself."

When I kiss her, it's nothing like last night. There's no desperation, no intensity, and no urgency.

After seeing that shithead angry with her, hearing what he did to her, and knowing he threatened her, I find myself wanting to give her exactly the opposite. Today, I kiss her the way she deserves to be kissed.

Brushing my lips across hers, I pull her head back, working my way down her throat. I hear her exhale as I kiss across her collarbone. Feeling her chest rise and fall, I continue back up the other side of her neck, tasting her and feeling her skin under my lips.

I whisper, "I feel different than I have in a while—a long while. I have a feeling it has everything to do with you, but nothing to do with you fixing my shoulder."

"Grady," she murmurs.

I kiss my way back to her lips, but stop when I get there. Lifting just enough to look into her light blue eyes, I ask, "You ever been with anyone besides him?"

She says nothing and I wonder if I crossed the line

before she gives her head two quick shakes, confirming my earlier assumption.

Looking down at her in my arms, arms that aren't just new to her, but really fucking new to her, I realize I need to take things slow. Especially after what she just told me about how that asshole treated her.

I nod before tilting her head up to kiss her again. When I finally pull away, I say against her lips, "You're not leaving, Maya."

I think my words yanked her out of her trance, because even with her quickened breath, she returns, "I'm not sure I can stay. I don't know what to do about Weston, and after what he said this morning, I really need to call my brother. I don't want to go back there, but I need to go see him."

"Tell him to come here."

She shakes her head. "It's not that easy. He has epilepsy. It's usually controlled with meds, but I'm worried. If Weston was telling the truth, there's no way he can travel. He developed Juvenile Myoclonic Epilepsy when he was twelve. It's always scary, but was awful when he first developed it. I was with him when he had his first seizure and had no idea what was happening. He fell and hit his head. I've never been so scared, and given the last few months, that's saying something. I'm not sure I'll ever get over seeing him suffer before the doctors got it under control. My guess is his meds need to be adjusted, but it doesn't matter if he's a junior in college, in my head all I see is my little brother. I *need* to see him."

I understand more than she knows about worrying about a sibling, but first I need to find out why she's so afraid to go back. "Why were they threatening you."

She pulls her lip between her teeth and looks away from me.

"Maya?" I ask, and she looks back up. "I have the means to help you if you let me."

She shakes her head. "You're underestimating them. There's no way to help when it comes to Weston and his family."

I raise my eyebrows and I hope my face is as serious as my tone. "No, you're underestimating me. I promise you, Weston and his family are nothing compared to what I've gone up against. You can tell me."

She shakes her head again, looking down at her hands, worrying them.

"Maya." I give her a little squeeze to get her attention.

Looking up at me, she gives me a resigned look, and slumps a bit in my arms. "Fine, you really want to know?"

I widen my eyes and say nothing, because she knows the answer.

Finally, she says, "Right before I left, he was doing everything he could to get me back. My mother hosted a party just so he could easily torment me. I walked in on him talking to his father. They were talking about business—*family business*—and after I overheard what they did, everything changed. That's when they started threatening me. Grady, I overheard them talking about how Weston killed someone. He's a *murderer*."

My body instantly turns rigid. As much as I try and fight my reaction, I can't.

I don't know what happened with Weston, but by the look on her face, I can tell how she feels about it.

Well, fuck me.

11

REGRETS

Maya

GRADY HAS ME wrapped up in his arms, and the way he kissed me left me wanting more. Way more. My insides churn, leaving my skin tingly with anticipation, eager for his touch. And his lips. And his tongue. A combination of the three would be ideal, but honestly, the way he has me humming, I'll take anything at this point.

He had me so comfortable, the words came rushing out. Maybe it's the way he's been with me the last few days. Maybe it's because I've hidden who I am from everyone for so long. Or maybe it's because he told me he contracted with the government. That seems legitimate. But then again, most anything would be compared to the MacLachlans.

When he pushed for a reason why Weston would threaten me—I caved, but now I regret it. His body which was warm and comforting just moments ago, is now tense, and his expression is strained.

"Grady?" I call for him, suddenly equally desperate to take my words back.

Grady's brow pinches and his dark blue eyes narrow. "You sure about that?"

"Yes." I try and wiggle to get out of his hold, but his arms cinch around me tighter, so I try to explain further. "He and his father both tried to deny it, but there was no mistaking what I heard. I sort of went apeshit, causing a scene. That was the day my life went from exasperating, trying to ward off his advances, to downright scary because of what I found out."

Grady tips his head minutely, and his voice comes at me harsh, even if controlled. I don't like either when he asks, "What exactly did you find out?"

I ignore his question and ask my own. "Why are you all of a sudden acting like this?"

Grady takes a big breath. When he exhales, I feel his body relax, but from the look on his face, I'm pretty sure it was forced. "I'm sorry. You surprised me. Tell me what you learned."

I guess it would be surprising to hear someone killed another person. I sigh, grateful to have his relaxed demeanor back. "Basically, I learned their family business isn't what it seems. They're in shipping. They own a fleet of cargo ships, but it's not only used for legitimate business. They were talking about smuggling, and I do know Weston killed someone. He practically admitted it that day by insisting I keep my mouth shut. Who knows, he's probably killed more."

Grady doesn't say anything for a moment, but his eyes drag over my face before his voice softens. "How did he threaten you?"

"Weston didn't really do anything. It was his boss,

the guy with him today at the Ranch, who does all the dirty work for Weston's father. His name is Byron Murray—he's basically a lackey. He told me—word for word—that it was time I got on board and married Weston," I pause to stress my next words, "*or else*."

His brows knit. "Or else?"

"Or else," I confirm. "Because I knew too much. And given what he said and how he threatened me, I knew what *or else* meant. Their business is a cover for organized crime—or whatever the modern-day terminology is for the mob. I had no choice but to play along, act like I was considering taking Weston back while still keeping him at arm's length until I figured out what to do. My only choice was to leave, but I still don't know how they found me. I've been so careful. I used cash for everything, got rid of my phone the minute I left town, and sold my car once I hit Pennsylvania, buying another down the street with cash and never registered it. I don't understand how they found me."

He takes another big breath and simply responds, "I see."

I grip his shirt at his shoulders where I'm hanging on and tell him what I'm really worried about. "I need to call my brother. I've been afraid to. Everyone there would know the way to find me would be through Joe, I have no idea what means they might have to track me. I wanted to call him with my prepaid cell, but I was too nervous to try. They know where I am now, so I guess it doesn't matter."

"If it makes you feel better, I have a phone you could use and you won't have to worry, even though they know where you are."

"You do?"

I see a shadow of a smile, but it's so faint, it almost looks like a regret. "I do."

I bite my lip when I feel the tears well in my eyes instantly. I've been riddled with regret and guilt over not contacting Joe. It's impossible to blink my tears away and they spill over, running down the sides of my face when I whisper, "Thank you."

His thumb comes up and swipes my temple. "No problem. Let me get it for you, you can talk as long as you want. I promise it'll be safe."

Relief and hope sweep through me, craving the chance to talk to my brother, let him know I'm safe, but most importantly, I need to know if he's okay. I don't know how I'm going to explain leaving like I did, but I'll figure that out. I do know I can't do anything to jeopardize him by telling the truth about the MacLachlans.

Grady leans down to kiss me. This kiss is soft like a few minutes ago, but this time I feel a bit of anxiety surrounding him. He's holding himself back, not kissing me the way he wants to.

When we stand, he puts a hand in back of my head one more time, pulling me to him where he puts his lips to my temple. Pressing his lips there, he says, "Stay here. I'll get you a phone and you can talk as long as you want."

With that, he starts to leave. He's about to turn the corner when I call for him. "Grady?"

He turns and looks at me.

"Thank you," I say. "It feels good to get all that off my chest. I hate keeping secrets. It's been a long and lonely few months."

He says nothing, but gives me another ghost of a smile with a nod before turning to leave.

I wipe my tears away and try to get it together. I get to talk to Joe. I'm not sure there's a sweeter gift than that right now, and getting it from Grady is even better.

Grady

STANDING IN THE clearing of the forest between the house and the biggest of the barns, I don't look away from the house when I say to Crew, "Could this be any more fucked up?"

"I don't know what to say." Crew is standing next to me, but facing the barn where Asa is in the doorway while the recruits battle it out on the mats. I haven't paid any attention to them since we got back. Crew told me to take as much time as I needed and I have.

Before what happened on the job from hell, I never would've taken time off. Idle time and I don't do well. For almost a decade, the most time I took off was to swing by and see my sisters for a couple days at most—then I was on the move again to my next job.

"You want her?"

When I glance over, Crew is turned to me.

I look back to the house, almost desperate not to take my eyes off it since she's there. Not that anything could happen to her, Crew's property is surrounded with surveillance and security. Still, it was hard for me to leave her to make her phone call in private. This must be a new low of obsession for me because even though I know she's safe, leaving her didn't feel right.

I shake my head and sigh. "It might not matter."

"You never know. Give it a chance."

Still not looking away from the house, I ask, "Addy ever balk?"

"She was surprised—probably more like shocked. Once I explained it to her, she was fine, especially when I explained my need to do it. It's not like you're a made man like her ex. Fuck, it's different and you know it."

"Just because I think it's different, doesn't mean she will. I can't even think about her finding out what happened with my dad."

"Hey," Crew calls for me and I look over. His face is hard when he stresses his words. "You don't want to be with anyone who'd hold that against you."

I look back to the house, not knowing if I want her to come look for me or hope she doesn't. "You didn't see her face. It was nothing but disgust."

"It should be," he says and I hear him shift on the gravel and brush, then he adds, "You should know that Asa called Bennett this morning."

This gets my attention. Bennett is our contact at the FBI. Even though we never work stateside, sometimes our cases are connected to activity here, especially since our focus has shifted to terrorism. Even though the sun is bright and winter has settled, I can see my own breath when I ask, "What did he find out?"

"Since Asa and Bennett have a good rapport, he asked what they had on him. The FBI have been working on the MacLachlans for a while. Found out they're closing in with RICO charges. First degree has only been a suspicion, they haven't gained solid evidence on anyone. Asa did find out the organization is wide and deep. You think she has any clue she almost married into the mob?"

Even though I'm grateful to have Weston's background confirmed. I'm not happy to learn it's worse than we thought to begin with.

"She does now, but it wasn't always that way," I confirm. "I don't think she knows all of it. She assumes, but that's it. Did Bennett say if they're close to pressing charges?"

"Not close enough, but she doesn't need to worry if she's here. You need to find a way to explain that to her."

"I'm not worried about her here, though I've gotta find a way to keep her safe at the assisted living center. I don't think I'll be able to convince her to let that job go, not after seeing her there this morning. What I'm more concerned about is her wanting to go home."

"Why would she do that?"

"Her brother. She's inside talking to him now. They're close and he's got health issues. I have a feeling if he's not good, she's gonna want to see him. I'm not sure how to keep her from doing that."

"They're the mob, not ISIS," Crew states. "They've imported bananas for years to cover their drug operation. They don't seem creative or overly-smart. If she needs to see her brother, you should take her, but don't leave her side."

"I thought the same thing. I don't want her near MacLachlan, and if we go, that could happen. I'll just have to deal with it."

"You think you can convince her to let you go?" Crew asks.

Turning back to him, I'm serious as shit when I say, "I promise you, she's not going anywhere alone. I'll make sure she does what she needs to do, but only with me by her side."

I hear a door and when I look back to Crew's house,

she's standing on the patio. Even from here, I see her send me a small smile with a little wave. I turn back to Crew one last time. "Do me a favor, tell Addy she won't be in for a while. And from here on out, I'll cover her rent."

Crew smirks and shakes his head. "Been there, done that. Maya's not gonna like it."

Since I don't care, I turn and start for the house where she's waiting for me. I don't give a shit what Crew thinks. In fact, for my entire life I haven't cared what anyone thinks of me.

Until now.

As I approach Maya, my insides tighten, wondering how I'm going to win her over. I can't keep who I am a secret forever. Eventually, she'll want details of my life—my past. I fucking hate secrets. I was raised keeping everything a secret—every bruise, cut, and wound. When my organization approached me with an offer, choosing to be a contract assassin was an easy decision. It was no different from what I'd done for my country. I've never had a regret.

But as I walk up the steps to my physical therapist, I might not feel guilty, but I am apprehensive. Because the woman who started to possess my mind over security cameras has turned into an addiction I can't turn away from.

When I get to her, I can't help myself, and reach for her hip. Pulling her to me, I ask, "You had a good talk?"

Hell if her eyes don't fill with tears again, something I could barely handle seeing the first time. She nods and swallows hard. "Weston was being honest for once—Joe's having seizures again. I made the excuse that I couldn't take the pressure from Weston or our mother any longer. My family has no clue what the MacLachlans are really about. I feel so guilty for not keeping in touch with him. He insists he's fine, his doctors are getting his meds evened out, but still, I'm worried and want to see him."

"I'll take you," I say, wrapping my arm around her back, pulling her flush to me.

She shakes her head and bites her lip. "I don't want you to have to deal with my family."

"I'll be fine. You should know that while you were on the phone, I read your background, and just for fun, I read MacLachlan's. You're not going anywhere near him or his family on your own. When do you want to see your brother?"

She's surprised, her watery blue eyes go big. "You read my background?"

"I told you I was going to. Don't worry, you told me everything important—other than the fact you played the flute." I can't keep the grin off my face. "This means you're good with your mouth. Bonus."

She rolls her eyes and gives me a little push, but I don't let go of her. "I don't know when I can get off work. I'm sure I'll have to give a little notice so Addy and the Ranch can plan for it. It'll have to be a quick trip, I can't afford to be off for too long. I'm already missing a few hours today."

I give her a squeeze before turning her toward the back door so I can get her inside where it's warm. "It'll work out. I can go anytime—I told Crew I'm taking you. I'm sure Addy will understand, and the old folks will be fine without you for a couple days." When we get inside I'm anxious to change the subject and feel the need for some therapy. "Since you've already electrocuted me today, we might as well see if it worked. I'm ready to get back to my weights and I need full motion for that. You feel like torturing me before going back to work?"

She smiles. "You're a quick healer. You already have a lot of your motion back, but you shouldn't be lifting for a while."

I shrug. "We'll see. I can run though, right?"

She nods, smiling bigger.

"Then get your running shoes. Tonight, we have a date."

She raises a brow. "A date?"

I tip my head, challenging her. "Or a race. Your choice."

She surprises me and narrows her eyes, showing me she has a competitive side. "Do you run for distance or time?"

I reach out, hooking my finger inside the waist of her jeans, and give her a good yank. "Both."

She catches herself by grasping my biceps, but doesn't try to push away. "I was All-State in track four years in a row and ran for Cornell on scholarship."

I lean into her, my addiction growing stronger by the second. "Told you I read your background, Maya. You're telling me things I already know."

She narrows her eyes farther, and I can't tell if she's annoyed or surprised that I know as much as I do. After thinking it over for a second, she squares her shoulders. "Then it's a race—an even 10K."

"You're competitive," I reply, my grin growing bigger. "How about a wager?" She instantly frowns, and I can't help but tease her. "What, I thought you ran for *Cornell*?"

She sighs. "Fine. I picked the race, you name the wager."

"A first date. A *real* date, planned by me if I win. Should you happen to win," I shrug and try not to grimace, "I'll eat a salad."

She tries to hide a smirk as she agrees, "It's on."

I lean in and kiss her quickly, sealing the deal, even though I want nothing more than to peel her clothes off and seal it a different way.

All in due time.

Until then, I pull away and say, "Should I take my shirt off for the torture? I'm more than willing to undress for you. If you'd like to torture something else, I can take my pants off, too."

So far today, I've seen her scared, nervous, apprehensive, and even having fun hula-hooping with an old guy. But when she bursts out laughing and slaps my chest, saying, "Stop it," it feels like I've accomplished a task so big and challenging, I almost forget about having to explain to her one day that I was a hired assassin.

Almost, but not quite.

Still, this doesn't stop her from torturing me.

12

HIS ILIAC FURROW

Maya

Even though it's late afternoon, the tasting room is slower than normal. So slow, that the women of Whitetail—Addy, Clara, Bev, and Evan's girlfriend, Mary—are all congregated at the bar. Bev and Mary are having a glass and they're all deep in chat. Or they were until Grady and I walked through the front door, and all eyes settled on my hand being held by Grady's. Chatting immediately ceased once they got an eyeful, and all their eyes got big.

Great.

My well-thought-out plan of not getting to know anyone, flying under the radar, and hiding in plain sight, has lost its steam. I certainly didn't mean to gain the attention of any man, let alone the one with whom I've become obsessed. The last time a man turned my head, I was sixteen and he was barely a man.

Between Weston appearing, worrying about Joe, stressing about paying my rent, not to mention, *or else*, I don't have time for a new man in my life. Obviously, *or else* wins, tipping the scales of my anxiety at the moment. If all this wasn't enough, I just agreed to let Grady travel home with me. I guess I deserve that since I basically threw him under the bus last night by pretending he's something he isn't in front of Weston.

Not that Grady wasn't flirty before last night. He definitely was. But ever since I threw myself at him, kissing him like he was mine to kiss, he's been acting like he's mine. What's more—he's acting like I'm his.

Not that I'm not interested, I am. Not that I don't like him kissing me, I do—I *definitely* do. Not that I don't like him touching me, or sitting in his lap, or even his teasing me. I like it *all*, and I think I like it too much. And now he's insisted on traveling to Buffalo with me so I can see Joe.

I'm not quite sure what's wrong with me, but I didn't even try to deny him. I simply accepted the fact he's coming home with me, to be subjected to my mother, who, prior to my leaving, incessantly pressured me to get back together with my cheating, good-for-nothing, murdering, mobster ex-fiancé. She did this solely because she wants a connection to the MacLachlans, as if being married to an Augustine isn't enough for her. She has no idea what the MacLachlan family is really about.

First things first, I need to talk to Addy about getting a couple days off. I'm looking forward to seeing Joe as much as I'm dreading seeing my mother.

Addy comes around from behind the bar, looking from me, to Grady, and back to me. Her smirk turns into a smile which turns into a knowing grin. I'm not sure what she thinks she knows, but if she knows something, I wish she'd tell me.

As she approaches, Mary and Bev are following with their wine glasses, and Clara is pulling up the rear. Clara is the event manager at Whitetail and I'm still getting to know her. She's almost full-term and expecting her fourth child in the next couple weeks. To say her personality is OTT would be an understatement.

Without my saying a word, Addy starts, "Crew told me you need some time off to see your family. Come on. Let's go talk about that in my office." In one fell swoop, she grabs my free hand, pulling me away. In the process, she looks over her shoulder and says to Grady, "Maya and I need to look at the calendar. Go have a dessert or something."

Surprised Addy already knows I need some time off, I look back at Grady and he shrugs, but doesn't seem to have an issue with it and heads to the bar. As Addy and I make our way to her office, I realize the rest of the Whitetail women are following.

When we get there, we file into her small, nondescript workspace. It's tight and boring in here compared to the charm surrounding her buildings and property. I'm about to ask why everyone is here just to look at the calendar, but Addy beats me to it. "Go see your family for as long as you need. We'll manage fine."

"But you can't miss the company Christmas party. It's Monday in Addy's Ordinary." Clara shuts the door behind her and motions for everyone to move out of her way so she can sit, her big belly paving the way. "I have a sitter. This will be my last hurrah before hellion number four starts to torment me outside the womb."

"Here." Addy sits me in the office chair behind her desk and pushes a bowl of candy in front of me. "Have some Laffy Taffy."

"Maybe you'd like a glass of wine?" When I look over, Bev is saluting me with her glass of red before taking a sip.

"Maybe I should grab a new bottle," Mary says with a sly smile on her face. "Or two. This could take a while."

My eyes widen, taking them all in. Finally, I turn to Addy and say, "I only need two days, that should be enough."

"I told you it doesn't matter. We're not here to talk about that anyway." Addy digs through the bowl of candy and pulls out three green pieces, handing me a purple one. "Do you like grape? We're here to get the scoop on you. And Grady. Then you and Grady."

Shocked, I absentmindedly take the purple candy and lean back in my chair.

"She needs wine," Bev states, and Mary immediately starts to stand, but I stop her.

"No-no. I can't have wine. Grady and I are running later—a 10K race. The way my life is going, one glass would turn into a bottle, and I can't be sluggish for the race. I need to be at the top of my game because I want Grady to eat a salad." I wait for them to say something, but they don't. They're staring at me, either frowning, wide-eyed, or confused. "What? He never eats vegetables."

When no one says a word, Mary finally sets her glass down on the desk. "Okay. Let's start from the beginning. Who's that shithead we heard about showing up at your door last night?"

My eyes widen, wondering how they know about Weston.

"Sorry." Addy tips her head as she unwraps a piece of candy. "Crew told me and I told them."

I realize my plan hasn't only lost steam—it's fallen off the track and landed in a deep abyss, never to be seen again. I guess now there's no reason to hide anything besides me almost marrying into a family of organized crime. They don't need to know that.

"Well, he's my *ex*-fiancé, although he's not happy about the 'ex' part. He's been trying to rectify that, but when I wouldn't budge, he became persistent. So much so that I left. I couldn't take it any longer—him, my mom, his family ... it was exhausting."

"Why did you break it off?" Bev asks.

I shrug, tired of rehashing this for the second time today. "I found out he was cheating on me."

"Son-of-a-bitch." Clara shakes her head while rubbing her tummy.

I go on to tell them all about my past with Weston, Joe's epilepsy, my pain-in-the-ass mother, and how I'm a physical therapist.

"That's it," I say, chewing on my grape candy. "Before this all happened with Weston, I was really boring."

"Don't you dare think you're done," Mary says, finishing her wine. "We haven't even gotten to the good part yet. Tell us all about Grady."

"Yes." Addy steps forward and half-sits on the edge of her desk. "We want to know about Grady. I hardly know anything about him. What's he like?"

I try to hide my smile by biting my lip. "He's sweet."

Instantly, they all look taken aback.

"He is?" Clara looks like she doesn't believe me.

"That's not what I expected you to say," Addy adds.

"Maybe she's just used to the asshole, so Grady seems, you know ... sweet ... in a way," Mary tries to justify Grady being sweet. "Or maybe Maya likes gruff, distant men who are full of themselves."

Now it's my turn to look confused. "Full of himself?"

"Poor choice of words." Addy shoots Mary a look. "Grady's not full of himself, not by a long shot. If anything, he doesn't like attention. However, he can be a little distant, and maybe rough around the edges."

"I guess I can see that if you don't know him." He was definitely that way to begin with, but not anymore. "He's different than he was when I first met him."

"I've always thought Grady was lovely," Bev states, taking her last sip of wine.

Addy smiles at her older friend. Mary pats her shoulder, but Clara rolls her eyes.

"We still haven't gotten to the good part," Clara demands. "For the past week, he won't order from anyone but you, he's sat in the tasting room for hours watching you work, now he's holding your hand, and tonight you two are running a race. Who even does that? So yeah, we want the behind the scenes VIP pass, Maya. Preferably before I pop this baby out—tell us *something*."

I tip my head, not knowing where to begin. Do I start with me being a creeper or about me being fascinated with his injuries? Neither is probably a good idea, even I know it's weird and I don't know these women very well. I'm still in the making-a-good-impression stage.

I decide to go with the less embarrassing option. "I

think maybe he warmed up to me when I started working on his shoulder."

"I knew it!" Addy exclaimed before looking around to the other women, smiling big. "I did that. I set up the physical therapy date. I set them up just like I set you up," she stresses, pointing to Mary, who smirks and shakes her head. "Just call me the matchmaker. My skills are honed to perfection. I can't wait to tell Crew."

Clara sighs and waves a hand at Addy before looking to me. "Tell us about it."

"He stood me up the first time I came to work on his shoulder, although I think he was home but just wouldn't answer the door. I stopped by the next day and surprised him, because he'd just gotten out of the shower. His hair was wet and he wasn't wearing a shirt. And he smelled good."

I sigh at the delicious memory of Grady in all his bare male beauty. I feel my face relax just thinking about touching Grady's bare skin for the first time.

When I look to my audience, they're listening with rapt attention, and something about the way they're looking makes me comfortable. I could be wrong, but I think they like me. It could be because I'm good at waiting tables, or I'm mostly on time, or I'm a good listener even if I haven't been a good sharer. Still, I'm one hundred percent sure they're not merely nosy because I'm Maya Augustine, daughter of the owner of one of the largest privately-held brokerage corporations in this hemisphere.

No, I'm pretty sure they're nosy simply because of the undiscovered female gene that makes everyone with a vagina nosy. They simply want the dirt about Grady holding my hand and why in the world we're running a race tonight. Something about this makes me relax, sort of like a truth serum, and the results will surely be like crack for their nosy gene.

"Yeah, he was half-naked. He had on a pair of sweatpants, but his chest was right there for me to perv on. I shouldn't have perved, I know this. I'm a healthcare provider, for the love of it all, I should've been professional. But it was hard and I think I failed because the whole moment was weird and tense. Very, very tense. It was honestly embarrassing."

Clara and Mary's expressions are absolutely greedy. Addy's trying to hide a smirk, and sweet Bev is sending me supportive vibes, relaying to me that I should keep going, so I do.

"It wasn't just his chest, but his arms are veined and honed to perfection. It was so hard to focus when measuring his range of motion, I fumbled and had to do it twice, which was even more embarrassing. I'm afraid he noticed, even though I tried to play it off as doing something important. When I was so flustered by his veins, I looked away only to see his iliac furrow."

"What?" Addy interrupts.

"Yeah, hang on." Mary leans forward in her seat. "You saw his what?"

"Please tell me the iliac whatever is some new slang for his dick and you got to measure it, too," Clara pleads and Bev frowns at her.

"Of course not," I shake my head. "It's the muscle below his abs going from his hip bone to his pubis."

"His pubis?" Mary echoes.

"Yeah." I can't help the smile that creeps over my face. "His pubis."

Bev pats Mary's arm. "She's a healthcare provider, dear."

"It's the V?" Clara guesses. When I grin and nod, she goes on. "We all know what that points to. So, I take it you didn't get to measure it?"

I shake my head and ignore her. "I felt him watching me the whole time, so I had to look away only to see his bare feet. There was something about his bare feet that was almost intimate, I couldn't help from getting turned on, so I looked back up, but there was the iliac furrow, and the muscles and the veins ... there was nowhere safe to look, so I started to blather on and lecture him about eating too much sugar."

"Eating too much sugar?" Addy gives me a confused frown as she chews on her Laffy Taffy.

I sigh, leaning back into her office chair. "Yes. I didn't know what else to talk about. I'm an idiot."

"You're a strange bird, Maya Augustine," Clara shakes her head. "But I like you."

"You do?" Like everything else, it pops out of my mouth before I can catch it and swallow it down.

Clara looks taken aback, and I'm not sure I've ever seen her that way. Nothing ever seems to phase her. "Of course, I do. Why would you say that?"

I shrug. "I've just ... never had a lot of friends, that's all."

"So, wait," Addy starts, looking distracted. "You said you met your ex when you were sixteen and even though it might've been bad at the end, you were together until recently, right?"

"Yeah," I answer.

"That's a long time. Have you ever dated anyone else?" she goes on.

I shake my head, biting my lip.

A big grin spreads across Mary's face. "No wonder his bare feet made you wet in the wonderland. You've only ever been with that asshole and now you have Adonis holding your hand and racing you through the woods. You're like an awkward fairytale for physical therapists everywhere."

I try not to wiggle in my chair thinking about Grady's bare anything, but the words just won't stop now that they've started. "My brother, Joe, has some health issues. I just found out today he's been having seizures again. Since Weston knows where I am, there's no reason for me not to go see Joe, even though I have no desire to be anywhere near Weston. Since that's a possibility, Grady said he'd come with me. I feel bad, but like a big fat chicken, I didn't argue."

"Why do you feel bad?" Mary asks.

"Because, when Weston showed up on my doorstep, I was shocked to see him. I was even more shocked to see Grady. I had no idea what to do, but I knew I had to do something, so I threw myself at Grady. I kissed him and acted like we're together, and now he's playing along, only it doesn't feel like he's playing. It feels real."

"Maybe it's because he wants it to be real," Addy says, with a faraway look in her eyes. She's probably patting herself on the back for her supernatural matchmaking skills.

"That man hasn't looked like he's been acting for the last week. He wants you, and you need to let him go home with you. How bad can it be, anyway?" Clara asks.

Thinking of my mother, my mobster ex-fiancé, and his organized-crime-laden family, I decide not to answer that question. To them, I'm just Maya, and I'd like to keep it that way for as long as I can. For the first time in my life, I feel normal.

But I know the answer to her question, and I think it has the potential to be bad.

Really bad.

I'm pulled from my thoughts when Addy's desk phone rings, and she turns to answer it.

"Really?" she asks into the phone, but looks to me as a smile spreads across her face. She stands and her eyes widen with excitement when she continues. "We'll be right out."

"What's going on?" Clara asks.

"Yeah," I add. "Why are you looking at me like that?"

Addy moves to the door, waving her hand for me to follow. "You got a delivery and Evan said it's something pretty! Well, he didn't say *pretty*, but he did say it was pink and girly, so it has to be pretty, right? Come on, let's go see what Grady sent you."

Why would Grady send me anything? He's been with me constantly—sending me something would be silly.

But I'm a curious girl nonetheless, so I hop up and am the first out the door.

When I round the corner to the tasting room, I see them, and Addy was right—they're pink and pretty. But they aren't just pretty, they're beautiful. A huge arrangement of pink blossoms are overflowing on the bar, but it's not a bouquet. They're brimming out of a basket and look more like a plant rather than cut flowers. It has to be over three feet wide and just as tall. I grew up with fresh flowers displayed in our house at all times, and this one would impress even my mother.

My heart stops as I'm halted in my tracks, the rest of

the nosy crew stopping with me. None of us utter even an *ooh* or *ah*, when the arrangement is completely ooh-and-ah worthy.

This is because Grady is standing next to my delivery and I instantly know it's not from him. Ever since I first laid eyes on him, he's been grumpy, brooding, teasing, sweet, or downright panty-melting hot. But I've never seen him angry, and it's radiating off of him.

"Umm." Clara breaks the silence from beside me. "I take it those aren't from you, are they, stud muffin?"

Grady doesn't move, but his eyes dart to Clara and narrow.

"No, I'd say these are definitely not from Grady," Bev guesses.

"They are pretty," Addy adds, hesitantly.

I feel someone touch my arm and hear Mary as she leans in close. "I think he might explode."

That was all it took.

Grady crinkles a piece of paper I didn't know he was holding and turns to roughly pick up the basket, heading to the kitchen.

I move quickly to follow, calling, "Wait, what's going on?"

But he doesn't wait or explain anything to me. Like he's been in the kitchen a million times, he stalks straight to the back door where the loading dock is located. Right when I clear the doorway, I see him at the dumpster just in time to hear the crash as he violently slams the flowery pink plant inside.

"Holy shit," Clara mutters from beside me. I agree wholeheartedly.

I move to Grady and look down into the dumpster

where the plant is now mangled with all the smelly trash.

But I don't care about the flowers. I look back up to Grady because all I care about is him being upset. "Are you okay?"

His rage is still festering, but I see him take a deep breath and he lowers his voice. "You're not going back to him."

Confused, I shake my head. "What? Of course, I'm not."

He takes a step and his hand comes to my jaw where he levels his eyes with mine. "You're not going anywhere without me, and I'll make sure you're safe."

I lift my hand to gently give his wrist a squeeze and soften my voice to calm him. "Okay, but you have to tell me what all this is about."

"Oleander." He lifts his hand up with the crinkled piece of paper to read it aloud. "*My dear Maya—An oleander for you as a reminder of how anything around you can be deadly if you don't choose wisely. It's time to come home.*"

My eyes widen and he instantly crinkles the paper again, throwing it harshly into the dumpster, with what I now know is a poisonous plant.

"It's signed *Byron Murray*," he growls. "He's not getting anywhere near you. None of them are—I promise."

I exhale and nod right before he pulls my face to his where he kisses me—deeply and passionately—showing me he'll take care of me.

"Holy shit," Clara exclaims again.

"You got that right," Mary agrees.

13

DON'T CALL ME A CARROT CAKE

Grady

This is the first time I've run since before I was captured.

I've been a long-distance runner since I joined the Army at eighteen. The Army didn't care whether I liked running or not. It had to be done and it was another way I could work at being the best, distinguishing myself from my peers. I've always been competitive, but that drive went to another level when I enlisted. I knew I needed something—a direction, a focus—and I knew I'd never find it in college.

When my organization approached me, explaining a top-secret group wanted to discuss alternative career options, they didn't have to ask twice. If there was ever a career created specifically for me, it was being a Soldier of Fortune. I was top-notch for nine years—on top of my game, had my specialty, and was in high demand.

Until I lost my focus. I let the guilt fuck with me.

When my fascination with Maya began, I'd notice

her running every night. That turned into watching her go from camera to camera. I'd wait for her. Like a pathetic dog knowing it was time, there I was. If she didn't come out for me to stalk, it almost hurt.

So now, after all that, to have her close to me and actually be running with her? I can't describe it, other than it feels like another piece of my puzzle has fallen into place. And after what happened with the fucking flowers today, there's no way I'll be able to tear myself away from her.

I asked her to point the way, even though I know her normal course. I can't let her know how much of a freak I am just yet. I keep her pace, which is a quick one, letting her lead as I follow. Now I'm glad I paid attention to the course so I'd know when to take the lead. Otherwise, I would be lost in the way her body moves effortlessly through the woods and hills.

After we finish mile four, I shift next to her. When she glances at me, she narrows her eyes, and instantly quickens her pace. We aren't jogging. She's fast and efficient with her strides.

We haven't said a word since we started, which I'm thankful. For the next two miles, I focus on her breathing and match my pace to hers. I keep my eyes on the path we're maneuvering side-by-side, letting myself absorb the feeling of being close to her, moving in tandem, like one, but still not.

I do this for six miles, and the whole time I have to work at not getting hard. It takes all my concentration and strength—listening to Maya Augustine breathe hard for that long is not easy.

We've just made the last bend and we're getting close to her tiny house on Addy's property. Since I've set my speed to hers, I can tell she's picking up her pace. I wait for my moment since our path is a narrow one. As efficient as her footwork is, I don't want to do anything to trip her up. I'd feel like shit if I won because she fell, even though there's no way I'm not gonna win this race —not with our first date on the line.

When the woods open into a clearing, I see her house in the valley. I move away from her and let loose. The last four-tenths of a mile goes fast, I hear her close behind me, but as I near the end, I lengthen my strides and I know I have it locked up.

When I cross the drive where her compact car is parked, I slow and turn to watch her do the same. When we're both stopped and facing one another on either side of her gravel drive, she puts her hands to her knees and breathes the word, "Shit."

"Tomorrow's Saturday—date night." My words come out quick while trying to catch my breath. It's been a long time since I've worked out. "Be ready. I have plans for you and they don't include a salad."

Her head pops up at the word salad.

Her fair skin is flushed red from the cold and the run, but her light blue eyes flare, and I can tell she's pissed. Only, I'm not sure what she's pissed about.

"I'm gonna start running for time again," she breathes, standing up and wiping her brow with the back of her forearm. "I hate losing."

She's pissed because she's competitive. I close the distance between us and she holds her ground, her face tipping back to look at me as I get close.

Before I kiss her like I plan, she asks, "How's your shoulder?"

"A little sore, but I'm good."

She tips her head to the side and barely smirks. "I should be happy it's sore since you beat me, but that wouldn't be nice since you're sort of my patient *and* you're traveling all the way to Buffalo with me. And you've been kind of sweet."

I step closer. "Kind of sweet?"

Finally catching her breath, her smirk turns into a smile. "Yeah. You're like dark chocolate compared to milk chocolate. Or carrot cake as opposed to devil's food with all the thick frosting."

I lose my smile and mean it when I say, "Don't call me a carrot cake. That's rude."

She grins broadly, taking a step back and throws her arms out low. "How about zucchini bread?"

"Now you're just being cruel." I move closer, making her take a few steps backward up her small porch.

She unzips a small pocket on her hoodie and pulls out a key. When she turns to unlock the door, she peeks at me over her shoulder and keeps talking shit. "Sweet potato pancakes?"

When she opens the door, I follow her in and watch her switch on some lights around the room. "What is it with you and health food?"

She tosses her key on the table and kicks her running shoes to the side before peeling off her sweatshirt. Between her leggings and compression shirt, it's easy to see every contour of her body.

"I have a minor in nutrition." She puts her hands on her hips and changes the subject. "So, this date tomorrow. What are we doing? I have to work in the tasting room all day. By the time we close and clean up, it'll be late. I guess I should've clarified that when I accepted your wager, but I really thought you'd be eating a salad. I shouldn't have let you keep pace with me for so long."

"We aren't seeing a movie and we don't have a reservation. Whenever you're ready is fine."

She smirks. "There you go again, being a candied butternut squash."

That's it.

I advance on her and when I do, her eyes get big, but her smile remains. She puts a hand up to stop me, but I move it out of the way and back her into the wall. With my body pressed into hers, I bring one hand up to her slim hip and place the other gently on the side of her face.

When I lean in close, I lower my voice. "Do you know what I want?"

Her smile shrinks. "No."

I lean in to kiss her so softly, her lips are barely a whisper against mine. "I want to be molten chocolate cake for you."

She sounds confused when she breathes against my face. "You do?"

"I do." I probably shouldn't, but I press my groin into her stomach, not able to keep from getting hard when I feel her body against mine. Her face flushes, this time having nothing to do with the cold. "Warm and moist, with chocolate oozing out. Have you ever had anything so good?"

Knowing full and well we aren't talking desserts any longer, she shakes her head twice. "Never."

I let my hand slide from her jaw into her hair, tilting her head to me. Brushing the side of her cheek with my thumb, it's all I can do to restrain myself from peeling her sweaty clothes off her and taking her against the wall. Instead, I let my hand on her hip move to cup her ass.

This doesn't help my resolve.

I force myself to focus on her eyes that flare at my touch. "Judging from the interactions with your ex, this doesn't surprise me. If you'll let me, I can give you sweet."

Her tongue instantly appears, wetting her lips before she catches her bottom one between her teeth. I feel her hands grip my sides where she's hanging on, but her voice is smooth and assured when she changes the subject. "What should I wear tomorrow night?"

I squeeze her ass, loving the feel of it in my hand. "I like these."

She tips her head. "Are we running again?"

"No. We'll be eating, drinking, talking, and maybe eating some more." I pull her away from the wall and fully palm her ass, making her eyes widen. I grin before leaning down to kiss her quick. "But I still like these."

She tries to look put out, but does it while suppressing a grin, and pushes against my chest. "I need to shower and you need to leave."

"You shower, but I'm not leaving. I'll get in after you."

Her eyes widen. "What do you mean, 'you'll get in after me'?"

"I mean, I don't want to smell like this all night and I doubt you want me to, either. I packed a bag. I'll shower after you. If you think I'm leaving you alone after what happened today, you're crazy."

"But," she starts before biting her lip again. I'm beginning to think it's a habit and can't help but feel a pang of jealousy. I'd love to bite on that lip freely. "I feel bad, there's nowhere for you to sleep."

I shake my head and turn for the door. "I'm not leaving. Either you shower or I shower," I stop and look back before I add, "unless you want to shower together. I'm up for that, too."

She looks down and sighs.

"Maya?"

Looking back, I can tell she's giving in because she raises her brows when she widens her eyes to silently acknowledge me.

"I want to know about your family—more about Joe and what I should expect from your parents. We'll talk about that as I watch your hair dry."

Again, she shakes her head, turning to her bedroom. But I catch it, the smallest of smiles, even if it wasn't for me to see, just before I lose sight of her face.

When I open her front door to go to my SUV and get my bag, I do my best not to think about her in the shower. Listening to her breathing hard during our run was rough enough, imagining her wet and naked is pure torture.

I was serious though, I need to know what to expect from her family. Reading her background, I know her dad's corporation has been listed on the Fortune 500 for years. Next week should be interesting, that's for sure. I've got three days to prepare—she told me today we're leaving first thing Tuesday morning. She's got two days off work, that means we'll be there for only one night.

I grab my bag and the two sacks of food I picked up this afternoon. As much as my obsession has taken over, I'm not about to become a vegetarian.

Maya

*H*E LICKS ME *from my opening to my clit.*

Oh, yes.

More, I need more. I try to lift my hips, but I can't. He has me pinned—deliciously pinned to the bed with his big hands behind my knees—holding me wide open for his painfully slow ministrations to my pussy.

I've never felt this before, I don't want the humming to end. I want to orgasm, but I don't want to lose his mouth.

"Please," I call to him.

He says nothing, and I didn't know it was possible, but his grip on my legs tighten, holding me stronger.

Then he circles my clit with the tip of his tongue before lightly scraping his teeth across it.

"Yes, that, more of that," I beg, but he lets me go.

I lose his tongue, his lips, his teeth, and his hold on me. But he does give me his weight—every beautiful muscle I've come to love is heavy and firm, pressing me into the bed. I bring my hands up to touch him, but I find nothing.

I frown as I look up into his blue eyes that shine brighter than they should through the dark. "I can't feel you."

"No, you can't. But can you feel this?" He slides into me, and as he does, he presses on my clit that's on the verge of igniting into a burst of hot sex flames. "Now you can come."

I lurch awake.

Breathing hard, I lean up on my elbows to look around my dark bedroom where I'm alone. My door is still closed, thank goodness for that. My gasping isn't quiet, and since my reality doesn't include Grady's face between my legs, he must still be asleep on my tiny sofa.

I fall back to my pillow and squeeze my thighs together. I've never had a sex dream, wet dream, or whatever it's called. Is it possible for a woman to orgasm in her sleep? If so, I'm seriously jealous. Why did I have to wake up right before the good stuff?

I roll to my side and groan. It's nowhere near morning. With thoughts of Grady between my legs and then inside me, I'll never get back to sleep.

"GIVE ME A SHOW OF HANDS, who got Madagascar?"

Grady raises his hand low, showing the world, or at least the brewery, he knew Madagascar produced two-thirds of the world's vanilla.

I raise a brow, wondering how he knew this bit of weird information.

He shrugs as he picks up his water. "I didn't know that one. That was a guess."

Grady has done everything he said he would. Last night after the nerve-racking ten minutes of imagining him naked in my shower, I watched his thick, brown hair dry into a perfect wavy mess before he ate enough for an army. He brought over a bevy of junk food, but he did eat two bananas with what looked to be a half a jar of peanut butter. I made a mental note to buy him the organic kind the next time I go to the store.

Putting the flower incident behind us, he was back to his normal self, and spent the night in my little house just as promised. I have no idea how he slept on the little loveseat Addy provided, but he said he was fine. I'm sure all of this spurred my subconscious, creating my erotic dream that I can't get out of my head. It took me forever to get back to sleep, and the only reason I didn't put my own hand between my legs for some relief was because I was afraid he'd hear me. Addy didn't name my little house a bungalow for no reason—it's small.

Still worked up into a sexual frenzy, I waited tables all day in the tasting room. Besides coming in for a quick lunch, Grady weirdly didn't stalk me at work today. Instead, he told me he was catching up on some things, he'd be by at six-thirty, and we'd leave whenever I was ready to pay off my bet.

It's strange how he won't leave my side at the Ranch, but at Whitetail he doesn't mind. I didn't have the chance to ask him about it—he seemed in a hurry to get wherever we were going, so I barely had time to change into a pair of jeans, sweater, and boots, plus touch up my makeup. We drove barely ten minutes to Old Bust Head, a local brewery in Vint Hill that I've never been to.

The place was packed, but Grady grabbed my hand and found a corner table where a group of four were leaving. Not only was it packed, it was loud because of trivia night. The guy on stage with the microphone was asking questions and we kept our own score.

Grady offered to play together, smirking the whole time and said I might not feel like losing to him again. That, of course, got the best of me. I'm competitive and it was time I beat him.

It was unlike any date I've ever had, but seeing as though Grady is only the second man I've ever been on a date with, it would be different.

Right after securing our table, he took my hand again, and we left the building through the back door. There, under a huge overhang near the brewery warehouse, was a truck with the name *French Kiss* scrolled along the side with a mass of people waiting their turn.

After taking our place in line, I looked up at him. "What's this?"

He tipped his head with a small smile, but spoke slowly as if I didn't speak his language. "Dinner."

"Like a concession stand?" I went on.

He turned fully to me. "You've never eaten at a food truck?"

"No." Sure, I've seen them around, especially when we went to New York City on shopping trips or if I had to go to downtown Buffalo. But Vanessa Augustine won't even eat at a chain restaurant, let alone from something on wheels. "I assumed all they sold were novelties, prepackaged ice cream bars, and popcorn."

"Oh, Maya. This is going to be fun." He grinned big and put an arm around my shoulders, pulling me into his large frame. Turning me to a large easel sitting next to the truck, there's a menu haphazardly scrawled on a dry erase board. "French Kiss is French food, not usually my thing, but I'll go out of my way to eat at any food truck. I don't care about the beer—we're here for the food. Order whatever looks good."

I read through the menu that included a full breakfast offering, savory crepes, fancy French bread sandwiches that would challenge Maggie's, cheese and meat platters, and a ton of sides that sounded mouth-watering.

"They have all that in this truck?" I asked.

"No, they make all that in this truck." He gave me a squeeze and I looked up to him. "You remember I read your background, right?"

I frowned, but nodded, not loving the fact he's been

able to read up on me while I still know so little about him.

"I understand why you might not have experienced a food truck. Trust me, it'll be good."

Well, it wasn't only good—it was great. I snagged the last of the parmesan fries that Grady ordered for us to share. They were tossed with parsley, sea salt, parmesan, and roasted garlic. I forked the last bite of my savory crepe with turkey, roasted asparagus, capers, and sun-dried tomatoes, and Grady inhaled his French dip sandwich. The meat and cheese platter that came with fruit was annihilated. It was the best meal I'd had in a long time.

I'm surprised it was made in a truck and now I'm wondering what else I've been missing out on.

Since sitting down for dinner and a delicious beer, all I've learned about Grady is he knows his geography and early American history well. He knows Australia is almost cut in half equally by the Tropic of Capricorn, and the Oneida Native Indian Tribe aligned themselves with Americans during the Revolution. I, on the other hand, am kicking his ass in science and literature.

"What measure of energy comes from the Latin word meaning *heat*?" the announcer booms over the PA system.

Easy. I know this before the options are given and scribble my answer down quickly before flipping my page over.

Grady leans in close, as it's the only way we've been able to have a conversation thus far because of the noise. I feel his breath on the side of my face when he boasts, "Madagascar put me ahead. You wanna bet again?"

Knowing we'll probably be back at a tie because he sucks at science and I doubt he guessed *calorie*, I turn my head to him and can't help but bite my lip from having him so close. Especially his mouth, and I find myself wondering if he's as good with his tongue and lips in real life as he was in my dream.

Shit. I need to focus.

"Another date?" I ask.

His eyes drop to my mouth. "You bite your lip a lot."

I instantly roll my lips out of sheer habit, before forcing myself to release them and relax. His eyes come back to mine, but I don't say anything. I know I do this, my mother has pointed it out my entire life, explaining to me it's not only unnerving for others to watch, but unbecoming. Still, I catch myself doing it all the time.

Grady doesn't let me explain, but goes on, "Makes me jealous."

To this, I lean back, confused.

His hand comes up quickly, wrapping around the back of my neck and the next thing I know, he's kissing me.

He doesn't kiss me long and deep, but his tongue does sweep mine. I taste the sweetness of his root beer he insisted on having since he was driving, along with a hint of our French Kiss dinners. I can't remember anything tasting better.

When he pulls away, he's looking at my lips when he mutters, "Makes me want to kiss them." His eyes shoot to mine. "Maybe even bite one of them myself."

"Let me see a raise of hands for *calorie*," the voice booms over the speakers.

Without moving, our lips almost touch when I ask, "Did you get that one right?"

His beautiful lips tip on one side. "Fuck no. Calories are something I work off so I can eat more of them."

I lean my head into his hand because it feels good and smile. "Then we're tied. You still want to bet?"

"Yeah. If I win, you make me dinner, but I get to choose what you make."

"And if there's more science and literature questions and you go down like a big fat loser?" I ask.

"Then you still make me dinner, but you get to choose what to make."

"Either way, I'm making you dinner," I point out the obvious flaw to his plan.

He grins big, unapologetically. "I know. I want you to make me dinner."

To keep from grinning, I bite the inside of my lip, but catch myself quickly when he narrows his eyes on my mouth.

Honestly, I love to be in the kitchen and there's nothing more I'd like than to cook for Grady. Even more so if I get to pick the menu. "I'll make you dinner."

He smiles and is about to say something before we hear the next question. "Name the author of *The Power of One*."

I scribble my answer and cover it up, but Grady doesn't try to hide his. When I see him write out Stephen Covey, I do my best to hide my smile.

"What?" He shrugs his shoulders. "I've never heard of *The Power of One*. It sounds motivational—it's my best guess."

I laugh and show him my answer when Bryce Courtenay is announced. All I say is, "You're going down, Grady Cain. I can't wait to make you dinner."

14

YOU GIVE GOOD DATES

Maya

"Tell me about your sisters."

I look back and Grady is pushing the cart, looking put out, but following along. He's just mad he lost at trivia, yet this was his idea. Apparently, I'm cooking for him tomorrow night.

It's late. We stayed at the brewery until closing, listening to live music, but it was louder than trivia, so I had no opportunity to interrogate him about anything. I'm shopping slow, trying to think out a menu while I bombard him with questions.

"What do you want to know?" he asks, looking bored since we're in the produce section.

I bag up a zucchini and he doesn't hide his scowl. "Are they older? Younger?"

He leans down with his forearms on the handle and starts pushing slowly again. "All younger."

I stop, so he stops in tandem. "Wow, I still can't believe your parents had five kids. All I have is my brother, and we were pretty quiet because we had to be. My mother wouldn't have it any other way. That must've been interesting for your parents."

"I don't know about parents, my mom did all the parenting when we were young, but that's it. We're really close in age. Gracie's the youngest and she's twenty-four."

I realize there's so much to learn about him. "How old are you?"

"Thirty-two."

I nod, but roll my eyes before moving on. "I suppose you know how old I am."

This buys me an unapologetic Grady-grin I'm quickly becoming obsessed with. "You'll be twenty-nine late next month. You can bake me a cake for your birthday."

Whatever. I move on and grab a small butternut squash.

"Are you close to your sisters?" I keep on.

He shrugs and when we finally move on to the next aisle, he perks up and starts tossing jars of pickles, olives, jellies, and more peanut butter in the cart. "I guess. I try to see them when I can—they're in Ohio. I'm the only one who left, and I did that right after high school. Joined the Army and never looked back."

We make it through more aisles, me adding needed ingredients and Grady adding junk food.

"I'm glad you're close to your sisters. I don't know what I'd do without Joe. He's my best friend," I say, thoughtfully. I stop again to look at him and mean it with all my heart when I say, "You don't know what it means to me that I get to go see him. I'm worried about him, but I also miss him. My mom's a pain in the ass, my dad's tied up in his business, but Joe and I have always had each other. And with the issue of Weston looming over me, I don't think I'd have the nerve to go back on my own."

Grady straightens from where he was leaning on the cart and takes a step, closing the small distance separating us.

"So, thank you," I go on, tipping my head back to look him in the eyes. "It means a lot to me."

He says nothing, but leans down just far enough to press his lips to my forehead.

When we finally make it through the aisles and head to the front of the store to check out, we come across the holiday department that looks as though Santa's dropped a Christmas bomb in Walmart.

"Do you spend Christmas with your family?" I ask.

I've never spent a Christmas away from mine, but I've hardly had time to think about it. Working seven days a week has distracted me from everything.

When I look over, Grady's gaze is on me.

"Sometimes," he answers. "It's been hit or miss for the last ten years. Depended on if I was working and could make it back. You okay?"

"Yeah, I'm fine," I look back at the artificial trees, stockings, and Santa tchotchkes galore. "I honestly haven't thought about Christmas until now. I've been ... busy."

"Maya," he calls for me. When I look back to him, he's got a small smile on his face and juts his chin to the aisles of holiday décor. "Go pick out what you want."

I shake my head quickly. "Really, I'm okay. You've seen my rental, I don't have room for anything else in that little house."

"There's room."

"There's not."

"There is."

"Fine, there might be, but I can't afford it."

He turns to me fully. "If you don't go pick out some Christmas crap, I will. Who knows what you'll end up with, but I promise it'll include the ugliest shit in this store. If you want to risk ugly Christmas shit around your house for the next few weeks, that's your call."

We have a stare down in the middle of Walmart.

"Go," he insists.

I sigh.

"Go," he repeats. When I don't make a move, he does. "Fine."

He starts down the aisle with purpose and literally starts to grab stuff off the shelves, tossing it on top of the food with barely a glance.

"Grady—you're going to squish the vegetables." I cringe when I see what he's thrown in the cart. "Eww, that is ugly."

I pull things out as fast as he throws them in. Pink reindeer, singing bears, a stuffed pig dressed in a Santa suit ... he's either got really bad taste or he's trying to piss me off.

"Nope." He moves forward as fast as he can, grabbing a box of Pokémon ornaments.

"Stop!" I yell, sort of laughing at the same time. "I just want some garland, maybe some lights and stockings. Nothing," I wave my hand at the stuff I just shoved back on the shelf, "like this."

He looks smug, like he won another bet. "Go pick out what you want."

I move around him to search for prelit garland just

so he'll stop. "This is why you're a carrot cake. You've honed the act of being sweet by being annoying. I never knew such a thing existed. How you do that, I have no idea."

"I told you, I'm good with women." When I look back, he's grinning, proud of himself. "Hurry up, but don't get a tree. We'll do that next."

"I don't have room for a tree."

"We'll make room, but I'll get you a real one."

I don't answer, but stop at the stockings for a quick second, hesitating. I don't have a fireplace, one stocking would look stupid, and even though he's been sleeping on my loveseat, I'd feel silly getting one for Grady. Shaking off the thought, I move on, to look at the lights.

"I thought you wanted stockings?" he calls from behind me.

I shrug it off without looking back. "I don't have a mantle."

"Maya," he calls for me and I look back. He doesn't stop until he gets to me, still pushing our cart. Reaching for my waist, he yanks me in tight, and I'm pressed up against his big, broad chest. "Have you ever spent Christmas alone?"

I sort of frown. Of course, I've never spent Christmas alone. Christmas is a production for my mother that she starts planning on Labor Day. The production grows by the year—not that she's ever lifted a finger to do any of it—and none of her decorations have ever come from Walmart.

"It's shit to be alone," he goes on, assuming my answer. His expression isn't as loose and relaxed as I've grown accustomed to over the past few days. It's serious and meaningful. "I've been alone for the last five. Even though it's shit, you do your best to talk yourself into it not being shit, but it is. Even though I'm taking you to see your brother next week, there's no fucking way I'm leaving you there, which means you'll be here for Christmas. I don't want to spend it alone this year. I want to spend it with you."

I bite my lip to mask my happiness. "You do?"

His eyes drop to my mouth and he frowns as his arms constrict around me. "Don't do that in the middle of Walmart."

I allow myself to smile this time and my eyes get big. "Sorry."

"Pick out two stockings, unless you're inviting someone else to Christmas that I don't know about."

I shrug. "I was going to invite Foxy, but since you've invited yourself and there's barely room for the two of us, I guess he'll have to make other plans."

"Does Foxy have family?" he asks.

"Yes."

"Then Foxy's not coming to our Walmart Christmas." He gives me a squeeze before giving me a quick kiss. "Hurry up, it's late and we still need to cut down a tree."

He lets me go, but I don't hurry. "I'm sure they have live trees outside. I doubt we'll find a tree farm open this late."

"We live in the middle of the forest, Maya. We don't need a tree farm, but we will need one of those things to put the tree in."

"A tree stand?" I grin.

"I told you I've been alone for the last five years, sorry I'm rusty on my Christmas lingo. Now, speed it up, we'll need shit to put on the tree, too."

“Got it.” I turn to pick out two stockings, which makes me immensely happy. “A tree thing and tree shit. I’m on it.”

Grady

I WASN’T LYING when I said I’d been on my own the last five Christmases. I also haven’t given it much thought until we were standing there, but at that moment, I realized how alone I’ve been.

I chose to be, I even know I needed to be after all that happened with my dad. But the last few months have been nothing but a sucker punch to the gut, and Maya has been nothing but a light in my darkness. Because of her, I’ve been desperate for changes, and Christmas is going to be one of them.

“I can’t get warm.” She yawns, standing next to me as we both stare at the tree it took for-fucking-ever to find. I’ve never cut a tree down before, but for some reason when we were standing in the middle of all the Christmas shit, something came over me.

I’m not quite sure if testosterone took over, but standing in the middle of Walmart, I decided there was no fucking way she was having a tree unless I cut it down for her. Now, standing in her tiny rental, I can admit I should’ve reigned in my sudden surge of caveman tendencies and thought it through.

Once we got back from shopping, I drove straight to one of Crew’s barns and found a saw. We trudged through the freezing forest in search of a tree. This is when I started to see the flaw in my plan. I’m assuming

Christmas tree farms are well organized and finding the perfect tree isn't hard.

But in the dark of night with only a flashlight leading the way, it took forever. Maya laughed at me the whole time, and the longer we searched, the less picky we became.

Finally, after an hour of trudging through the forest with the cold sinking in, we settled on one.

I cut it down and dragged it back to her tiny house.

Rubbing the back of my neck, I look at the disaster in front of me. "I'll get you another one."

"No," she says, rubbing her hands together to warm up. "It's going to look better with lights and ornaments. What kind of tree do you think it is?"

I turn to look at her. "I'm not a forest ranger, but I'd say a fucking ugly one."

She laughs. "It's not ugly. A little sparse, maybe, but not ugly. There's lots of room for the ornaments to hang, right? I think once we string the lights, it'll be beautiful."

My brows rise. "Beautiful?"

I shake my head and turn to her. It's late, well into the morning hours, and she's got to work tomorrow. She's already changed into what she must sleep in. She's in loose, soft pants cinched around her waist and a big hoodie. I can't see one curve on her, but if there's anything beautiful in the room, it's definitely not the ugly-ass tree we just searched over an hour for.

"Yeah, beautiful," she says, looking away from the ugliest tree on earth to face me. Her voice goes soft and low when she keeps on. "You make losing bets worth it, Grady Cain. This was only my second first date ever, but it was perfect. Thank you."

Forgetting about the tree, I let that sink in at the same time I try not to think about her other first date, because the thought of that pisses me off.

Instead, I hook a finger in the neck of her hoodie and pull. "If you want to lose some more bets, I can make that happen."

I kiss her, feeling her relax in my arms. I dip my hand under her sweatshirt, and the touch of her warm skin under my hand makes my dick twitch. When I slip my tongue in her mouth, she melts into me further, so I move my hand up her back to find it bare. Fighting my urge to yank off her sweatshirt, I press in between her shoulder blades, making her arch into me.

Fuck.

I deepen my kiss, wanting nothing more than to learn every contour of her body with my touch, and then, my tongue.

But for some reason, I stop. It doesn't matter how she responds, this isn't the time. I have no idea why it's not. I want to bury myself in her more than I've wanted anything, but it's not right. If for no other reason, I just took her on her second first date, and knowing who gave her the first, gives me all the determination in the world to be everything he wasn't. This alone is all the willpower I need to pull away. But I'm no saint, and press my cock into her stomach first.

When I drag my lips away from hers, her face is flushed, and she's catching her breath. Gripping my shoulders, she holds on tight, looking confused as to why I pulled away.

"You should go to bed," I mutter, still holding her tight, not wanting to let go of her bare skin. Getting a hold of my voice, I go on, "You've got to get up early."

As tired as she looked before, there's a hint of disappointment on her face, and I can't lie, it makes me fucking ecstatic. This also gives me more resolve that now's not the time, after a long day, even though it feels fucking good to know she wants it.

I kiss her one more time before making myself let go. "Go to bed."

"You're staying again?"

"I am." I step back and start to unbutton my shirt as I turn to my bag.

She closes herself in the bathroom for what seems like forever. When she finally comes out, I've changed into a pair of sweatpants and am ready to settle in for another long night of little sleep that has nothing to do with her miniature size sofa.

Standing at the door to her bedroom, she leans into the door jamb looking at me and calls softly, "Goodnight."

I don't get up and go to her. If I touch her, kiss her, or feel her melt into me again, I'll lose my resolve.

"Sleep well," I answer, wishing I could expect the same for myself.

She says nothing more, but nods before turning to her room and I lose sight of her. Her light flips off and I'm swallowed by darkness. I turn to my phone to check messages, thinking when we get back from Buffalo, it'll be time to get back to work.

When I open my email, not only do I find updates on the recruits, but a forwarded one with the subject matter of Weston MacLachlan. I read through and sigh, relieved for now, but wondering what next week will bring in Buffalo.

Asa's FBI contact confirms Maya's ex and his friend

have been home for almost a day. They know nothing more than that, but at least I know he's not in Virginia. Not that I'm taking a chance they won't send someone else for her. If she's not at work in the tasting room, I'll be with her. She'd probably be fine here in her little house by herself, but I'm not leaving for the sheer fact I can't stand to be away from her.

I hear the bed move again and her roaming about. I look up to see her shadow standing in the door frame. She's got on the same pants, but is wearing another thin tank.

"Grady?" Her voice comes at me hesitant and small.

"Yeah?"

Accustomed to working in the dark, it's easy to see her fingers grip the woodwork she's leaning against.

"Well, I feel bad you're out here. You've got to be uncomfortable."

"I'm good."

She stands up straight, quickly gesturing in back of her and her voice is shaky. "You could come in with me. You know, to sleep ... and stretch out, and be comfortable."

I feel my mouth tip on one side. "Are you inviting me into your bed, baby?"

I see her eyes narrow and she turns defensive. "Fine, get a backache. I was only worried about your shoulder."

I set my feet down from where they were propped on her coffee table and stand, tossing my cell to the sofa. It takes me four strides to close the distance, and when I do, she shifts to make room for me. Looking at her, I lightly drag my fingertips down her bare arm, and I swear she shivers.

Lowering my voice, I murmur, "I think I'd really enjoy being in your bed, but I'm trusting you not to take advantage of me, Maya. Don't disappoint me."

Fuck me, she bites her lip again as she shakes her head.

It's my turn to narrow my eyes.

I turn and leave her in the doorway. When I make it to her bed, I turn back to her and put my thumbs at my waist, pushing my sweats down. Her eyes get big, as they follow my pants until they hit the floor. When I kick them to the side standing in my boxers, I hold out my hand for her. "You coming or are we switching places for the night?"

I hear her quick exhale, but she doesn't delay. She comes to me, taking my hand. Turning, I guide her into bed, and I follow so I can face her, lying on my good shoulder.

Having her this close, wanting to feel her against my bare skin, I wrap my arm around her waist and I pull her to me.

Finally.

After all this time—allowing this woman to consume my thoughts, her being the only reprieve from my fucked-up memories—I'm here. Close to her, in her bed, where she invited me to be.

I've had her in my arms enough to know she's tense. I yank up the back of her thin tank, wishing I could rip it off to feel her tits against my chest, but I don't. I'll settle for the bare skin of her back and start to stroke her skin lightly. "Relax."

She sighs, whispering, "I hope you sleep better here."

It's my turn to sigh and really fucking mean it when I say, "Me, too."

"Grady?"

"Yeah?"

"You give good dates."

I smile and I think she can feel it because her body relaxes a bit. "That's good to know. Haven't had a date in a long time."

She pushes back to look at me through the darkness. "You haven't?"

I can't tell her there's no way to have a constant anything when one is traveling the world as an assassin. Instead, I pull her to me and kiss her before settling us again. "No."

A few moments go by and it's not hard to sense she's wide awake now, her being chatty is the first clue.

"And thank you for spending Christmas with me," she goes on.

I start stroking her back again, feeling her words against my neck. "I thought you were spending Christmas with me, but if you insist."

I feel her body laugh, which feels fucking good against mine.

"Do you want to come to the Whitetail company Christmas party with me? It's Monday night in Addy's Ordinary."

I smile and roll until she's on her back. Looking at Maya under me, her body covered by mine, it takes all my resolve not to grind into her. "Are you asking me out?"

She shrugs. "I guess I am."

"Do you give good dates?" I give her a little more of my weight.

Her face softens. "There won't be a food truck, but I'll do my best."

"Now you ask me out," I complain. "After I let you strip me down to almost nothing, maneuver me into your bed, and practically get me to second base. Taking me to your Christmas party is the least you can do."

Laughter bursts from her lips, but it feels even better than it sounds, her body moving under mine. I dip my face to take her mouth as she continues to laugh. Kissing her, pressing her into her bed—I can hardly take it.

I roll, taking us back to our sides before I rip her clothes off. When I pull away, we both catch our breath. As she presses her face into my neck, I say, "You'd better go to sleep. You'll barely get a few hours before work."

I feel her breathe against my skin again and she sighs. "I think I might need to run before work."

Knowing exactly what she means, I couldn't agree more.

"Motherfucker." He's not fighting back anymore, but I don't give a fuck.

"Grady, she won't open her eyes." Raine is crying in back of me, but I don't stop to look.

"Never again. You won't touch them ever again. Fucking asshole." I pull his head up by his hair and pound it into the tile.

Holly and Peyton are crying in the background, but I don't process it.

Sirens.

I look down at my hands. Wet and sticky, covered in blood.

His blood.

When I look down at the man who gave us life, but was too weak to be a father, I fall back on my ass.

Resting my elbows on my bent knees, I hold my hands up in front of me and slowly blink.

Things start to come into focus. The blood, my sisters crying, my father ... and the blood. His blood—all-fucking-over me.

The sirens get louder.

"They're almost here, Gracie. Wake up," Raine begs through her sobs.

Only when I hear the sirens stop and pounding at the front door, do I feel how deeply my chest is heaving. So much, it's almost painful.

That's when I blink one more time. I look around.

It all comes into focus. I see it.

As the police file into my childhood home that's been nothing but hell ever since our mother died—it happens.

The police try to talk to me, EMS start to work on Gracie, my other three sisters continue to cry.

Even though EMS start to work on him, I know.

Only then do I realize.

It's over.

"Grady?" Her voice is rough with sleep.

My eyes fly open and I feel myself gasping for a breath.

"You jerked awake. Are you okay?"

She's leaning up on a forearm looking down at me through the dark. Her eyes are worried.

Shit. I slept. Not like I've been sleeping with naps here and there, not allowing myself to really rest, because when I do, I dream, and I'm so sick of that motherfucker taking over my head. I can't believe I let it happen the first time I'm in her bed. The last thing I remember is enjoying her soft hair against my skin.

I roll, pulling her into my arms, and just when I thought she felt good there earlier, it's nothing compared to now.

"I'm sorry," I whisper. Even though my actions don't mirror my words, I offer what I don't want to do. "Sometimes I don't sleep well. I'll go back to the sofa so I won't wake you again."

"No." She burrows deeper in my chest, holding me to her. "Don't go."

I should leave her to sleep, but I'm selfish. "I'll try not to wake you again."

"I'm good," she murmurs against my chest, and sounds like she's already close to sleep.

I hold her tight and close my eyes.

That one was different. In all the years since it happened, I've never dreamt about that day. Lots of other days, but not that one.

I don't even know what that means.

I do my best to even my breathing so she can sleep and put it out of my head.

When her breath becomes steady again, it's not hard. I need to focus on her, maybe that will help me forget my demons. At least for tonight.

I close my eyes, and for the first time in a long while, I allow myself to go back to sleep after the nightmares.

I sleep until her alarm goes off.

Weston MacLachlan

My phone rings over the speaker. I cringe when I see it's my father because, between the shit going down with Maya and my new idea of moving drugs across the border instead of shipping them with produce, it's been a long couple of days. I can barely control myself when I think of her with him. I've never felt more on edge, thinking of someone else touching her— tainting my sweet pussy.

"Yeah?" I answer, fisting the steering wheel and trying not to sound how I feel.

"Your mom just called. Vanessa has invited us to dinner next week. Son, Maya's coming home."

My heart stops. "She is?"

"For a visit," he adds, his voice strained and I can tell he's trying to temper his words. "She's coming to see Joseph, but she's bringing someone with her. I was told to warn you, but Vanessa wants you to see Maya. This may be your chance to convince her you're ready to settle down."

I hear what he's saying, but all I can think about is her not being alone.

"She's bringing him?" I bite out.

My dad sighs into the phone. "She is. But we don't know what that means. I'm trying to find out what I can about him, but I'm coming up blank. It's like he doesn't exist. You need to keep your cool and do your best to convince her."

I hang up on my dad without another word. Desperation isn't something I'm used to, but it's becoming a familiar feeling as the days wear on.

I look to the road as I steer myself home, but I don't

see anything. Nothing but red. My dad's right. This might be my only chance. I need to do everything I can to convince her—the stakes are too high. I can't even think about what I'll have to do if she doesn't come around ... if she stays a liability.

I slam my hand into the steering wheel, causing the car to swerve.

Fucking desperation. I don't know how much more I can take.

15

FRIENDS

Grady

"YOU LEAVE TOMORROW?" Crew asks.

"First thing in the morning. I booked the flight. We're flying out of Manassas, coming back the next day. She said one night was enough, she just needs to see that her brother's okay, although I can tell she's not looking forward to seeing everyone else. We're staying at her parents' home so she can be close to her brother. She doesn't want him to have to leave in case he has another seizure."

"Talked to Asa who talked to Bennett at the FBI. They know you'll be there. The wires are still up, and somehow, they got a bug in the MacLachlan house—in the big man's office. If they hear of anything about Maya, I'll call you."

"I read about how secure it is—how did they get ears in there?"

Crew shrugs. "We might all play for the same team,

but still, we don't. I'm surprised Asa's gotten as much out of them as he has."

I look to Crew and shake my head. "Asa has too many friends."

"Contacts," Crew corrects me, suppressing a smile. "Pretty sure I'm his only friend."

"Friend," I huff. "I guess he and I both have that in common then."

I take a sip of my beer. I rarely drink, just enough to be social and not have people ask why I don't. I don't hate it—just hate the way it makes me feel. I had my benders when I was younger, but now I prefer to stay in control. Not that I judge, I don't. Especially when I look across the room and see Maya throw her head back, laughing with no inhibitions. I don't think it's the wine. She's becoming more relaxed with everyone around her.

The past couple days have been good. I've learned from Asa's FBI contact that MacLachlan has stayed put in Buffalo, which is a relief. Maya made me dinner last night in her little house, and damn if it wasn't delicious. And hell if I didn't eat butternut squash and zucchini since I lost the bet. The squash was fine, the zucchini was less than fine, but I ate it anyway because I'm learning the longer I'm around Maya Augustine, I'll do practically anything to make her happy. That's not me, and it's really not me when it comes to food. She's thrown me off my game. Not that I've had a game in years—I haven't. Still, I can't believe I'm eating vegetables just to make her happy.

Even though she knew MacLachlan was back in Buffalo and she'd be fine on her own, I was back in her bed last night without question. I did nothing more than kiss her until she was breathless after we talked, and I gave her shit about making me eat vegetables, but it was all worth it.

I held her in my arms as she slept. I did my best to doze—there was no way I wanted to risk my fucking dreams coming back. But hours after we went to bed, I succumbed to it before her alarm woke me this morning. After two nights of the best sleep I've had in a long time, it feels good. Not only that, but sleeping next to Maya is by far the best thing I've ever experienced, and I haven't even had her yet. I don't know why I keep holding back, but I do.

Maybe it's because I know I'm only the second man she's ever kissed, let alone the second for everything else. Maybe it's because she doesn't really know me—my work, the shit that happened with my family. Maybe I think I'll fuck things up even though I'm trying hard not to.

I'm sure it's a little of all that. All I know is every moment I spend with her, I want her. More than I've ever wanted anything. Falling into a dreamless sleep with her last night just makes me more obsessed.

I contemplate all this as I watch her. She's standing with Addy, Bev, and another woman with pink hair who I don't know. We've been here for two and a half hours—the food is good, the people are friendly, and it's been fine. It's been the first time I've done something normal in a long time. Things like this have never been my normal.

"You seem good," Crew says. I turn to him and raise a brow and he amends his comment. "Okay, you seem better. Maya still working on your shoulder?"

"Yeah, and I've been going at it strong. It almost feels back to normal."

"You sleeping?" he asks.

I shrug, and tell him the truth but not why. "Better."

"You ready for her family and the MacLachlans?" he continues his interrogation.

I nod and look back to her. "I've thought it through, every scenario we could run into. So yeah, I'm ready."

"Sorry! Sorry we're late."

I look over and another one of Addy's employees, Clara, comes rushing in, her big pregnant stomach leading the way. She's followed by three boys, and bringing up the rear is a man who doesn't look like he's feeling so hot.

"Okay," Clara announces loudly, talking to the room at large, before motioning to the three children who have since scattered around the large brick room. "I'm sorry, *so sorry* for them and the ruckus they'll no doubt cause. Our sitter didn't show. I tried to call our parents, and if you can believe, their social lives are busier than ours. Or they're liars—really, it's a toss-up. But I made everyone get out of the house to come. I'm a ticking time bomb—I could pop at any minute, but I'm not missing this, come hell or high water. Anyway, I texted Addy, she insisted we bring the kids, but we're even later since Jack is moving slow because he's trying to pass kidney stones."

"Really?" Her husband grimaces, though I'm not sure if it's from the kidney stones or her public announcement of his current situation. "Is it necessary to tell everyone?"

"We're all friends." Clara waves him off and goes to the makeshift bar at the side of the room and tags a bottle of sparkling water out of the ice bucket. Turning back to us, she waves a hand in front of herself as she goes on. "I mean, all you have to do is pee through a strainer. I, on the other hand, will be on display for a room full of people while squeezing out your fourth baby. So, I'm sorry, but since I'm about fifteen months pregnant and look like a petite hippo, I've lost my filter."

Her husband shakes his head, and winces as he follows her to the bar and pours himself a scotch, asking his wife in a way I doubt he's looking for an answer, "Have you ever had a filter?"

"You're supposed to be drinking water," she announces.

"I need this and maybe three more, then I'll drink water."

"Nick, don't touch that," Clara snaps her fingers and moves across the room to the youngest boy.

When I turn to Crew, he's grinning at the show going on, so I ask, "You ready for all that?"

Without losing his grin, he looks over at me and raises a brow, but doesn't say a word.

"Really?" I ask.

He nods, raising his bottle to his lips and leaves it at that.

I shouldn't be surprised. Doing what we've done is surreal at times, so much that when it ends, it's an adjustment to realize the rest of the world has continued their lives, going on as normal without taking a hiatus from life like we did.

Crew sets his beer down and heads to one of the boys to help wrangle them. The Ordinary is centuries old. Surely, they can't do that much damage, but I've heard about Clara's kids.

Looking back at Maya, her dark blond hair that I've

come to love has fallen around her face as she talks to one of the boys.

Staying where I am, my eyes wander to the right to see more people who work for Addy. Morris, Evan, and Van are in deep conversation about who knows what, and Van has his arm around a woman I've never seen. There's a fire burning in the massive stone fireplace that's so big, I could almost walk into it. We're surrounded by exposed brick that's centuries old, and in the corner stands a practically-perfect lit and decorated tree. It's so different than the one I cut down for Maya's little house, it's laughable.

Crew has wrestled Clara's oldest into a headlock, but the kid doesn't seem to mind since he's laughing his ass off. The third is shoveling sweets into his mouth at the buffet.

I've visited my sisters a couple times for the holidays early on after I left home. But for the most part, I've avoided shit like this for fifteen years. Even before that, the holidays weren't great.

The noise of the room starts to blend as I stand off to the side, taking it all in. Co-workers, friends, spouses, lovers—together to celebrate the season. Together, not only because that's what people do, but more importantly, they're right where they want to be.

I don't know how long I stand here, soaking it in, but the longer I do, the more foreign it seems.

Is this me?

Or more importantly, could this be me?

Crew never had a problem. He didn't even hesitate—as soon as he found what he wanted, he was all in.

Just when the noise from the room becomes a

distant hum in my head the way it does when I get lost in it all, I feel a pull. My eyes go directly to her.

Standing in the middle of the group with a boy tugging on her arm, she tips her head, sending me a curious look through the crowd. She doesn't break my gaze, even as the kid pulls and yanks on her. Her expression softens the longer I hold her gaze.

Fuck, I wish she could *really* see me.

Because I really see her. I know it all—that asshole she was hiding from, her pain-in-the-ass mother, her distant father, and the brother she loves more than anything. Even with the shit swirling around her, she's simple.

She's Maya.

Two months ago, I never would've thought this, but after Maya Augustine walked into my life, I'd give anything to be simple.

No, right now, I'd give everything to be transparent.

Maya tips her head to the other side and I can tell she's trying to shake the kid off her arm, when a voice breaks our trance.

"Clara, babe, we've gotta go."

I look to the entrance of the Ordinary from Addy's house where Clara's husband, Jack, is stepping into the room holding a cell phone between his thumb and index finger since it's dripping with water.

"What did you do?" Clara asks, her eyes going big at her husband.

He scowls, holding out the cell farther in front of him. "I was in the bathroom, but when am I not in the bathroom with all the water you're forcing me to drink? I thought I felt ... something pass, so I had to use the flashlight on my phone to look. Then I dropped it in the toilet."

To describe Clara's face as twisted would be an understatement. Holding her lower back, she shakes her head vehemently, exclaiming, "Why didn't you use your strainer?"

Jack rolls his eyes, shaking his head. "I'm not bringing my pee strainer to a Christmas party."

Now Clara's face really contorts, but not directed at her husband. Holding her back with one hand and her belly in the other, she winces before looking down. "Are you kidding me?" she complains.

Bev rushes to her. "What's wrong?"

"Clara?" her husband calls to her, still holding his toilet drenched phone out to the side.

"My water broke," she groans, and everyone in the room starts to move. She looks at the ceiling and shakes her head before she sighs, saying to no one in particular, "Nothing is easy. I just wanted to go to a party."

"Come on, boys," Jack calls for his kids, his face suddenly lit up. "This is good. I'm pretty sure I just passed my stone, but now I don't have a phone, damn it. I'll use Clara's."

Jack goes to his wife, probably trying to help her out, but she waves him off and starts for the door, groaning, "I can't believe we have to bring the boys."

"No, don't bring the boys," Addy shakes her head quickly. I notice Crew frown, but she dismisses him and smiles big, excited for her friend. "They can stay here with us. Now go—go have a baby! But call as soon as you can. On your phone, not Jack's. Yuck."

Maya has shaken off the kid who goes to say goodbye to his parents. She doesn't wait, she comes straight for me, and when she gets to my side, I lean in and whisper, “You want to get out of here before we get stuck babysitting?”

Pressing her front into me, I feel her squeeze my bicep, trying to suppress a smirk. “I was just thinking the same thing.”

I grab her hand as I look down at her happy, open face. I’ve been ready to leave for an hour. “Let’s go.”

We say quick goodbyes to everyone, Crew appearing resigned to the fact they’re stuck babysitting. When we walk out the door, he has a kid sitting on each foot and wrapped around his legs, with another on his back. He shakes his head as we leave, probably wondering how to keep them from tearing the house down.

It’s cold and the wind is becoming bitter. I hurry Maya to my SUV, opening the door for her on the passenger side. I make the short drive to her little house on the vineyard property, it’s close but too far to walk in the cold, especially in her tight black dress, not to mention her heels. I’ve done my best not to stare at her all night, although my best wasn’t very good.

My resolve is starting to break, so I focus on our trip tomorrow, wondering what that will bring.

16

I WANT YOU

Grady

Maya unlocks the door and turns to look up at me. She threads her fingers through mine, giving me a small, almost shy smile, as she turns to walk into her house. I need no encouragement. I'd gladly follow her anywhere.

After sleeping with her the last couple nights, she'll have to kick me out if she doesn't want me. My obsession has reached a new level. I'm not sure what to think about this, so I'm choosing to ignore it.

Because really, I don't give a fuck.

I want her.

She makes her way straight to her bedroom, and as much as I want to follow, I let her be. After a couple minutes, she calls, "Can I get you anything?"

"I'm good." I open her fridge and grab a bottle of water. When I turn back, she's standing in her doorway. Tonight, she's wearing a pair of loose short shorts with another tank so small and thin, I have to force myself to focus on her light blue eyes, however, I can't suppress my slow smile that creeps across my face. "You look comfortable."

She bites her lip again, damn it, and that makes me lose my smile instantly, wanting nothing more than those lips on mine. And eventually, around my cock.

"Are you," she pauses, "staying?"

I don't say anything, and set my water on the counter before I go to her. After closing the distance, I reach for her hip, pulling her to me, and do exactly what I wanted. When my lips touch hers, I don't waste a second before tasting her. Backing her into the door jamb, I deepen my kiss, pulling her bottom lip between mine. She arches, pressing her tits into my chest.

Shit, my resolve practically evaporates into thin air.

I pull away, seeing nothing but her flushed face, her eyes telling me she wants me when I point out, "Spent my morning doing Gentle Yoga while sitting in a chair, and the only reason I did it was so I could watch you move and stretch. After that, you electrocuted me again, and I drank coffee while the old ladies knitted, asking me every question under the sun. While you finished your work, I ate a low sodium lunch with nothing for dessert but Jell-O. If you think I'm leaving you now, you're crazy."

She smiles and it lights up her whole face. Sliding her hands up my arms, she ignores my rant about my new volunteer position and changes the subject. "Thank you for coming with me tonight. I really like everyone here, they're different than anyone I've ever known. Did you have fun?"

Looking down at her eager face, I try to remember the last time I've done anything for fun, but don't share that. "Not as much fun as I had watching you lead yoga, but yeah, I guess I had fun. Though, their Christmas tree sucks compared to yours."

"Ours," she corrects me, grinning and pushing me away to walk into her bedroom before she goes on sarcastically. "I agree. I think our tree rivals Rockefeller Center's. It doesn't remind me of Charlie Brown's whatsoever."

I follow as I start to unbutton my shirt while watching her put a knee to the bed, tagging a bottle off the bedside table on her way. She shifts and turns to sit, popping open the bottle and spreading lotion on her hands and arms. Dropping my shirt to the floor, I go to the button on my pants, wasting no time to get to her.

"If you say so." I step out of my pants and watch her watching me.

When I flip the covers back, she crawls to the other side, and repeats what she's said countless times over the last couple days. "I'll pay you back for the airfare—both your ticket and mine. I really thought we could drive, but you're saving me from missing another day of work."

I shake my head, because if she has trouble making her rent, she'll never be able to pay me back. "I told you it's no big deal."

"We'll see," she says, as I pull her into my arms. I dip my head into her neck to kiss her as she wraps herself around me, whispering, "Grady?"

"Hmm?"

Her hand comes to my head, fingering through my hair as I let my tongue slide down her collarbone. "I'm nervous about tomorrow. I mean, I want to see my brother and spend time with him, see that he's okay, but

I can't stress enough how *unpleasant* my mother is to be around."

I roll so I'm on top of her, but support most of my weight on my forearm above her head. "I've dealt with some really scary people in my day. I'm pretty sure I can handle your mom."

"My mom is best friends with Weston's mom. My dad is okay, but he's distant and wrapped up in the world he's created. Not to mention, Weston will be close. After the last week, that worries me."

"Baby." I lean down to kiss her softly before finishing. "This is why I'm coming with you. I don't want you there by yourself, but you'll be fine with me. I think I've already proven it with the Gentle Yoga, but I won't leave you on your own until he's taken down."

"Speaking of." She pauses and bites that damn lip again. "How come you won't leave my side at the Ranch, but when I'm working in the tasting room, you don't seem to care?"

I look down at her and sigh. I might as well tell her. Maybe it'll make her feel better. "You know Crew owns the property next door and runs his business there, right?"

"Yeah."

"His property is heavily secured. When Addy had her drama, Crew extended that security to her property. When you're here, both at home and at work, you're covered."

"Covered?"

"Yeah. Covered."

"Grady, I've lived in a heavily-secured property my entire life. I'm familiar with security systems and I don't have one. What do you mean by covered?"

"Cameras, surveillance, motion detectors. It's a good system. You're safe."

"And you're still here?" She gives me a squeeze to reiterate her words.

I can't help my voice from coming out rough. "I am. I'm here because I don't want to be anywhere else."

Her face relaxes and she finally whispers, "I've never wanted anyone to be here as much as I do you."

Fuck, she's killing me. I lean down to kiss her and roll us to our sides. Her hands land in my hair again and I can't help but to run my own down her side, brushing her tit with my thumb on the way. When she gasps against my mouth, I move to her nipple, sweeping it back and forth across her tip, creating a deeper exhale this time. She pulls her head back to look at me, and her eyelids are heavy, but underneath, those light blue eyes are telling me what she wants.

When I palm her tit and lightly squeeze, I lose her eyes as a small moan sounds from low in her throat. I thought that moan was the sexiest thing I've ever heard until I roll her nipple, making her arch her back, pressing her chest into my hand.

There's no point fighting my dick getting hard, it's already there, but tonight's still not the night. Not for me anyway, but for her?

Absolutely.

There's nothing I want more than to watch her fall apart by my touch.

Sliding my hand up her tank and touching her for the first time, her soft skin is more than I imagined. Her nipple is hard and when I give it a gentle twist, her arms convulse around me.

But I can't drag my eyes away from her face. When I

keep at her, massaging and teasing, she finally drags her eyes open and I say against her lips, "Don't worry about the trip. I'll be with you every second."

She says nothing, but nods slightly.

"I need to touch you. I can't wait another day." I let go of her tit and run my hand down the side of her body.

"Holy shit," she says on a quick exhale.

I don't ask, but I'll take that as a yes.

I run my hand down her spine and immediately slide my hand into the back of her shorts to only find skin. More soft, smooth skin.

"Maya," I kiss her as I squeeze her bare ass, "have you been sleeping next to me commando?"

"Maybe." Her voice is breathy as her hands grip my neck. When the next words come out of her mouth, I swear I hear a smile. "I guess you'll never know."

I yank my hand out of her pants to pull her knee over my hip. "Open up for me, baby."

When I bring my hand up the back of her thigh to finally touch her, something I've been itching to do, her hand slides down my chest and lands on my dick.

I thought having her touch on my bare skin was incredible before, but her small hand grasping my raging hard-on is something else altogether.

Just when she slides her hand down to go for my balls, I catch her wrist to stop her. "Not tonight."

"But," she pulls her head back enough to look at me. "I want to touch you."

"Maya," I start as I direct her hand back up to my chest before returning mine to her thigh. "Your experience is limited, am I wrong?"

A small frown comes over her face and she doesn't answer, but her silence is answer enough.

"I thought so." I trail my hand up the back of her thigh, my touch so light, I feel the effect on her skin. "For tonight, I don't want you stressed—I want you relaxed and rested. Tonight, I want to focus on you."

"But what about you?" She presses herself into my hard cock.

"I'll be fine. I have been since the day I laid eyes on you." My finger trails up and it's easy to find her with her shorts so loose. She's spread wide, but I want more, and hitch my knee raising her leg higher.

When I touch her for the first time, the look on her face alone is worth the wait. Her lids close right before she presses her face into my neck. She's turned on and wet, wanting my touch just as much as I want her. Sliding my fingers through her pussy, I tease her with barely a touch. "I like you opened wide for me, baby."

She groans and I swear if her fingers could dig into my chest, they would.

I add more fingers, learning her body. She's so wet for me, my touch glides through her easily. When she presses into my hand, I ask, "You gonna relax for me?"

I feel her exhale against my neck when she nods.

I slide a finger inside, doing my best to focus on her and not imagine the day I really get to make her mine, but it's hard. Especially when she presses down on my hand wanting more. I add another finger and move slowly as I brush her clit with my thumb at the same time. I lift my knee farther, opening her more. With each slow slide of my fingers, it's easy to feel her body heat as it's pressed against mine.

When I add more pressure to her clit and move my

fingers quicker, her body jerks, and I have to hold her tight to me with my other arm to keep her where I want her.

"Look at me."

She drags her head up, her face flushed and her eyes heavy, but she manages. It's at this moment, before she comes for me for the first time, that I decide.

I never want to look at another face again. I feel that in my gut and know it in my chest like I've never known anything else.

"I want you." The words fall from my mouth before I can stop them.

She's breathy, on the verge of coming in my arms when she says, "I told you I wanted to touch you, and I want—"

"No," I stop her from speaking as I keep finger fucking her but take pressure off her clit. I'm not ready for her to come yet. "For my entire life, I've survived. Never have I stopped long enough to want anything, but I want you. More than anything else, I know this is right."

"Grady," she moans, pressing into my hand, wanting more, and I give it to her. I can't wait another second.

It barely takes anything to push her over the edge, she falls, and she comes hard. It's the most beautiful thing I've ever seen.

When she slumps in my arms, trying to catch her breath, I run my hands up and down her back, and playing with the loose curls at the end of her hair. We lay like this, her body seeping into mine by the second, and just when I'm wondering when I can make this happen again just to see her face, she mumbles against my skin, "Triple chocolate."

My hands stop. “What?”

She doesn’t move a muscle, but her words keep coming. “I’m gonna make you a triple chocolate cake with fudge icing and raspberry sauce—and not from a box. I’m gonna make you the good stuff, with two layers so you get extra icing.”

I smile into her hair. “Do I get cake every time I give you an orgasm? ‘Cause I can make that happen a lot.”

She lifts her head to give me her eyes—eyes that are sleepy, sated, and happy. Her face breaks into a small smile to match her eyes. “You’re sweet.”

I grin. “You’re just saying that ‘cause I let you feel me up.”

She barely pushes my shoulder. “Stop.”

“You stop,” I counter, pulling her body up mine so we’re face to face. “Don’t think you can bake me a cake just to get in my pants. I’m not that kind of guy.”

She starts laughing, her whole body shaking against mine.

“Now you’re not relaxed *and* I’m hungry for cake,” I say. “We have a trip tomorrow and I need to be on my game to deal with mobsters and your mother. I’m not sure which I’m most worried about.”

That seems to dampen her spirit, because she sighs and sinks into me again. “It’s a toss-up.”

“Go to sleep.”

We lay like this for a long time. So long, I think she must have dozed off when she shifts and whispers, “Grady?”

“Yeah?”

“I think I want you, too.”

That, I feel in my gut, my chest, and my cock.

I pull her up to face me and when I look into hers, I see it.

To confirm this, she nods with a hesitant smile. I kiss her, long and deep before we finally settle. After that, Maya really relaxes and falls into a deep sleep.

After fighting it for a few hours, I finally do, too.

Dreamless.

17

BRANDED

Maya

I THOUGHT THIS morning might be awkward after last night, but it wasn't. Grady's my second ... everything. My second kiss, the second man I've slept next to, the second man to touch me, and boy, did he touch me. But I wanted him so much, he could've done anything and everything to me.

I know my experience is limited to Weston. I gave him my virginity at the sweet age of seventeen. Looking back, I'm surprised he was patient as long as he was, because he is not a patient man. I might not know what to expect from men in general, but I sure didn't expect Grady to ward off my advances, insisting to take things slow. Him giving me a body-rocking orgasm like I've never experienced was a million times better than any dream. But this morning, he's back to his easy-going self.

I'm learning that nothing is awkward with Grady. In fact, everything with him is easy. So easy, I'm officially obsessed. But really, I've been obsessed since I started creeping on him.

As addicted as I might be, I'm also confused at the moment. I turn to Grady who just threw his SUV into park. "What are we doing here? We're going to be late—we're already cutting it close as it is."

He turns to me, resting his forearm on the console, and studies me a moment before he answers. When he finally speaks, it sounds like he's choosing his words carefully. "I don't fly commercial."

I tip my head to the side, not understanding. Sure, I've flown commercial some, but what I'm not anxious to tell him is that I'm accustomed to traveling in one of the company jets—my father has not one, but three.

"Sooo…?" I let my voice trail off letting him know I don't understand.

He pulls in a big breath and on an exhale, goes on. "In my work, or my previous work, I had to be prepared to protect myself. In the worst-case scenarios—like I told you about what happened on my last job—I needed to defend myself. That job might've gone bad, but I'm still very good at what I do. Now, thanks to you, my shoulder's back to normal and—"

"Your shoulder's nowhere near normal," I interrupt. He keeps trying to tell me he's going to start back to his weights and regular workouts, but I don't care what he says—he's not ready.

He sighs. "It feels back to normal, but that's another discussion. Right now, I'm telling you I feel good, but I can't take you to see your brother with the MacLachlans around and not be able to protect you or myself. That means I need to carry and I can't carry on a commercial flight."

"Carry?" I ask, wanting to make sure I know what he's talking about.

"Fly armed." He confirms my assumption, still choosing his words carefully. "I'm not a federal agent—not even close. I can do a lot of things, but I can't get around that. So, when I fly, I charter. We're flying a Learjet today—they're nice."

I know Lears are nice—my dad has two. I turn to look out the window, because I don't know how much a chartered flight would be. There's no way I can pay him back, not without touching my trust fund, and I'm ready to break away from that part of my life. If I want freedom from my mother, I have to be financially independent or she'll hold that over me in a heartbeat.

"Hey," he calls for me, and I turn back to him. "Don't worry about it."

"We could've driven. It would have been time consuming, but I could've made it work. But this?" I jut my thumb over my shoulder. "I don't think I can pay you back for this."

"I know. That's why I didn't tell you. When I say it's not a big deal, I mean it."

I bite my lip and sit back in my seat. Feeling guilty, I decide to bite the bullet and tell him something about myself. In a matter of hours, he'll figure it out anyway. "I have a trust fund."

"I know," he responds quickly.

I'm taken aback. "You do?"

Reaching over, he takes my hand in his. "I told you I read your background, and it was a very complete file. I also know you've never touched it. I also know that besides the time you were at Cornell, you've always lived in your parents' house even though you worked. I don't know exactly why, but now I'm assuming it has something to do with your brother."

I feel my face relax a bit. "Mostly."

"If your mom's such a pain in the ass, why else would you stay?"

I tell him the truth. "Joe is in school, but the last few years with Weston were so bad, I felt safer there. When Weston started pressuring me into marriage and then getting back together after I broke it off, living there was the barrier I needed. If I had been out on my own, I'd have been too accessible. Like I said, you'll see. It's easy to make yourself scarce there. I've done it all my life."

"Ah." He nods and then smirks. "See, I don't know everything about you."

I roll my eyes and move to open my door. "Doesn't seem that way."

My phone dings and when I unlock it, I have a text from Evan that makes me smile and I announce, "Clara had a girl. Jack must be so happy. Her name is Kate Elizabeth."

He gives me a grin when I meet him at the back of his SUV. I reach in for my bags, but he beats me to them, grabbing the big one. Grady's looking as hot as usual this morning in a pair of jeans and a casual button down with a jacket.

I picked my outfit carefully, as my mother always made us dress to travel. She always said, "One dresses to their status if they want to be treated as such." So just to piss her off when we get there, I'm wearing a pair of skinny jeans so faded, ripped, and worn, they could be decades old, when in fact, I've only worn them twice. They show as much skin on the front as they do denim. I'm also wearing my pink Converse, because my mother hates canvas shoes, and have topped it off with a camo print jacket. I look like a teenager hanging at the mall.

"You know," I start and grab my carry-on since he's not letting me carry my own suitcase. "I might just have to bribe Crew for a full report on you. The scales are uneven. I don't know nearly enough about you when you know everything about me."

He looks at me curiously while efficiently carrying our suitcases. Even though we're going for one night, I had to explain to Grady you never knew what to expect from my mother, and dinner is rarely a casual event. We packed for every eventuality.

"Enlisted in the Army right out of high school, never played an instrument, and basically checked out of life while I was a contractor. That's it."

I fall in beside him and look up at his profile. In the midmorning sun his golden highlights shine bright and I do everything I can to take him in—a man who's gone out of his way to protect me, to make a holiday special for me in his own way, to get to know me, and finally, to want me for me.

He wants *me*.

Who knew when I ran away from my previous life I would be on a path leading straight to Grady Cain. Many months later, when I should be scared out of my mind to go anywhere within the same state as Weston, I'm not scared at all.

Grady gave that to me.

"I guess it doesn't matter," I say with a smile before I call to him. "Grady?"

When we reach the office building attached to the hangar, he juggles a suitcase while opening the door for me, but I don't go through. He looks down at me and raises a brow in silent question.

I take a step and put my hand on his chest. "Thank you, again."

The next thing I know, Grady drops the suitcase and I'm caught in the steel of his arms, being branded by his kiss.

Branded.

And I took it all, never wanting anything else as much as him.

Grady

"Can you pull over really quick?"

"Why? We're almost there."

"Just do it. Here—pull in here."

I don't pull over. I keep driving.

"What are you doing? Grady, pull over!"

I sigh, and pull the rental over to the side of the road. It's much colder than it was in Virginia and there's a foot of snow everywhere.

I put it in park. "What?"

Her words come out quick and almost desperate. "My mother's ostentatious and selfish. My father is mostly absent, but doesn't see it that way. He sees it as providing for us. Joe is usually fun, but he's been home all semester because of his epilepsy. I don't know what kind of mood he's going to be in because he swore he'd never live at home again."

"Baby, you've basically told me all this."

"No, Grady," she stresses. "There are housekeepers

who come daily. Cooks who manage my mother's kitchen, and a staff to serve meals three nights a week because the rest of the time my parents are out."

I try to keep from smiling, because I told her I know everything. "Does this mean the food will be good?"

"You don't understand." Her voice turns harsh and she fully turns to me. "They're uppity, pretentious, and my mom's basically a bitch. Who knows if my father will even be there because of work, and my mom will be downright mean to you because she wants me with Weston."

I unhook my seatbelt, leaning into her and lower my voice. "Are they going to capture me, hang me by one arm, and dislocate my shoulder?"

A horrified look comes across her face and she whispers, "What?"

"Are they going to beat me with a pipe, break my ribs and put a gash in my head?"

Her trembling hands come to the sides of my face. "That ... that's what happened to you?"

"That and more."

"Who did that to you?" her disturbed voice goes high.

"Doesn't matter. What matters is I doubt that's gonna happen to me today or tomorrow, so I'm trying to tell you that I don't care if your father is there, I can deal with your mom being a bitch, and I'm looking forward to meeting your brother."

She runs her index finger lightly over the scar on my hairline. It's still red, but over time it should fade. She murmurs, "I can't believe that happened to you."

"Maya," I call for her and she gives me her troubled, light blue eyes. "I want you."

She exhales as her fingers tense on me. Her face goes slack.

"Even with all I've been through, because I want you, I'll endure anything for you."

Her eyes well instantly and she moves up in her seat to put her mouth on mine. I cup the back of her head to keep her close.

When she pulls away, her eyes are still wet, but she doesn't look as troubled, so I ask, "How does your mom feel about dessert?"

She gives me a small smile. "You can't have a proper five course meal without dessert."

"Something to look forward to," I murmur before pulling her to me again. When I finally let her go, I say, "Let's get you to your brother."

She nods, sitting back in her seat and buckles. I pull out onto the road and she directs me the rest of the way.

A few minutes later, I pull into a drive with security cameras everywhere, and an attendant waiting in the security booth. Before I roll my window down, Maya reaches over and squeezes my forearm. "Let me handle this."

When I look over at her, all of a sudden, she's sitting up straighter and has a weird air of confidence I'm not used to seeing. "Whatever you say."

When I roll down the window, the security guard walks up, holding an iPad and walkie-talkie. He's about to say something when Maya interrupts him. "Hello, Charlie."

Charlie does a double take, his eyes widening, looking across me to the passenger seat. Surprised, but in a pleasant way, he greets her happily. "Miss Augustine. You're back."

She smiles. "I am. How are you? Your family?"

"Very well, Miss Augustine, thank you. The baby's finally sleeping through the night."

"That's great. Can you let us through please? We'll be staying overnight, but leaving around lunchtime tomorrow."

He types something into his iPad, but looks up and with a little grimace. "I just need to search your vehicle. Mrs. Augustine's orders."

My gun's on my ankle but I have another in my bag. My eyes dart to Maya, and she's shaking her head smiling, not at all concerned. "But, Charlie, it's me."

"Ma'am." He nods and apologizes. "I'm sorry, but your mother was adamant. Every vehicle."

"Really?" she acts shocked. "She couldn't have meant me. Don't worry, you won't hear a thing about it. I'll speak to my father at once."

Charlie seems to be warring with himself over dealing with Mrs. Augustine. From the sounds of it, I don't blame him.

"I guess," he reaches for a remote hooked on his belt and the heavy gates open in front of us.

"Give that baby a squeeze for me," Maya calls as I'm closing my window. It's not until we're through the gates that she says, "See? She's a bitch."

I look over at her. "You think she did that to fuck with us?"

She sighs. "I think she did that to fuck with you, to throw her power around. Fucking with me is just a bonus."

I shake my head and reach over to squeeze her hand. "Child's play, baby. Don't worry about it."

She says nothing but sighs again as she looks out her window.

The property is large, and we wind around a few times before the house comes into view—if you can call it a house. It's fucking huge. I pull up the drive that circles the front with a turn off to the many garages on the side.

When I put it in park, I hear from my side, "I'm sorry for all the bullshit that's about to happen."

When I look to her, she appears as excited as one would be to step into an ice bath.

I grin. "I'm not worried. I told you I'm good with women. I can handle it."

I turn to get out and meet her on her side, locking the car on the way up to the house. Grabbing her hand to hold it tight, we move up the wide massive steps toward the double doors.

"You're really slumming it at the vineyard, huh?"

I hear a laugh burst from her, and when I look down, she's shaking her head. "Shut up."

We barely hit the top step when one of the heavy doors opens for us. A middle-aged woman dressed in black pants and a white shirt greets us with a warm smile, but speaks to Maya specifically. "Welcome home, Miss Augustine."

I might've been surprised, thinking she exaggerated about her mom if I hadn't done my research and know this is definitely not Maya's mother.

"It's good to see you, Marilyn," Maya says.

We step through the front door, and the only thing in sight is a Christmas tree, standing in the middle of the spacious opening. I'm not sure where someone would get a tree this big, or even how they'd get it through the door.

I barely get the chance to take in the house Maya grew up in, not at all seeing the object of my obsession fitting into this environment, when I hear footsteps echoing through the vast space. Heels, more specifically. The quick cadence of a woman who's walking with attitude. I stand casually, and brush the back of Maya's hand with my thumb when I feel her tense.

Just like the Christmas present from hell, she appears from around the side of the perfectly-decorated tree.

I recognize her from the pictures included in Maya's background, but instead of a smiling, pleasant woman from a posed portrait taken at a charity event, she's scowling. Dressed in white pants, it's clear to see she's not only taken care of, but also takes care of herself. Her black sweater strategically hangs off one shoulder, leaving it bare to show off her jewels. The woman is dripping in diamonds. It's just after lunch, for fuck's sake.

Vanessa Augustine barely gives me a glance before she takes in her daughter from head to toe while shaking her head. Putting a hand to her hip while hitching her heeled foot, she takes the universal bitch stance when she says to Maya, "Well, Joseph said you were bringing a man. I didn't believe it, but here you are." She tosses out her hand that's not perched on her hip, and adds, "I can't believe you traveled like that."

I look down at Maya, not understanding what Vanessa means, because Maya's hot. It was all I could do not to put her back to the couch on the plane and relax her again. Not that my hand would've fit down her jeans —they're that tight.

Maya sounds nothing but exasperated when she replies, "It's lovely to see you, too, Mother."

"Don't *Mother* me," she snips. "You've been gone for months and think you can just waltz in here with no ramifications. Do you know what you've put us through?"

"Mother—" Maya tries again, but she's interrupted.

"It's embarrassing." Vanessa leans forward to enunciate her words, as if anyone would think she's shitting us. "I have had to make excuses, telling our friends you were traveling, staying at the Villa in Turin, trying to *find yourself*. Nancy's been worried sick because of what you've put Weston through. I hope you plan to get yourself together soon." Her eyes shoot to me for a second, before looking back to Maya. "And come home for good. *Alone*."

Ignoring her mom's words, Maya holds her ground and gestures to me. "Mother, I'd like you to meet Grady Cain." Maya looks up to me with a raised eyebrow, silently giving me an *I told you so* look. "My mother, Vanessa Augustine."

I try to hide my smirk and look back to the Wicked Witch of New York. Letting go of Maya, I step forward offering my hand and do my best not to sound sarcastic. "It's a pleasure."

Even though she doesn't look like she wants to, I'm sure her social niceties take over and she puts her cold, firm hand in mine for a quick shake. "I'm sure it is." Looking back to Maya she goes on. "Your room is ready and the guest room is available for *him*."

I'm about to object, but Maya beats me to the punch. "We'll take the guest house."

Well, that's even better. I should've assumed there'd be a guest house.

Vanessa's face turns hard. "You will not."

"We will," Maya counters. "Now, if you'll excuse us, I came to see Joe and want to do that right away."

Vanessa narrows her eyes, but doesn't say another word about the room assignments. But what she does say, surprises us both. "Dinner will be served at seven, cocktails at six-thirty."

"Seriously," Maya complains. "There's no reason for all the pomp and circumstance. I'm only here to see Joe, we'll be gone by noon tomorrow."

Vanessa Augustine drops her arms and stands as straight as she can. A smile creeps over her face, and I can see if she weren't being a bitch, she could be pretty. Not as beautiful as Maya, but still, pretty.

That's until her smile turns into a sneer. "We're having guests—the MacLachlans. Ron and Nancy would like to see you, and I'm sure you can imagine Weston has been out of his mind worried. He's anxious to make amends and offer you a fresh start."

"Mother—" Maya exclaims.

"Ah, I remember Wes," I interrupt and Vanessa finally acknowledges me with a scowl. I go on to note, "Interesting guy. He can't seem to take no for an answer, but you've gotta give him credit for persistence. What's for dinner?"

She doesn't tell me what's for dinner, but she does glare at me and I can't help but wonder if Maya was switched at birth. There's no way they can be related.

"I suppose I'll arrange for your bags to be delivered to the guest house," she says.

"No need," I answer quickly. "I can get our bags."

It seems only commoners carry their own bags, because she rolls her eyes, and turns to walk away with more attitude than before, if possible.

We're left standing alone, under the monster Christmas tree and within the walls of the massive structure Maya grew up in.

I'm not sure if Maya's either more surprised or freaked about us having dinner with her mobster ex fiancé and his mobster family, so I turn to her and say, "Well, this is gonna be more fun than I thought. We should stay for a week."

She pulls her hands up and runs them through her hair, tightening them at the back. "Fucking hell."

"Your mom could've gotten a bigger tree. She didn't try very hard," I go on.

Maya shakes her head. "I hate her."

I agree and have nothing else to add, so I ask, "Is there anything to do? There's gotta be a bowling alley or an indoor basketball court."

"She arranged for him to come to dinner. I knew she'd do something, but not this."

I pull her into my arms, and point out the obvious, "They can't make you marry him. We'll eat dinner—hopefully the food will be good—and finally prove to them all you will not be marrying Weston MacLachlan. What can happen?"

She looks up at me and sighs. "The possibilities are endless."

"You're right, they are," I agree. "Don't worry about it

now, let's go see your brother. When we're done bowling, I want to see the guesthouse."

She finally smiles. "There's no bowling alley."

I try to frown, but it's hard while watching her smile. "Well this mansion fucking sucks. I bet Charles Schwab has a bowling alley. Or ... I don't know, some other old, rich guy."

She laughs and lifts up to her toes to kiss me. "Come on, let's go see Joe."

"Okay," I agree and take her hand to let her lead me to her brother. "Just don't leave me alone—Vanessa will corner me just to glare at me some more."

With that, her laugh echoes through the paneled walls and marble floors.

All I can do is think about dinner, and for once, I'm not thinking about the food.

18

I SETTLED

Grady

After leading me through long hallways decorated with more Christmas shit, we finally reach the library. And it's just that—a huge fucking library with books lining the walls from floor to ceiling. The minute we step through the double doors, Maya screams and tears her hand out of mine, running to her brother. She throws herself in his arms and he catches her, only stumbling back a step or two.

Joe is lanky and taller than Maya by a few inches. Even though his hair is darker than hers, they share the same light blue eyes, and it's clear to see they're related.

I lean back into the leather sofa as I watch her with her brother. She talks about Joe a lot. I can tell they're close. I understand why she was so upset to find out he's had multiple seizures in the last few months and needed to see him. I guess it was so serious, he withdrew from his classes at St. John's in Brooklyn, where he's in his junior year.

Joe's seven years younger than her. Maya said he was probably an accident—as her mother isn't the mothering type. It's why she felt the need to see for herself that he was okay, especially after not talking to him for months.

We've been talking to Joe for almost two hours, and Maya has grilled him on everything from doctor appointments to his medication. Joe gave her the lowdown—how he had two episodes at school before their dad forced him to come home, and how he thought he was doing okay until he had another just last week. He wasn't happy about leaving school, complaining about having to be home, but since he's been back he's been working with a medical response dog that will soon be with him full-time.

He finally puts a stop to her line of questioning, and leans back in his chair across from where we're sitting. "Was it that bad? That you had to run away?"

She leans into my side since I have my arm thrown over the back of the sofa behind her. She looks down to her hands before back to her brother. "I left, didn't I? I don't want to get into it now. I can't."

He looks from his sister to me and tips his head curiously. "How did you meet my sister?"

I shrug my bum shoulder that's feeling almost back to normal. "She's my physical therapist."

He narrows his eyes. "How long have you known each other?"

"A few—" Maya starts to answer, but I interrupt.

"A while." I look down at Maya and I can tell she's trying to hide the surprise in her eyes. "It's hard to believe, huh?" I tighten my arm around her, pulling her to me and look back to Joe. "The days fly by."

Joe nods and looks to his sister inquisitively, speaking directly to her. "Not that I mind, Weston's an asshole. I've been trying to tell you that for the last couple years, but the jury's still out on this guy. I know nothing about him."

I hold up a conciliatory hand, and add, "I'm not perfect, but I'm also not his brand of asshole. *That*, you don't have to worry about."

She gives me a small smile before looking back to Joe. "We're still new."

"We're not that new," I counter.

She sighs, shaking her head and looks back to her brother. "You know mom invited all the MacLachlans for dinner?"

Joe shakes his head. "I'd ask why the fuck she'd do that, but I'm not surprised, and you shouldn't be, either. She grilled me when I told her you were bringing someone. She wouldn't give up, so I told her I know nothing about your new guy. Tonight should be fun."

Maya brings her fingers to her temples, looking pained. "I can't even think about it."

"Hey," I give her a squeeze. "It'll be over soon."

Joe looks at his watch. "Sorry, I have a meeting with my new dog and the K-9 trainer. She won't be ready for a couple months, but having her means I can go back to school next year. And she'll be a chick magnet, not that I have a problem in that department." He grins before adding, "I guess I'll see you at the dinner from hell."

"Yeah, we'll see you for *cocktails*," Maya mocks her mother and gets up to hug Joe. When she lets him go, she adds, "Whatever you can do to divert the attention away from me tonight, I'd appreciate it."

Joe grins, and by the look on his face, I'd say he's

looking forward to it. “Maybe tonight will be fun. I love a chance to piss off mom.” He looks from Maya to me and instantly loses his smile. “You’d better not be an asshole.”

“Stop it.” She says as he leaves.

I grab her hand and ask, “You feel better now that you saw him?”

“Yes,” she says, relieved. “He makes it sound as if having episodes isn’t a big deal, but after watching him go through many, it’s a huge deal and very dangerous. What he didn’t tell us, but I know from all the years he’s dealt with this, is if the meds don’t work, it could require surgery. I hope it doesn’t come to that.”

“I hope not, too.” We make our way back to the monster tree and I ask, “Since there’s no bowling alley, what do you want to do before the big event? We’ve got two hours.”

She pulls in a big breath. “I could use a run. Do you mind?”

I put my hand to the back of her head and pull her to me for a kiss. “I followed you all the way to Buffalo. You think I won’t go a few more miles?”

“Good.” She smiles. “I definitely need to work out my nervous energy.”

We head to the front door so we can get our bags.

“You know, there’re other ways to release your nervous energy.” I look back at her and she smirks at me.

I can’t wait for the day I can help work her nerves out in other ways.

Maya

My fucking mother.

She's such a bitch.

Gah.

I need to settle down. If I don't, I'm going to end up with an angry makeup application and that would be scary.

Grady and I ran six miles, but this wasn't a race. This was me running and Grady keeping pace with me but two strides back. I think it was his way to be close but give me my space, and I needed it.

I'd say Grady is perfect, but he's not. Ever since I threw myself at him in front of Weston, he's done exactly what I needed, even when I didn't know I needed it. He's protected me, he's stood by my side, and he's never wavered. In that way, he's more perfect than I deserve.

But he's not proper, he's not formal, and he makes inappropriate comments all the time. He makes bets that, no matter the outcome, I end up cooking for him and he gets his way. And he relentlessly teases me. These are not perfect qualities.

Or so I've been taught.

But Grady's not perfect qualities are what makes me want him even more as our hours and days together add up. Having him meet Joe probably seemed like a non-event for everyone else, but not for me. I couldn't wait for the most important person to me to meet the new man in my life, whose imperfect qualities make me weak.

Even though running usually helps when I'm tense, it didn't help today. I'm more wound than I've been in a long time. I lean over the vanity toward the mirror to apply my mascara, and I see Grady standing in the doorway behind me.

I sound funny since I can only apply mascara with my mouth open. "Hey."

"Hey, yourself."

Freshly showered, Grady's wearing suit pants in a gray so dark, they're almost charcoal. His dress shirt is pressed to perfection, making me wonder how it traveled so well, but only for a second. Because all I see are his eyes, brighter than normal because of the deep blue of his shirt.

But his eyes don't meet mine. They're traveling my body, and if I'm correct, right now they're on my ass.

Maybe I should've picked a more modest dress, but I'm attending a dinner in the house I grew up in with a new man. A man whom, at this point, I'm itching to impress. Not that he's made me feel like I have to, but I want to.

It seems to have worked. I think he likes my dress.

And this does nothing to help my frazzled nerves.

Without taking his eyes off my back, he approaches until I feel his hands low on my hips. I finally get his eyes when they meet mine in the mirror.

"Beautiful." His voice is lower than usual, even a bit rough. When the word beautiful passes his full lips, I feel his hands tense on me.

"You clean up well, too, Grady Cain," I say and bite my lip, twisting my mascara shut and tossing it to the counter.

His hands start to move on my navy dress, a blue so dark, it resembles the color of the ocean at night. It's stretchy and fits like a glove from my thighs to my collar bone, but only on one side. My left arm and shoulder are bare, the dress dipping under my arm, but my right has a full sleeve that flares just above my wrist.

I haven't slipped on my shoes yet, so I feel smaller in front of Grady, his large frame surrounding me from behind.

"What's wrong?" he asks, as his hand comes up and sweeps my hair over my shoulder, putting his lips at the base of my neck.

I can't help but close my eyes. "I don't think the run helped. I'm wound up. I still can't believe my mother put me in this position when she knows I want nothing to do with him."

"You need to calm," he murmurs against my neck, his lips working their way up to my ear. His hands start to roam, traveling my body.

"Grady," I breathe and lean my head back on his shoulder. "This isn't helping my nerves."

His left hand comes up to cup my breast, and I lose his lips on my neck, so I look up into the mirror. There, his blue eyes are heated—on fire.

"No baby," his voice is soft and smooth this time. "You need to *calm*."

His hand drops to the hem of my dress and pulls it up around my waist. Not wasting any time, he reaches and dips his hand inside the front of my panties. There he is—roaming, touching. And just like last night, it makes me melt, and is better than any dream. I give him all my weight, and the second I do, his arm tightens around me. It's a good thing too, I otherwise might've fallen to the ground.

"Grady, we're going to be late for dinner," I breathe.

"We've got time." His fingers work me lightly and I feel myself become instantly wet. "Look at me."

I open my heavy lids and look at us in the mirror. Me, my dress hitched around my waist, with Grady wrapped around me, his big hand dipped in my panties.

"When I said this isn't new, I meant it. Since the day I got back after I was captured, I've been watching you over the surveillance system."

His fingers move slowly, roaming and exploring, almost like he's trying to memorize me. But I don't understand what he said. "What?"

"I wasn't just fucked-up, baby, I was fucked *up*. Watching you come and go, run, sit outside and stare into the woods—it kept me from losing my mind. I didn't even know you, but I was obsessed with you even then." His words come at me softly, and learning that he was watching me should freak me out, but for some reason it doesn't. "You didn't even know it, but you saved me from some fucked-up demons. I didn't want to be anywhere, talk to anyone, but when I watched you, I settled."

His eyes, burning into mine, are open and honest, and even as he works me into a state of sexual frenzy, I ask, "What are you saying?"

He circles my clit harder and slips a finger inside me, making my breath catch.

"I'm saying we're not new. You might not have known it, but I've been with you for months. I'm saying," he adds more pressure, creating an ache between my legs, "that you took care of me all that time and you didn't even know it. That made me want you even then, before I was in a place where I could make you mine. I've wanted you since the beginning, baby, before you even knew there was a beginning."

I barely shake my head—stunned, turned on, and kind of freaked out, but all in a good way.

"Let me take care of you." He puts more pressure on my clit and starts to finger fuck me. "Whatever happens tonight, if anyone upsets you, you let me handle it."

I say nothing, but turn my face into his neck. I'm breathing so hard, I can't respond.

His words keep coming. "I'll handle your mom, that asshole, and whoever else decides to jump in the ring. No one's gonna fuck with you, not with me standing in the way."

He adds a second finger, and oh, it feels good.

"Maya?" he calls. When I open my eyes, he's looking into mine. Just before he puts more pressure on my clit, he asks, "You gonna let me take care of you tonight?"

I nod, unable to talk.

Then I gasp, moan, and my body shudders in delicious shakes. The whole time, Grady holds me tight and milks my orgasm to a point where I feel so weak, I'm certain he's the only thing holding me up.

"Fuck," I hear him mutter and I lose his hand from between my legs.

The next thing I know, I'm turned around and he's circled me in his strong arms, his mouth landing on mine. Kissing me deep with his hand tight in my hair, I have a feeling he's showing me exactly how he's going to take care of me. If it's anything like this, there's no way I can argue.

When he finally loosens his hold in my hair, his kiss turns soft, his lips barely brushing mine. He looks down at me, his gaze meaningful and sweet when he asks, "You better?"

I nod. "Yes."

"Did I freak you out?" he asks, his brows puckered, honestly concerned about what I'm thinking.

"Yes." His frown deepens and even though I'm still catching my breath, I quickly add, "But not in a bad way. In a surprised and sort-of-pleased way that I could do something for you when you needed it. Even though I didn't do anything."

"You did." He kisses me again softly before changing the subject. "You ready?"

"I think I'm going to need to touch up my hair and makeup."

His eyes move over my face in a way I know he doesn't want to go to dinner, and he pulls me tight with one arm but the other goes slack. When his hand comes around, he smirks as he puts his index and middle fingers in his mouth. I feel my eyes go big as he tastes me, sucking his fingers clean.

When he slides them out of his mouth, he licks his lips and leans down to kiss me quick before letting me go. "Hurry up, baby. I'm hungry."

He gives me one more devilish grin before leaving me in the bathroom. When I finally turn to the mirror, I smooth my dress and groan at my hair. My makeup fared well, but I cannot go to a dinner in my mother's house with my ex in attendance wearing sexed up hair.

But, I think I like the way I look being sexed-up by Grady, and we haven't even had sex yet. I run my fingers through my loose, chunky curls turned away from my face, trying to piece them back together. Since I wore the dress for Grady, I'm thinking my half-sexed hair fits it well.

Although he might've relaxed me for a short time, it makes me ache to think about what he said. I don't know much about what he went through when he was injured, but I do remember his anguished eyes and desolate demeanor during the weeks while I was a creeper. To know he found some sort of comfort in me during that time? That makes me feel funny, and not in a bad way.

I reach for my lipstick as my stomach twists and turns. Between learning that Grady considered me his lifeline before I even knew him, having dinner with Weston and his parents, and dealing with my mother, the night seems impossibly long. Grady did say he'd handle tonight, after all.

Knowing all the possible scenarios, I might just let him.

19

I'M ATTACHED

Maya

As we round the pool from the guest house through a path of cleared snow in the cold December air, I'm not sure what's louder—the sounds of my heels on the stone patio or my heart pounding in my chest.

"Relax," Grady says, squeezing my hand as we approach the French doors to the back of my parents' house.

"Stop telling me to relax," I clip. "The more you tell me to relax, the more I can't relax."

"Okay," I hear him say with a smile as we walk up the steps. He moves ahead quickly to open the door for me. "So don't relax. We'll get through the night either way."

I turn to look at him, rolling my eyes, before stepping inside the formal living area. Grady trying to relax me in the bathroom made us late, and my mother doesn't do late unless it's her. She's always late to social events—she thinks she's just that important.

"Well." I hear her voice the minute we step over the threshold. "We thought you decided not to attend your own homecoming dinner."

I do what I trained myself to do years ago—change my expression to an impassive one since I know it pisses her off. "We went for a run. And I didn't know this was a homecoming dinner. We're leaving tomorrow, so for all it matters, it could be a going away dinner."

My mother narrows her eyes before turning to a server I'm not familiar with who must be new. "Lidia, make my daughter a cosmopolitan and take *his* order."

Of course, she wouldn't ask what I'd like to drink, but arguing would be exhausting, so I don't.

"Maya." I cringe and turn to see Weston heading straight for us with a crystal highball glass in his hand filled with his favorite scotch, but his eyes—angry and hard—are on Grady. Grady's fingers tense on the small of my back, but other than that, I don't notice a change in his demeanor whatsoever. Across the room, Weston's parents are standing with Joe, all of them watching us with bated breath. My father is nowhere to be seen—I'm sure he's still at work.

"Wes," Grady greets my ex-fiancé like they've been friends for years before I have a chance to say anything. Without letting me go, Grady offers his right hand. "Never thought I'd see you again after our last meeting."

Weston doesn't take his hand, and I slip my arm inside Grady's suit jacket to give him a squeeze. He knows about Weston's shady side, there's no reason to antagonize him. We need to get through dinner with as little drama as possible. It's the only way to handle Weston.

Weston glares at Grady right before his eyes move, and I shift my weight at the way his eyes rake over me. I wonder how I ever found him attractive. Now, he just looks like the slimeball he is.

"You look beautiful," he says, and pins me with an intense look. "We need to talk."

I tip my head and sigh. "I didn't want to talk to you when you came all the way to Virginia. I'm only here to see Joe, so don't ruin my visit. I have nothing more to say to you."

He leans in closer and lowers his voice. "I get it. I made a mistake and hurt you. But it's over. It's time to fix this—you know we are meant to be together. Give me five minutes alone to explain."

I lower my voice for only him to hear. "Explain how you were fucking someone else while you were engaged to me?"

"Ma'am, your cosmopolitan." A drink appears in front of me and I look over to see the server speaking to Grady. "Can I get you something from the bar?"

"I made a mistake," Weston goes on, ignoring our server.

"Beer," Grady answers. "Anything's fine."

When the server steps away, I take a sip of my drink, but I can't help if I sound a little sarcastic when I say, "You should move on. You didn't have trouble doing that while we were together—it should be easy now." I've been so worried about dinner all afternoon, I'm not quite sure where my sudden boldness is coming from, but I even swing my hand out while holding my glass, yet don't spill a drop as I continue. "Just think, no hiding, no sneaking, you won't have to juggle two phones, because Lord knows that was difficult, wasn't it?"

"Enough," Weston clips and takes my drink out of my hand, setting it on an end table. He didn't even use a coaster—my mother's sixth sense will eagle-eye that in no time. He has the nerve to grab my free arm. "I don't know when you started acting like this, but it probably has something to do with him." Weston jerks his head toward Grady.

Until now, Grady has remained a calm bystander, allowing my new-found assertiveness to do its thing. But the moment Weston laid a hand on me, that changed.

His body gets tight, his arm around my waist becomes a force of nature as he pulls me to him and out of Weston's hold. "Keep your hands off her."

Weston looks straight at Grady and seethes, "She'll never be yours."

"We'll see. That's up to Maya—but it looks like you need to get it through your thick skull she'll never be yours."

Weston's about to argue further, when I hear his mother say smoothly, "Weston, this isn't the time or place. Please allow me to welcome Maya properly."

I've always liked Nancy. Even though she's best friends with my mother, she's always been genuine, like a real mom who wants the best for her kids, but to get that, her kids don't have to be the best, like I did.

So when she pulls me into her arms for a warm hug, I let her. "You look lovely, dear. It's good to have you home."

"Thank you, and it's good to see you, too, but we're

leaving tomorrow. I have to get back to work and only came to see Joe."

"Maya," Ron MacLachlan greets me, standing beside his wife. He tips his head, but his expression is bland, and that makes me nervous. He raises a brow and says pointedly, "I do hope you'll rethink your decision and come home for good."

Nancy grabs my hand and gives me a squeeze. "Please rethink this, Maya. Come home … give things a chance to mend."

I shake my head and smile, because as much as Weston's father scares me, I know Nancy loves her son and wants everything for him. But it's not my fault he turned out to be a lying, cheating, murdering asshole—and I don't think it's hers, either. Her husband, on the other hand, I do blame.

"You're a waitress and a glorified babysitter, Maya. You can leave your jobs at a moment's notice," Weston says, shaking his head.

"You're a waitress?" my mother exclaims.

"Cool, she's a waitress." I hear the smile in Joe's voice. "This is going to be fun."

Grady corrects them as the server returns with his beer in a frosty glass. "She works in the tasting room of a vineyard and she's the activities director for seniors. They love her and she's good at it."

"It was bad enough she didn't pursue music in college like she should have." My mother sighs and flips a hand toward me. "First you insist on physical therapy, and now you're a waitress. This is embarrassing."

I'm about to roll my eyes when I hear from behind me, "She's back."

I turn around and see my father. As always when he

enters a room, his presence demands attention, but his is only on me. He's just as I've known him to be all my life—tall, with dark eyes and hair that's now peppered with gray, but it only adds to his demeanor, making him even more dapper and refined. He's dressed the way he always is during the week, in a custom-made suit, fit to perfection.

My father is nothing like my mother. He's not an asshole, but I wouldn't enter him into any father of the year contests, either. He built his empire through hard work and long hours. Maintaining his spot on the Fortune 500 is no fluke, but by doing so, he had no time for his family.

He's not an asshole—just absent. Even if he doesn't see it that way.

Still, he walks straight through the crowd that has formed around us and comes straight to me. Leaning down to kiss my cheek, he says, "It's good to see you, sweetheart. You look beautiful. I told everyone not to be worried, you were doing what you thought you needed to do."

I give him a small smile. "Thanks, Dad."

"Clint, talk to your daughter," my mother starts in. "She's working as a waitress and doing something at a senior center. It's time for her to come home."

My father looks down at me with a smirk. "You were never shy of a hard day's work. Good for you."

"Dad, this is Grady Cain. Grady, my father, Clint Augustine," I introduce them.

My Dad shakes Grady's hand and doing what he does best, he takes over the situation, but not before glaring at Ron. He's never liked Weston's father. "I'm the only one without a drink and I'm hungry. Let's eat."

"I'm always hungry," Grady agrees, and hands me my Cosmo.

Thankful for the evening to move along so we can be done with it, I take Grady's hand and we move into the formal dining room. But the second I walk up to the table set for nothing less than a five-course meal, I'm stopped in my strappy heels.

"Find your place setting," my mother directs as she takes her seat at the head of the table.

I feel my blood boil again as I look down at the finest china and crystal. Of course, my name is placed right next to Weston's, and Grady is across from us. If I didn't know better, I'd say my mother was still in middle school. If she thought she could pull this off, she's crazier than I've given her credit for.

I step forward, grabbing Weston's paper tented name, scrolled in calligraphy, and toss it to the other side of the table. When I look up, my mother is scowling. I return her look with a smug one as I turn to Grady. "My mother does a lovely job of welcoming guests into her home. Have a seat."

I'm surprised Weston has the decency not to argue. Still, he appears to be holding a grudge as he rounds the table to the open chair. We all take our seats—Joe to my left, Grady to my right, and Weston across from us, flanked by his parents.

The minute we sit, the staff flocks, and my napkin is placed in my lap. I'm grateful for Joe—he starts telling our father about the training session with his medical service dog this afternoon, diverting any attention placed on Grady and me for a bit.

We're served petite crab cakes for an appetizer, lemon garlic orzo soup, and our salad dishes have just been cleared. Until now, the conversation has remained bland, but I had a feeling it wouldn't last long.

"Grady," my mother starts, clearing her voice as she demands, "tell us about yourself."

I tense and look over to Grady, who's been nothing but relaxed all night. I wish I knew how he did that.

He asks, "What would you like to know?"

"Tell us about your family," my mother goes on in a tone signifying she doesn't give a shit about his family.

Grady shrugs. "I have four sisters."

"And your parents?" my mother probes. "What do they do?"

"My parents are deceased."

My eyes widen even though I try to control it, doing my best not to look surprised. I've never asked about his parents, only his sisters.

My father frowns and picks up his bourbon. "I'm sorry to hear that."

"It's been a long time," Grady says.

Not satisfied, my mother keeps going. "What is it that you do?"

I feel Joe kick me under the table before he announces, "I've decided to change my major."

Everyone looks at my brother, surprised, especially my father, and he asks, "Excuse me?"

"Not now, Joseph," my mother clips. "Grady?"

Grady wipes his mouth before returning his napkin to his lap, and if we weren't sitting in front of my ex, his parents, and my family, I'd throw myself at him. He ate his entire salad without a peep. I know he ate it to not ruffle my mother's feathers, but by doing that, he did it for me. I obviously can't reach over and kiss him at the moment, but if I could, I would.

"I'm a government contractor—specializing in overseas security. I'm fluent in seven languages and even more dialects."

I try again not to look surprised, because I should know these things about the man I'm sleeping with and who's had his hand down my pants. Even if we're only actually *sleeping* together, the act itself has been incredibly intimate, especially when he was relaxing me.

"Who exactly do you provide security for?" my mother keeps on.

"I'm tired of finance," Joe continues, as if he was asked. "Sorry, dad. It's boring."

"Joseph." My mother throws him the look from hell.

Grady picks up his water, leaving his mostly full beer to go warm, and takes a drink. "All sorts of organizations. Corporations, foreign dignitaries, Americans traveling abroad. I used to travel exclusively, but I'm home now."

Grady looks to me when he finishes, his eyes searching my face, though for what, I'm not sure. But he does lift his arm up around my shoulders, settling it against the back of my chair.

He goes on. "It's hard after traveling for so many years, but I'm getting settled. I think Maya is, too."

I reach out for him, touching his thigh, hoping to communicate that I am.

Joe, who's doing his best to redirect the focus of conversation away from us, continues. "I'm thinking about switching to Fermentation Sciences. I want to learn how to make beer without poisoning anyone."

I look to Joe to see if he's serious, and I honestly can't tell. What I'm sure of, is my mother hasn't heard a word he's said. She's too focused on her own agenda.

"Well, don't get used to it," my mother spouts. "Maya will eventually tire of spinning her wheels waiting tables and whatever else she's doing."

I straighten in my chair and turn to my mother. "I'll have my Virginia license in a matter of weeks and I have a PT job lined up for the beginning of next year. I don't plan on tiring of anything and I'm not coming back."

"But I'll also learn how to make cheese," Joe adds. "You know, as a backup career."

"Come back for a week." Weston leans forward and speaks to me in a tone that surprises me. If I didn't know better, I'd say he almost sounded desperate. "Give me a week to make things right, Maya. Please."

"Or, I could do both," Joe raises his voice, vying for someone's attention. "I'll move to Wisconsin and open up a brewery. Beer and cheese curds. It'll be a fermentation utopia."

"They've been together since she was sixteen," my mother says, looking straight at Grady. She waves a hand toward Grady and me as she continues. "You can't give her the life she's accustomed to. She'll eventually get bored and come home. Whatever you think this is, you're wrong. Maya got her feelings hurt, she's licking her wounds, but eventually she'll find her way, so don't get too attached, *Grady Cain*."

"Mother!" I exclaim.

"Vanessa," my father warns from across the length of the table. "Watch yourself."

My mother tips her head and scowls first at my father, then me. "You can't be serious about him. You've known him, what? Weeks?"

"Months," Grady corrects her.

"Whatever." She throws him a dirty look before

returning her glare to me. "It's time to get over it and move on."

"That's it," Grady declares.

Moving his arm from in back of my chair, he narrows his eyes at my mother and reaches in the breast pocket of his suit jacket. Deftly, a small velvet box appears, and quicker than naught, he flips it open with his thumb.

And I lose my breath.

What the hell?

"What is that?" I breathe, barely able to hear myself speak.

Grady says nothing, but reaches across my body for my left hand. He removes the round metal object with a really big, bright, sparkly thing on the top, and tosses the box haphazardly to the table.

I feel my breath quicken, not able to hide my reaction from what's happening in front of me. I'm pretty sure he's moving quickly and efficiently, but my brain is functioning in slow motion.

It's a ring.

Why does he have a ring, and why is it aimed at my hand?

Holy shit, it's a really beautiful ring.

From somewhere outside of my head, I hear my ex-fiancé growl, "What the fuck?"

But I can't give that any mind space, because Grady is sliding that beautiful, shiny piece of metal that circles to infinity on my left ring finger. When it slides all the way to the base, miraculously fitting perfectly, his thumb brushes the side of it right when I feel a hand at my face.

When he lifts my chin to look into his eyes, his

expression is possessive and hot. When he dips his face, his lips touch mine—demanding and warm. It's the most perfect kiss he's ever given me, and there have been plenty.

He pulls away hesitantly, his tongue reaching out to taste me quickly before I open my eyes to find him looking contentedly down at me. "You'll let me take care of you?"

I exhale, thumbing the underneath side of the ring sitting at the base of my left ring finger. A ring I'm not totally sure the meaning of, but to the rest of the world, I know what it looks like. Even if I don't know what it means to Grady, there's nothing more I want at this moment than for him to take care of me.

I nod. Once.

Still, it's the universal sign of yes.

"Yes?" he confirms aloud.

I nod again, this time adding a throaty, "Yes."

A look takes over his handsome face. An expression I've never seen, but on Grady Cain, it's the most beautiful thing ever. He leans in to kiss me again, and when he pulls away, wraps his arm around me.

Still stunned and staring down at the ring on my finger, wondering what just happened, I hear Grady say, "As you can see, it's too late, Vanessa. I'm attached."

That's when I hear a crash.

I jerk from the noise and look up to see Weston standing, his chair thrown back with such force, it broke the glass doors of my mother's built-in china cabinet. Glass is still settling as Weston yells from across the table, "This is not happening. This is not fucking happening!" He points straight at Grady. "This is your fault. You'll pay for this—I swear."

With one last vicious glare, he stalks out of the room. His parents stand quickly making multiple apologies before they hurry out after their son.

"I cannot believe this," my mother seethes at me. "Look what you've done!"

I've had it.

Pushing my chair back, I stand quickly, and Grady stands with me.

"I hate him." I point to where Weston left the room. "He cheated on me, he controlled me, and he threatened me. Never again will I allow that to happen. This is why I left when I did. And if it means never stepping foot into your house again to not be put through this, then so be it. I'll go to the city to see Joe or I'll bring him to me when he's okay to travel. But never again will I allow you to do this. I'm done."

"He threatened you? Why didn't you tell me?" I turn to look at my father, and it's clear to see he's livid from what he just heard, his voice demanding answers. But he's looking straight at my mother. "Did you know about this?"

"Clint—" she starts, but I interrupt.

"I've had enough for tonight." Looking over at my father and Joe, I add, "Goodnight. I'll see you both tomorrow before we leave."

With that, I turn, making my way back through the formal living room and toward the back doors. Grady's right beside me but doesn't say a word. Even though he's not touching me, I know he's close. If possible, through the cold night, I feel the heat of him at my side.

When we reach the guest house, I'm trembling—but not from the cold—from my adrenaline crashing after the high I just went through. Not only from dealing with my mom and Weston, but from Grady sliding a ring on my finger. Everything—it's all too much. I fumble with the door, not able to get it unlatched, when Grady's big, steady hand covers mine and opens it for me.

I move through first and immediately kick my shoes off to the side. When I turn around, I look down at the ring he slid on my finger, needing to know, but afraid to ask.

I don't even know what I want it to mean. He said he was with me before we even spoke a word to one other, but it hasn't been that long. It took me almost twelve years to figure out Weston was toxic, and that was before I learned of his dark-side business dealings.

When I look up, Grady has already rid himself of his suit jacket and is pulling his tie off, unbuttoning the top three buttons of his shirt. He does all this without taking an eye off me—assessing me.

Is it possible to *know* in a matter of weeks?

Then he does nothing, says nothing. He stands there —half the room separating us—*doing nothing.*

Finally, I hold up my hand, the one showcasing the supersized, brilliant cut diamond in an exquisite setting, flanked by baguettes running down the band.

"Grady, please," I call for him, my voice unstable and hoarse. "Tell me what just happened."

20

HEAVY?

Grady

NEVER IN MY life have I been as anxious about the outcome of my actions as now.

Not when I joined the Army, not when I was recruited, not on my first assignment. Not even the first time I ever put a bullet through someone's head, officially making me an assassin. Even though that day didn't officially make me a killer—I'd been one for years at that point.

I especially wasn't anxious the day I made sure my dad would never fuck with us again. That day was nothing but a relief.

But now, standing in front of her, having to explain my actions, yet prove to her it's her choice? That it'll only ever be what she wants?

I'm fucking anxious.

In a short time, this woman has stirred emotions in me I never knew existed, and before that, she just plain saved me.

It's not helping that her face is a mix of wonder, fear, and fuck me, I think she's got tears in her eyes. She has no idea what that does to me.

I bought that ring with only one intention—to make her mine. I knew I'd use it if I needed to make a statement. I had no idea what to expect from her family or that asshole ex of hers. I knew I'd be taking a chance if I was forced to put it into play. It's not too soon for me, but I can see how it might be for her.

Throw all that in a pot and stir it up along with what just happened at dinner, it's a lot of shit for her to deal with. That makes me even more anxious.

"What just happened?" she repeats, more forcefully.

Never good with words, I hope like hell I don't fuck this up.

"I'm curious." It's a lame start, but I'm buying time. I shift my weight and cross my arms, but I really need to know, so I jerk my chin toward her. "How does it feel?"

Her brows instantly pucker. "How does it feel?"

"Yeah," I confirm. "I know it fits, but how does it feel?"

She spreads her fingers out in front of her, and her other hand comes up to touch the diamond I just slid on her finger. She doesn't look away from her ring as she shakes her head. "I'm not sure."

"You've gotta feel something, Maya," I insist, dropping my arms and taking a step. I don't like all this space between us.

"I mean." She twists it back and forth a bit, not looking away from her hand. "I don't know. It feels," she looks up at me, confusion still clouding her features, "heavy?"

I frown, wondering what the hell that means. "Heavy?"

She nods, looking back to her hand. "Yes. Heavy."

"Heavy..." I let the word hang on my tongue, not sure if I want to know what that means. "Like I bought a big enough diamond-heavy? Or oppressive-heavy?"

"No," she says quickly, shaking her head. "It's plenty big. I mean, yes, it's heavy-big. It's beautiful—perfect. I can't believe it fits." She looks back up to me, bewildered. "How did you get it to fit?"

Well, fuck. If that's not the heavy she was talking about, that's not good. I take another step and lower my voice. "It wasn't hard. I'd memorize every inch of you if you let me, baby."

Looking up to me, her eyes are definitely wet.

"Tell me what *heavy* means, Maya," I demand.

I see her swallow and she drops her arms to her sides. "Significant?"

I tip my head. "Is that a question or an answer?"

She changes the subject to one I don't like. "I've only known you for a matter of weeks, Grady."

I narrow my eyes, not liking where this is going, but quickly say, "I've known you longer."

She ignores me. "You know how my last relationship ended. It took me twelve years to realize it was bad and wrap that misery up, finally putting an end to it. It makes me question my judgment."

I counter, "I've only ever questioned my judgment once, and that was after the fact—when I almost got myself killed. Besides that one time, I never once regretted a decision in my life."

"So tell me then, Grady." Her voice insistent and

strong now, holding her hand out to me. "What does this mean?"

I take another breath and ask one more time, needing only one answer from her. We can figure the rest out later. "Don't think about your past and don't overthink this. Just answer one question. Do you want me?"

She shakes her head slowly as a tear falls, and I swear, she might as well have turned a knife in my gut. All that pain I experienced months ago—the rope, the pipe, the broken bones, dislocated joints, and concussion? Nothing compares to now.

Now, it's crippling.

Until she knocks the wind out of me when she utters, "Yes."

I take a moment to let that sink in. But a moment is all I need. Right now, it's the sweetest word in the world.

Maya

I SAID YES and I meant it.

But I think I might be losing it.

What the hell am I doing? I have no business wearing a man's ring after only knowing him for such a short time. Not after knowing the last one for so many years and it turning out as badly as it did.

But something in me doesn't care, because this feels different. *I'm* different. And it doesn't have anything to do with taking a chance on Grady. He's Grady, after all—solid, sweet, protective, and loving. He is who he is, and there's not a single disingenuous bone in his body.

I don't know how I know this to be a fact, but I do. I feel it.

This is different because of *me*. Finally, after twenty-eight years, I'm in a place where I feel comfortable in my own skin. After living my life being told what I should want, what I should do, and who I should do it with because of some status that needed to be upheld, I've finally found my place.

Who knew it would be in the middle-of-nowhere-Virginia and with a bruised, battered, and irritable man, who underneath it all is none of those things.

But I barely have a second to process this, because just a moment ago when I admitted I want him, Grady was many strides away from me. The next instant, my face is being held in his big hands with his mouth on mine.

His kiss is bruising and desperate as he holds me tight.

He tears his face away but stays close when he questions, "Yes?"

Loving his eyes, especially the way they're looking at me now, I don't hesitate. "Yes."

"Fuck," he clips, and his hands move low on my hips.

Digging his fingers into my skin through the thin material of my dress, he fists and pulls. The next thing I know, my dress is being yanked up and over my head. Standing here in my strapless bra and panties, I reach for his shirt, wanting to touch him—really touch him. Not like when I'm working on his shoulder or snuggled up to him before sleep. I want all of him.

I rip a button off his shirt trying to get them undone. After taking his time to run his hands along my bare skin, my hips and ass, he cups my breasts lightly before one hand reaches around, nimbly unhooking my bra with one single flick of his fingers. It instantly falls to the floor.

I keep at his shirt, wanting nothing between us. The second I push it down his arms, I lift, pressing my bare breasts into his muscled chest. His light dusting of chest hair rubbing against my sensitive nipples radiates pleasure through my body.

"Never wanted anything more than you," he says as his hands move on my bare back, gliding down to my ass. "Never let myself want anything before."

His words only cement what I already know.

I need him, but even more, I want to give him everything he needs.

"I want you, Grady. All of you," I confess.

I feel his thumbs dip in my panties at my hips and he pushes. When I'm standing bare in front of him, he rocks back a half-step to take a look at me. His hungry gaze rakes over my body, leaving me warm and tingly all at the same time.

His eyes come back to mine, his hands go to my ass, and I'm up. My legs circle his waist and I wrap my arms around his shoulders to hang on. Holding me with one arm, I feel his fingers drag through my wet pussy right before he fills me with two fingers, and I can't help but press down on his hand.

"Do anything for you, Maya. You'll never know how you saved me from myself. I was at my lowest, had no one. Just watching you on those fucking cameras was the only thing that got me through. To have you here, like this? Never thought this would happen."

As I let his words sink in, he carries me into the

bedroom, coming down with me as my back hits the bed. Kissing me one more time before letting go, he runs his hands down the front of my body. Teasing my breasts on his way, his eyes never stray from his touch, his fingertips rough on my overly sensitive skin.

"Wouldn't even let my mind want you like this in the beginning. That would've been too painful, to think of you like this, you giving yourself to me. If I allowed myself those thoughts and this didn't happen? I'd come undone."

"Grady," I moan. He's killing me with his words.

His hands go to his waist and he swiftly undresses, standing over me bare. His cock—hard, thick, and veined—is as beautiful as the rest of him. He drags his eyes over my body while holding his erection, and slowly, methodically running his fist up and down his length. My breath catches, watching him hungrily take me in, as if he can't decide where to start.

When his eyes settle between my legs, without looking away, he murmurs, "Spread for me, baby."

Holy shit.

I pull my knees up slowly before letting them drop to my sides, doing exactly what he asked, spreading myself for him. For my Grady.

Without looking away from his target, he bends and his mouth is on me. There's nothing slow or sweet about his touch.

He's hungry.

It seems all the time he said I was his before I even knew it, and all the time I spent being a creeper, fascinated with everything Grady, has come to fruition. Not to mention the tension that's been building between us.

The culmination of it all is too much for me, and I can tell it is for him, as well.

There's no control.

His lips and tongue devour me. Sucking, licking, and kissing. He's absolutely consuming me.

I can't get enough. Putting my feet to the bed, I push up to get more, and he gives it to me. Squeezing my ass with one hand to hold me to his face, he slips his thumb inside my pussy as his tongue teases my clit right before his lips encompass it and he sucks.

I throw my arms out to the side to fist the bed, needing something to hold onto. Lightning shoots through me and I lose my grasp on reality. All I've dealt with—my family, my worries, threats made against me, it all disappears. Everything.

As my body shakes with my orgasm, I realize I can't move. Grady's easily holding me to his mouth in his strong arms, still sucking, teasing, and gently grazing his teeth over my clit, not giving me any reprieve.

Just when I think I'm spent and can't take another second, Grady lets me go.

"Maya," he whispers, and I feel his hand at the back of my knee, pulling my leg up.

When I drag my eyes open, he looks into mine and slides into me. Slow, smooth, and perfect. And inch by inch, I see it spread across his features.

If his eyes speak the truth, he just made me his.

"You feel that?" he asks, his voice rough and gravely.

With his forearm bent to the bed above my head, his other hand travels my body and down my arm. When he reaches my hand, he pulls it above my head, and cupping it in his, he holds the ring he just slipped on my finger between his forefinger and thumb.

"Yes," I breathe, feeling him pull out, just to slide back in as slowly as he did the first time.

I'm still sensitive from my orgasm and feel it every time he fills me. Wanting more, I try and arch my back, but he gives me his weight and takes over.

"Fuck, baby." He starts to move, giving me what I want, but doing it on his terms. "Even if I thought I knew before, now I know. Don't want anyone else besides you for the rest of my days."

He picks up his pace. Holding my hand and the diamond on my left ring finger, staring intensely into my eyes—Grady is solely focused on me.

Focused. On. Me.

I've never had that—ever. Sex has always been sex. To have it focused on me, but be about us?

It's never been so good.

Staring into my eyes, he starts to move. Really move, as if he's losing control and can't help himself. His eyes close and his breath comes across my face, short and labored, all the while he never lets go of my left hand. Never takes his fingers off the ring.

He angles his hips with every thrust, hitting my sensitive clit. I do my best to move with him, to arch, to do anything I can for more.

Just when I thought he'd already lost control, I was wrong. With each strong thrust, every muscle in his body tenses. Running my free hand over his shoulder I've worked on so many times, I move down his back to his ass, loving the feel of his body. He's like a work of art I can't get enough of.

When it comes over me again, that heat feeling better with Grady moving inside me, it unfurls, consuming me.

He bows his back, thrusting into me two last times, and groans, coming right after me.

Breathing hard, he gives me most of his weight, pressing into me one more time.

Taking my mouth, his kiss lingers before he rolls to his back where I end up on top, my knees to his sides. I snuggle my face into his neck as he strokes the outsides of my thighs from my knees to my ass, and back again.

After our long day—dealing with my mother, the stress of dinner, and now having the most amazing sex of my life—I'm spent.

"This is new." He doesn't stop stroking my skin. "But you give it time, baby, I promise I'll make this good."

Without moving, I close my eyes, feeling as if I could sleep here, with his light touch, and filled with his cock.

I'm almost startled when his hands stop abruptly, grabbing my ass. I swear I feel him tense underneath me, as well.

I try to move but one hand comes to my head and he holds me to him, murmuring, "Shh."

I'm so tired, I relax again, and Grady goes back to stroking. This goes on for many minutes when he finally calls for me softly. "Baby?"

"Hmm?" I answer, pressing my face deeper into his neck.

"I meant what I said."

"About what?" I ask sleepily, without moving.

"You know I want you. I'll do everything in my power to make this good. As soon as the shit settles with your ex, and the FBI hopefully does their job faster than slower, we can focus on the future. You've got that ring on your finger to prove it. You know that, right?"

"Yes. You don't have to prove anything to me."

"Good." I feel him take a breath before he keeps talking. "That didn't go the way I wanted it to. It was fast. I mean it when I say, I'm okay either way. But, baby, are you on birth control?"

What?

My eyes fly open.

He must feel the change in my body, because his arms come around me like a steel cage, holding me where I am.

"Maya?"

"Oh, fuck." I try to push up, but he won't let me.

With a hand on my ass, and one angled up my back, he keeps me where I am. "Hey—"

"I didn't even think." I struggle against him. "Who does that? I'm a grown, responsible woman."

"Maya," he raises his voice to get my attention and I push up enough to look at him. "After my accident, I was tested for everything under the sun because of where I was and what happened to me. I'm clean. Don't worry about that."

"Holy shit." I freak out even more. "I didn't even think about that. What's wrong with me? And I work in health care for fuck's sake."

He puts a foot to the bed and rolls. I struggle, but I can't get out from under him. He pulls out of me when he's on top again and looks at me with a frown playing on his face. "Don't ruin this."

"Ruin it?" I exclaim. "Grady, I had myself tested back when Weston cheated on me. I'm good, and I told you I haven't been with anyone else. But I'm not on birth control. I left Weston well over a year ago, there was no reason."

His face softens and he leans down to kiss me. I

don't have much of a choice since he has me pinned where I can't move. But where I was exhausted and sated just moments ago, now I'm very much awake and tense. And have Grady leaking out of me. And very possibly, could be on my way to being pregnant.

Oh, fuck.

He pulls his head up to look at me again and smiles.

What the hell is he smiling about?

"Don't worry." He looks happy as he tries to calm me, but there's no way I'm not going to worry. "I told you I'm good either way."

"Please move," I almost beg. "I need to clean up."

He leans down to kiss me one more time, then finally rolls off. I scurry from the bed, not even noticing Grady getting up to follow me.

When I finish, I open the door and there he is. He's leaning against the vanity with his arms and feet crossed waiting on me. He's also still naked.

Naked and beautiful.

Even though I am too, I can't help but stop and take him in. After being his physical therapist, I now have a whole new appreciation for his body.

His arms fall to his side and he holds a hand out low for me. "Come here."

Feeling self-conscious for the first time, I go to him fast so I'm not standing here bare. Pressing myself to him, his arms come around me and I bury my face in his neck.

I feel his lips at the side of my head. "I'll use a condom next time."

I sigh, but melt into him, resigned. "What's done is done."

I feel him shrug. "Okay, then, I won't use a condom next time."

I look up at him quickly and shake my head. "No, no. You'll use a condom."

He smirks, reaches for my hand, and plays with the diamond on my finger. "Like I said, I didn't mean for that to happen, but I told you I'm good."

I gesture to the ring. "Seriously, does this mean we're officially engaged? Because as much as I want you and you want me, you have to know this is more than a little crazy."

He drops my hand and wraps me up tight. "Leave it on. Let's just see how it feels."

I sigh. "You keep saying that."

He leans in close, but doesn't kiss me. Against my lips, he murmurs, "We'll take it day-to-day. Now, let's go to bed. I'll bring a condom this time."

"Grady." I shake my head and give him a small smile. "You're practically impossible to resist."

He smiles back, proving he's irresistible. "Good for me."

21

I'LL BRING THE CONDOMS

Grady

As I STAND in the big-ass kitchen, across from the big-ass family room, in the big-ass house Maya grew up in, I pop the last bite of my fourth blueberry muffin in my mouth. I was starving when we woke up since the drama last night interrupted dinner.

But I'd fast for a month if it meant having Maya, especially for the first time. I never meant to take her bare, I have never gone without a condom in my life. But I also didn't lie when I said I was good with whatever happens.

I look across the room as Maya laughs with her brother, spending their last hours together before we have to leave. She looks happy, not at all stressed like she was last night.

We did go straight to bed, and just like I said I would, I relaxed her. I made her mine again, but with a condom.

When we woke up this morning, she seemed quiet, but explained it was about dealing with her mom before we left. She told me as much as she's enjoyed the time with her brother, she couldn't wait to get home.

It made me feel really fucking good she doesn't consider this monstrosity her home anymore.

Sensing something from my side, I turn as he's heading into the kitchen—Clint Augustine.

"Good morning," he greets.

"Morning," I reply and watch him head straight to the coffee, reaching for a mug in the cabinet above.

Talking to me as he pours himself a cup, he goes on. "You're leaving today?"

I tip my head, not sure if he's referring to me or us, so I decide to set him straight. "Yes. We leave for the airport in about an hour."

"I see." He nods and turns fully to me. He's in suit pants, a dress shirt, and tie, looking very much the part of a Fortune 500 business man. He leans against the counter and assesses me before continuing. "My wife left early this morning, you won't need to worry about another run-in. I'd apologize, but..."

He lets his words trail off. I'm guessing a lifetime with Vanessa Augustine would leave one tired of apologizing.

"So, you and my daughter," he continues. "The engagement was a surprise. I can't say I'm upset, though. My Maya, she's nothing like her mother. I never could figure out what she was doing with Weston. When she found out he cheated on her, I told her to dump his ass. I had no idea she was threatened in any way—it was worse than I thought. I wish I had known, I could've done something."

I say nothing but nod, happy to see her dad cares about her, even if Maya says he was never around much.

He keeps going. "She seems comfortable with you in a way I've never seen her before. Regardless of her mother's behavior, we'd like to see more of her."

"I can make that happen if she wants it," I concede. "But I don't like her stressed. I will tell you she's happy in Virginia. She's got people there who care about her and she's starting to open up to them."

He takes another drink before setting the mug down and crosses his arms. Leveling his eyes on me, he's no-nonsense when he lowers his voice and lays it out. "Grady, regardless what Maya might have told you about me, even though I'm a busy man, I care about my family. You think I'd let my daughter disappear off the face of the earth without doing everything I could to find her? I have the means to hire the best and I did. I've known where she's been the whole time. She did what she thought she needed to do, and so did I. Once I found out she was safe, I gave her the space she needed. Had I known she was running because she felt threatened, I never would have allowed her that space."

I tip my head, surprised. "You've known where she was all this time? I thought Weston's been looking for her."

"He was, but he and his dad are morons, and Vanessa didn't need to know. I told her our daughter needed time away and we should give it to her. Maya did what she needed to do and found you in the process. You, on the other hand, I'd like to know more about."

I shrug and keep my face neutral. "Told you I work in security. What else do you want to know?"

He shakes his head and looks toward his daughter. "I only want her to be happy and provided for."

"I can do both," I answer immediately.

He nods slowly. "I hope so. She deserves it. Now if you'll excuse me, I need to say goodbye to my daughter and get to the office. As long as Maya's happy, you're welcome here anytime."

I'm pleased to know I have her dad's support. "I'll bring her back whenever she wants."

He pushes away from the counter and moves past me to his kids. I watch him wrap up his daughter in a hug and talk to her quietly.

With the side of her face pressed into her dad's chest, she looks across the room at me and smiles.

Yeah, I'll do whatever I can to make her happy.

Maya

I FEEL HIM take my hand and I look from my window to him.

"You okay?" Grady looks concerned. He's done so much for me. I hate to see that look on his face.

I give him a smile and hope it looks genuine. "I'm good. Thank you for coming with me. I can't imagine dealing with all that happened last night on my own."

He gives my hand a squeeze as he watches the road and smirks. "Not that I would've let you come alone, but after seeing you handle your mom and ex, I'll think twice before going head-to-head with you." He looks over to me quickly. "You're no damsel in distress, that's for sure."

I narrow my eyes and pull my left hand out of his to wiggle my fingers. "I'm not so sure about that. You sure swept in at the end, didn't you?"

We're close to the airport and Grady makes the last turn. When he pulls into the lot and parks, he turns fully to me. "The way I see it, I just sped up the inevitable. This was going to happen Maya—sooner rather than later."

I lean in and smirk, lowering my voice. "You seem very sure of yourself."

He smiles smugly. "I am, and seeing as though our need outweighed our brains last night and we might've made a baby, it's a good thing you're wearing my ring. At least we'll get to tell him we had a plan."

That's something I can't get out of my head—Grady's sperm.

I've been trying to calculate where I am in my cycle all morning. If his swimmers are as strong and resilient as the rest of him, the chances we made a baby last night are not low. I don't know if they're high, but the possibility is definitely there.

"Hey," he interrupts my thoughts. "Don't think about it. Whatever happens, I'm happy."

He's said that more times than I can count since last night, and I believe him. The more I let that settle, the more I'm unsure about myself. Last night, I freaked after our irresponsible first time together, but what I'm more worried about is that I'm not truly worried.

Worrying about not being worried might be even more stressful because who doesn't worry about a pregnancy scare?

That's not me, or at least it didn't used to be. But this is the new me, who I'm pretty sure is engaged to a man I creeped on long before we barely spoke a word to one another. And to top it all off, I could be pregnant with his baby and not be in a panic about it.

Who the hell am I?

Now *this* is something for me to worry about.

I don't tell him about my lack of worry about *maybe* being pregnant, because I'm afraid he'd jump me right here in the car. And I'd probably let him. And he probably wouldn't use a condom. And even worse, I'm afraid I might be okay with it.

So instead of admitting to what a freak I've become, I say, "It could be a girl, you know."

He smiles bigger. "I grew up with four sisters. The universe wouldn't do that to me. It'll be a boy."

Holy shit, he really doesn't mind if I'm pregnant.

Not knowing what to say, I do what I always do when I get nervous, and start to blather on without a filter. "But you don't know where I am in my ovulation cycle. I don't know if it's true, but I've heard girl sperm swim faster than boy sperm. If I'm ovulating, it will most likely be a girl, if not, the boys have more of a chance to get there. They might be slow, but they live longer. But, if it's all an old wives tale and the opposite is true, I'm still not quite sure where I am in my cycle, it's not like I take my temperature every morning. So, who knows? What I do know is the universe has nothing to do with it."

His smile grows into a devilish grin and he closes the distance between us, laying a hot, heavy kiss on me. Cupping the back of my head with his big hand, he kisses me possessively, but does it smiling the whole time.

Gah. Grady kissing me while smiling about his boy and girl sperm is too much.

I pull away from him and he smiles even bigger.

"I don't know what to say," I admit.

He reaches for his door. "You should talk about my sperm and your ovulation cycle some more. I'm learning a lot."

I get out and meet him at the back of the rental. Watching him lift the bags, I warn, "Be careful with your shoulder."

He looks over, still smiling. In fact, I don't ever remember him ever smiling this much. "You weren't worried about my shoulder when I picked you up last night."

Oh shit. He has a point.

"Come on." He tips his head toward the office that's attached to the hangar at the private airport. "The rental company is picking up the car here, we're scheduled to leave in ten. We're cutting it close."

After he checks in at the desk, he hands our suitcases over to the same pilot who flew us here. I stand next to Grady, feeling guilty again about him paying for the private flight when there's no way I can pay him back.

When he's done, he takes my hand and leads me out the same door the pilot exited.

"You know," he starts as he looks down at me with a smirk, "the flight's long enough, I might tell the pilot we don't want to be disturbed. It'll be your choice if we use a condom or not."

I shake my head, looking up to the gray winter sky, yet can't keep from grinning as we walk to the plane. "You're too much. The answer from now on is yes—"

But I don't get to finish my sentence, because Grady yanks me to him with such force, it's enough to take my breath away.

When I look up, his face has turned to stone as he stares over my head. He holds me to his side and his other arm comes up, elbow out.

I finally realize what's going on, and see Byron, the old guy who works for Weston's dad—the same one who showed up at the Ranch.

"Get her!" Byron yells, and I realize there's a younger man, faster and in much better shape who I've never seen before. His dark hair is cut short, and he's tall and fit. But his eyes are on me since he was given a directive.

My heart races, and I fist Grady's shirt as he tries to maneuver me behind him.

Byron advances on Grady again right as the other guy reaches for my arm. He grabs my bicep and it makes me yelp in pain.

Oh fuck.

Grady

We were walking to the tarmac as these guys appeared from the other side of a nearby plane. I knew we'd have trouble right away when I recognized the old, heavy-set guy. He was the one with Weston at the Ranch. The second I made eye contact with them, they made their move. I tried to pull Maya out of the way, but they were close.

When the old guy goes for my throat, I do the only thing I can with one free arm since I've got Maya in my other. I go for his pressure point on his jugular with my thumb. The guy's eyes widen and his grip on me loosens, but he doesn't give up.

That's when I hear Maya yell and feel her being pulled from me.

The younger guy has his hands on her. No fucking way is anyone going to take her from me.

"Damn it, Trevor. Get her!" the old guy yells again.

I try to pull her in back of me, but the old guy goes for my hair and chin, trying to yank my head back.

Amateur move.

I swing my free arm up and over, easily dislodging his hands, and quickly kick, putting a foot to his chest. He loses his footing, landing hard on his ass and back.

"No!" Maya screams and I tighten my arm around her waist. The younger guy is big, strong, and seems to be ten times the adversary compared to his friend who's lying on the ground. Even so, for as big as he is, he doesn't seem to be trying very hard.

Turning Maya as much as I can, I lift my leg and put a foot into the side of the younger guy with all my might. He stumbles back a couple feet, but out of the corner of my eye, I see movement.

The old guy is rolling to sit on the ground and when he brings his gun up, I don't have a choice.

I'm forced to let Maya go, and yell, "Get on the plane!"

I hear a scuffle behind me, but don't take my eyes off my target. I swear, every hair on my body stands on end when I hear Maya let out a painful cry.

By the time the old guy's arm swings forward, gun in hand, I've made the three strides it takes to get to him.

He's still on his ass, so his hand is an easy mark. I circle my leg just in time.

He gets a round off, but he's fucking slow. My boot already made contact and the shot goes astray, his gun flying through the air.

Then I put my boot to the side of his head.

His body follows, flipping over to his side and rolling onto his face. I bend, yanking up the leg of my jeans and reach for my gun that's holstered at my ankle.

"Grady!"

I stand and turn with my weapon, but I'm too late, the younger guy has her. Her back is plastered to his chest with her wrists bound in one of his big hands. It's not enough, and he's doing everything in his power to keep hold of her.

This is because she's struggling, kicking, and twisting her body. Even though he's twice her size, she's strong, in shape, and making him work for it. But her face is full of fear and I grit my teeth when I see blood seeping from scratches on her cheek.

I take two steps to the right so the old guy isn't behind me, although I'm pretty sure he's knocked out.

The young guy glances quickly at his unconscious friend as he struggles with Maya.

I raise my gun, making him my target. "You're fucking crazy if you think I can't put a hole in your head without touching a hair on hers. Let her go."

His eyes narrow, shifting quickly between me, my gun, and his friend lying on the ground. I'm not sure what I expected, but he instantly gives in, lifting his chin, and lets Maya go, giving her a little push in my direction. He raises his hands to show me he's done.

Once freed, Maya runs to me. Without taking my

gun off my target, I wrap her up in my free arm and move us sideways to the plane. When we get there, I push her up the stairs first and the pilot reaches for her hand to pull her in the rest of the way.

After we board, he yanks the door quickly and locks it before looking from me to Maya. This is the same pilot Asa, Crew, and I have used for years, so he doesn't question me as to what just happened, but says quickly, "We're cleared, let's get out of here. Get yourselves belted in and then get her some ice after takeoff—she hit the ground hard."

Looking to Maya, she's sitting on the sofa holding her head in her hands. I feel my phone vibrate in my pocket at the same time I bend to look out a window. The young guy has moved away from the plane and toward his friend on the ground, but what's weird is he just stands there, with a hand on his hip while running the other through his hair.

Making sure he doesn't turn on us, I don't take my eyes off him until he's out of view as the pilot taxis to the runway.

"We're going, Cain. Buckle up," I hear him call to me from the cockpit.

But I don't buckle. I go to the galley and brace myself as we speed down the runway. With nothing else to use, I wrap ice in a towel, and wet another one to clean her face.

Feeling my phone vibrate again, I ignore it and move to Maya, who's visibly shaking. My gut wrenches as I gently lift her face. Her beautiful face—that's wet with tears, laced with fear, and now seeping blood—has what looks like road rash across her cheekbone.

"I'm sorry, baby. So sorry I had to let you go. He pulled a gun—I had no choice."

She shakes her head and shifts into me, but I need to check her out.

I lift her face to mine again to get a good look. Wiping away her tears gently, I ask, "What happened?"

As she finds her voice, I wipe the blood from her scratches before applying the ice to her cheek.

She winces. "He works for Weston's dad. Holy shit, they don't mess around."

I know all this, but don't want her to think about it, so I ask again, "Not that. Tell me what happened when I had to turn my back. How did you get hurt?"

Her hand comes up to mine to hold the ice to her cheek. "I was trying to get away from him. I thought I had, but he grabbed me and I fell, sort of skidded. I've never seen that guy before, just the older one with the gun."

"How hard did you hit your head?" I turn on my phone light and lift her chin farther to check her pupils.

She blinks rapidly as I flash the light in and out of her eyes. "Not that hard. Stop it."

I feel the plane lift off the ground and breathe a sigh of relief when my fucking phone vibrates again.

I see Crew's name across my screen. Frustrated, I answer, "What?"

"Answer your fucking phone," he clips. "We got word they're gonna make a move on Maya. Where are you?"

"How do you know this?" I ask.

"Asa's contact at the FBI got a tip. Where are you?"

"They got their tip a little too late. Our plane just took off, but we were jumped at the airport. One of them was the same guy who showed up at the Ranch that day with her ex. I don't know the other. One pulled a gun on us. I took care of it, but not before Maya got tossed around and scraped up."

"You're good then?" he asks with more meaning than I like, but I get that he might wonder where my head is.

I look at Maya as she takes the ice away from her face and shifts into me. I put my arm around her and say into the phone, "I'll talk to you after I get her settled."

I end the call without saying goodbye and pull her to me tighter.

"Ouch," she winces.

I release my hold. "What's wrong?"

She rubs her arm before she sinks into my chest again. "He hurt my arm when I was wrestling with him. It's over. I'm fine."

I lean back, pulling her to me more gently this time. I scoot us down in the couch as she settles into my chest.

"Grady?"

I close my eyes and try not to think about how bad that could've been. "Hmm?"

"I'm sorry," she murmurs into my chest. "You were shot at because of me—because of my shitty history with Weston."

I rub her arm gently. "Don't worry. They had no idea what they were doing and that's not the first time I've been shot at."

My words make her body go tense again and she pushes from my chest to look at me with big eyes. "How many times have you been shot at?"

I try and give her a reassuring smile and pull her back to me. "That's a conversation for another day. I will say, I hope it's the last time anyone fires a gun at me. Slid a ring on your finger last night, bonded with your dad over muffins this morning, and might've made a baby with you. I'm ready to move on to other things than being shot at."

She sinks into me. "You bonded with my dad?"

"Yeah, he wants to see more of you. I told him I'd bring you back whenever you wanted, but after what just happened, there's no way you're leaving the vineyard until something happens with the MacLachlans."

She nods against my chest and we lay like this for a long while.

Maya eventually breaks the silence. "This ruined your in-flight sex plans."

I sigh, finally relaxing. I put my lips to her soft hair. "I'll charter a plane just to fly around in circles to make that happen. You give me the word and it's a date."

"Okay." She burrows in farther. "I'll bring the condoms."

22

ONE, TWO, THREE, AND FOUR

Grady

ONCE THE PLANE lands, I hurry her to my Escalade while making sure no one follows us. I don't think they'll try to make another move so soon, but you never know.

I checked her eyes two more times on the plane for signs of a concussion. She's got swelling on her cheek that's sure to bruise and the scratches are starting to scab. Her pupils aren't dilated, she hasn't fallen asleep or been sick—but I'm not taking any chances, so I tell her I'm taking her straight to a doctor to get checked out.

This is when we have our first argument. It isn't ridiculous banter about food or Christmas trees, either. It's a hands-down, lay-your-shit-out disagreement.

She insists she's fine.

I tell her she's going to the doctor—end of discussion. She's not the one looking at her face with a constant reminder of what just happened. She even admits to having a slight headache.

She retorts that anyone who skidded across a tarmac on their face would have a headache, and again, repeats that she's fine.

I tell her she doesn't have a choice—we're going.

She says I'll have to wrestle her out of the car and that would just be embarrassing, because she isn't going and—fucking again—says she's fine.

I ignore her, insisting she go.

Then she explains in a high-pitched tone that she's the only health care professional in this vehicle and if she gets sick, she'll go. She even goes so far as to add in a sarcastic tone that she'll be sure to throw up all over me so I don't miss it.

I start my car, and as we leave the parking lot, put my foot down. She's going to see a doctor.

As I pull onto the highway to find the nearest emergency clinic, her voice fills the car, but this time it's small and shaky.

"Please, Grady," she starts, and when I look over, her eyes are filled with tears. Damn it. That, mixed with seeing her beautiful face marred, is enough to gut me all over again. "I just want to go home after all that's happened. I promise I'll tell you if I don't feel good. Please."

I sigh and turn back to focus on the highway. Reaching over, I take her hand and, fuck me, I agree. Seeing tears in her eyes nearly does me in.

This doesn't bode well for me.

But I try to save face and tell her I'll only take her home if she takes a couple more days off work to make sure she's okay.

Surprisingly, she doesn't argue. I'm out of pawns to negotiate with, so I'm relieved she gives in. Plus, there's no way I was going to let her go to work anyway, so it saves me another argument.

The rest of the car ride is quiet, but when my phone rings and I see that it's Crew, my stomach tightens, wondering what it could be now.

I don't put it on speaker, just in case. "Yeah?"

"Hey, I know you've had a busy day already, and trust me, I wouldn't bother you for anything else, but if I were you I'd want a warning." I've known Crew for more than ten years. I probably know him better than anyone, so I can tell by his tone of voice, this isn't an emergency. If anything, he sounds amused.

"Okay," I drawl, waiting for him to finish.

"I was in the middle of a training session with the men, and then, boom—it was like a tornado hit."

"What are you talking about?" I growl and feel Maya squeeze my arm.

When I look over, her face is as confused as I feel.

"Well." I hear him move the phone and muffle a laugh. "Let's just say the Cain Quartet rolled into town and now my old farmhouse looks like Rudolph threw up all over the place."

"What the fuck?" I feel my face fall as Maya's expression turns from confused to concerned.

I've been putting my sisters off for months, even more since I was captured and fucked-up. I didn't need them to see me that way. They know my job as a contractor could be dangerous and I told them I'd had an incident, but was fine. They don't know the truth about my prior job.

I guess I put them off long enough, they made a surprise attack. Damn them.

"Yeah, you heard me. They said they were tired of you giving them the runaround, so they came to you. Did they ever. I wouldn't believe it if I hadn't seen it with my own eyes. There was no way I could stop them, and man, they've only been here for thirty minutes. They're a force to be reckoned with."

I look back to the road, but slow down. I was in a hurry to get her home, but now I'm wondering if we can get back on the plane and head for Fiji. I can keep her safe in Fiji, not to mention, we can fuck on the beach.

Just when my thoughts go to how many ways we can fuck on a private island, Crew keeps talking. "Tell me you're close. They're talking my fucking ear off and I left the men with Asa. I've carried in all their shit and eaten enough Christmas cookies to get me through Independence Day. I think I'd rather go to the depths of hell for you again than entertain them."

I shake my head and turn onto the two-lane road that leads us home. "I've decided to take Maya to Fiji."

"Fuck you," Crew clips.

"I'll see you in five," I concede and we hang up.

"What's wrong now?" Maya asks.

"I feel bad," I start, trying to break the news that we'll be bombarded the second we get home. "I had no idea they were coming, but they're crazy and can do shit like this from time to time. I know it's really a bad time after last night and today. I wanted to bring you home to peace and quiet, not to the whirlwind we're about to walk into."

"Grady, what are you talking about?"

"My sisters." I look over at her. "They're here. They

like this spur-of-the-moment shit. I'm sorry, baby, but from the sounds of it, there'll be no peace and quiet today."

Her hand comes to her face and she instantly pulls down the mirror on the visor to inspect her scrapes.

"Hey," I call for her. "They're a pain in the ass, but only the good kind. They'll love you so much, it'll make you sick to your stomach. But still, if you throw up on me, don't think you can blame it purely on my sisters. You're going to the doctor to get checked for a concussion."

"I'm a mess," she says into the mirror. "I can't believe I have to meet them looking like this. Can you just take me home? I'll meet them next time."

I shake my head as I pull onto the road that leads to Crew's house. "Sorry, baby. I need to get my sisters off Crew's back and I'm not letting you out of my sight."

She flips the mirror closed, giving up. "It's useless anyway. Who knows when my face will heal."

"It's not deep. It should heal soon." I look over at her and raise a brow. "But I shouldn't have to tell you that. You *are* the health care professional here, right?"

She closes her eyes. "Shut up."

I pull slowly up to the house, park next to a brand-new minivan with temporary tags and add, "Warning—they'll attack you with the energy of a pack of puppies who just downed a double espresso. And since it's Christmas, they could be on a sugar high. Just go with the flow, I promise you'll make it out alive."

Her eyes get big right before I hear them and look toward the house.

Maya

When the door bursts open, I get the feeling Grady wasn't exaggerating. Four women come filing out—one in a flat-out run, one skip-running, and the other two at a quick clip.

When Grady opens his door, I hear excited screams and shouts from the women, but I stay where I am. I know I can't hide in Grady's SUV forever, but for now, I feel safer in here.

All four women have darkish hair similar to Grady's. They all have his coloring, especially the most enthusiastic one running to him. Even from here, I see she has the same vibrant blue eyes I've been falling for.

Shorter than me, she's petite. When she gets close to Grady, she jumps, leaping into his arms where he catches her, leaving her feet dangling at least six inches off the ground. She wiggles from side to side, excited to see her big brother.

But I barely have a moment to appreciate her love for Grady when the other three reach him. At least they don't run and jump, but they do attack him. It's like he's turned into a huge tree smothered in vines.

It's honestly one of the sweetest things I've ever witnessed. I know I'm the same way with Joe, but to see Grady being loved on by his family, especially after I learned their parents are gone, makes it even sweeter.

They finally give him some breathing room, breaking away even though they all seem to be talking a mile a minute. But just when I think I'm safe, tucked away in Grady's big SUV, one of the sisters looks over and catches my eye.

I can't help but tense when she doesn't look away.

I'm not a professional lip-reader, but it's easy to see she just asked who I was as she gestured to where I'm hiding. When they all look over, I give them a half-smile with a little wave. Grady gazes straight into my eyes, and his smile is bigger when he lifts a hand, crooking a finger for me to come to him.

Well, I'd look like a freak if I just sat here, but none of my mother's incessant lessons in composure taught me how to meet the family of the man I'm sleeping with when my face is scraped, swollen, and starting to bruise. It's not like I can simply explain that my ex-fiancé and his mob family are after me and my face skidded across the tarmac of a runway. They obviously love Grady, they're going to want more for him than some woman with baggage so big and heavy, it requires an eighteen-wheeler to haul it around.

But the longer I sit here, the longer they'll stare, and the weirder they'll think I am.

I finally reach for my door handle and climb down from my seat. The second I start toward the Cain huddle, Grady breaks away from his sisters and moves to me. I instantly feel at ease when he reaches for my hand and pulls me to his side with his arm around my shoulders.

He turns me to our captive audience and announces, "This is Maya Augustine. Maya, these are my sisters."

I open my mouth to greet them, but it's like I never had a chance. They prove just what I thought—their interest in the woman standing with their brother is off the charts.

"You're dating someone?"

"No wonder he won't return our calls."

"Obviously, he's been busy."

"Look how cute they are."

"How long have you been together?"

"You're the most hypocritical man *ever*. You demand to know everything about us, and you didn't tell us you have a girlfriend?"

"I mean look, with her blonde hair against his dark complexion? They're *soooo* cute."

"I agree."

"I bet they've been together a long time, it's why he hasn't come to visit. He's been relationship-busy."

"But he's never been in a *real* relationship."

"That's why he's been so busy—he doesn't know what he's doing."

"What happened to your face?"

"Seriously, Grace? You need a filter."

"Sorry. But really, what happened to your face?"

Holy shit, the way they talk, I doubt they ever need anyone to answer. I'm usually good with people, but really, it's four versus one. I'm not sure what to say, who to answer first, or how to lie about my face.

Grady's arm tightens around my shoulders and he tucks my front to his side. I try not to look pained when I offer a little wave accompanied with a lame, "Hey."

"What the hell?" the tallest of the Cain sisters screams, staring at my hand. "You're engaged?"

I quickly pull my hand back, but Grady catches it in his.

"Okay," Grady starts in a voice that sounds practiced and clearly demands attention. "I should've told you about Maya. But fuck, have you all ever heard of an invitation? Or at least a phone call to warn me of this shit?"

"No, and no." The woman with blonde highlights

steps forward and juts her hand out. At first I thought she wanted to shake mine, that is, until she rips my left hand out of Grady's to inspect my ring. "It's huge. And beautiful. And huge." She looks up at her brother and smiles. "To think you did this without our help. I'm proud of you." Looking back to me, she adds, "I'm Peyton, number two."

Overcome by ... everything really, all I can think to do is question, "Number two?"

"Yeah, sister number two," she confirms. She waves her hand toward another sister, the one with shoulder length dark hair and a fuller face. "Raine thinks she's special since she's number one." She flips out her other hand to the side toward the younger ones and continues, "Holly is number three and Gracie is four."

Holly's the one who announced how cute Grady and I are, and Grace was the one who jumped into her brother's arms.

It's hard not to be overwhelmed but ... I am.

I open my mouth again to properly greet them when Grace hits Grady's arm and exclaims, "You're getting married and didn't tell us? Wait. You're not already married, are you?"

"No," I respond quickly. "We're not married. We're," I pause to collect my thoughts so I don't ramble. "He gave me a ring just last night, in fact. So, it wasn't that he didn't tell you, there just hasn't been time. He did tell me about you all, though. But, ah, not enough. Still, he wasn't keeping anything from you. It's just been a busy..." I think about it, not wanting to admit it's only been weeks, although Grady would insist it's more like months, "time."

"You just got engaged last night?" Holly exclaims

and grabs my hand, dislodging me from Grady. She pulls me into a huge hug. “Congratulations!”

“Well, it seems we got here just in time,” Peyton says, with a hint of sarcasm. “Who knows how long it would’ve taken Grady to call us. They probably would’ve been pregnant before we heard from him.”

Holly just releases me when these words float through the air, making me gasp.

“It’s cold.” Grady changes the subject and puts a hand to the small of my back, giving me a push. “Can we take this inside?” I’m about to take a step through the gaggle of sisters when Grady stops and states, “You look funny. What’s wrong with you?”

When I look back, his arms are crossed, and he’s glaring at Raine, sister number one.

Raine smiles big, her shoulders rise, and her arms come out to her sides. “I was going to wait to tell you, but it’s hard to keep it a secret anymore. I’m pregnant!”

I start to smile at her news until I hear Grady growl, “What the fuck?”

When I look up to him, he doesn’t appear happy about becoming an uncle, even if Raine seems overly happy about her announcement.

Raine rolls her eyes. “Would you stop? I’m married—get over it.”

Really confused now, I look back to Grady and he’s closing his eyes and shakes his head.

Honestly. I don’t know when I’ve ever been more confused.

Sisters one, two, three, and four don’t seem a bit phased by Grady’s unhappiness about number one being with child, and they all turn toward the house, but not before Grace threads her arm through mine and pulls me with her.

When I look over, she leans into me as if she's telling a secret, but in the same boisterous voice only the Cain sisters have managed to perfect, says, "Don't mind him. Raine's hubby, Alex, is the bomb. Grady knows it down deep, and even paid for their wedding, but he only did it because he loves Raine, and the whole time he grumbled about poor Alex. I mean, Alex is an accountant, and a good one. He does all our taxes. It's convenient. Grady just refuses to believe any of us have sex." She turns around and gives her older brother a glare when we reach the front door.

I don't have a chance to turn to see Grady's expression, because the next moment, Raine opens the front door and Christmas music is blaring from inside the house.

Grace doesn't miss a beat. "Come on, Crew told us about the vineyard next door. We're going to do a tasting and you're coming with us." She looks straight into my eyes and is as serious as serious can be when she demands, "And you're going to tell us all what happened to your face."

I let out a little puff of air and look over at the man whose ring I'm wearing, whose baby I could be pregnant with, and whose sisters just ran roughshod all over us. I widen my eyes and silently plea for help.

And damn him, what does he do?

He leans down and kisses me.

Then I hear catcalls through the Christmas music.

What. The. Hell?

Weston MacLachlan
Somewhere outside of Buffalo

I SEE HIM. He's standing with Jeff and my dad. Trevor is off to the side with his arms crossed and looking intently at the scene in front of him.

I look back to Byron. He's got an enormous knot on the side of his head where he's holding ice. Besides that, I don't see any other injuries, but I wouldn't because I'm not looking for them, and I'm not looking because I don't give a fuck.

They all watch me as I approach, but I don't stop. When I get close enough, I put my hands to his chest and shove with all my might. "You went after my woman?"

Byron goes reeling, landing on his ass first before falling to his back.

I sense someone at my side and I hold my hand out to stop them before looking to my dad. "Do not fucking tell me you ordered that to happen. Do not tell me you ordered him to go after her."

My dad's face tightens and he looks to Byron, who's slowly pulling himself up from the ground. "I did not."

Byron looks worse for the wear, but even so, he looks straight at me and yells, "It needed to be done and you never talk to your Lieutenant that way! You're a fucking mess and not held to the same rules because you're a daddy's boy." He takes another couple steps toward me and puts a finger in my face. "You're a soldier. Don't *ever* question anything I do."

I couldn't give a shit who the fuck he is or if I'm supposed to answer to him. He made a move on Maya. I know I've gotta find a way to get her back and I'm in the process of making that happen. Nothing in my life has made me crazier than seeing her with *him*. That won't last for long, though.

But Byron going after her on his own? No one fucking does that without answering to me. I don't give a shit who he is.

"Did you hurt her?" I counter, hitting his hand out of my face and taking a step to get into his. I stay where I am, but turn to look at Trevor and demand, "Did you?"

Trevor's eyes shoot to me and his face tightens. His chest is rising and falling, but I don't give a fuck. I can tell by the look in his eyes something happened.

I pull my gun out of the back of my pants, point it at Trevor, and shout, "Fucking answer me. Did you hurt her?"

"Weston!" my dad bellows at the same time Jeff yells, "Stand down!"

But I don't take my eyes off Trevor. His hands come out, palms up as he lowers his voice, even though it holds steady. "I took my order and did what I was told. I tried to be careful, but there was a scuffle. Other than some scrapes, she looked fine."

"Put the gun down. That's an order," Jeff warns again.

I don't give a shit if he was trying to be careful, I barely move my gun a centimeter and squeeze the trigger. Trevor falls to the ground, but not because I hit him.

"What the fuck?" he yells from the ground where he fell for cover, and scrambles back to his feet.

"Weston!" my dad growls.

"That's a warning," I seethe, glaring straight into Trevor's eyes. "If Maya ever gets so much as a scratch on her again and you're involved, you're dead."

Only because he's a recruit and I know he was taking an order from my shithead Lieutenant, do I take a step back and swing my arm around to Byron.

"Weston!" I barely hear Jeff yell for the rage ringing in my ears.

"What're you gonna do, pretty boy?" Byron eggs me on. "You'll pay for this. You're a soldier, nothing more. Don't forget you report to me. You don't take a stand against your superior. Ever. I don't give a fuck what your last name is."

I lower my voice and look at him through the sight of my 9mm. "You hurt what's mine. No one goes after what's mine. I'll get her back, but in my own way."

"She knows about us. It was necessary, she's a liabili—"

Without moving my gun, I shout, "No one calls her a liability!"

"Put the fucking gun down," Jeff demands.

"Weston," my dad calls for me.

I ignore them both.

"I'll get her back on my own and get rid of that other guy in the process," I inform Byron. "Don't ever think about her again. She'd better not even enter your fucking brain."

Byron takes a step and narrows his eyes. "I'll do what I need to do for this family. Liabilities are eliminated, and she's a fucking liabil—"

That's when I pull the trigger.

All I hear is the gunshot ringing through the abandoned warehouse as he hits the floor. I don't hear the commotion, the yelling, or the men running to Byron where he's starting to bleed, lying on the cold concrete. That's when his eyes roll back in his head.

I know he's dead. That's what he gets for going after Maya.

"Fuck!" Jeff yells and turns to my dad. "What are you going to do about this?"

"No one fucking touches her," I warn and turn my gun on the rest of the group, including my father. I look to Trevor, who doesn't take his eyes off me. "The only reason you aren't dead, too, is because I know you were taking an order." His chest heaves, even though he's standing stock-still. I look back to the rest of them. "I'll get her back and that asshole who took her from me will pay. But no one makes a move on Maya Augustine. Ever."

I don't give a shit about Byron, I've always hated him and now he's out of the way. I walk backwards, not taking my eyes off them when my dad calls for me, "Weston, stop."

As soon as my back clears the door, I turn and move. It's time to bring Maya home and take care of that asshole who took her from me for good. I shoot two tires on every car but mine.

I have a task.

Fuck the consequences. All I can think about is her.

23

YOU'VE SUNK ME

Grady

"I CAN'T BELIEVE you're engaged."

I look over and Crew raises his beer to his lips as he watches the huddle of women at the bar with their empty bottles of wine scattered about.

Wine "tasting" turned into everyone having a glass and then another. The next thing I knew, Addy closed the place down and brought out platters of food as Evan started popping corks. That's when the wine tasting turned into a party.

I take a sip of my water and make no comment. Maya and I still haven't spoken the word *engaged* out loud, let alone anything else. At this point, I'm just happy she's still wearing my ring. It's a step in the right direction, but I'm not about to tell Crew.

"You beat me," Crew goes on and turns to me. "I'm giving Addison some time—she needs it after what went down with O'Rourke. But we're getting married in the spring as long as she's good. She just doesn't know it yet."

"Happy for you, man," I say, because I am. There are times I look back on what we did, when we were in the thick of it. Seems like forever ago, when really it hasn't even been a year since we officially retired. It seems like another life—a hallucination compared to the last couple months.

"You gonna tell her?" Crew asks.

I sigh and look at my obsession, sitting in the middle of my sisters. Three of them are drunk and cackling up a storm with Addy and her friend Mary, but Raine and Maya haven't had a drop. They've been deep in conversation for some time.

"I'm working on it," I answer. "Just when I think I have a plan, new shit is thrown at us. The latest being my sisters."

"I just found out two of them are staying with us at Addison's since I only have one bed at my old house." He looks over at me and raises a brow. "You're welcome."

"I have no idea how long they're staying, but at least they all have jobs. They have to leave eventually," I grumble. "Speaking of jobs, I know Maya's ex and his family are still a threat, but once that's under control, I think it's time for me to come back. I've taken too much time as it is."

"No problem. Whenever you're ready."

"I'm ready," I say firmly. "This time around, I'm all in. I see what you did when you got us out—I'm not taking it for granted again. I'm committed."

Crew looks to me and nods once before turning

back to the women, saying, "It's time. Time for us to sit back and reap the benefits of doing our duty."

I lean back in my chair farther and think about the benefits. I'm so ready for the payoff, I can barely stand it.

But first, I know things need to happen and information needs to be shared. And that makes me antsy.

Maya

I TIP MY head to the side. "I don't understand."

I've latched onto Raine since she isn't drinking and I don't want to drink, just in case. I'm pretending to be the supportive, non-drinking friend since it's annoying to be around drunk people.

She gives me a little frown and asks, "Has he started drinking?"

I think back on our time together. "He did a wine tasting here and he took me to a brewery. But now that I think about it, he never had a beer because he was driving. He never finished a drink at my parents' house, either. I never realized it until you said something."

"Oh, that's normal," she flips out her hand before popping another piece of cheese in her mouth. "He doesn't have a problem with alcohol, he just doesn't like it. Given the circumstances, who can blame him?"

I try not to look confused, but I am. "Circumstances?"

She levels her eyes on me. "Yes. Our father." When she realizes I have no idea what she's talking about, her eyes get big. "You mean he hasn't told you about our father yet? How long have you two been together, like a week?"

I shake my head quickly and try to brush her off, even though she's closer to the truth than she probably realizes. "Since Grady and I met, there's been a lot going on. You know..." I point to my face and shrug as an explanation. I gave all the Cain sisters the abridged version of what happened this morning at the airport, telling them I have a little issue with an annoying ex-boyfriend.

She nods, thankfully accepting my non-answer as if she understands completely. I'm learning these women have a knack at communicating through a one-way conversation, and even sometimes, telepathy.

"I totally get you." She dips a cracker in hummus and keeps talking with her mouth full. "I'll tell you this. None of us would've survived our childhood had it not been for Grady. Our dad was a first-class asshole, in the worst way possible. Our mom died soon after Grace was born. I'm not sure why they had so many kids, I was only seven when we lost her. She had breast cancer and since she was either pregnant or nursing for almost a decade, her boobs were in a constant state of flux. She didn't notice the lump until it was too late. I remember things were good before she died. Or at the very least, they were normal."

Listening to how they lost their mom at such a young age is heartbreaking.

"That's kind of when I started remembering things. The other girls barely recall her, they were too young. From then on, things progressively got worse with our dad. He started drinking. The drugs came later, when we were older."

"That's awful," I utter, not knowing what else to say, but also feeling like a heel for not asking Grady more about his family.

"Yeah, we were basically raised by babysitters, and not great ones, either. I don't remember at what point it eventually got so bad, but he'd come home late and drunk, and take all his aggravations of raising five kids out on us. We couldn't do anything right. The beatings were bad and Grady usually took the brunt of it."

"What?" I whisper.

"Yep," she shrugs as if she's told the story a million times, which who knows, maybe she has. "When we were little, we all got it. That is until Grady grew as big as him, then the old man couldn't fuck with us while Grady was standing in the way."

"Holy shit," I mumble and look over to Grady sitting across the room with Crew, deep in conversation.

"Grady managed him the last couple of years, but the day he came home to find dad wailing on Grace—that was it. Grace was only nine and so little for her age. Who knows what she did to piss him off that day, but it got to the point where it didn't matter. When Grady saw that Grace was almost unconscious, he lost his shit. Put dad in intensive care and he never woke up. I'm sure Grady saved Grace's life that day and took care of our dad for good."

"That's how your dad died?"

"Mm-hmm. Best day ever. Grady joined the Army, the girls and I went to live with our aunt and uncle from our mom's side. Happily ever after." She pops an olive in her mouth. "You know, I'm gonna gain a gazillion pounds. I'm so hungry, I can't stop eating."

I try to keep our conversation going as I process

everything she just told me, and try not to sound distant when I offer, "You need to listen to your body, you're starting the second trimester. The baby is growing a lot."

Raine smiles big. "I love you already. You just told me to eat whatever I want. You're awesome."

I give her a small smile, and almost jump out of my skin when I feel a hand wrap softly around my chin and lift. Grady is standing above me looking down. "Time to go. I need to check your eyes."

I give him a small smile. His thumb brushes my cheek when he comes down to kiss my forehead.

He looks to Raine. "Can you get the drunks to bed?"

Raine stands from her barstool. "It's not like I haven't done it a hundred times before. Besides, we're going into DC tomorrow to see the sights. You're not the only person we came to annoy. Abraham Lincoln, here we come."

"At least he's sitting so you don't knock him on his ass," Grady mutters as he takes my hand and pulls me from my stool.

Raine looks to me and rolls her eyes. "He thinks he's funny."

After we say our goodbyes, Grady takes me home. Fifteen minutes ago, I would've done anything to go straight to bed, but after Raine told me what she did, I'm very much awake.

Grady

I HEAR THE water turn off. The moment we hit her small house, she said it had been such a long day, she needed a shower. Before that, she was just plain quiet on the short trip home.

When I hear the bathroom door open, I look up from where I'm sitting on the edge of the bed waiting on her. Her hair is pinned up high and she's wrapped in a short robe. But my eyes go directly to her hands where she's sliding my ring back on her finger. All of that, with her eyes on me and coming my way, makes my cock twitch.

When she doesn't stop, I open my legs and she comes right to me. Her hands come to my bare skin and her eyes follow her touch.

She finally looks into my eyes and her voice is soft. "You haven't done your exercises in three days."

I wrap my arms around her waist and run my hands up her back. "I've been busy."

She doesn't smile, just shakes her head and starts to massage my shoulder with one hand, but otherwise doesn't move.

"You okay?" I finally ask. The number of things that could be clouding her head are countless.

Her ministrations continue, a touch so light but healing, she'll never know its significance.

She finally looks into my eyes. "Raine told me about your dad."

It's everything I can do not to tense. I do my best to control it, but in an instant, I'm pissed at my sister and worried about what she knows.

I tip my head. "What did she tell you?"

Maya's hands work their way up my shoulders, neck,

and into my hair. She finally looks down into my eyes. “She said you saved Grace’s life.”

I exhale, still not relieved, so I offer, “It was a bad day.”

She leans forward and kisses my forehead, her voice like a feather on my face as she whispers, “Raine said it was the best day ever.”

I narrow my eyes, wondering where this is going. “That’s another way to look at it.”

Her hand comes up, her thumb lightly tracing the scar down my hairline and she whispers, “Grady?”

I run my hands up her back and pull her tight to me, her tits pressed into my neck. My voice is rough when I look up into her eyes to try and figure out what she’s thinking. “Yeah?”

She pauses a long moment and both her hands frame my face, her voice filled with nothing but compassion. “You killed your dad?”

I search her face for something, but all I see is my beautiful Maya. “I did.”

“To save your sister?”

“To save us all.”

“Grady,” she whispers again. “Just when I thought it wasn’t possible to fall deeper, here I am. You’ve sunk me.”

“Baby,” I breathe, and when I do, she dips to kiss me.

Her lips move light over mine, but after the last few moments, wondering what she thinks, how she sees me? I need her.

I put my hands to her waist and pull her to me. She climbs on my lap, putting her knees beside my hips to straddle me, and I get what I have wanted all day.

Her.

I pull the big clip out of her hair and toss it to the floor. I cup her head and take over her kiss, wanting nothing more than to be as close as possible. I reach between us and pull the tie on her robe.

When I dip my hand inside, I become instantly hard. I tear my mouth from hers long enough to push the robe down her shoulders.

She's completely bare.

Just when I allow my eyes to drag over her body, she interrupts me by reaching for my dick. When she wraps her small hand around me through my boxers, I press into her hold.

She dips her hand inside and I feel her, skin-to-skin.

"I want you, Grady."

She does. I see it in her eyes. Just when I think there's nothing more beautiful she can do, she tops it.

With her needy gaze and her hand wrapped around my cock, I can't wait another second.

"Hold on to me." I wrap an arm around her waist and stand just enough to push my boxers down.

When I sit back down, she immediately comes up on her knees and sinks down on my cock.

I groan.

Her head falls back with a whimper and she closes her eyes, her fingers digging into my shoulders.

I pull her face to mine and kiss her. "I want nothing but you, baby. For the rest of my life, to have you like this, to be wrapped up in you."

She opens her eyes, bringing her hands to my face, she lifts right before impaling herself again.

"Baby?" I call for her but reach for her clit while trying to control my breathing.

She doesn't answer, so I start to play with her and

she arches to get more as she fucks herself on me. When her head falls back and her eyes close, I've never seen anything more beautiful.

Damn, she's making this difficult.

"Maya." I try again. "Baby, you want me to get a condom?"

When she straightens her head, she looks like it's the most painful thing in the world to pry her eyes open and look at me.

But she doesn't stop moving.

And I don't stop circling her clit.

"Maya?"

"I don't know." If her eyes tell the truth, she's conflicted. "Just ... don't stop."

I give her clit more pressure and I get a little moan as a gift in return. But she also starts to move faster, which does little for my self-control.

"Baby, you keep fucking yourself like this, I'm not gonna be able to stop. I'm okay with it, so you're gonna have to be the one to say the word."

Damn if she doesn't move faster, and I have to take a deep breath. It might help if I could shut my eyes, but there's no fucking way I can look away from her, not when she's riding me for the first time and so close to falling apart.

I didn't lie when I said I was good with going bare. She's wearing my ring and I don't plan on her ever taking it off. We make a baby now, that's just more goodness for us.

Just when I'm thinking about our future, she answers my question. "Please. Oh, please don't stop now."

She moves faster, and I rub harder. That does it. She releases a guttural moan and her body tenses.

I pull her down on my dick and hold her there. Her pussy milking my cock is the sweetest feeling I've ever had—I want every second of it. And if she keeps moving, I'll come faster than we can ask if it's pink or blue.

When she drags her eyes open to look into mine, she starts to move again. Fuck me, I guess I'll let her, but as much as I've enjoyed this, I need more.

I wrap my hands around each globe of her ass and stand. Turning, I put her back to the bed. Picking up her feet to hold her legs high and wide, I really start to fuck her. When I look down, her eyes are on me, her tits moving, and she's grasping the covers below her.

I feel it in my balls. I'm not sure how much longer I'll be able to hold on between her tight pussy and looking down as I fuck her. I drop her feet and bend, putting a hand to the bed beside her head. When I lean to kiss her, I pull out and fist my cock as I come all over her stomach, shooting up to her tits.

At this point, we're a fucking mess, so I give her my weight. We lay here like this until we breathe evenly and I turn to kiss the side of her head. "Pulling out as a form of birth control sucks."

She starts to laugh and turns to me. "That was my fault."

I raise my brows and smirk. "Oh, I know that was your fault."

She puts her hands to my face and tries to keep from smiling. "I'm sorry."

I shake my head and kiss her again. "I need to clean us up. Hang on, I'll be right back."

By the time we're cleaned up and settled in bed with the lights out, I sigh. "I forgot to check your eyes."

"Geeze-Louise, it happened hours ago, I'm fine."

I pull her to me, close my eyes, and decide to give in.

After a few moments of quiet, she whispers, "Grady?"

"Hmm?"

She presses into me tight and announces, "I hate your dad."

My eyes fly open and stare into the dark.

"I mean, obviously, you hate him, too. But I hate what he did to you and your sisters. I hate that you had to live so many years in that nightmare, and I hardly know any of the details. I hate you had to do what you did to save your sister, but at the same time, I'm grateful you're the person you are and had the will to do it."

I roll so I'm facing her and breathe in her soft hair, but say nothing.

"You saved me today, too."

I look at her through the dark.

She brushes my lips with the tips of her fingers. "Thank you."

I put my hand to her face, but quickly move it into her hair so as not to hurt her raw skin, before I put my mouth on hers.

When I finally pull away, I kiss her forehead and pull her to me. Not sure I can take more of her words, I whisper, "It's been a long day. Go to sleep."

She nods and I feel it against my skin.

A few moments later, just when I think she's about to drop off, she adds, "And I was serious before. I've fallen so deep, there's no way to find my way back."

I rub her back. “Baby, the path I’ve walked to get to you? I’m never going back.”

I feel her exhale against me and her body finally releases some of its tension.

Then, for the first time in more than a year, when I close my eyes, my body fully relaxes. And lying next to Maya, who’s wearing nothing but my ring, who just admitted she’s in so deep she doesn’t want to find her way out, and who could be pregnant with my baby, I sleep.

Really, sleep.

24

OR ELSE

Grady

I STAND AT the opening of Crew's barn and watch as Jarvis lays another man, Stafford, out flat. Stafford, who is lying face down, just laid the rest of them out, so he's no slouch. After being away for so long, seeing their improvements is impressive, but Jarvis stands out.

I fought for him to be here, so it feels good to be right.

This is the first time I've been back since I was captured. I had an early morning appointment I've been anxious about and decided to stop in here before getting back to Maya. I left her with my sisters at Crew's house so she'd be close to him while I was gone. But I need to get back to her. The girls are heading into the city for the day, thank fuck.

"I think he's ready." I look over at Crew and he juts his chin toward Jarvis. "He's tested out of three languages, but he was already fluent in French and

Spanish. He can keep working on the Middle Eastern languages as he goes, but he has a good enough start, he should be able to travel with no problem."

"Has he learned to control himself?" I ask, as I watch Jarvis unnecessarily pressing the guy who's clearly pinned, into the mat with his knee.

I hear Crew huff one laugh. "Enough that he won't get himself killed. The rest of his intensity should only serve him well—I think it's what makes him who he is. He'll be in high demand soon enough."

I turn to Crew and cross my arms. "I'll be back once all this shit gets settled with Maya. She's agreed to take a couple days off work, but eventually she'll need to get back to the Ranch, and I'll have to be there with her. After that—count me in."

"I wouldn't speak too soon if I were you." I look out the door and it's Asa.

As he approaches, his eyes are on me. "I just got off the phone with my source at the FBI. You're gonna be getting a phone call, and before you chew my ass for giving them your information, know that I had to convince them to contact you instead of Maya. They want to talk to both of you, but they have a laundry list for her."

As he speaks, my phone vibrates. I step outside to take the call that's listed as unknown on my screen. "Cain."

"Mr. Cain, this is Special Agent Jason Gordon from the FBI Organized Crime Task Force in Buffalo. I need to speak to you about an incident that happened yesterday at the regional airport there. We have surveillance video of a gunshot and standoff before you boarded your plane."

I pause even though I'm not worried. If they've got video, they know we did nothing wrong. But he doesn't wait for me to respond.

"I also need to interview Ms. Maya Augustine about yesterday, regarding her connection to Weston MacLachlan."

"What about her connection to Weston MacLachlan?"

"We'll discuss that in person. I'm en route as we speak, and should be in your area soon. I'd appreciate your cooperation as this is urgent and time-sensitive. Where can we meet?"

I have never dealt with the FBI, we've always let Asa take on that responsibility as our main contact. Time sensitive and urgent can't be good when it comes to them.

"There's a vineyard close to where I'm located. Whitetail. Give me your ETA, we'll meet you there. I'll make sure we have a private place to talk."

We work out the details, and I've got some time before they get here to explain to Maya we'll be having a conversation with the FBI about her ex.

When I turn back to Asa, he says, "Sorry that happened so fast, but it seemed urgent when my guy called to get your information. You have nothing to be worried about, they only want information."

"I'm not worried." I slide my phone into my pocket. "We're not the ones who ambushed others on the tarmac, and they have the surveillance video. I'm ready for this to be over."

"My guy didn't give me much, but I got the feeling something's happened to move their case along. Up until now, they've been in a holding pattern," Asa adds.

"If it means they're close, I'll take it." I turn to Crew. "I told them we could meet at the tasting room—they don't need to be here. Can you call Addy and set that up?"

"Sure," he pulls his phone out to make the call.

"You back, Cain?" I look over and Asa's got a shit-eating grin on his face.

I shake my head, and as I turn to make my way back to the house where my sisters are surely torturing the woman who's wearing my ring, I answer, "Yep, but only because I missed fucking with you, old man."

As I walk away, I faintly hear Asa say to Crew, "It sure hasn't been the same without him."

Maya

"Byron Murray is dead."

I feel my body go tense and Grady instantly squeezes my hand, but otherwise he doesn't show any signs of alarm.

"Come again?" Grady calmly asks for clarification from where he's sitting beside me.

"But," I start and try to find my breath, my voice edging on hysterical. "You just said you have video surveillance at the airport. He might've been knocked silly, but I'm almost certain he wasn't dead."

"Ma'am—"

"No, I'm positive—he *was not* dead," I interrupt. "He was still sort of fidgeting around on the ground when we got on the plane, kind of like a turtle stuck on his back."

"We—"

"Tell him," I turn to Grady, "that he would've shot you had you not knocked the gun from his hand. *Tell him.*"

"Baby," Grady lowers his voice and squeezes my hip where he's got his arm around me. "Let him talk."

We're sitting in the basement inglenook at Whitetail for privacy. Grady and I are on the big sofa and the agent is sitting across from us in one of Addy's big leather chairs.

Grady came to get me this morning and told me the FBI wanted to question us about what happened yesterday. We just sat down and he started by informing us Byron is dead—even though he was very much alive when we escaped yesterday.

"We know he was alive when you left the airport. We have solid information he was killed later in the day, although we haven't located his body yet. We're working on leads," Special Agent Gordon explains.

"Oh." I breathe a sigh of relief. Honestly. He could've shared that bit of information first, but who am I to tell the FBI how to conduct interrogations? Even though he assured us this is nothing more than a fact-finding trip, talking to the FBI is worrisome, nonetheless.

"Ms. Augustine, can you tell me what you know about MacLachlan Industries?" He flips a piece of paper on his notepad to take notes.

"They're importers. More like shipping, I guess. They ship a lot of produce from Central America," I share.

"Do you know of anything else, anything questionable? I know you were with Weston a long time, you're bound to be close to his family, too. Ever hear anything?"

"No, everything always seemed on the up-and-up, but I didn't ask or even think to be on the lookout back then," I answer.

"How long have you been estranged from Weston MacLachlan?" Gordon asks.

I can't help but grimace. "I broke off our engagement well over a year ago. But he's an insistent man and wouldn't take no for an answer. When the pressure got to be too much, I left. No one knew where I was until recently."

"Ms. Augustine—" Gordon starts before I interrupt.

"Please, call me Maya." I've been called Ms. Augustine my entire life, even as a young girl. I hate it.

"Maya," he goes on. "Before yesterday, have you ever felt in danger? From Weston MacLachlan or anyone around him?"

I look over and Grady gives me a nod, so turning back to Gordon, I reluctantly lay it all out. "Yes, that's why I left. Weston never threatened me directly, but Byron, the one you said is dead? He did."

"How did he threaten you?" He leans forward, resting his elbows on his knees.

"I overheard something. It was at my parents' house before I left, during one of my mother's attempts to get me back together with Weston. After that, I was approached by Byron and was told if I didn't get on board, I'd be in trouble. That was when I figured out they were involved in some type of organized crime."

"What did you overhear that would cause them to give you such an ultimatum?"

My eyes go big and I bite my lip.

"Maya." Gordon gives me a small frown. "Your ex-fiancé is involved in nefarious activities and incidents. Please don't feel the need to protect him."

"Oh, no." I shake my head quickly. "I have no desire to protect him. It's just, I overheard him talking to his dad and he said he *killed* someone. They realized I was there, tried to cover it up, but in the end I didn't believe them. That's when Byron came to give me my options. And my options weren't good. They told me to either get back together with Weston, *or else*. I figured I knew what that meant and decided to get the hell out of there."

I feel Grady give me another squeeze, and this time I relax into his side.

I watch the agent lean back in his seat with an assessing look—and I don't like it one bit.

I must not have imagined it, because Grady demands, "What aren't you telling us?"

"You were right to feel threatened. We have inside intelligence that says you're considered a liability by the MacLachlan family, and therefore, a target."

Well, shit. It's one thing to assume I might be unsafe, but to have it confirmed by the FBI who has *inside intelligence*? That's another level of scary.

"When Byron Murray was killed, things changed and we've lost our ears. We have other sources of intel, but feel those will be gone soon, as well. We don't currently know where Weston MacLachlan is. He fled yesterday and can't be traced by either his phone or car. He has business associates all up and down the east coast. We assume he'll reach out to some of them for help, but I need to advise you to take extra precautions."

"I've got her covered," Grady announces. "He knows she lives and works here, along with a second job at a nearby senior center. I'll get you the address before you leave."

Agent Gordon gives me his business card. "You took quite a fall, we saw it on the film. It's good to see you're okay. I'll be in touch."

"Thank you." I stand and Grady gives him the information he needs. When he finally leaves, I turn to Grady. "This has to be over soon."

"It will be." Grady takes my hand and pulls me to the stairs.

When we get to the main tasting room, Mary, Bev, Addy, Evan, Van, and even Morris, are crowded around the bar. When we get closer I see what they're all looking at. The crowd parts and a sleepy but happy Clara is sitting there holding a bundle of pink blankets with baby Kate peeking out the top.

"Awwww," I drawl and get closer. "I'm sorry I wasn't here to visit you in the hospital. Did you just get home?"

Clara smiles. "Yesterday. The hospital is so much more relaxing than my house. I tried to fake complications so I could stay longer, but they were on to me and kicked us out."

Everyone laughs, and after being around her boys at the Christmas party, I don't blame her for trying to spend extra time in the hospital.

"She's perfect." Jack beams as he looks down at his newborn before announcing, "I think we're done having kids."

Clara more than enthusiastically agrees. "Oh, we're done. You're making an appointment to get snipped, sooner rather than later." Little Kate stretches, arching as she starts to wiggle. "We'd better get going. We left the boys at home with my parents and she'll be ready to eat soon."

We all say our goodbyes after they pack up the baby and all her necessities. After hanging out most of the morning with Grady's sisters, then eating a late lunch with Grady in the tasting room, followed by my first ever interrogation by the FBI, the day has flown.

I guess Grady is done hanging out, because he takes my hand and we leave, following Clara and Jack out the door. He turns back to me and his face is serious when he says, "I have something I want to show you."

When he starts driving toward the exit of the vineyard, I ask, "Where are we going?"

Grady fists his steering wheel, but doesn't look at me as he turns left onto the two-lane highway. "Not far."

He didn't lie. We barely drive a half-mile when he turns onto another lane which is surrounded by a slatted white fence. We're hardly off the road when Grady approaches a security gate and rolls down his window to punch in a code.

"Um, where are we?"

He looks back to me and smirks. "Across the street."

I narrow my eyes instantly. "I know that."

The gates open in front of us and Grady drives through rolling pastures, mixed with patches of woods and tree lines scattered about. Even though everything is dormant and brown, I imagine how pretty it would be lush and green, or better yet, colorful in the fall. As we come up a hill, a large home sits at the top. It's not a typical Virginia colonial. It's decorated in stone with crisp white trim to match the slatted fence surrounding the property, dark gray siding, and a dark stained front door and shutters.

"Seriously, Grady." The suspense is wearing on me. "Are we here to visit someone?"

He ignores me, turns off the engine, and climbs out of the SUV. I follow suit, because I'm curious, but I also don't like him ignoring me.

He doesn't wait, but jogs up the steps ahead of me and goes straight to the front door.

"Grady," I call for him again, but he's now at the door handle and pressing more buttons on an electronic lock.

Finally, he turns to me as he opens the door and gestures for me to enter first.

I stand where I am and demand, "What's going on?"

He still says nothing and reaches for my hand, pulling me through the threshold.

What I find is stunning.

And empty.

I take a few steps, barely glancing at what would be an office with French doors, flanked by a formal dining room across from it. I keep walking, the heels of my boots echoing on the dark hardwoods through the vast, empty space. I move until there's nowhere to go because I've reached the floor to ceiling windows overlooking the property that appears to go on forever. The way the home is situated on the rolling hills, there's no other structure or buildings in sight besides the enormous barns that match the exterior of the house we're standing in. Off the back of the house is a stone patio, and down another few steps, is an inground pool covered for winter.

Thinking I know exactly what's going on here, I turn slowly, vaguely taking in the spacious family room with stone fireplace that's open to an oversized kitchen. My eyes land on Grady standing in the center of the room. His stance is wide and his arms are crossed. But unlike me, who's taking in the details of our surroundings, his focus is solely on me.

"Are you thinking about buying this place?"

25

YOU SAVED ME

Grady

"WELL, ARE YOU?" she asks again.

I narrow my eyes, studying her but don't answer. Instead, I ask, "What do you think?"

She frowns slightly. "Of this empty house or you acting weird?"

I shake my head. "Maya."

She mirrors my stance and crosses her arms, but smirks in the process. "Because I think it's weird that you're acting so weird."

I drop my head and study the floor in front of me. How do I even begin?

When she gets tired of waiting, her voice sounds frustrated. "Grady?"

I exhale and pull my hand through my hair as I look to her. She's dropped her arms, impatient for an explanation.

"I was in the Army for four years," I state.

She looks perplexed. "I know. You told me."

"I was a Ranger assigned to Special Warfare."

She tips her head and frowns. "Um, okay."

I started, I can't stop now. "Right before I left the Army, I was recruited to Delta Force."

Really confused, she sounds like she's playing along when she responds. "I assume that's an honor?"

I raise my brows and make an understatement. "Yeah. Delta Force is not for the weak."

"Grady." She sighs. "You brought me across the street to an empty house for a reason I still don't know, and now you're speaking in riddles. There are moments when I feel I know you well, but right now I have no idea what you're getting at."

I decide to just say it. To get to where I want us to be, she needs to know. "My recruitment to Delta Force was a big deal. I caught the attention of a secret group and was recruited to contract overseas for our country and allies. For the past ten years, I was paid to eliminate threats. And I did. I eliminated a lot of them."

"Right," she agrees, impatiently. "You told me you worked in security."

I relax my features and try to gauge her reaction. "I guess a certain security was obtained as a result of my work. But no, security is a cover for what I really did."

I try not to let it affect me, but a hint of hurt bleeds through her features. "I don't understand."

"Terrorism, cartels, organized crime. You name it, if a country or organization couldn't manage it, someone like myself was hired to take care of it."

She crosses her arms protectively and takes a step back. "Take care of it?"

"Yes," I confirm. "To eliminate the threat. A threat they couldn't handle on their own."

Her face falls and she whispers, "Wait. You mean if it couldn't be dealt with legally?"

I put a hand up to stop her thoughts. "More like they couldn't handle it legally in a timely manner. Sometimes the threat outweighs the time it takes because the system is slow. Especially if the system is corrupt."

"What are you saying?" Her face is etched with uncertainty and I fucking hate it. She didn't look this way when she found out I beat my dad so bad I put him in intensive care and he never woke up. Not when I threatened to kill the guy on the tarmac if he didn't let her go. Not even when I slid that ring on her finger.

I don't answer, but try to explain. "You know how I grew up—what my sisters and I dealt with for years. The day I walked in and saw my drunk-ass and high-as-a-kite father wailing on Gracie, I'd had it. She was so little, not even crying because she couldn't. She was half out of it from his blows, curled into herself, barely whimpering. I fucking *lost* it, Maya. By that time, I was big and ten times stronger because of football. When the police showed up, I was covered in his blood. I swear to you, it's the only time in my life I've lost time. One second I walked into the house to find my baby sister cut, bruised, and bleeding, and the next, I'm sitting on the floor by my lifeless father."

"Grady," she whispers, and takes a step toward me, but this time I put my hand up to stop her.

"He died two days later in the hospital—the same hospital Gracie was recovering in. I was never charged. It was reported as self-defense. Gracie was evidence enough, all the questioning they did after the incident was only procedure. Detectives told me if I hadn't done it, the cops who showed up would've wanted to. They made it clear I did nothing wrong."

"You didn't," she softly agrees.

"I know." I take a breath, wanting to finish more than anything, yet finishing could mean an outcome I dread. "Three months later I joined the Army. Besides football and protecting my sisters from our dad, I found something I was good at. But just weeks after I was recruited to Delta, they showed up on my doorstep with an offer. As soon as they laid it out for me, I signed and never looked back."

She pulls her lip between her teeth and doesn't say a word.

Damn that lip. I need to make her understand.

"Maya," I pause and take a breath. This could close the door on our future for good, but I'll do everything I can to put a wedge in it. I can't lose her. "I was a paid assassin for a secret organization for ten years."

That made her release her lip. Right before she takes another step back.

"Assassin?"

"Yes. Terrorists, insurgents, cartels. I worked solely overseas, never in the US."

"You were paid to kill people?" Her eyes are big but I can't tell what she's thinking.

"Bad people," I insist. "The worst."

I see her chest rising and falling quickly, but she says nothing.

"And Maya," I add. "I was good at it."

She frowns deeper.

"Until I wasn't."

This surprises her. "What do you mean?"

"A while back, I got a call from Raine that Gracie wasn't doing well. She was in her last year of college, quit going to classes, and she couldn't sleep. She was hardly eating. The girls got her to a doctor. She'd fallen into depression. After we got her into therapy, we found out it wasn't only because of our fucking father, but me killing him because of what he did to her. Her head was fucked up, and for some reason, she was feeling guilt."

"But." Her words come quick, and if possible, she defends me to me. "That wasn't anyone's fault. It sounds like he could've killed her if you hadn't stepped in. You saved her."

I soften my voice and take a step closer. "I know. But seeing Gracie have to deal with that? She was in a bad place and it fucked with me. Knowing what I did might've caused her to slip away from us? I didn't recognize it then, but it messed with my head, too. It consumed me and I got careless. Crew and Asa saw it, tried to warn me, but I wouldn't listen. That's when Crew took it into his own hands and got us out."

Her eyes grew big. "Crew and Asa do what you do?"

"Yeah, but not anymore," I correct her. "We're all retired and now train others to do what we did. That's what's happening on Crew's property."

"Oh. So, you're retired from um ... assassin-ing?" she asks, her face is screwed up as if it disgusts or perplexes her. I'm not sure which.

"Yeah. But I got antsy, thought I wasn't ready to retire. Looking back, I needed something to focus on. Gracie was in therapy and getting better, but I still carried that guilt. I thought work would give me some focus. I went back and got myself in trouble. I'd be dead if Crew hadn't been there to save my ass."

"That's when you were hurt?" she guesses.

"Yes."

"That wasn't very long ago," she points out.

"Seems like another lifetime since I met you."

She shakes her head and looks to the side out the big windows toward the back of the property, but she doesn't appear to be actually looking at anything. She's thinking and unfocused.

I don't like it.

"Maya?"

She looks back to me.

I lower my voice. "I'm not him."

She frowns.

I keep on. "My assignments were to take out targets who would've caused mass destruction through terrorism. Or who've killed, or made the order to kill, just so they could take over drug territory. I've taken out rebels who've raped women and children just to—"

"Okay!" She holds her hand up. "You'll never have to convince me of that. I know you aren't him. But why are you telling me all this now?"

I tell her the truth. "I love you."

Her eyes widen and she breathes, "What?"

"You saved me."

"Grady, I—"

"You did. Didn't know what I wanted to do with my life. Thought I needed to work as long as my body would let me. I never thought to want more, let alone search for it. Then I was captured, tortured, and almost killed. When I came home from that, I was lost. My only refuge was watching a woman over the surveillance system when she ran. I'd wait for you, baby. Everyday. I'd wait, and when you showed, I'd get lost in you."

She pulls that damn lip into her mouth again as her eyes well.

"Who knew when I barely survived the depths of hell, my path would lead to you."

Her hand comes up and she swipes a tear from her scraped cheek. "Why now? Why are you telling me all this now?"

"Because you're wearing my ring." I take a step, only a couple feet separating us. "Even though things might've happened in the wrong order, you deserve to know everything. I want you to know who you're spending the rest of your life with."

She swallows hard as another tear escapes.

"Because of you, I'm ready. I'm done with you seeing how that ring feels on your finger. It means something. I should tell you it means you're mine, but fuck, Maya, you don't even know it, but you've got me. You standing right here in this empty house—you're holding my heart, baby. It's yours. I want our life to start and I want it to start here." I point to the floor. "And I want it to start today."

She doesn't look away as she tries to blink back her tears. I can't take it another second—I need to touch her.

Closing the small distance between us, I don't stop when I reach her. Putting my hands low on her hips, I move her backwards into the kitchen, and she doesn't try and stop me. When I get to the marble island, I put my hands to her waist and sit her on the counter so I can look her straight in the eyes.

Her hands instantly come to my chest and I slide my palms up the inside of her loose dress to feel her skin on mine.

"You know everything there is to know about me.

Everything. If I need to, I'll take that ring off your finger and ask you properly, but baby, I need to know that you're in. If you aren't, then I need to know what to do to make you in, because I'm not letting you go."

She wraps her boots around my waist and pulls me to her while shaking her head. "You're not taking my ring off."

I slide my hands up to grip her ass and press my cock in between her legs. "It's my turn to ask what you mean."

Her face softens into the expression I fell in love with when she asks, "Do I know everything about you now?"

"I have never told anyone about my work. Not even my sisters. No one knows what I've done but you, and I know I couldn't ask you to be with me forever without you knowing."

She gives me a small smile as if she's relieved. "You might've been a tough Delta whatever and traveled the world taking out bad guys, but you'll have to wrestle me to the ground to get this ring off my finger."

"Baby." I exhale and lean my forehead against hers. "I look forward to wrestling you to the ground, but I'll never take that ring off your finger." Looking into her eyes, I ask, "Does this mean you're in?"

Maya

I PRESS MY breasts into his chest, getting as close as I can. "If that's your official proposal, then yes, I'm in."

And I am. As sweet and protective as Grady is, I

knew he had an intense side he wasn't showing me. So even if it was surprising that he didn't simply work in security—it wasn't. If anything, I feel closer to him and want nothing more than to make him happy. Because during my short time with Grady, life has never felt so perfect. Where I'm at right now fits, and I'll do anything I can to brighten his life like he's done mine.

He leans in to put his mouth on mine with a desperation I've never felt in him before. Dipping his hands into the back of my panties, he squeezes my ass. I bring my hands up to his hair to hold him close and moan into his mouth.

His hand comes between my legs where my panties are soaked, and he pushes my legs farther apart as they dangle off the counter when he mumbles, "I should show you the rest of the house."

"Yeah," I agree, but I'm sure my expression doesn't. When he hooks a finger inside my panties, my pussy doesn't agree, either. He slides through me easily, creating tingles throughout my body.

"The house can wait," he growls. With both hands, he starts to pull my panties and demands, "Lift."

"Should we do this here?" I ask, wondering if it's a good idea to have sex in a house being shown to potential buyers. Still, I put my hands to the counter and lift so he can easily pull my panties down.

"It's fine," he assures me and does his best to quickly wrangle them down my legs and over my boots.

Yanking the buttons on his jeans, he pushes my legs farther apart before flipping the hem of my dress up around my waist. "Lean back."

Holy shit—this is going to happen in a stranger's kitchen. But with the heated look in his eyes, I lean back on my hands immediately. When I'm reclined for him and he's got me spread before him, he slides his hands up my legs again, but slower this time.

"You're really mine." He looks into my eyes.

Sliding a finger inside me without breaking eye contact, he keeps talking.

"This is mine," he puts his other hand to the counter and leans to me, "forever."

He comes closer to kiss me as he starts to finger fuck me. When his thumb circles my clit, I scoot to the edge and arch my back. I've never felt the way Grady makes me feel.

When he releases my mouth, I look into his eyes and whisper for the first time, "I love you."

He stops finger fucking me and almost freezes. His heated, bright blue eyes burn into mine before he kisses me again, and this time it's possessive, deep, and long. Finally ripping his mouth from mine, I lose his hand and he yanks his jeans down just enough to free his cock.

Wrapping a hand around the small of my back, he pulls me forward. He drags the smooth tip of his cock through my wetness, and his voice is low and guttural. "I'm taking you bare."

I don't argue.

"Okay."

With that, he doesn't inch his way in, he doesn't take his time, and he doesn't savor it.

He consumes me.

Then he proceeds to fuck me. Hard.

And I lean back and let him. Every other time with Grady has been amazing, but this is life-changing.

"Look at me," he demands.

I open my eyes and look into his. I have to wrap my legs around his waist to hang on—he's slamming into me. Each thrust is better than the one prior, hitting that spot inside, forcing me to pant, and making it hard to hold myself up. When his other hand returns to my clit, I moan out loud, not able to handle it another moment.

It comes over me, my arms tremble and Grady's hold around my waist tightens, pulling me to him with each beautiful thrust. I feel myself start to shake, moan, and call out to him.

"Fuck," he growls. "Your pussy milking me, I can't take much more."

My orgasm starts to fade when he slams into me two more times, and I get to watch his beautiful face when he comes. Every muscle and vein in his corded neck is tense and flexed—the most gorgeous sight I've ever seen. And every bit of him is mine.

When I put my arms around him, he holds me to him tight, his cock still buried deep.

"This is just the beginning, baby," he murmurs in my ear, pressing into me again. "From this moment on, our paths that brought us here end—they're done. We're starting a new one—one we'll navigate together."

Pressing my face into his neck and kissing him there, I nod against his skin and breathe him in. "Yes."

He gives me a squeeze. "Never want anything between us, baby. We'll talk about what that means. You want to be on birth control for a while, I'm okay with that. If not, I'm more than good with that, too. But there'll never be anything between us again."

I smile because that's more than okay with me, and pull away enough to put my lips on his. When I look around the empty house we just had sex in, I finally give myself a chance to take in its beauty. "Are you really thinking about buying this house?"

He looks away from me and over my head to study the kitchen behind me. "It's not quite the mansion you grew up in. Do you like it?"

I pull back and put my hand on his cheek to get his attention. "I don't want to live the way I grew up. Not even if I could. I want a quiet life."

"You didn't answer my question."

I tip my head. "What's not to like? From what I've seen, it's beautiful."

"Well, I hope you like the rest, too, because I closed on it this morning."

I feel my eyes go big. "You bought this house?"

"Yep, and the three hundred and sixty acres it sits on. Plus the barn and the pool. We even have a corral, though, I have no idea what we'll do with it. Previous owners were horse breeders. It was a quick sale because I paid cash."

I can't help the surprise in my voice when I ask, "You did?"

He presses his cock into me one more time and grins. "Doing what I did—it paid well. I wasn't lying to your father. I can take care of you, baby."

I roll my eyes. "All I want is you. I don't care where or how we live."

He leans in to kiss me softly. "You ready to see the rest?"

I actually can't wait to see the rest, but instead of telling him that, I ask, "It depends, do you have any toilet paper in your new house since we're doing away with condoms?"

He grins. "Ours. Our house, baby. And I don't know. Let's go find out."

Weston MacLachlan

It's all I can do not to break through those fucking glass doors. I want to put a bullet through his head, but I can't do that from here, and especially not in front of Maya.

But to see him touch her? Fuck her?

My Maya?

I can't take it. They surprised me when they left that vineyard and only drove across the street. I had to wait and once I found out there was an electric gate, I parked up the road and had to climb a fucking fence. By the time I found the house and came around back, they were going at it in the kitchen.

I don't know what the hell they're doing there, the place is empty. All I know is it won't last much longer. She's mine and I'll get her back. No more fucking around.

I only need a moment to get to her, but he never leaves her. One thing I know, it's going to happen soon.

26

THINGS AREN'T AS THEY SEEM

Elijah Pettit
FBI Field Office – Buffalo, New York

STANDING HERE WATCHING Ronald MacLachlan, for once appearing worried, through the one-way glass window is fucking frustrating. Jeffrey Acogi is sitting in an interrogation room down the hall, and more soldiers are being rounded-up as we speak. It's barely seven in the morning, but more than half the organization is in custody, and we're working on the rest. Scrambling units for a roundup at a moment's notice all the way up and down the east coast wasn't easy, but it couldn't wait.

But what's really frustrating is the young MacLachlan is still on the lam.

Bennett, my supervisor, falls in beside me. I finally look over when he says, "They found the body. We've got physical evidence and an eye witness. If that doesn't convince these fuckers to talk, we might have to send you in."

"I want to go to Virginia and be the one to take down that asshole. I deserve that after going under all these months. He needs to be found before he gets to the Augustine woman."

"We warned her when we were there yesterday." He looks at me and raises a brow. "I can't say more, but I know for a fact her security is good. They know the threat is real."

I look back to the senior MacLachlan as he sits with his arms crossed. He just invoked his Miranda rights and is waiting on his attorney.

I glance at my watch. "I'm wasting my fucking time here. If you have the body, there's no need for me to stick around. The plane leaves in twenty and I want to be on it. We'll be on the ground in Virginia in no time. Let me do my fucking job and finish this."

Bennett looks to me and shakes his head. "You had a good run and you're a good agent, but you know what this means, right?"

I'm pissed I couldn't do more. Still, I'm not a good agent, I'm a fucking great one. I know exactly what's gotta happen, but that doesn't mean I'm happy about it, so I growl, "I know. Now let me finish this in Virginia before I have to move on."

He ignores my demand. "You're not gonna get to choose where you go."

I exhale, because I didn't know that. That pisses me off. Just for that, he better let me finish this. "Dammit, Bennett. I've gotta be on that plane. The clock is ticking. You gonna let me go or am I gonna go against orders? Either way, I'm taking down Weston MacLachlan."

He shakes his head. "Don't fuck it up, Eli."

Finally.

I smirk. "I'm a good agent, remember? I deserve one more hurrah before you send me off to Timbuktu."

He looks to the one-way glass and crosses his arms. "I've heard the word Texas mentioned, not quite Timbuktu. I'll still miss you, even though you're a pain in my ass at times."

I don't waste a moment. I need to grab my bag and make it to the plane.

"Pettit," he calls, and I stop, frustrated. He narrows his eyes on me and lowers his voice when he stresses, "I want that little fucker alive. Now that we have him for multiple charges of capital murder, I want his ass rotting in a cell for consecutive sentences. Get it done fast, I'm ready to wrap this up."

I say nothing but nod. After months of dealing with the MacLachlans, I'm ready to wrap this shit up, too.

Grady

Rolling Hills Ranch, hours later...

"MOST OF THE Buffalo crew is in custody, including your dinner buddy, Ronald MacLachlan."

As I listen to Asa brief me over the phone, I watch Maya from across the room. She was leading Bingo, but now she's dancing around with the residents doing the Chicken Dance, of all fucking things. I'm not sure if it's the news that the MacLachlans are out of business or watching my fiancée shake her ass with the old ladies, but one of the two makes me smile.

That is until she moves to Foxy and he rubs his old

ass against hers. That's enough to wipe the smile right off my face.

"Did you hear me? And what the hell's going on there?" Asa asks.

"Yeah, sorry. I heard you. They're dancing. It's good for their circulation." I turn away before I'm forced to watch Foxy go in for the bump and grind. "Won't be very many more years until you'll be moving in here."

"I'm only forty, jackass," he bites out before moving back to the topic at hand. "They have an eyewitness—Weston's the one who killed Byron Murray."

"No shit?"

"Yep. When they find him, he'll be charged with first degree at the very least. Who knows what else they've got racked up on him. Agents from New York, along with some from the Northern Virginia office, are in the area. I know you are, but be on the lookout," Asa warns.

"I am. I'm not even leaving her on her own in the tasting room."

The music ends and Maya returns to the front of the room for more Bingo. I take my seat next to Miss Lillian Rose and grab a new card off the stack being passed around the room.

"I wanted to update you," he finishes. "If you need anything, call."

I hang up and slide my phone back into my pocket.

"I can't believe you and our little Maya are engaged." Miss Lillian Rose smiles at me. "Have you set a date? Will we be invited?"

When we got to the Ranch first thing this morning, I sat down to eat breakfast with all the ladies, but that didn't stop them from zeroing in on Maya's left hand. There must be an extra chromosome in the female body alerting them to new diamonds in their vicinity. They almost found it faster than my sisters and their excitement was off the charts.

I can't help but grin. "No date and I don't know what Maya wants. But if it's around here, sure, you're all invited."

"Whoop!" she exclaims. "Did y'all hear that? Grady said we're invited to the wedding!"

As the room erupts, and I only have eyes for Maya as hers go big. I'm not sure if she approves or not, but she loves these old codgers, so I'm not worried.

"When's the wedding? I want to put it on my calendar and make sure I have an appointment to have my hair set," Emma Lou yells.

"We'll let you know," I say loudly, so she can hear. "Maya needs to shop for a houseful of furniture first. That's gonna start today."

"You bought the house." Maya smirks at me. "Maybe you should start shopping for furniture."

Shrugging, I talk across the room for all the seniors to hear, "I've done my share of furniture shopping for the next decade—I bought a chair. That's all I need. If you want anything more, you'll have to go shopping."

"You need more than a chair, you silly boy." Miss Lillian Rose frowns at me before turning to Maya. "You need to set up that home he bought for you. You'll need a full set of formal china for the holidays. I'm sure brides these days don't register for silver, but you should. It's time to make your own heirlooms your grandchildren will want someday."

Maya shakes her head quickly and opens her mouth, hopefully to tell Miss Lillian Rose we don't need silver anything when Betty agrees. "Yes, don't skimp.

Beautiful flatware is important. Sure, you might have to polish it, but it's worth it in the end."

The look on Maya's face is one that tells me she doesn't give a shit about that stuff. I clear my throat and I hope to make my point. "I think we can start with a couch and TV. Go from there."

"Let's get back to Bingo," Maya says, and narrows her eyes at me, but since she's biting her lip, I know she's not complaining.

I showed her the rest of the house last night, but it was getting too dark and cold to walk around the property. Since I just closed yesterday, I don't have surveillance set up yet and wasn't taking a chance walking around the woods with Weston on the loose. I talked to Crew about extending his system across the street, he thought it would be easy, and made some phone calls first thing this morning to get it going. As soon as I can get her to buy some furniture, we're moving in.

I can't wait. It's been a long time since I've had a home. I never considered my childhood house a home since my mom died. After that, it was basically a hellhole we were forced to survive in. But starting a new life with Maya? I can't wait.

She starts calling out numbers again while Miss Lillian Rose talks my ear off about what we need to set up a proper southern home. But when Maya hesitates mid number, I look to her.

She's tense and staring at the back of the room. Before I have the chance to turn and see what's caught her attention, she screams.

I'm not far from her, but I instantly reach for my left ankle as I turn in my seat. When I look to the opening of the activity room, there's Weston. But he's not alone.

He's grabbed the first person he could reach and has an arm around his neck with a gun to his head.

Weston's voice barrels through the room, "I swear, Maya, I'll blow his fucking head off if you don't come with me right now."

Maya

No.

No-no-no-no.

I hear faint screams and voices from the residents I've come to love over the past few months. They're confused and scared, and rightly so. I'm terrified for their safety. Especially one in particular—my favorite of the bunch.

Weston's here—and he has Foxy.

But he wants me.

I stand quickly from the table I'm sitting at, and scream, "Let him g—"

But Grady interrupts me and when I look over, he's standing at the side of the room with his gun drawn and pointed directly at Weston, demanding, "Drop the gun."

Weston jerks, causing Foxy to lose his footing and claw at Weston's arm that's cinched around his neck to keep hold. As spry as Foxy is, it's easy to see he's in pain. Especially when Weston roughly shoves the nose of his gun into his temple.

"Come with me and I'll let him go, Maya. Do it fast, I'm tired of this shit. And I'm tired of seeing you with *him*." At the last word, Foxy moans from Weston jerking him again.

"You stay right there, baby," Grady says to me without taking his eyes off Weston. When he starts to move efficiently, stepping sideways toward the middle of the room, he keeps talking. "I just got an interesting call, Wes. Your dad and most of your cronies were taken down this morning. They're being interrogated as we speak."

Weston processes that bit of information for two beats before he looks back to me. "You're coming with me!"

Miss Lillian Rose screams, "You let Foxy go!"

I move quickly and wrap my arm around her. Her old hand grasps mine as tight as she can, and I feel her body shake with fear.

Grady holds steady and speaks without hesitation. "Guess what else? I hear they have an eye witness as to who killed your buddy, Murray." Grady moves two more steps, but I can still see Weston, and his face falls just a touch, but I caught it. Grady keeps talking. "That's right. It's over, Wes. Let the man go."

"No," Weston breathes and his hold on Foxy tightens.

"Yes," Grady confirms. I have no idea what they're talking about.

"Let me go, you damn little bugger." Foxy tries with all his might to get away, but it doesn't help.

"Please, Weston," I cry. "You're going to hurt him. Let him go."

He doesn't let Foxy go, but he shakes his head and looks straight into my eyes. "I can't lose you."

"Weston." I lower my voice. "You haven't had me for

a long time. I'll never come back to you. Now please," I feel my voice crack with emotion and tears fill my eyes, "you're going to hurt him. He's done nothing to you, let him go."

"Don't make me kill you," Grady says, his voice low. "I can, I will, and I'll do it gladly."

"Maya," Weston calls for me one more time, but before he has the chance to say anything else, I see movement in front of me.

Betty is sitting next to where Weston is standing with Foxy, and by the look on her face, she's determined. She doesn't take her eye off Weston as she slowly brings her cane up, then all of a sudden, stabs him right in the crotch.

I have to hand it to her, she got him pretty hard for as frail as she is.

Weston buckles at the waist from the jab, loosening his hold just enough for Foxy to twist away. Weston tries to reach for him, but Foxy moves fast enough to escape his grasp. That's when we hear scurrying in the hall.

But Weston, even keeling over in pain, lifts his arm enough to point his gun right at Grady. "She's not yours!"

"Grady!" I scream.

Grady's prepared, but his whole-body tenses right when someone from behind Weston clocks him on the side of his head. Weston's wrist is lifted, his gun pointed to the ceiling before being twisted out of his hand. Weston instantly collapses to the ground on his hands and knees.

More men come rushing in, and I scream, "Grady, it's him!"

It's the man who grabbed me at the Buffalo airport,

the man with Byron Murray who attacked us. This is the same man who just basically knocked Weston out and disarmed him.

"FBI, get your hands up!"

FBI?

A team of men file into the room, but I can't take my eyes off the one who had me on the tarmac in Buffalo. Trevor, I think? He looks the same, yet still, very different.

He's tall with thick, dark hair and a trim body with a muscular frame. He's bulky, wearing a bulletproof vest with FBI printed across the front and black utility cargos. If the bulletproof vest wasn't enough to give it away, the badge clipped onto his belt loop is.

Trevor, the guy who tried to kidnap me, isn't a bad guy?

He's an FBI agent?

Miss Lillian Rose exclaims, "It's the FBI! My stars, it's just like my evening shows."

Grady, who's between the action and me, quickly pulls his hands back, pointing his gun toward the ceiling. "I've got a C and C."

"Cain," Trevor calls to Grady. "We know who you are and were expecting you to be close. You can holster your weapon—we've got it from here."

The agents move to Weston, and since he's still reeling from Betty's brave shot to his groin and hit to the head, he complies easily.

The second I see it's safe, I run to Foxy and stoop low to look into his eyes. "Are you okay?"

He crooks his head this way and that way, stretching from where Weston was holding him. I reach for his neck to rub it for him, hoping he just needs to loosen his muscles. The scene alone was frightening enough, let alone for someone at the ripe age of eighty-eight.

"I'm fine," Foxy tries to brush it off, but it's easy to see the relief in his face. It cuts through me he had to endure that because of me.

I put my arms around him, and he follows suit. "I'm so sorry. Are you sure you're okay? I can get a doctor to take a look at you."

However, I know he's fine because he pulls me into him tighter and starts to rub my back almost to my ass with one hand, and fingers my hair with the other.

That's when I hear Grady growl, "Are you kidding me?"

With all that's happened, I have to laugh.

When I finally disentangle myself from Foxy's old-man grope, I look over to see Weston being cuffed by Trevor, and it seems Weston is just as confused as I am.

"You're a pig?" Weston yells. "You fucker, I should've killed you when I had the chance."

Trevor looks bored. "Probably, because now I'm an eyewitness to you murdering Byron Murray. Don't think you'll be able to plea manslaughter for that one. I also just got word you've got soldiers flipping for lesser charges. We've got agents on the way to locate two additional bodies and it's not even noon. Looks like your time's up, MacLachlan." Trevor looks to a fellow agent and says, "Mirandize him." We all watch Weston being led out of the activities room before Trevor turns back and offers his hand to Grady. "Eli Pettit."

Grady puts his left arm around me and shakes the hand of the man we knew as Trevor-the-bad-guy. But as it turns out, he isn't. Grady mutters, "Things aren't as they seem. Nice work."

Eli Pettit turns his attention to me. “Sorry about your fall, Ms. Augustine. I did everything I could to keep Murray from touching you—it wasn’t easy. Sorry I didn’t do a better job at keeping you safe.”

After all that’s happened, I melt into Grady’s side, not quite sure what to say, so I wave him off. “It’s, um … it’s okay. I’m fine, really.”

I feel Grady exhale. “Glad I didn’t shoot you.”

“I’m glad you didn’t either, but trust me, that wasn’t the first time I about got my head blown off working this case. I’m glad this shit’s over.”

Grady wraps his other arm around me and puts his lips to the top of my head. “So am I.”

Pressing into Grady, I watch Eli Pettit turn and follow the other agents and Weston as they file out of the activities room of Rolling Hills Ranch. “I can’t believe it’s over.”

“Took long enough,” Grady mutters before he sighs again. I feel his hand on my cheek that’s not scraped. “You okay?”

My face softens into a small smile and I lift up on my toes to kiss him. “Yeah. I think I’ll be okay until forever.”

“Forever is good with me.” He gives me a squeeze before he kisses me back, and we hear clapping around us from my favorite group of senior citizens.

27

ORGASM PURGATORY

Maya

THE LAST WEEK has been surreal. But it's been surreal because it's been normal.

I haven't had normal in a long time.

When I get right down to it, I'm not sure I've ever had normal. I know I didn't grow up normal, and running away from the mob and my ex-fiancé was anything but. And being engaged so quickly to a man I creeped on is definitely not normal.

No one is after me because they're all in jail. Grady spoke to our new undercover FBI friend a couple of times since last week. Eli assured us they have enough charges on the MacLachlans and the rest of the higher ups, they'll all remain in jail while awaiting trial. He also added they have enough charges stacked up against them that I should be safe roaming the countryside until I'm at least eighty.

I'm free to come and go, work, and even socialize

without having to look over my shoulder. It's seriously been a strange sensation.

It took a whole week, but Grady finally convinced me to give notice at Whitetail. I knew in my heart I'd have to give up that job eventually, but actually telling Addy I would only be able to work for two more weeks was hard. I know they'll be shorthanded until she can hire someone else but, as always, Addy was gracious and didn't make me feel bad.

She grabbed my hands and smiled big. "I wondered what was taking you so long. You have a houseful of furniture being delivered later today and you're getting married—you have no business working seven days a week anymore. I'm happy for you, and I'm super happy we'll still be neighbors. You'll be here drinking wine all the time anyway, I won't even know you're gone."

She then proceeded to make sure Grady and I were still coming to her farmhouse for Christmas dinner.

Well, that's done.

Addy's right. We do have furniture being delivered today. Grady dragged me out every free hour we've had over the last week to shop. It might seem like a houseful of furniture is being delivered, but it's really not. That's because the house that Grady bought across the street from Whitetail is pretty big. Don't get me wrong, it's no mansion, and this makes me happy. I love it so much I can't ever imagine wanting to live anywhere else. So today, furniture is coming for the family room and master bedroom. That took long enough to pick out, the rest will have to wait.

The property is beautiful and goes on forever. However, I have no idea what we'll do with the barns. The previous owners bred horses, so they're quite fancy as far as barns go. Grady keeps teasing me that he's going to buy me some cows. I hope he's not serious.

I just got off early from my shift at Whitetail and I'm on my way to pick up Grady at Crew's house. Winter has officially arrived in Virginia, and the recent snow will give us a white Christmas.

As I pull onto Crew's property, it's still hard to believe what they do here. Grady has answered all my questions, and doesn't pretend he's not relieved I didn't freak out and leave him after he told me. I explained it just needed to sink in, but over the last week, I've come to find what he did fascinating. Now I have a million questions about what they do to train their up-and-coming replacements.

Grady felt guilty for being away from Crew's operation for so long and wants to dive in to make up for his long absence. He explained how some of their recruits are ready to start working on their own.

I park outside the barn where I dropped him off this morning and decide I want to see it firsthand. When I get out of the car and walk to the door of the barn, I pull it open, but I'm stopped in my tracks.

Holy shit, I cannot believe the sight in front of me.

"Grady!"

Crew's standing there with his arms crossed, grinning, not at all surprised to see me. He says nothing, but he does look up to Grady. "Man, I told you she was here."

I step into the warm barn, slamming the door behind me and exclaim, "What do you think you're doing?"

Grady doesn't answer and I can't see his face. He's got his back to me, with no shirt on, every muscle in his back and arms are taut. He's doing pull-up after pull-up, but not just that, his legs are bent at the knees where he's holding a barbell steady with enormous plates on each end. Who knows how much weight he's lifting besides his own. All I know is any pull-up is bad for his shoulder and these are worse.

"Grady, stop!"

He listens this time and drops enough to hang from the bar, but doesn't let go. Crew steps forward and lifts the barbell before Grady drops his legs the rest of the way and falls to his feet. All he has on is a pair of loose athletic shorts hanging low on his hips and a pair of tennis shoes. It's clear to see he's been working out well beyond what I just witnessed.

But looking at him here, mostly bare, with his muscles taut, and skin glistening with sweat—I struggle to hang on to my irritation. If possible, he's more beautiful than ever, and this makes my panties wet.

He's breathing heavy from the workout he should not be doing and grins. "You ready to go?"

I shift in my snow boots and cross my arms, trying to pretend I'm not affected by ... all of him. I toss my hand out between us. "You shouldn't be doing any of that. You'll reinjure your joint."

He looks unapologetic when he keeps on grinning. "I'm fine. It feels good, thanks to my physical therapist."

"Speaking of," Crew butts in, grinning almost as big as Grady. "You never billed me."

I roll my eyes and shake my head. "Honestly."

Grady bends and tags his shirt off the floor and starts for me. When he gets close, he puts his hand to my lower back and pulls me in for a kiss. "Let's go. I'm anxious for furniture, and since all we own are clothes, moving in will take less than fifteen minutes."

"See you tomorrow," Crew calls, as we walk out through the snow to Grady's Escalade.

Truth be told, I'm looking forward to furniture, too, but I'm really looking forward to starting a life with Grady.

GRADY TAKES MY hand and pulls me out of the kitchen. "We can finish this tomorrow."

After the furniture was delivered, Grady was on a mission. He loaded me up again and we headed for Target. When we got there, he pushed a cart my way and told me we were to divide and conquer.

I was told my mission was simple—buy "shit to sleep on and shit to eat off of."

I grinned and asked if he was serious. The look on his face told me how serious he was, right before he told me to hurry.

But I didn't hurry. I reached up and gave him a kiss before turning to Starbucks. I needed a coffee and he, of course, headed for the food.

Since we got home, we've been washing new sheets and towels in our new washer and dryer, setting up our bedroom, putting dishes away, and eating. Grady even bought me four bags of the Flamin' Hot Fritos.

Now it seems he's tired of setting up house. He leads me through the family room to our new bedroom.

"I was almost done," I say as we round the corner where our new bed, mattress, and other furniture fill the room. Even with the room full, it still feels empty and I make a mental note that we need stuff to hang on the walls.

Grady moves to the side of the bed and turns. There, he pulls me to him and his hands instantly come to the hem of my shirt. After he lifts it up and over my head, his eyes are heated. "Time to break in our new bed."

Even if I feel that between my legs, it reminds me of earlier when I walked in on him working out in the barn. I run my hands over his arms and shoulders. "I'm still upset about the pull-ups no matter how hot it was."

He smirks. "You liked that?"

I bite my lip and my eyes go big. "There was a lot to like. But you still shouldn't put that much strain on your joint yet. You could've at least started with normal pull-ups, not the super-uber-strongman kind."

His fingers start to work the button and zipper on my jeans, making quick work of taking them off. "I have been doing the normal ones. I had to work up to the weights, it's been a while."

I step out of my jeans and kick them to the side at the same time I give him a little push, only it was just for effect. It didn't move him an inch. "How long have you been working out like that?"

Reaching around my back, he efficiently pops my bra. "Long enough. But trust me, I'm fine. I know my body."

"I'm the physical therapist. I think I know better than you what your body is ready for."

Grady pushes my panties down until they're lying on the rest of my discarded clothes on our brand-new area rug. He's just undressed me in record time.

"If you know my body better than me, then I'm determined to know yours better than you." He leans down to kiss me as he twists my nipples, creating sensations in my lower belly that shoot straight between my legs. I rub my thighs together, because if I thought I was wet before, now I'm soaked.

When he releases my lips, I open my eyes and ask about his state of dress compared to my state of nakedness, "Are you not joining me?"

His hand runs down my tummy and his fingers slide easily between my legs, making my eyes heavy. "See? I knew you'd be wet. I'm getting to know your body better every day."

I exhale and am forced to find my voice to point out, "If you told me to do something in my best interest, I'd listen to you."

"You about done talking, baby? I'm in the mood to play with you. Trust me, it'll be in your best interest."

I shake my head at him, giving in, and he sees it. He grins as he takes a step back and sits on the side of our new bed, holding his hand out. "Come here."

I put my hand in his and step toward him where he pulls me between his legs. His hands go straight to my ass and his lips straight to my nipple. I press myself into him as I moan and feel him squeeze me in his big hands.

He rolls his tongue around my nipple right before he pulls it between his teeth, biting down just enough for me to feel it everywhere.

I close my eyes and let my head fall back to enjoy every second of it, because I know with every ounce of my being that Grady would never hurt me. I feel it every time his eyes land on me, every time he touches me, and every time he tells me he loves me.

Every. Single. Time.

He sucks me into his mouth one more time before releasing me with a pop. His hands make their way up and down my ass and thighs when he looks up to me. His expression is heated, his eyes warm, and his voice heavy when he asks, "You gonna let me play?"

Oh.

I've lost my voice. Instead, I nod.

"Turn around, Maya."

I close my eyes, but I turn.

Still standing between his legs, his hands start to move lightly on me. I lean back into him and melt.

"This is where it begins."

I moan when he brushes a light finger over my clit, and I spread my legs just enough to let him know I want more.

"You saved me when we lived across the street, but this is a new start. From here on out, it'll be nothing but good." His fingers go from light on my clit to firmly cupping me between my legs, and his other hand squeezes my hip. "Sit."

I do as he says and lower my ass into his lap. It's easy to feel his hard, thick cock through his jeans, and knowing that's all for me—forever mine—I sink back into his chest.

His face comes to the side of mine and when his lips touch my ear, he whispers, "I'll make sure this is good." His hand comes up to my lower belly, making my breath catch, and he presses in. "For us."

I turn my face and put my lips on his. Once I made my decision, I have never doubted it. I know life with Grady is going to be good.

His hands slide down my body to my thighs. When

they reach my knees, he pulls my legs apart to straddle his.

Then he spreads his legs—spreading me.

I exhale as my head falls back to his shoulder.

His voice is as smooth as his fingers running through the wet between my legs. "There you go."

Not knowing where to put my hands, I grasp his thighs below me. The more he touches me, the firmer I grip. His hand roams—teasing, massaging, and even twisting my nipples. All the while, his other one never stops its constant torture on my clit.

He wasn't kidding when he said he was in the mood to play.

When he spreads his legs even farther, really far, he whispers in my ear, "I just decided I'm a big supporter of yoga."

I'd laugh if I could, but I can't. Instead, I exhale loudly and arch my back for more of his touch.

"You like that."

Oh, I do, but I don't answer. It obviously wasn't a question, I'm pretty sure he knows I like it. His fingers continue to tease, until finally, one fills me. Deliciously and divinely.

"Please," I whisper, doing my best to press into his hand, but his other arm drops to my waist to hold me tight.

"You want more?" he asks.

"Yes." I nod at the same time the word falls from my lips, trying to relay how much I want more. I really want more. Hell, I want more so much, I can't even think straight.

Then perfectly, just like my Grady has been since

the day I first worked on his shoulder, he gives me what I need.

He gives me another finger and more pressure on my clit. But he also holds me tighter, angling an arm up to cup my breast possessively.

"You gonna come for me, baby?"

My body is humming from head to toe as he teases me, giving me more, then less, evilly delaying my imminent orgasm, leaving me hanging in the balance of the most beautiful purgatory ever.

Orgasm purgatory—it's like walking a sexual tightrope that only Grady can balance.

One of my hands comes up to the side of his face when I beg, "Grady, baby, please."

"Hmm," he breathes in as he puts his lips to my neck. "Love you, Maya."

Then he really finger fucks me while giving my clit more pressure. I gasp and arch and call out for him. All the while he holds me tight.

And finally, I'm consumed.

When I lose his hand between my legs, I feel myself going up. He turns and the next thing I know, he's laying me face down on the bed. I've barely had a chance to catch my breath when I feel Grady pull my hips up until I'm on my knees, he instantly fills me from behind. "Oh, yes."

He's surrounding me from above, enveloping me where I feel him everywhere as he starts to move. He doesn't take his time as he did when he was in the mood to play. I feel his need as he pounds into me.

"Never felt this," he growls into my ear where he's hovering. "Never get enough of you."

"I hope you never do," I breathe and arch my back.

"Love you, too, baby."

As if my words lit a fire in him, he moves, and I feel every muscle in his body as he makes me his. I'll always be his.

When he finally comes, thrusting into me the last time, I feel his body tense over mine. Totally spent, I let my knees slide out from under me and he follows, staying connected.

After many moments, I feel his breath finally even, and turn my head. "Grady?"

He kisses my forehead. "Hmm?"

I exhale. I'm not sure now is the time, but if it's not, I have no idea what will be. Today has been busy. But now, being connected as we are, it seems to be as good a time as any. "My period was due today."

He freezes momentarily, but I doubt I would've even noticed had he not been touching me everywhere. Pressing his still hard cock into me, he gives me a squeeze.

When he doesn't say anything, I go on. "I'm pretty regular, you know, give or take a day or two every once in a while."

He leans up enough to reach my lips and kisses me. "I'm more than good with that."

I open my eyes wider to look into his and smile small, whispering, "I am too."

His face turns serious. "I'm gonna marry you."

My face softens. "I know."

"Soon, baby."

"Okay," I agree.

With that, it looks like we'll be getting married in the very near future. And whatever that future looks like, I know it will be perfect.

28

BALLS TO THE WALL

Maya

I SMACK THE balloon with my pool noodle toward Butch.

When I woke up in the middle of the night thinking about how I'm almost two days late, somehow this popped into my head. Before work, I made a quick trip to the store and bought an armful of pool noodles with bags of balloons. After I cut the noodles in half and blew up some balloons, I gathered the residents. We're sitting around tables that have been pushed together playing balloon tennis.

I named the activity *Smack It*, but now I'm rethinking this because I think Foxy is getting into it on a whole other level.

"That's right, smack it like you mean it, Butch!" Foxy yells across the table.

I don't know whether to grimace or laugh.

"No one's hittin' it to me," Betty complains.

"Here." I pop the balloon up with my noodle and

lob it to her so she can have a turn.

"This is stupid," Miss Lillian Rose whines. "Donuts and Dominos was on the schedule. We can't eat donuts while we're smackin' a balloon."

Foxy leans up out of his chair, and you'd think it was match set at Wimbledon as hard as he hits it. It flies as fast as a balloon can fly and hits Erma right in the face.

Foxy raises his noodle in the air. "Score!"

"Foxy!" Erma screams. "You're a buffoon."

His only rebuttal is to point at her with his noodle. "I win!"

"There's no winner." I try to frown at him, but I'm sure it comes across lame. I bet this is why parents have trouble disciplining children—sometimes their bad behavior is too cute.

At the reminder, I sigh.

Children.

This brings my thoughts back to why I woke up in the middle of the night.

I don't feel different, but I also don't feel like I'm about to get my period. I do know for a fact I've never once analyzed how I feel as much as I have in the past two days. Do I feel pregnant, do I not feel pregnant, what does being pregnant even feel like? Am I bloated, do I need chocolate, am I emotional?

And if I am pregnant, what kind of mom will I be? It's not like I have a good example. At least I know what kind of mom I won't be—Vanessa Augustine was no role model.

Suddenly, I have the overwhelming desire for a donut.

Does this mean I'm pregnant? Or is it just because I smell donuts? And can I smell the donuts because my senses are heightened or is it just because there are donuts on the next table?

Honestly. I'm so over myself, I can't stand it.

I toss the balloon and hit it down the table to Betty as I berate myself for over-analyzing my uterus and my sense of smell.

"Spank it, Betty!" Foxy yells.

"For the love of it all," I say but can't stop myself from grinning. "It's *Smack It*. I should've just named it Tap the Balloon."

"Oh, Maya." Foxy narrows his eyes and slides back and forth in his seat. If I didn't know any better, I'd think he was constipated, but this is Foxy. He's giving me his sexy eyes and doing one of his little dances. "I'd tap that. Bow-chicka-wow-wow."

I can't help it. I burst out laughing and throw my noodle across the table at him.

And Foxy shows me how spry he really is, because he catches it in midair as he keeps moving in his chair. "Boom—now I can spank with both hands."

Oh my.

Grady
The next day…

I CAN'T WAIT for her to be done working two jobs. I want her here more. She doesn't need to work at all, but she loves being at the Ranch, and it looks like that PT job will officially be hers soon. She seems excited about that. Lucky for me—she can electrocute me any time she feels like it.

When I push the button to lift one of the garage doors, I'm surprised to see her small compact car already parked for the day. She's home early—it's barely five o'clock.

Seeing her car reminds me we need to buy her a bigger one. It snows enough here she needs a four-wheel drive, plus, if she is pregnant, we'll need it sooner than later.

I go to my phone to unarm the security system, and I shake my head when I see it's already unarmed. We've only had the system for two days, but I've told her when she's here, it needs to be set. It also needs to be set when she's not here, and so far, she doesn't seem to understand how strongly I feel about this.

As I walk through the mudroom and into the back hall, I round the corner and find her in the family room, tucked in the corner of the enormous sectional that was delivered a few days ago. "Hey, you're home early."

Her eyes dart to mine, surprised. She was staring at the ugliest Christmas tree on earth, as she insisted we bring it from her rental at the winery. She said the memory of me cutting it down is one of her favorites, and told me next year she expects me to do it again. When she filled me in on this, I immediately decided to have a grove of trees planted on the back half of our property. If I plan for it now, at least we'll have decent trees in the future.

But I can't take my eyes off her face. Her expression is almost void of emotion, and it's not one I'm used to seeing. "You okay?"

She shakes her head, but just like she's done to me before, her words contradict her expression. "I'm fine."

I drop my workout bag, forgetting all about talking

to her about the alarm, and move straight to her. She tilts her head back, looking at me as I get close and moves her legs for me to sit. Frowning, I ask, "What's wrong?"

She shakes her head again. "I thought I'd be relieved."

My frown deepens. "Relieved?"

She sighs. "It must have been all the activity or stress of the last few weeks. Or, who knows, maybe it's all the Flamin' Hot Fritos I've been eating and my system is off. I can't remember the last time I was three days late."

I try not to let my disappointment show, because as our days together have added up, especially the last few, I've been doing my best not to get excited.

We're new. Not only are we new, but we've just moved in together, we have a non-date set in the very near future to get married, and as much as I know I love her and this is right, it doesn't change the fact that we're new.

Still.

I didn't lie when I told her I was good if there was a baby. The last couple days when she told me she was late and wanted to give it a few more days before taking a test, I was becoming more and more good with the thought of being a father. A *different* kind of father.

A *good* father.

No—a fucking *great* father.

I try not to let my disappointment show, because I don't know what she's thinking. I bring my hand up to her chin and turn her face to mine. "What?"

It's her turn to frown. "What?"

I raise my brows. "What are you thinking?"

She bites that damn lip, and just like every time it happens, my cock twitches.

But fuck, her eyes start to well. She'll never know how deep that cuts me, and I'll never tell her because I never want her to hide it.

She shrugs as her eyes fill and her voice cracks. "It's silly—I know. Especially after I freaked about us being careless, but I was sort of getting used to the idea."

I brush her jaw with my thumb and let out the breath I was holding. Leaning in to kiss her, I taste her tears as they fall to our mouths. When I let go, I put both hands to her face, wiping the wet from her cheeks with my thumbs. I'm serious as shit when I lower my voice. "We didn't give it a full go. You teach me about your ovulation cycle and come January—it's balls to the wall."

Damn it, she smiles but her tears come stronger, and this time she nods her head in my hands.

I can't take her crying, so I pull her into my arms and stuff my face in her hair where I mumble, "Like I need another reason to make love to you. January's gonna be a fun month."

She nods as her face is stuffed in my neck. "I'm sorry. You didn't sign up for this, but I'm a little emotional while I'm on my period. I swear, I'll get it under control. It'll pass soon."

This makes me laugh as I rub her back. "Then it's a good thing I'm good with women."

And fuck me, she starts laughing as she continues to cry into my neck.

I hold her while looking at the ugliest Christmas tree ever that sits in our new house and I see our future. A new path—our path. A path that can only be good.

EPILOGUE

THREE YEARS LATER

Grady

"THIS MUST BE take your kid to work day," I say, and look over at Crew who's holding a wiggling Vivi in his arms. She's grabbing at his cheeks and lips as she arches her back to get down.

We're in the middle of summer. The sun is out and it's hot, but for some reason the one-year-old little girl is wearing rain boots with her sundress.

"She wants Cayden," he says, flipping her around so her back is to his front where she has no leverage. Holding her easily with one arm wrapped around her middle, her dark hair falls around her little face as she continues to wiggle. "Addison doesn't know we're here, but she will if I let her climb all over the tires again. Last time I brought her home covered in dirt and grease, I got a lecture about making sure she's dressed for boot camp. I have a feeling this isn't what Addison had in mind when she dressed her this morning."

I look back out to where Cayden is climbing over the

old rubber creating black smudges all over his arms and legs. Now his face is covered and his clothes are filthy.

Nothing a dip in the pool won't fix.

I smile when he pulls himself to his feet and looks at me waving. "Daddy, watch!"

He jumps off the side of the tire and lands in the center before starting the climb to do it all over again.

"Good job, bud," I yell back. "Two more and we've gotta go."

He starts to scramble faster.

"With the new group starting next week, our schedule will be tight. I'm not sure how available Asa's gonna be. For now, we'll have to pick up the slack."

Given the sabbatical I took years ago, I have no problem with that. Especially given Asa's current situation. I'm more than enjoying seeing him spin his wheels, so I shrug. "It won't be a problem. Maya's going part-time. I finally talked her into it since she's in the homestretch."

Crew wrangles Vivi, flipping her upside down before he lifts her to blow in her neck. Baby squeals fill the air and she starts to belly laugh. "Even though Addison says she works four days a week she's at the tasting room almost every day. I think she's gonna offer Evan the general manager position. It won't be soon enough."

It didn't take long for Maya to become tight with Addy and her group. One thing about our women, they're busy and like their work. But Crew and Addy had a tough year before Vivi was born, so I know he's ready for his wife to slow down. Crew and I don't talk about this shit, but Maya told me how Addy's ready to try for another baby, but Crew's hesitant.

I look back at Crew and change the subject. "I want to make some changes to the course. I'll outline it and we'll talk tomorrow. It can be done easily by next week."

"Sounds good." He flips Vivi back upright and sits her on his shoulders. "I'll see you tomorrow."

I lift my head and move to Cayden. If I don't go get him, he'll never come on his own. He's as rough and tumble as boys come.

I step over three tires and reach for him when he's not expecting it. Picking him up under the arms, I turn him to me, not caring he's covered in black tire soot since I just got done working out myself.

"Noooo," he complains.

"Let's go see your mama and get you cleaned up."

He jumps in my arms, because he knows what cleaned up means when he's with his old man. "Simming!"

I grin down at my son whose blue eyes shine bright. "Yeah, we'll go swimming."

Maya

"Don't touch anything," I hear Grady call after the garage door slams.

I sigh, because I know what that means. Since Cayden learned to crawl, he always comes home in need of a bath after being out with his dad.

As I'm cooling down on my yoga mat in the middle of the family room, I can't help but smile when my son comes running around the corner. It's just as I thought. He's covered in black, probably from climbing around on the tires again. I keep telling Grady we need a swing set for him here at home, but Grady says there's no reason when he can go across the street to Crew's property and climb on anything he wants. But with the baby due in two months, I think Grady finally sees the need.

My sweet boy comes running and throws his little dirt-covered body at me. I catch him and rock back a bit from his weight.

"Careful for the baby," I hear Grady say. When I look over Cayden's dark hair, just like his dad's, I see my husband walk in almost as sweaty and dirty as our son.

"You two are a pair." I snuggle my boy, but look up to my husband.

We were married three years ago this past spring and I never looked back. Just like Grady said it would be, it's been nothing but good. That day in early April, we said *I do* on the deep porch of Addy's winery overlooking the budding countryside. Our families, friends, and all the residents of Rolling Hills Ranch were in attendance. Oh, and I was also two months pregnant.

Just like his promise of a good life, Grady also made good on his other promise. We went balls to the wall—I was pregnant quicker than we could throw a wedding together. And unlike our pregnancy scare, there was no hesitation or indecision. We were happy.

Ecstatic.

My mom, on the other hand, was not so ecstatic. Because it would be uncouth to miss her daughter's wedding, she attended in all her uptight glory. She had to, as at the time, she was basically eating crow after the fall of the MacLachlan family. It was a surprise to everyone. But my mother, being who she is, separated herself as quick as possible. I do believe this made it easier for her to swallow her crow after all the efforts she made to tie me to Weston, especially since he's spending the next seventy years in prison for multiple counts of first degree murder, drug smuggling, and other RICO charges. I think my dad might've had something to do with her change in attitude, as well.

My dad, on the other hand, is happy for us, and is more involved with Cayden than he ever was with Joe and me. That's okay, because if it means my son will get everything I never got from a grandparent, I'm good.

Joe comes to visit every now and again. He graduated with his degree in finance and now works for my father. His epilepsy is stable and it seems he was right—his medical dog is a total chick magnet. I never hear him talk about the same woman twice.

On the other hand, One, Two, Three, and Four—the infamous Cain sisters—have become staples in our lives. Raine's daughter is only six months older than Cayden. She and I are bound and determined these cousins will be close, so they visit often, with the rest of the Cain sisters in tow. It's a good thing Grady bought a big house. We've certainly put it to good use.

I kiss my stinky baby on the head. "You need a bath."

Cayden looks up to me with the same bright blue eyes I fell in love with—his father's—and gives me a toothy grin. "Simming!"

I roll my eyes and look up to Grady. "Of course you're going swimming in lieu of a bath."

Grady smiles and steps forward to offer me a hand. "Come on, we'll take a dip before dinner."

I take his hand and let him heft my big pregnant self off the floor. "He still needs a bath, Grady."

My husband smirks but doesn't comment. Instead, he puts a hand to our unborn baby and lays a kiss on me. "I'll rub your back tonight, then we'll see how well pregnancy yoga is keeping you limber."

I can't keep from grinning. Pregnancy tends to send me into an abyss of hormones, making me almost a sex maniac, something Grady enjoys. So much so, I had to hold off the making of baby number two. If it's up to him, who knows how many we'll have.

I put my hand over his and say, "I'll go change. But you're giving him a bath before I let you touch me."

"I bet I can change your mind." He grins big.

I bet he could too, and he usually does, but instead of denying the truth, I lift up on my bare toes to kiss him. "I don't doubt it. You've proven to be very persuasive over the years."

His grin shrinks into a soft expression that's only for me. "That's because I've loved you from the beginning and I'll never stop proving it."

Standing in our home with our son playing at our feet and unborn daughter doing somersaults in my belly, I've never been happier, and I smile up at my husband. "Love you, too."

Thank you for reading. If you enjoyed *Paths*, the author would appreciate a review on Amazon.

Read Eli Pettit's story in *Bad Situation* – The Montgomerys, Book 1

Read Crew and Addy's story in *Vines*
Read Asa and Keelie's story in *Gifts*
Read Jarvis and Gracie's story in *Veils*

Read Cole and Bella's story in *Scars*
Read Ozzy and Liyah's story in *Souls*
Read Evan and Mary's story in *The Tequila – A Killers Novella*

The Next Generation
Read *Levi*, Asa's son

OTHER BOOKS BY BRYNNE ASHER

Killers Series

Vines – A Killers Novel, Book 1

Paths – A Killers Novel, Book 2

Gifts – A Killers Novel, Book 3

Veils – A Killers Novel, Book 4

Scars – A Killers Novel, Book 5

Souls – A Killers Novel, Book 6

The Tequila – A Killers Novella

The Killers, The Next Generation

Levi, Asa's son

The Agents

Possession

Tapped

Exposed

Illicit

The Carpino Series

Overflow – The Carpino Series, Book 1

Beautiful Life – The Carpino Series, Book 2

Athica Lane – The Carpino Series, Book 3

Until Avery – A Carpino Series Crossover Novella

Force of Nature - A Carpino Christmas Novel

The Dillon Sisters

Deathly by Brynne Asher

Damaged by Layla Frost

The Montgomery Series

Bad Situation – The Montgomery Series, Book 1

Broken Halo – The Montgomery Series, Book 2

Betrayed Love - The Montgomery Series, Book 3

Standalones

Blackburn

ABOUT THE AUTHOR

Brynne Asher lives in the Midwest with her husband, three children, and her perfect dog. When she isn't creating pretend people and relationships in her head, she's running her kids around and doing laundry. She enjoys cooking, decorating, shopping at outlet malls and online, always seeking the best deal. A perfect day in Brynne World ends in front of an outdoor fire with family, friends, s'mores, and a delicious cocktail.

- facebook.com/brynneasherauthor
- instagram.com/brynneasher
- amazon.com/Brynne-Asher/e/B00VRULS58/ref=dp_byline_cont_pop_ebooks_1
- bookbub.com/profile/brynne-asher

Made in the USA
Las Vegas, NV
25 November 2024